AN UNOFFICIAL MINECRAFTERS GRAPHIC NOVEL FO[R]

A BATTLE BEGINS

THE S.Q.U.I.D. SQUAD #4

MEGAN MILLER

SKY PONY PRESS
NEW YORK

Copyright © 2021 by Hollan Publishing, Inc.

Minecraft® is a registered trademark of Notch Development AB.
The Minecraft game is copyright © Mojang AB.

Sky Pony Press books may be purchased in bulk at special discounts for sales
promotion, corporate gifts, fund-raising, or educational purposes. Special editions
can also be created to specifications. For details, contact the Special Sales
Department, Sky Pony Press, 307 West 36th Street, 11th Floor, New York, NY
10018 or info@skyhorsepublishing.com.

Sky Pony® is a registered trademark of Skyhorse Publishing, Inc.®, a Delaware corporation.

Minecraft® is a registered trademark of Notch Development AB.

The Minecraft game is copyright © Mojang AB.

Visit our website at www.skyponypress.com.

10 9 8 7 6 5 4 3 2 1

Library of Congress Cataloging-in-Publication Data is available on file.

Cover design by Kai Texel
Cover and interior art by Megan Miller

Print ISBN: 978-1-5107-6300-5
Ebook ISBN: 978-1-5107-6781-2

Printed in the United States of America

Introduction

is a dire time in the world. The Evil Pillagers are conquering villages and destroying the villagers' re and libraries. But far out at sea live the Book Guardians, a secret group of miners and villagers ng to save the libraries' precious books. The Book Guardians bring chests of books, before they ce destroyed by Pillagers, to the Book Guardians' hidden underwater ravine headquarters. Here all group of three families collects the books and stores them for better times—for when the ers are defeated.

nile the grownups are checking deliveries, securing books, making plans, and double-checking e plans, the children—Inky, Luke, and Max—are meeting new friends and solving mysteries! And s not all. The Dolphins were so happy for the trio's help, they gave them the GOLDEN DUST IC OF SPEAKING TO CREATURES. So, yes, the children can talk to their underwater neighbors, nderwater creatures, fish, and squid they share their new home with. And now the intrepid three, S.Q.U.I.D. Squad," are ready to take on any undersea mystery, no matter how deep or treacherous!

Meet the S.Q.U.I.D. Squad

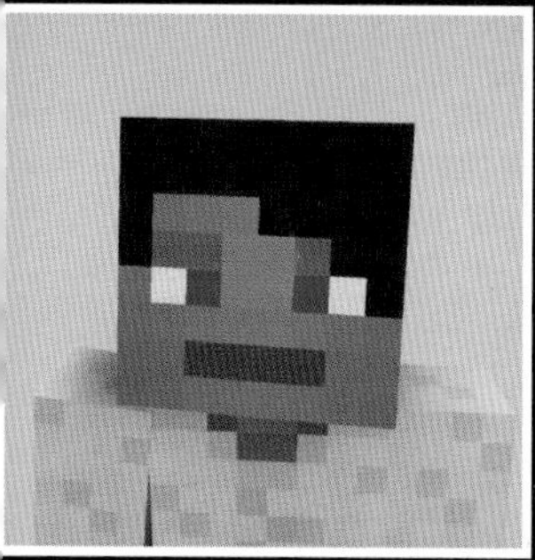

INKY

Clever. Enjoys organizing stuff. Faced too many squid to count. Knows what words like *acronym* mean. Mostly likes to play by the rules.

LUKE

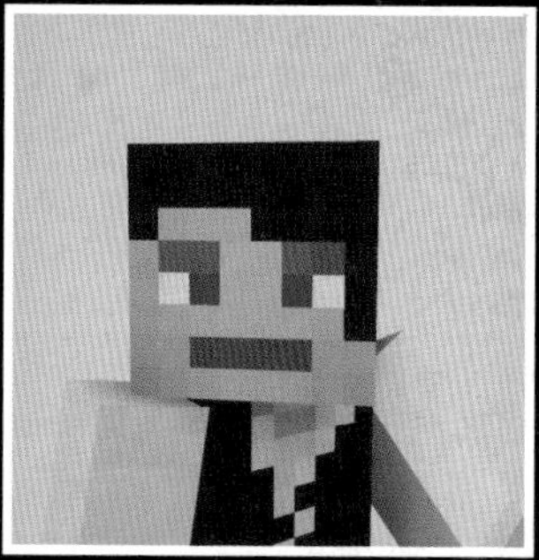

A little rebellious. Enjoys delivering a good speech. He sees himself as the leader, but Inky and Max have other ideas.

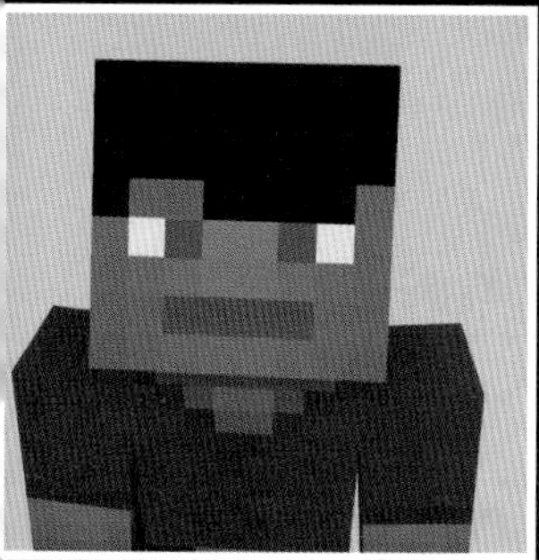

MAX

Brave. Leaves Inky and Luke in the dust when it comes to crafting stuff really, really fast. Their secret club name was his idea—the Super Qualified Underwater Investigation Detective . . . er . . . Squad. Just say "S.Q.U.I.D. Squad," it's easier.

And also, meet ...

EMI

Special friend to the squad, she also fled to the oceans to escape the Pillagers. She lives secretly in a cottage on the other side of the coral reef.

SOFI

Inky's mom. Redstone engineer in charge of the book delivery system. And she has ALREADY figured out that Inky, Luke, and Max have made their OWN secret underwater cave headquarters INSIDE OF the Book Guardian's own secret underwater ravine headquarters. She hasn't even told anyone else about it!

ABS

Sofi's brother. He can haul chests of books like you wouldn't believe.

ZANE

Max's dad. He goes on a lot of secret missions to find new villages that want to save their books.

NEHA

This is Zane's sister. She's learning the art of potions!

PER AND JUN

Luke's mom and dad. Per is fond of speeches and Jun tries to let him know when they go on too long. They go out on secret missions, too.

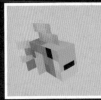

MABEL

Friend to the Squad, unafraid to say what she thinks!

Chapter 1
A Place at
the Table

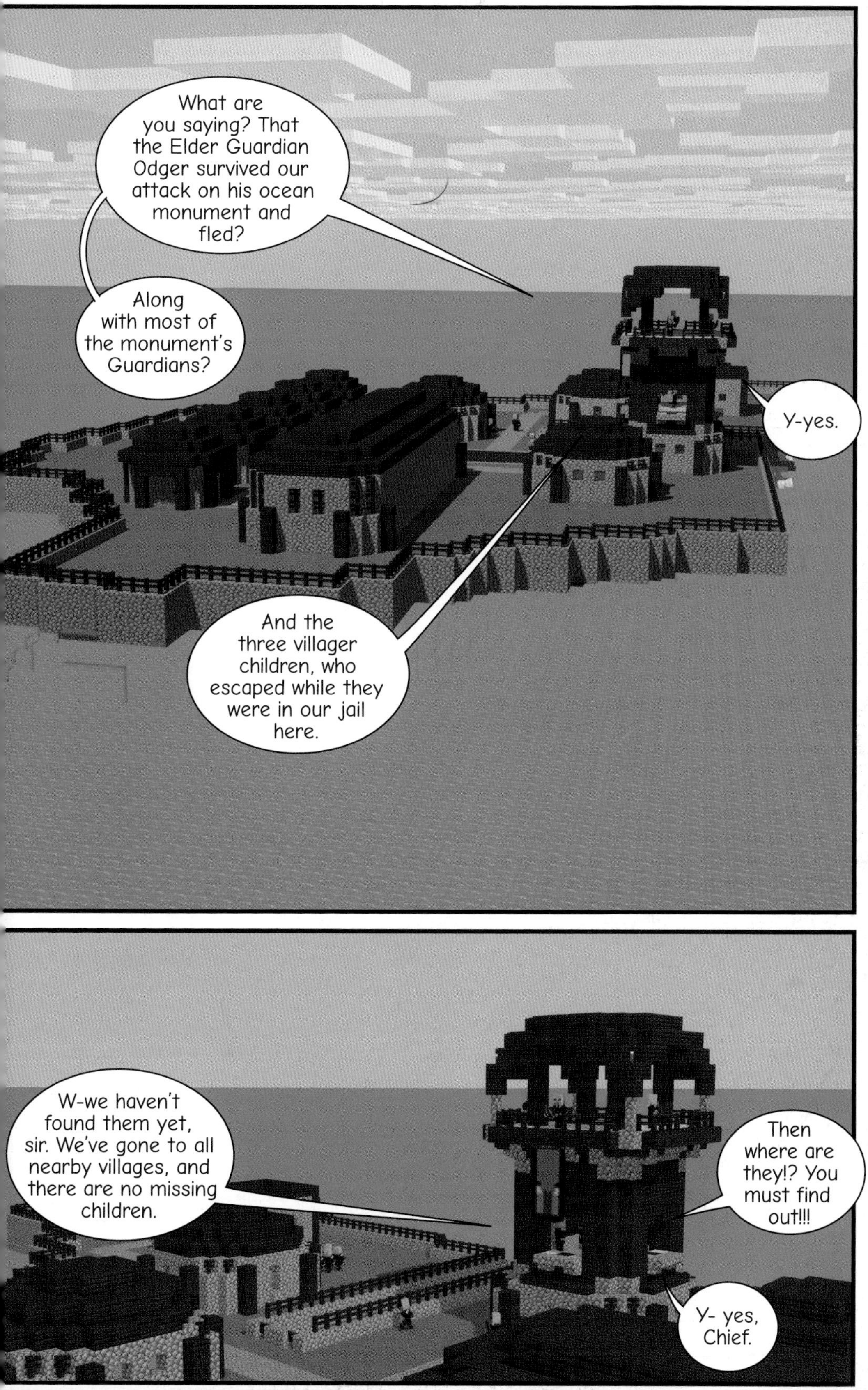
What are you saying? That the Elder Guardian Odger survived our attack on his ocean monument and fled?
Along with most of the monument's Guardians?
Y-yes.
And the three villager children, who escaped while they were in our jail here.
W-we haven't found them yet, sir. We've gone to all nearby villages, and there are no missing children.
Then where are they!? You must find out!!!
Y- yes, Chief.

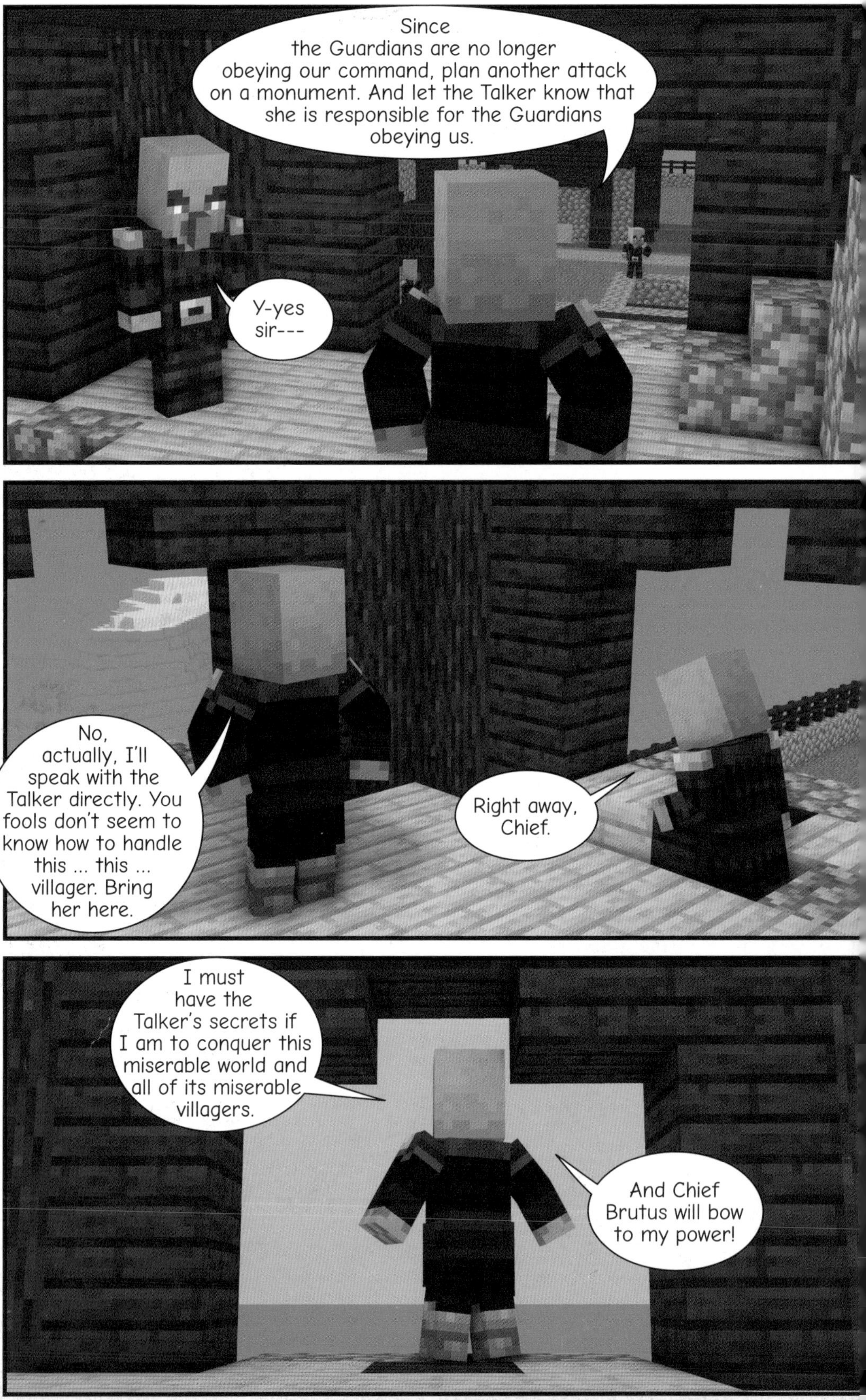
Since the Guardians are no longer obeying our command, plan another attack on a monument. And let the Talker know that she is responsible for the Guardians obeying us.
Y-yes sir---
No, actually, I'll speak with the Talker directly. You fools don't seem to know how to handle this ... this ... villager. Bring her here.
Right away, Chief.
I must have the Talker's secrets if I am to conquer this miserable world and all of its miserable villagers.
And Chief Brutus will bow to my power!

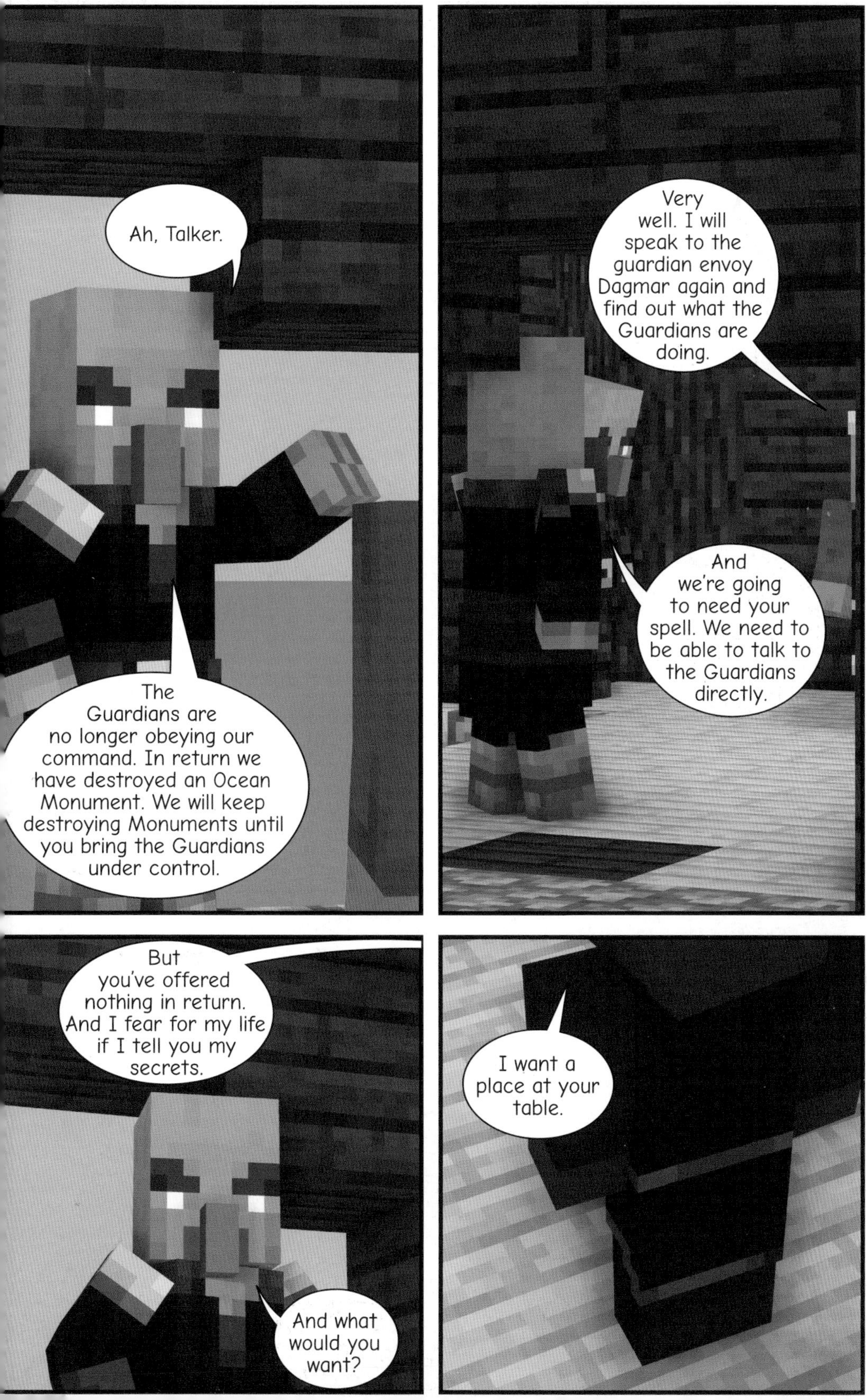
Ah, Talker.
The Guardians are no longer obeying our command. In return we have destroyed an Ocean Monument. We will keep destroying Monuments until you bring the Guardians under control.
Very well. I will speak to the guardian envoy Dagmar again and find out what the Guardians are doing.
And we're going to need your spell. We need to be able to talk to the Guardians directly.
But you've offered nothing in return. And I fear for my life if I tell you my secrets.
And what would you want?
I want a place at your table.

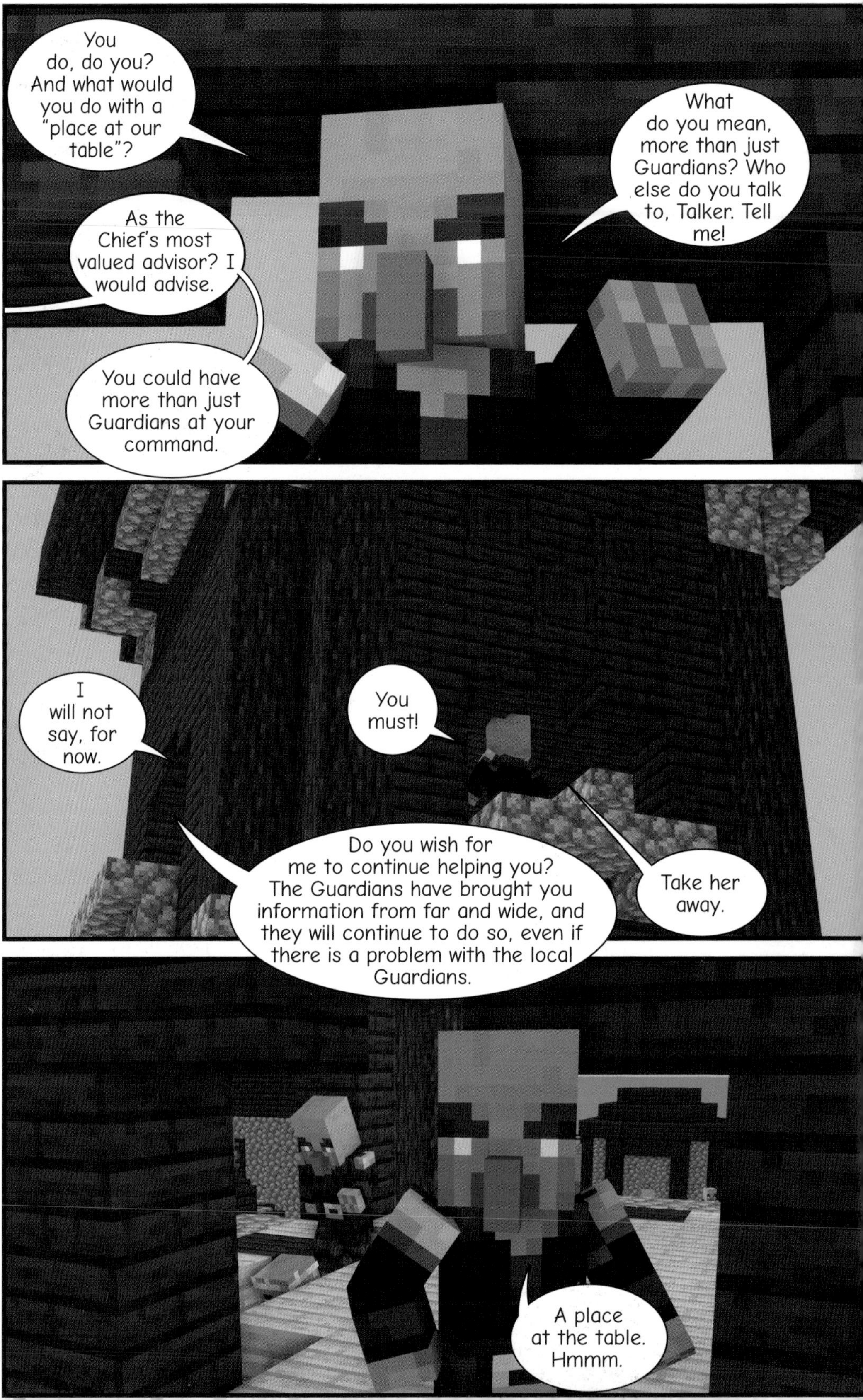
You do, do you? And what would you do with a "place at our table"?
As the Chief's most valued advisor? I would advise.
You could have more than just Guardians at your command.
What do you mean, more than just Guardians? Who else do you talk to, Talker. Tell me!
I will not say, for now.
You must!
Do you wish for me to continue helping you? The Guardians have brought you information from far and wide, and they will continue to do so, even if there is a problem with the local Guardians.
Take her away.
A place at the table. Hmmm.

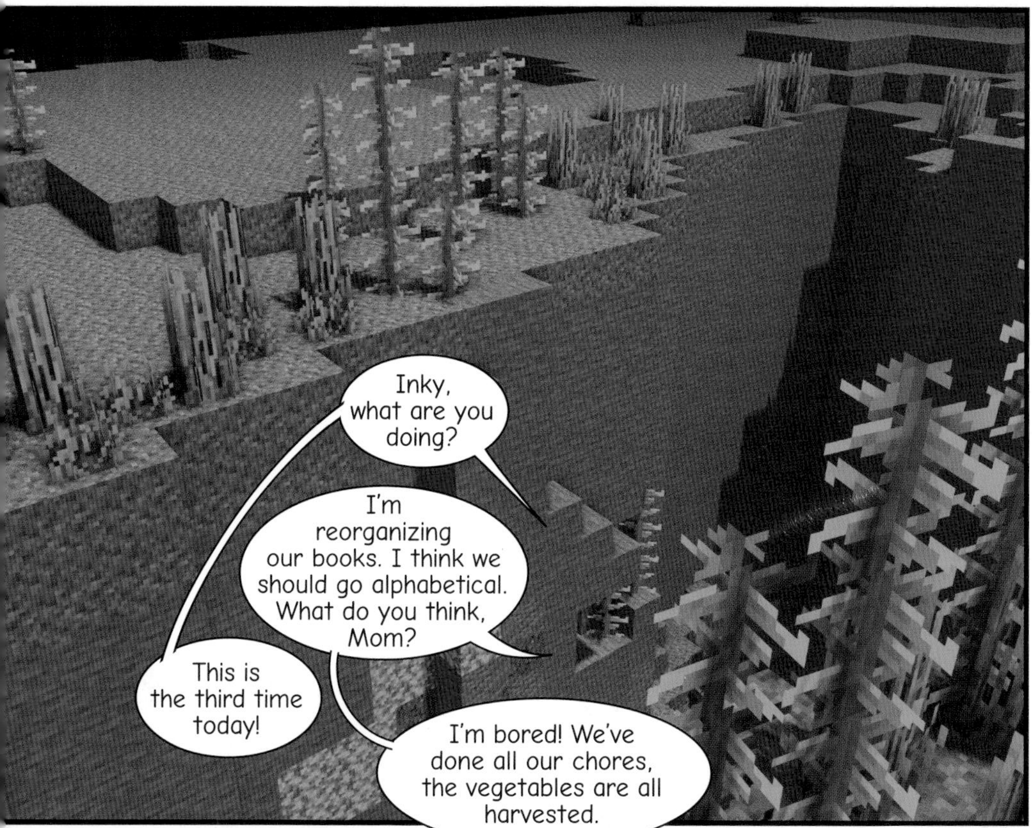
Inky, what are you doing?
I'm reorganizing our books. I think we should go alphabetical. What do you think, Mom?
This is the third time today!
I'm bored! We've done all our chores, the vegetables are all harvested.

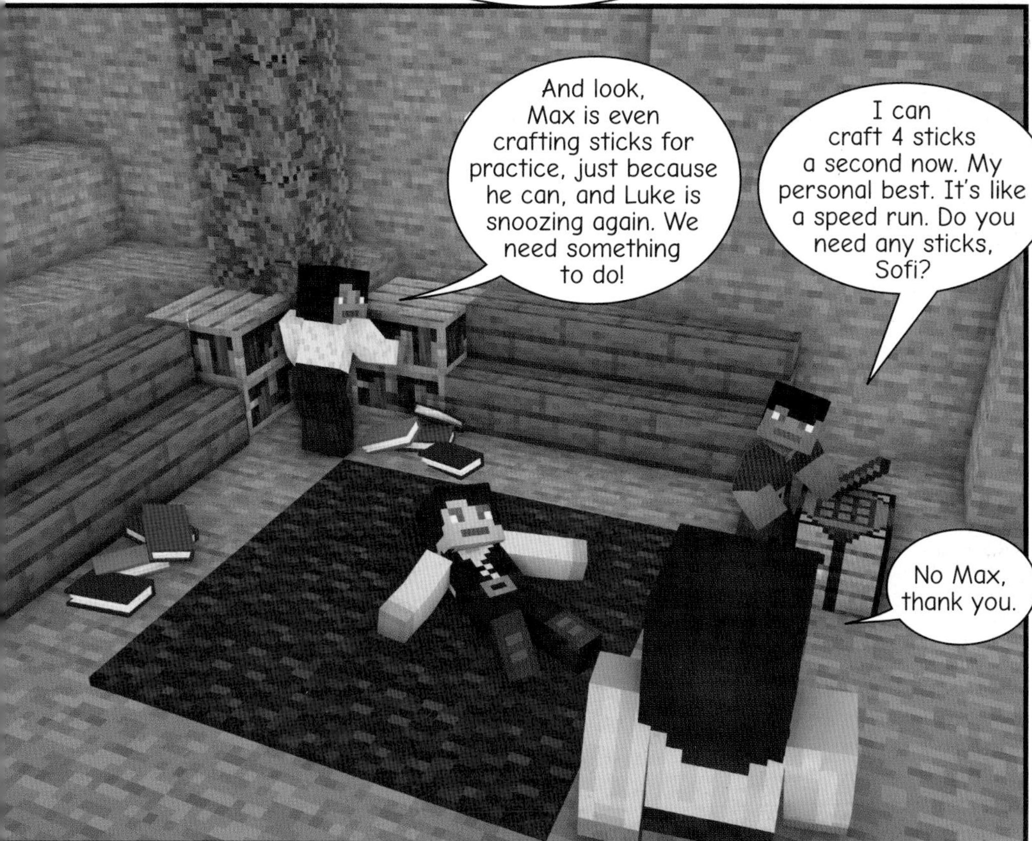
And look, Max is even crafting sticks for practice, just because he can, and Luke is snoozing again. We need something to do!
I can craft 4 sticks a second now. My personal best. It's like a speed run. Do you need any sticks, Sofi?
No Max, thank you.

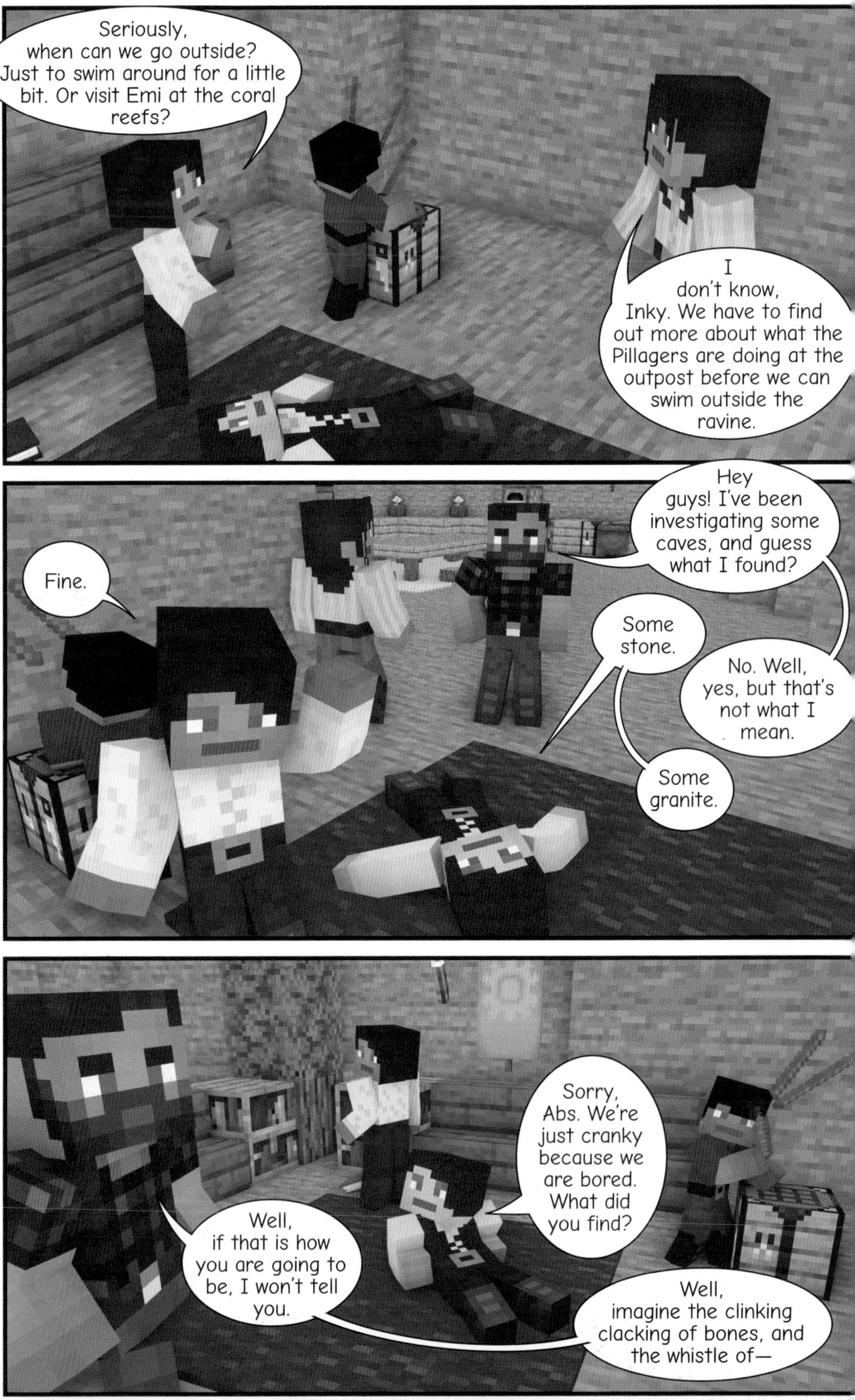
Seriously, when can we go outside? Just to swim around for a little bit. Or visit Emi at the coral reefs?
I don't know, Inky. We have to find out more about what the Pillagers are doing at the outpost before we can swim outside the ravine.
Fine.
Hey guys! I've been investigating some caves, and guess what I found?
Some stone.
No. Well, yes, but that's not what I mean.
Some granite.
Well, if that is how you are going to be, I won't tell you.
Sorry, Abs. We're just cranky because we are bored. What did you find?
Well, imagine the clinking clacking of bones, and the whistle of—

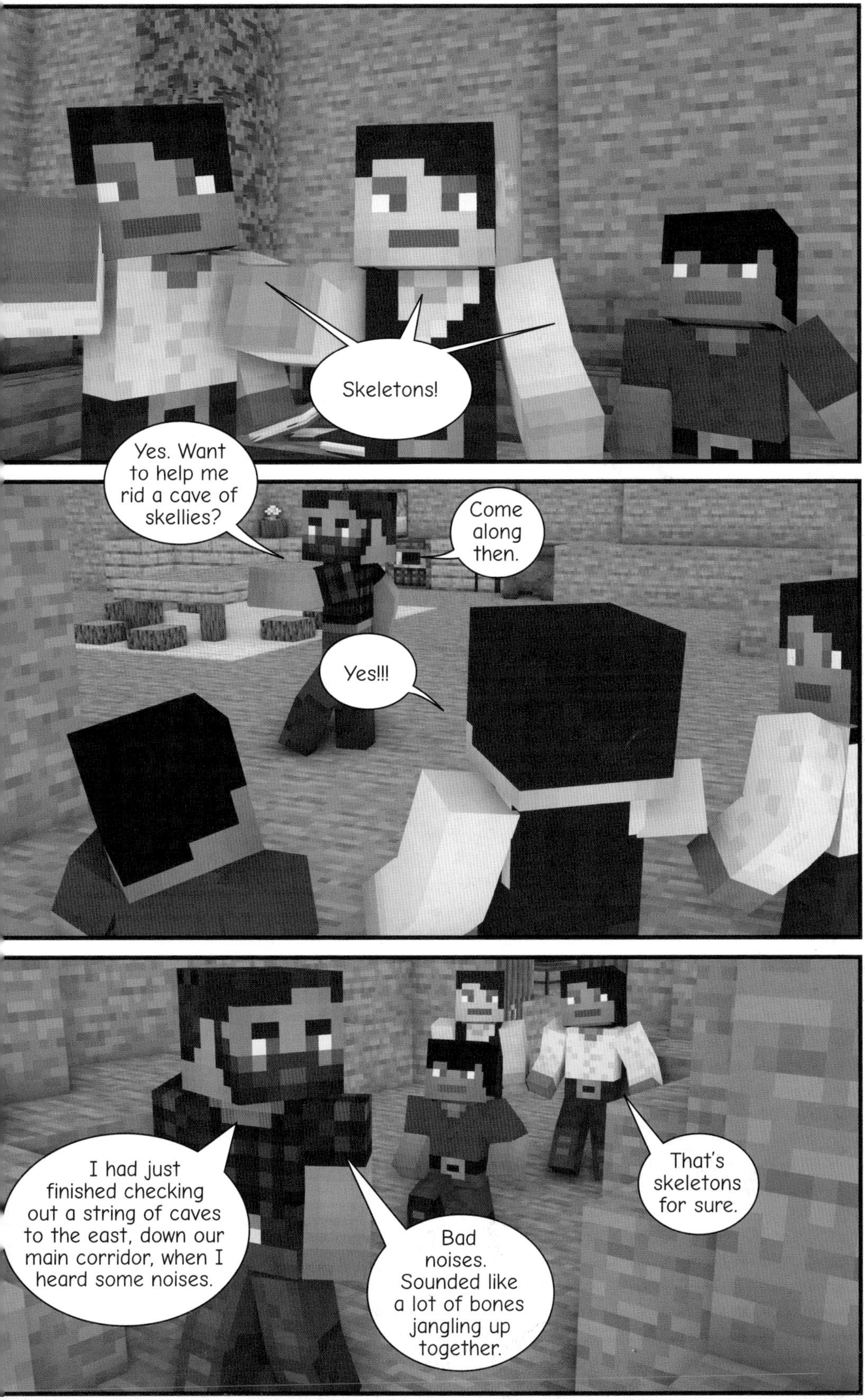
Skeletons!
Yes. Want to help me rid a cave of skellies?
Come along then.
Yes!!!
I had just finished checking out a string of caves to the east, down our main corridor, when I heard some noises.
Bad noises. Sounded like a lot of bones jangling up together.
That's skeletons for sure.

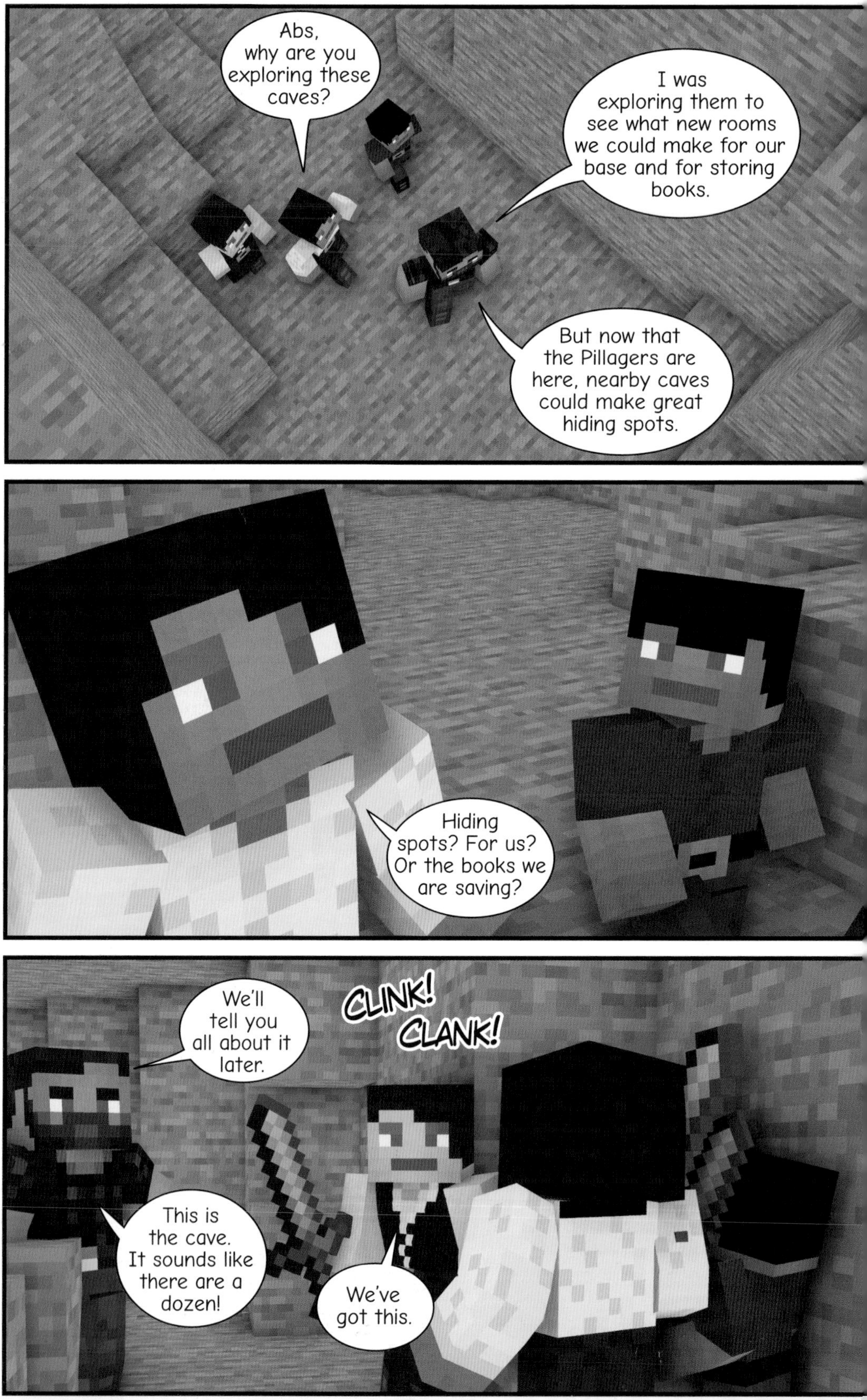
Abs, why are you exploring these caves?
I was exploring them to see what new rooms we could make for our base and for storing books.
But now that the Pillagers are here, nearby caves could make great hiding spots.
Hiding spots? For us? Or the books we are saving?
We'll tell you all about it later.
CLINK! CLANK!
This is the cave. It sounds like there are a dozen!
We've got this.

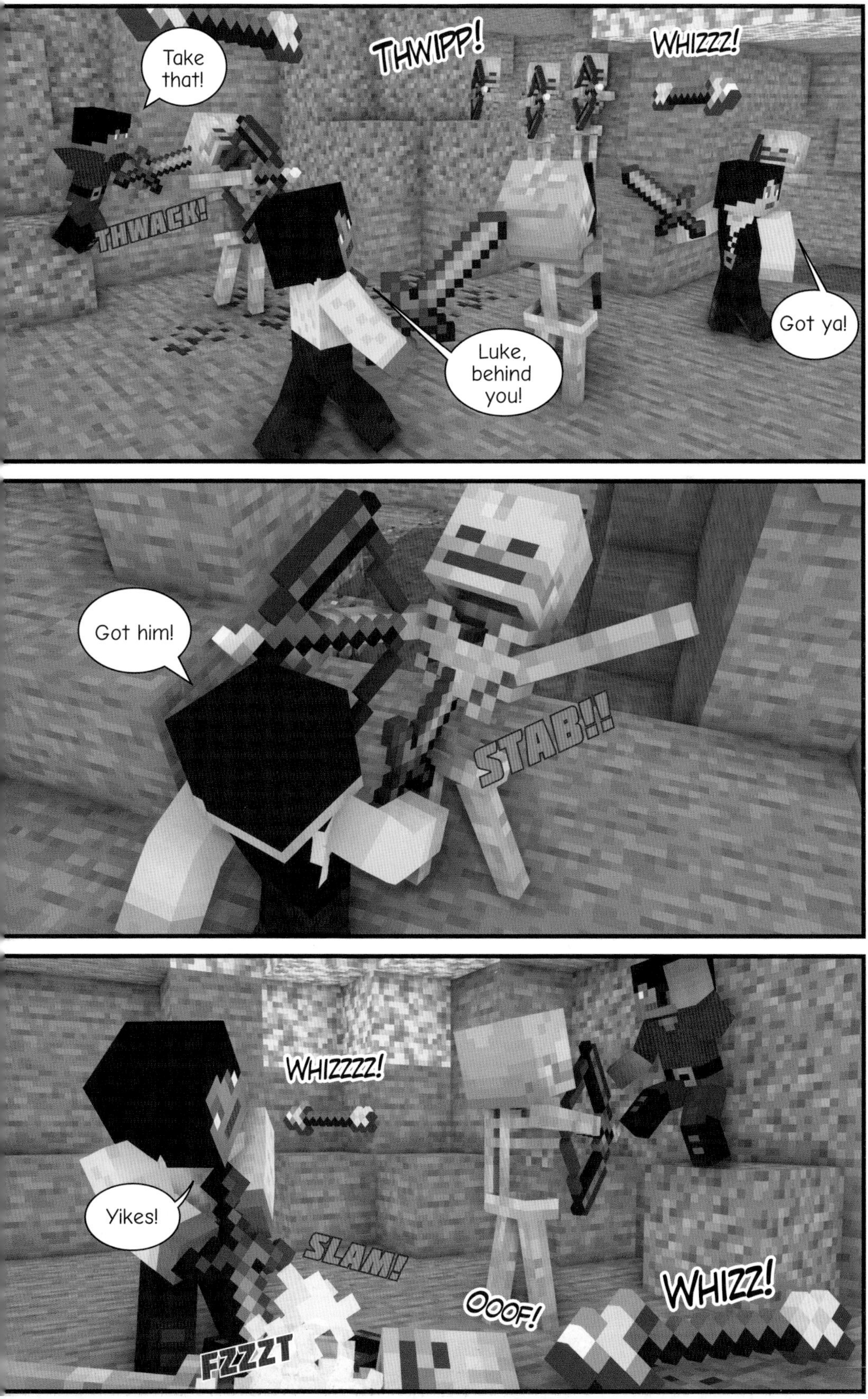
Take that!
THWIPP!
WHIZZZ!
THWACK!
Luke, behind you!
Got ya!
Got him!
STAB!!
WHIZZZZ!
Yikes!
SLAM!
OOOF!
WHIZZ!
FZZZT

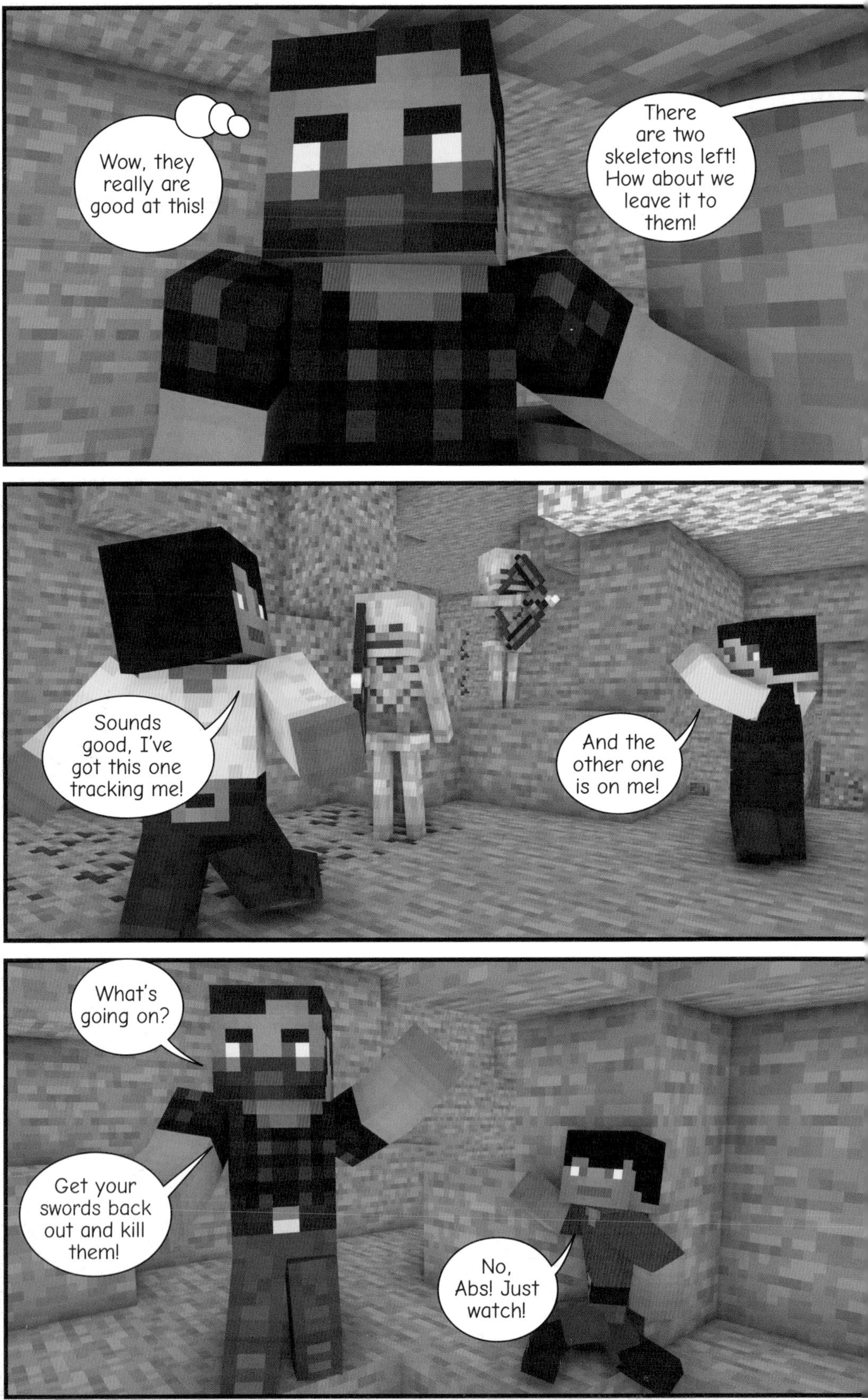
Wow, they really are good at this!
There are two skeletons left! How about we leave it to them!
Sounds good, I've got this one tracking me!
And the other one is on me!
What's going on?
Get your swords back out and kill them!
No, Abs! Just watch!

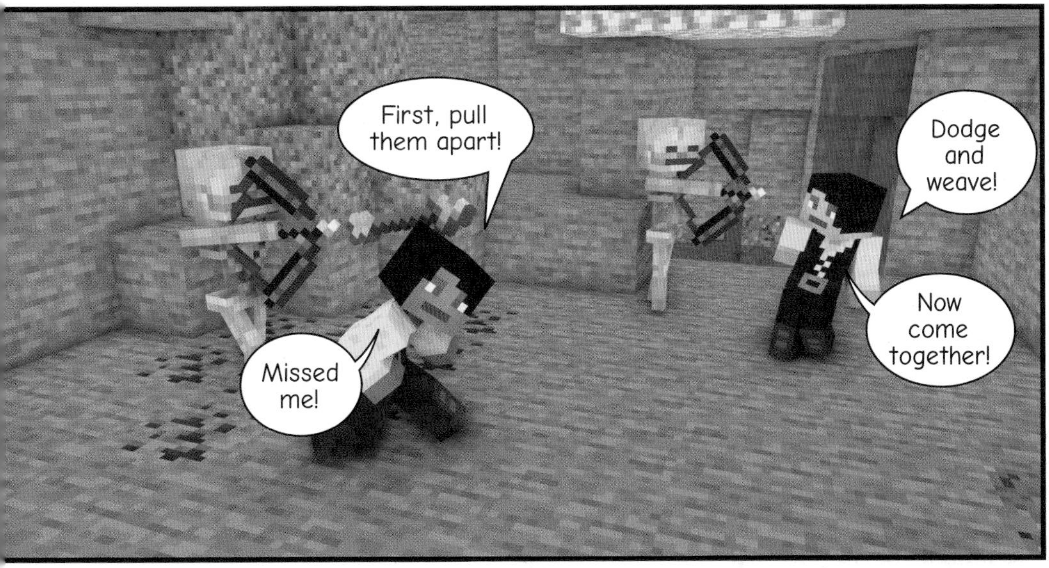
First, pull them apart!
Missed me!
Dodge and weave!
Now come together!

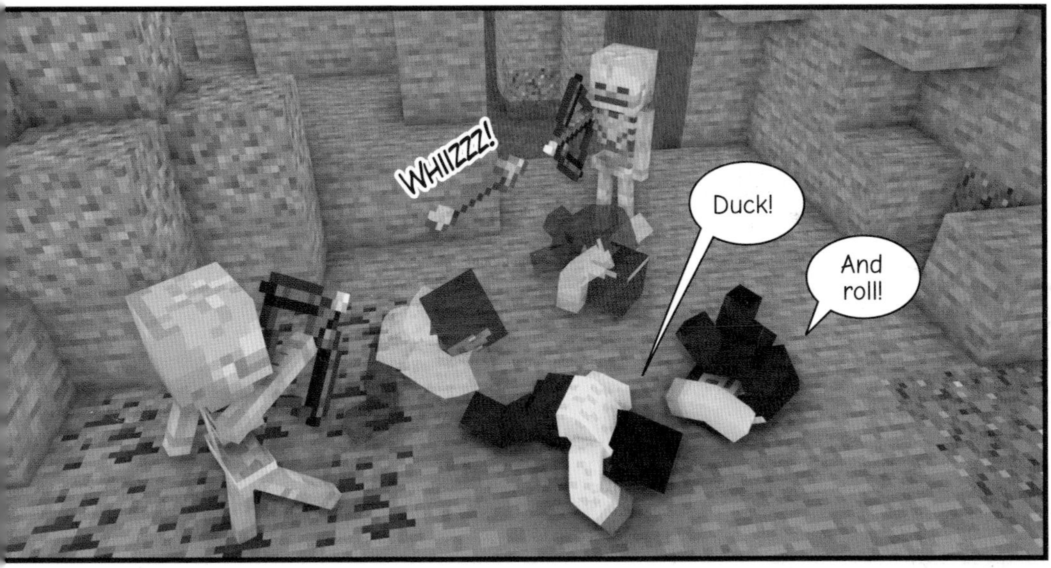
WHIIZZZ!
Duck!
And roll!

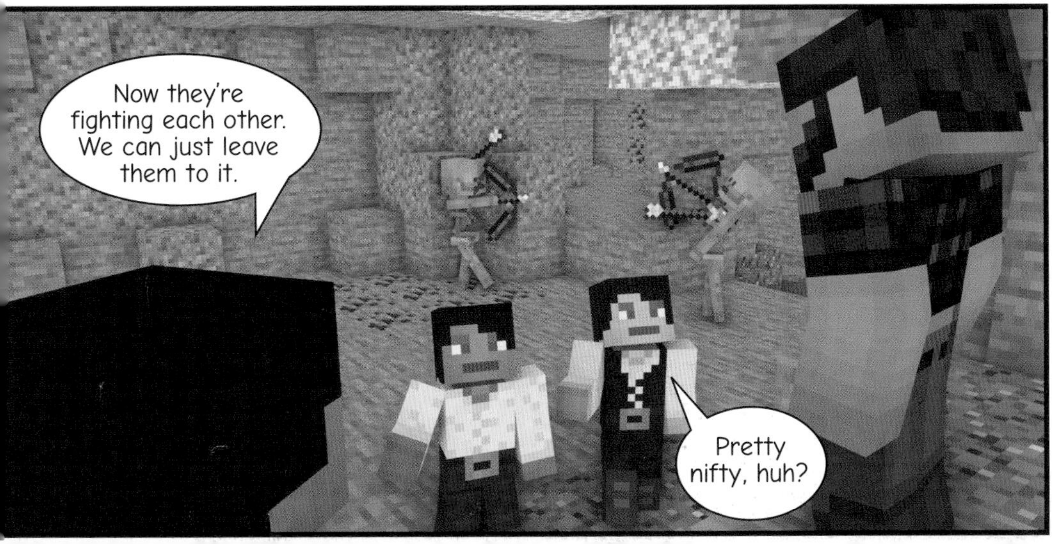
Now they're fighting each other. We can just leave them to it.
Pretty nifty, huh?

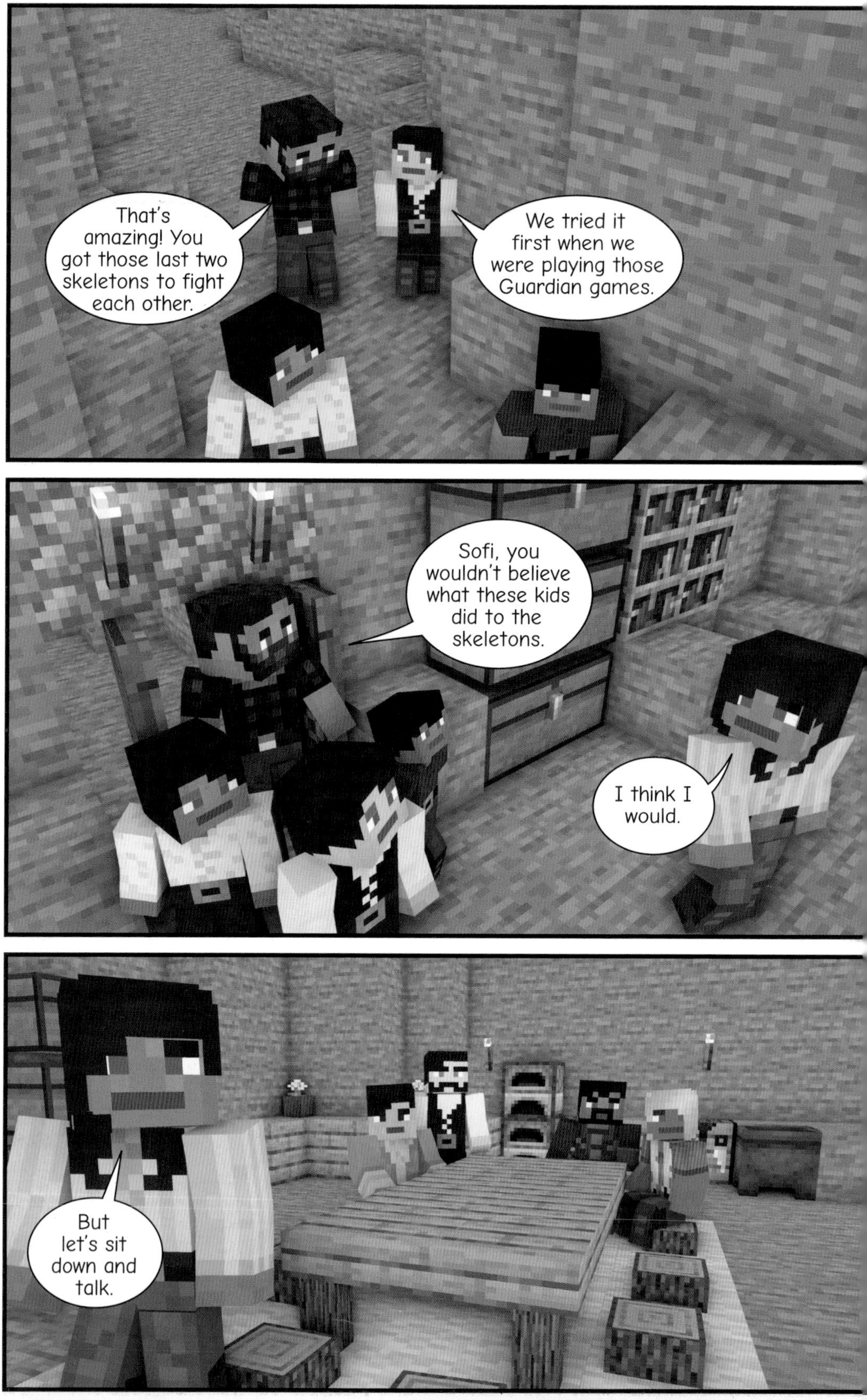
That's amazing! You got those last two skeletons to fight each other.
We tried it first when we were playing those Guardian games.
Sofi, you wouldn't believe what these kids did to the skeletons.
I think I would.
But let's sit down and talk.

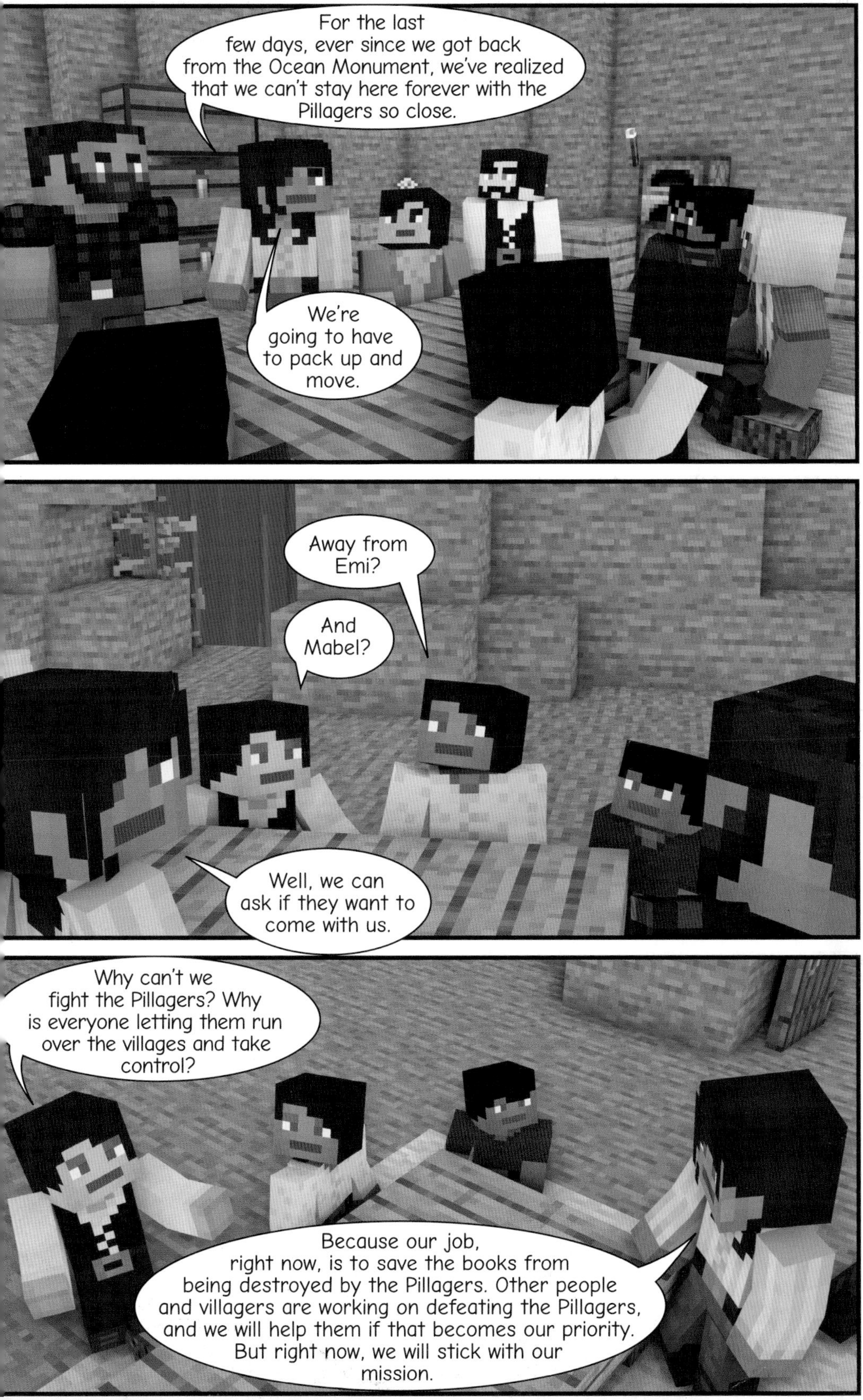
For the last few days, ever since we got back from the Ocean Monument, we've realized that we can't stay here forever with the Pillagers so close.
We're going to have to pack up and move.
Away from Emi?
And Mabel?
Well, we can ask if they want to come with us.
Why can't we fight the Pillagers? Why is everyone letting them run over the villages and take control?
Because our job, right now, is to save the books from being destroyed by the Pillagers. Other people and villagers are working on defeating the Pillagers, and we will help them if that becomes our priority. But right now, we will stick with our mission.

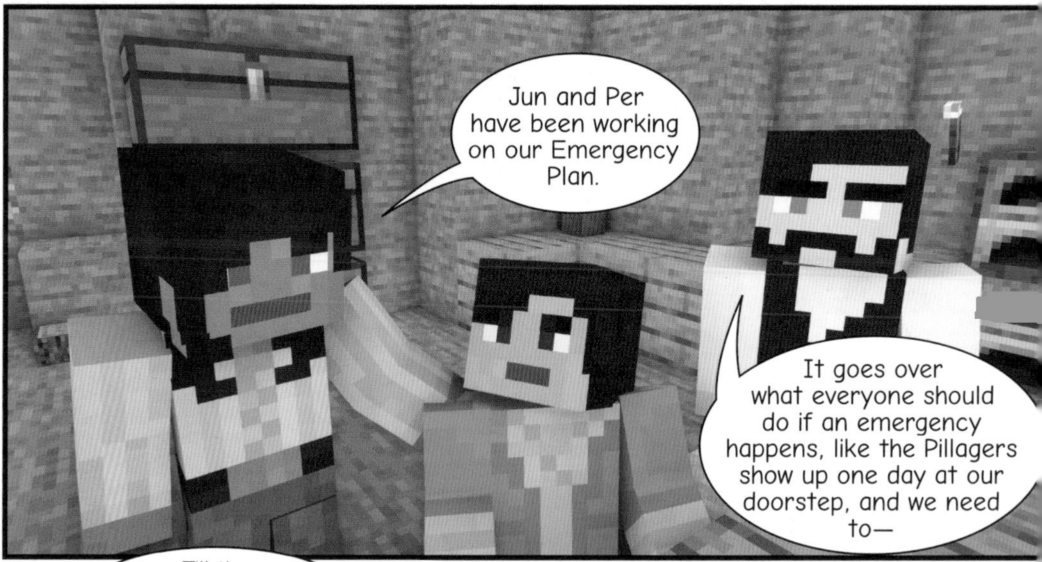
Jun and Per have been working on our Emergency Plan.
It goes over what everyone should do if an emergency happens, like the Pillagers show up one day at our doorstep, and we need to—

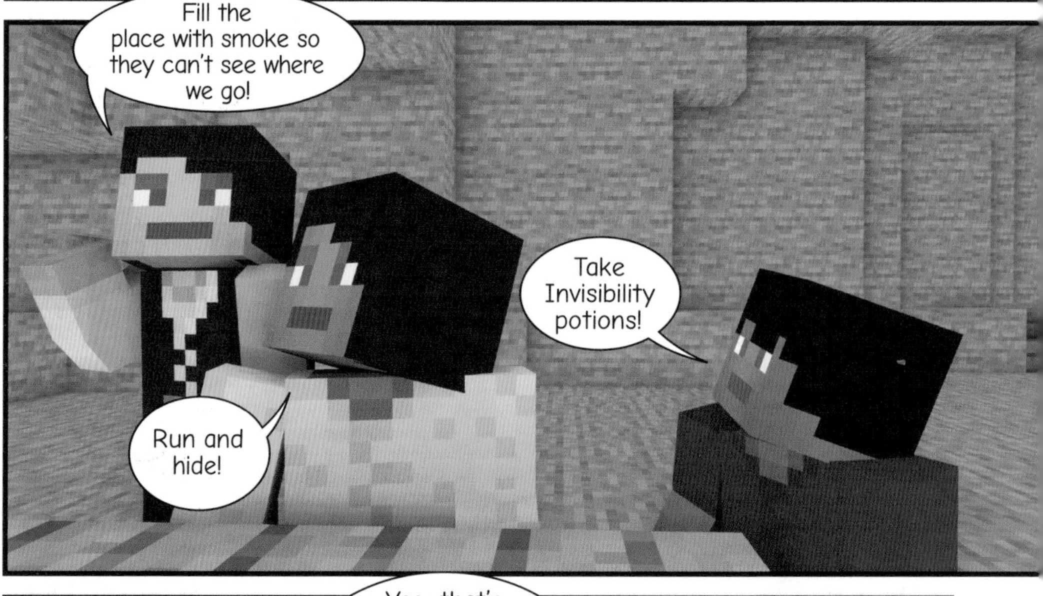
Fill the place with smoke so they can't see where we go!
Take Invisibility potions!
Run and hide!

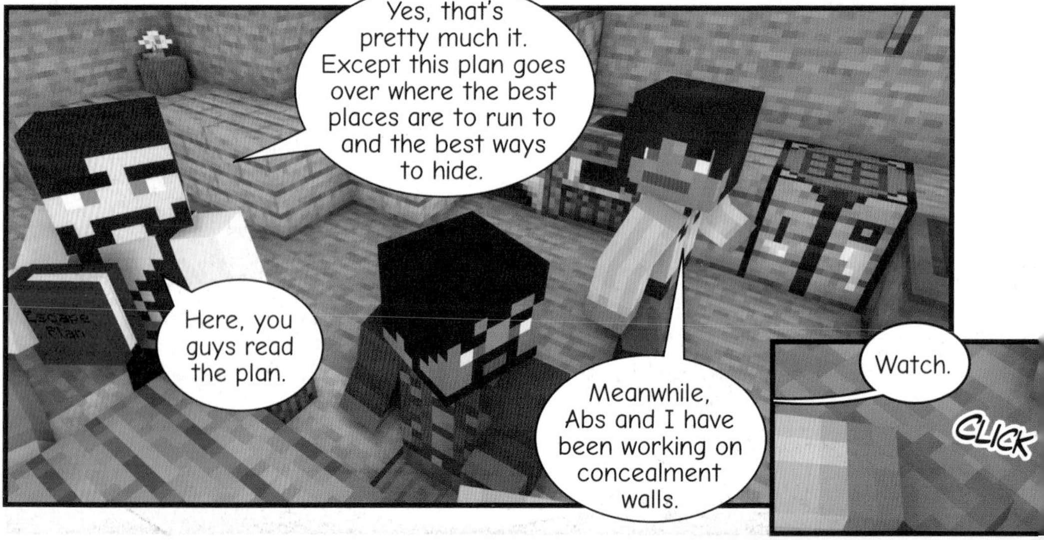
Yes, that's pretty much it. Except this plan goes over where the best places are to run to and the best ways to hide.
Here, you guys read the plan.
Meanwhile, Abs and I have been working on concealment walls.
Watch.
CLICK

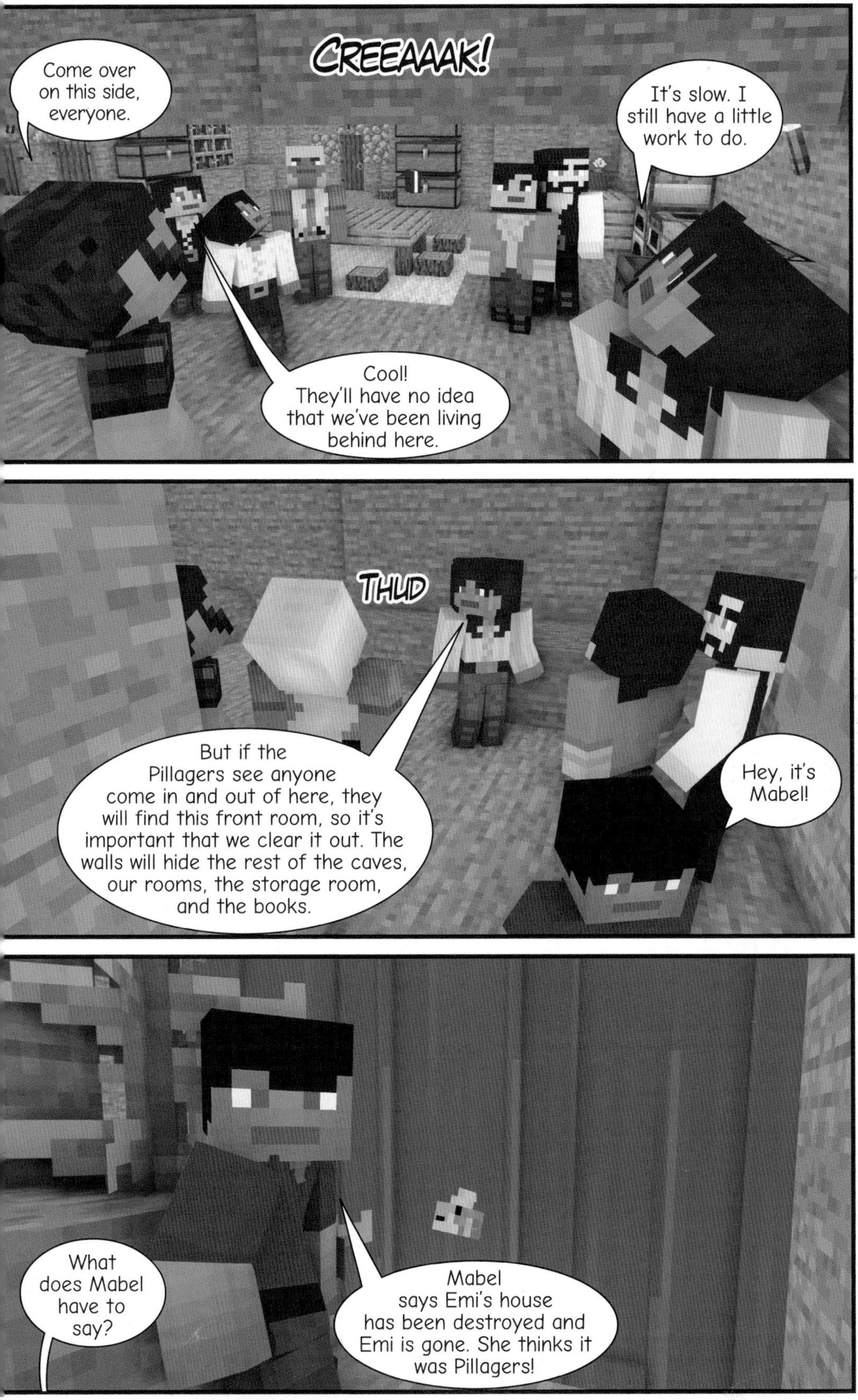
CREEAAAK!
Come over on this side, everyone.
It's slow. I still have a little work to do.
Cool! They'll have no idea that we've been living behind here.
THUD
But if the Pillagers see anyone come in and out of here, they will find this front room, so it's important that we clear it out. The walls will hide the rest of the caves, our rooms, the storage room, and the books.
Hey, it's Mabel!
What does Mabel have to say?
Mabel says Emi's house has been destroyed and Emi is gone. She thinks it was Pillagers!

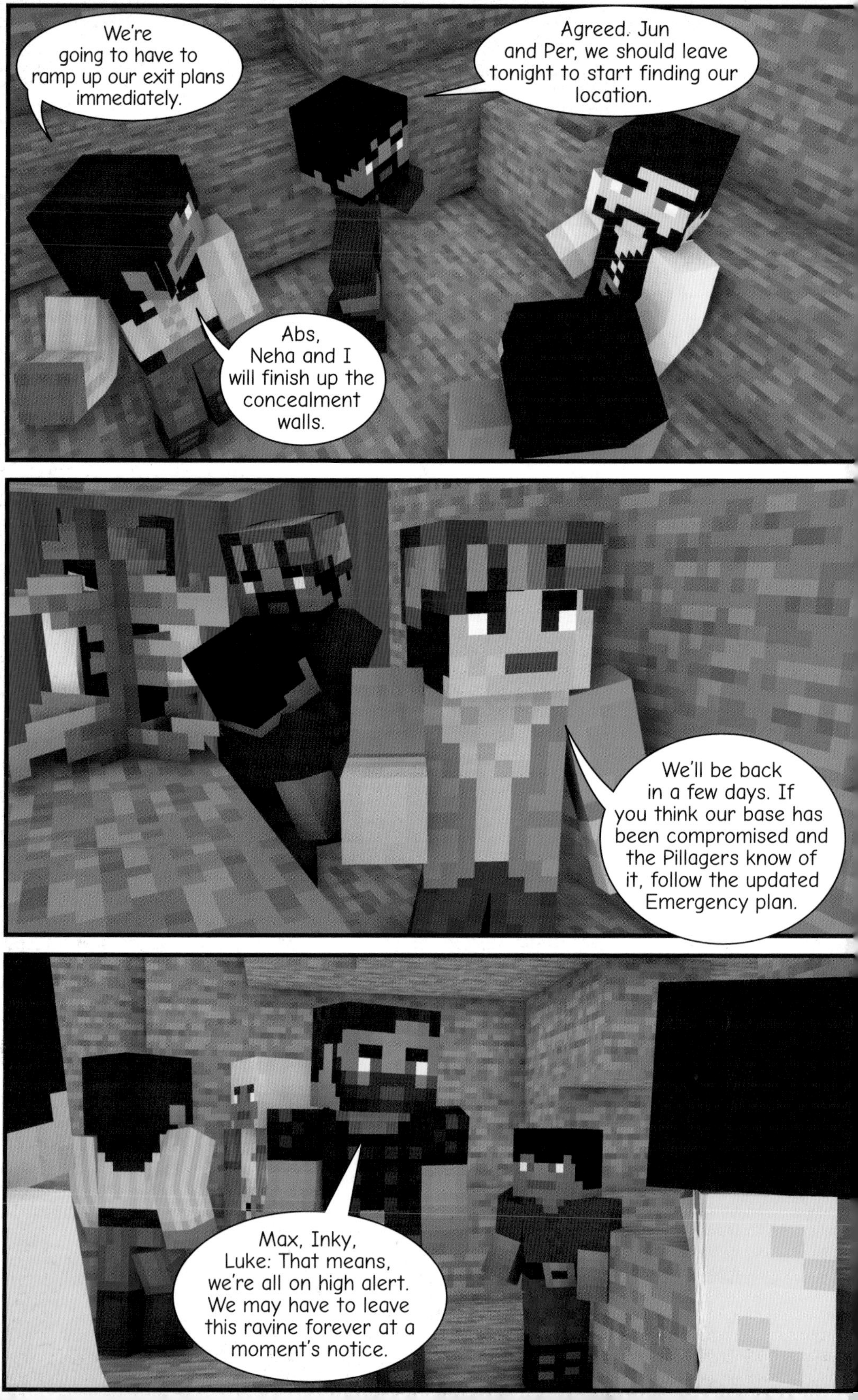
We're going to have to ramp up our exit plans immediately.
Agreed. Jun and Per, we should leave tonight to start finding our location.
Abs, Neha and I will finish up the concealment walls.
We'll be back in a few days. If you think our base has been compromised and the Pillagers know of it, follow the updated Emergency plan.
Max, Inky, Luke: That means, we're all on high alert. We may have to leave this ravine forever at a moment's notice.

Chapter 2
A Pillager Chat

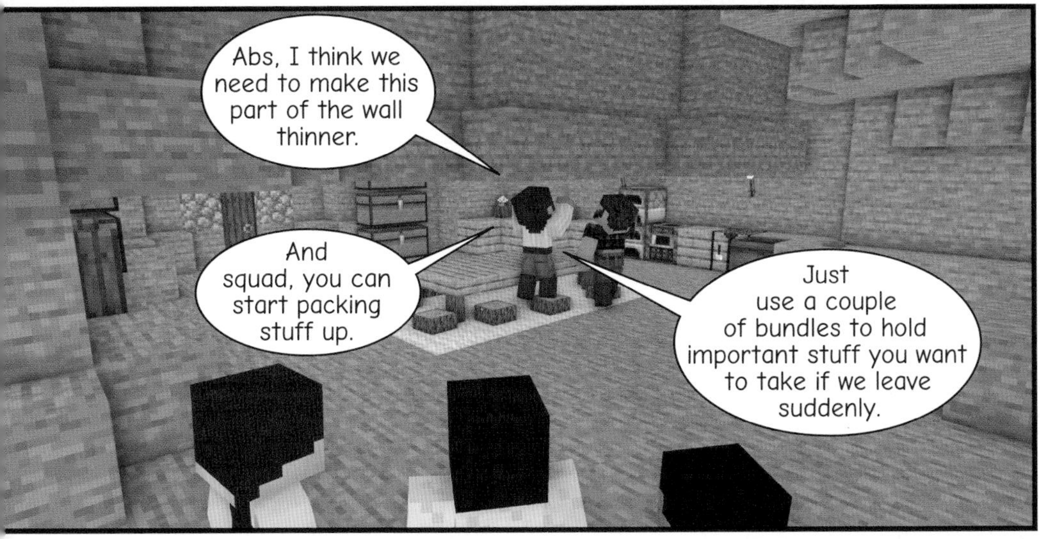
Abs, I think we need to make this part of the wall thinner.
And squad, you can start packing stuff up.
Just use a couple of bundles to hold important stuff you want to take if we leave suddenly.

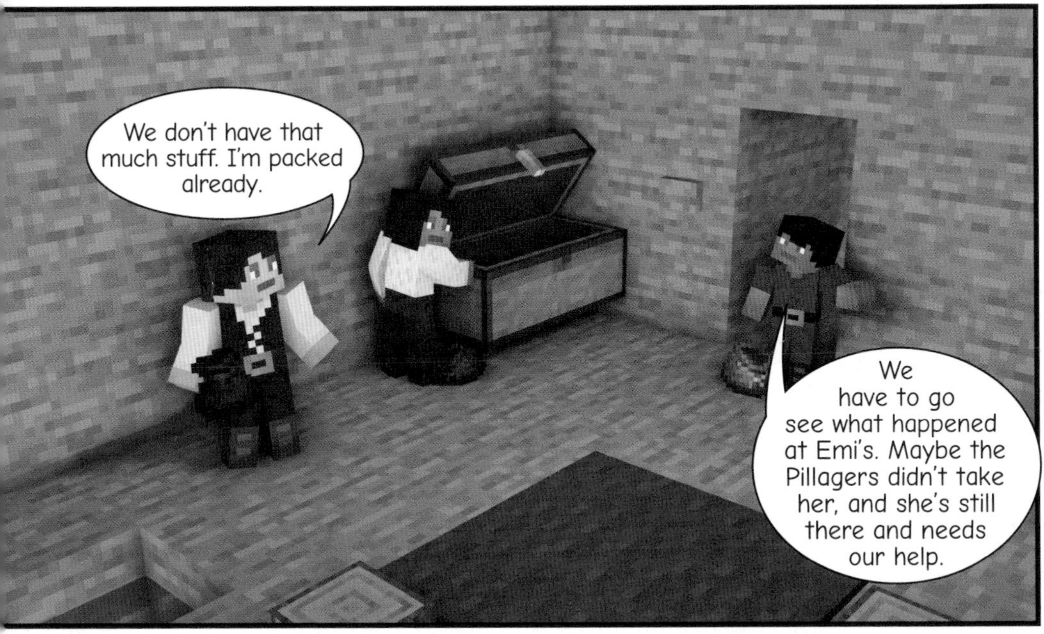
We don't have that much stuff. I'm packed already.
We have to go see what happened at Emi's. Maybe the Pillagers didn't take her, and she's still there and needs our help.

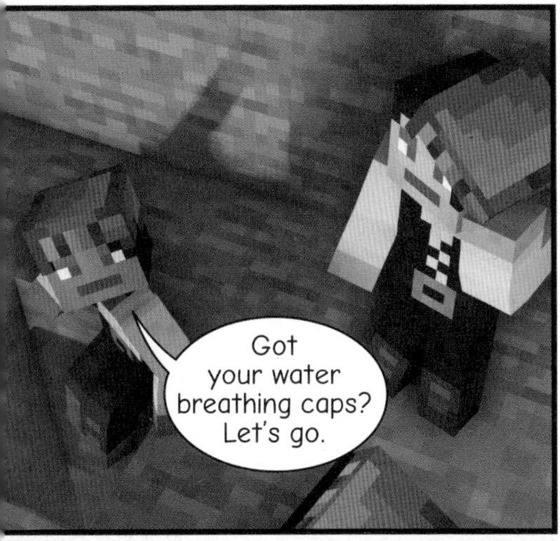
Got your water breathing caps? Let's go.

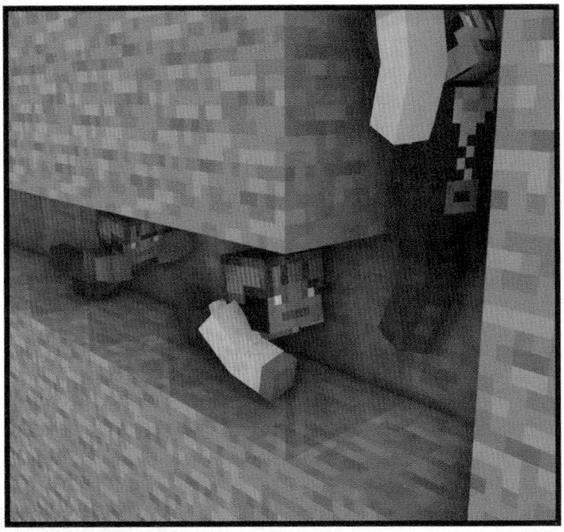

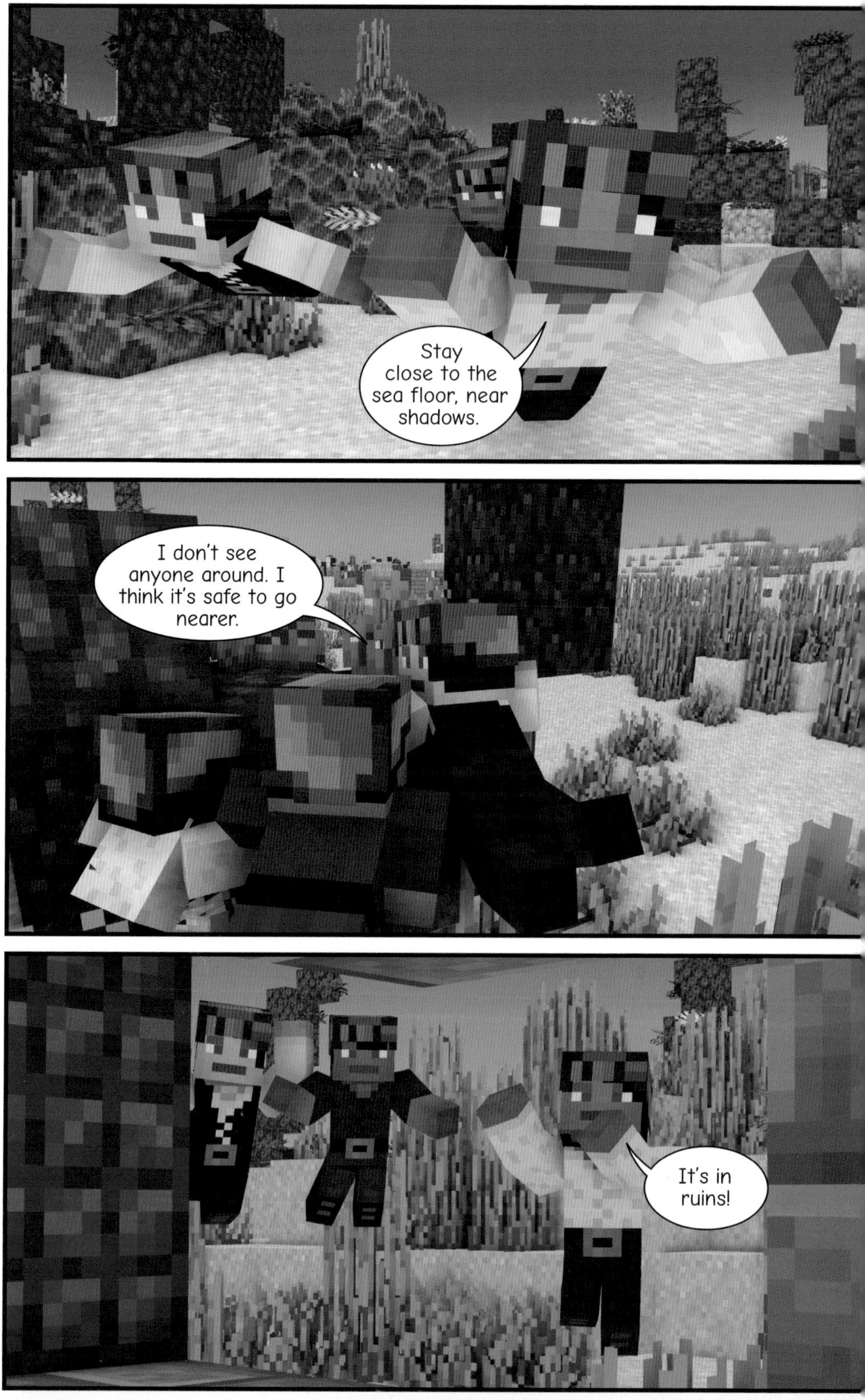
Stay close to the sea floor, near shadows.
I don't see anyone around. I think it's safe to go nearer.
It's in ruins!

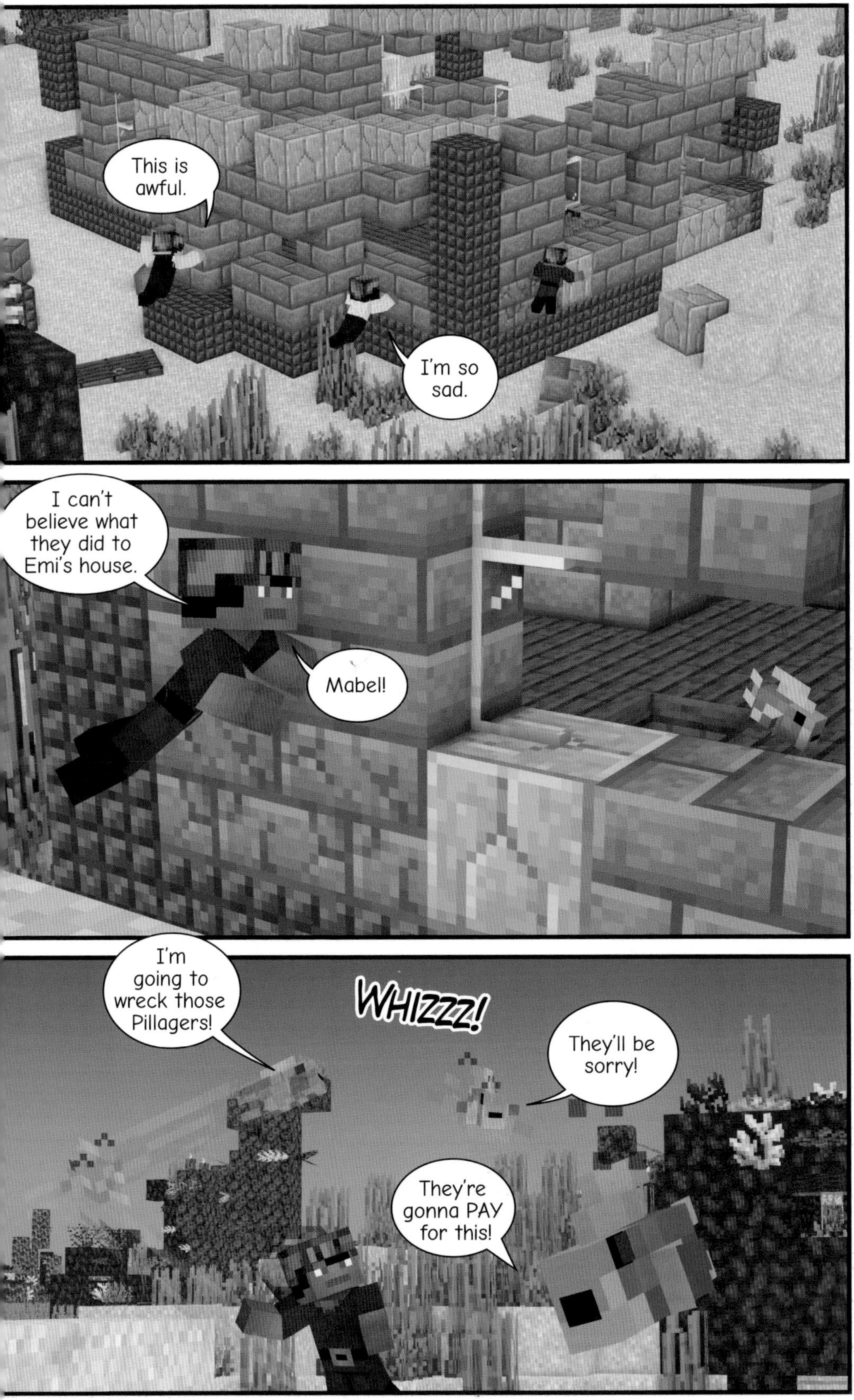
This is awful.
I'm so sad.
I can't believe what they did to Emi's house.
Mabel!
I'm going to wreck those Pillagers!
WHIZZZ!
They'll be sorry!
They're gonna PAY for this!

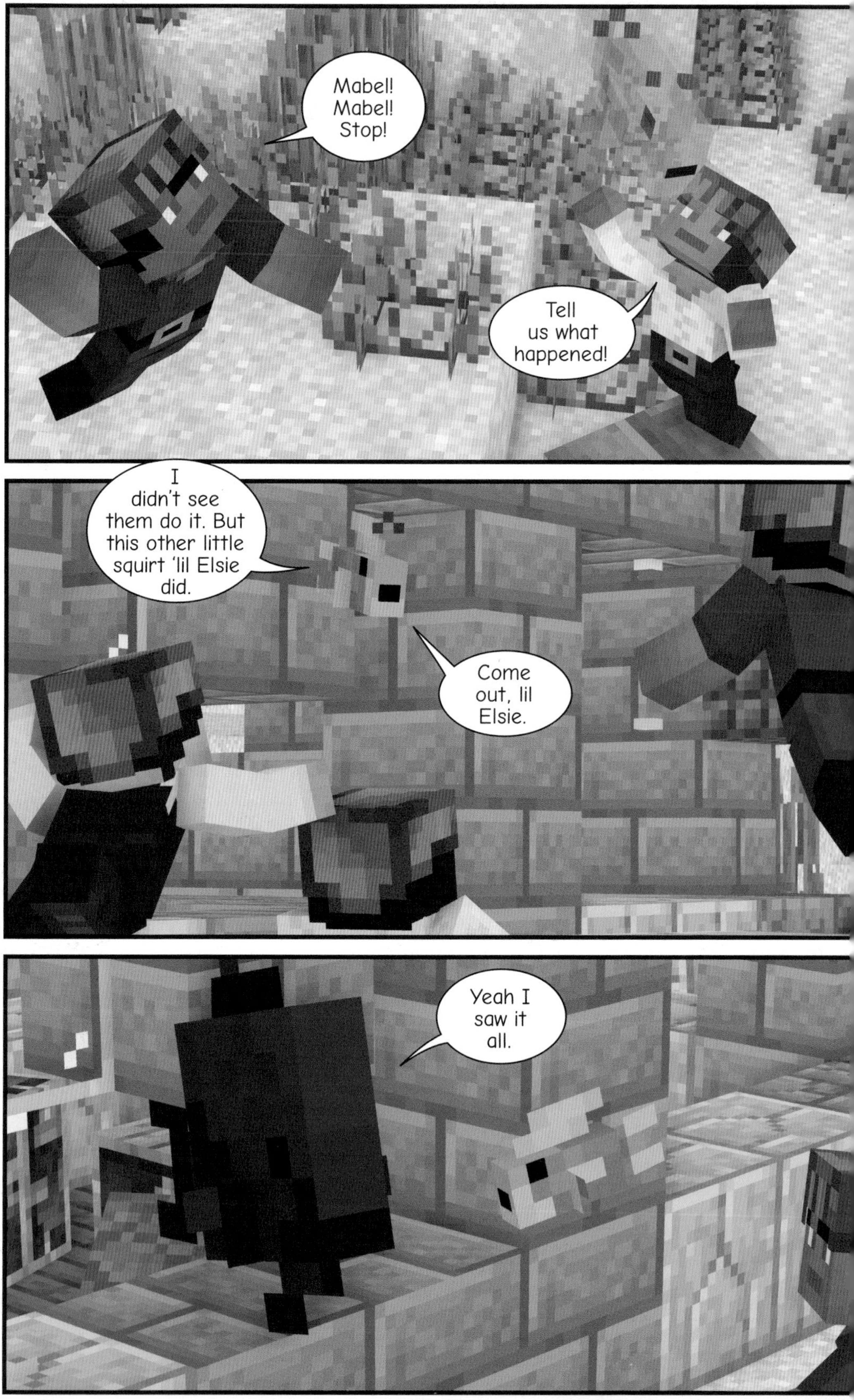
Mabel! Mabel! Stop!
Tell us what happened!
I didn't see them do it. But this other little squirt 'lil Elsie did.
Come out, lil Elsie.
Yeah I saw it all.

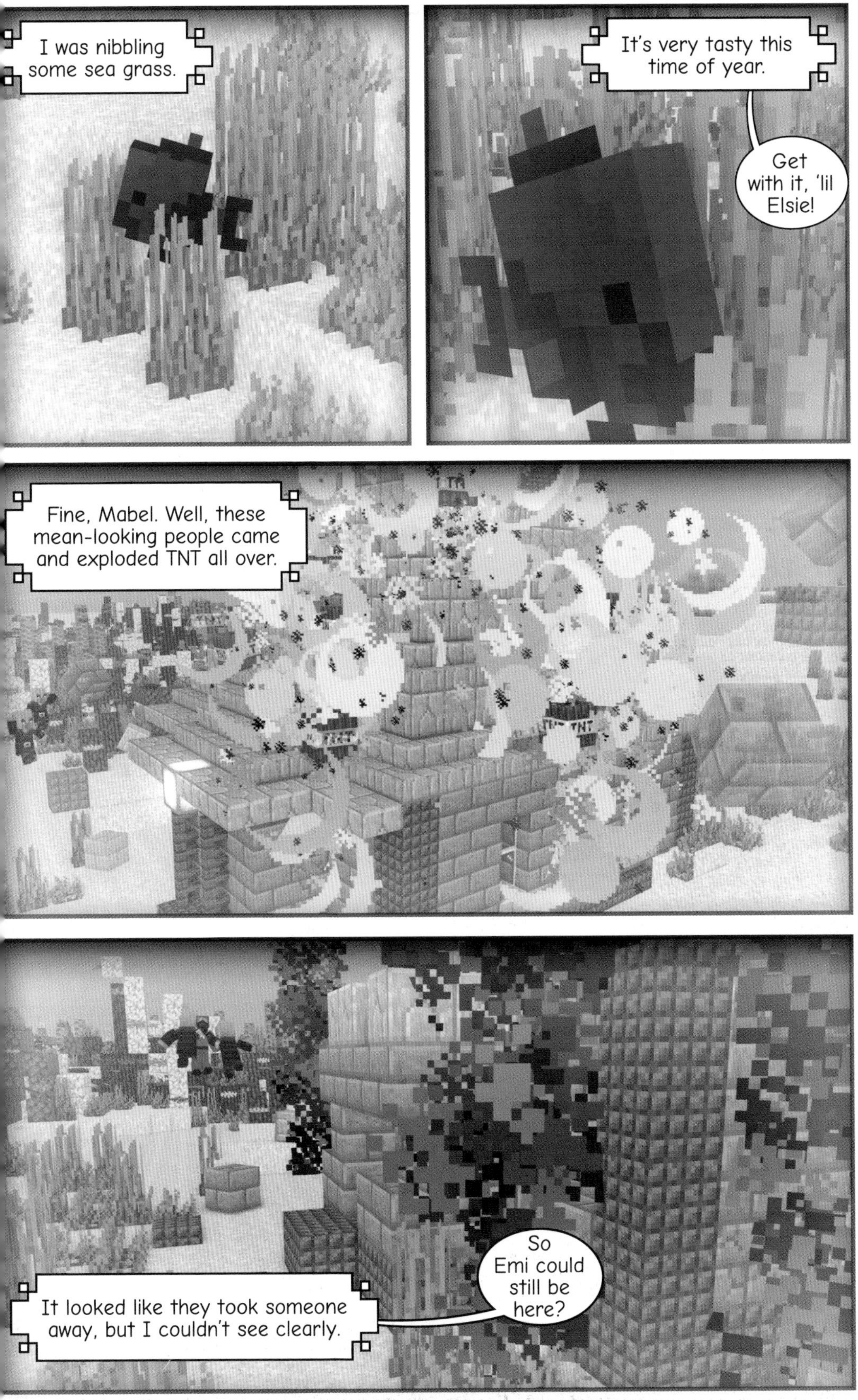
I was nibbling some sea grass.
It's very tasty this time of year.
Get with it, 'lil Elsie!
Fine, Mabel. Well, these mean-looking people came and exploded TNT all over.
It looked like they took someone away, but I couldn't see clearly.
So Emi could still be here?

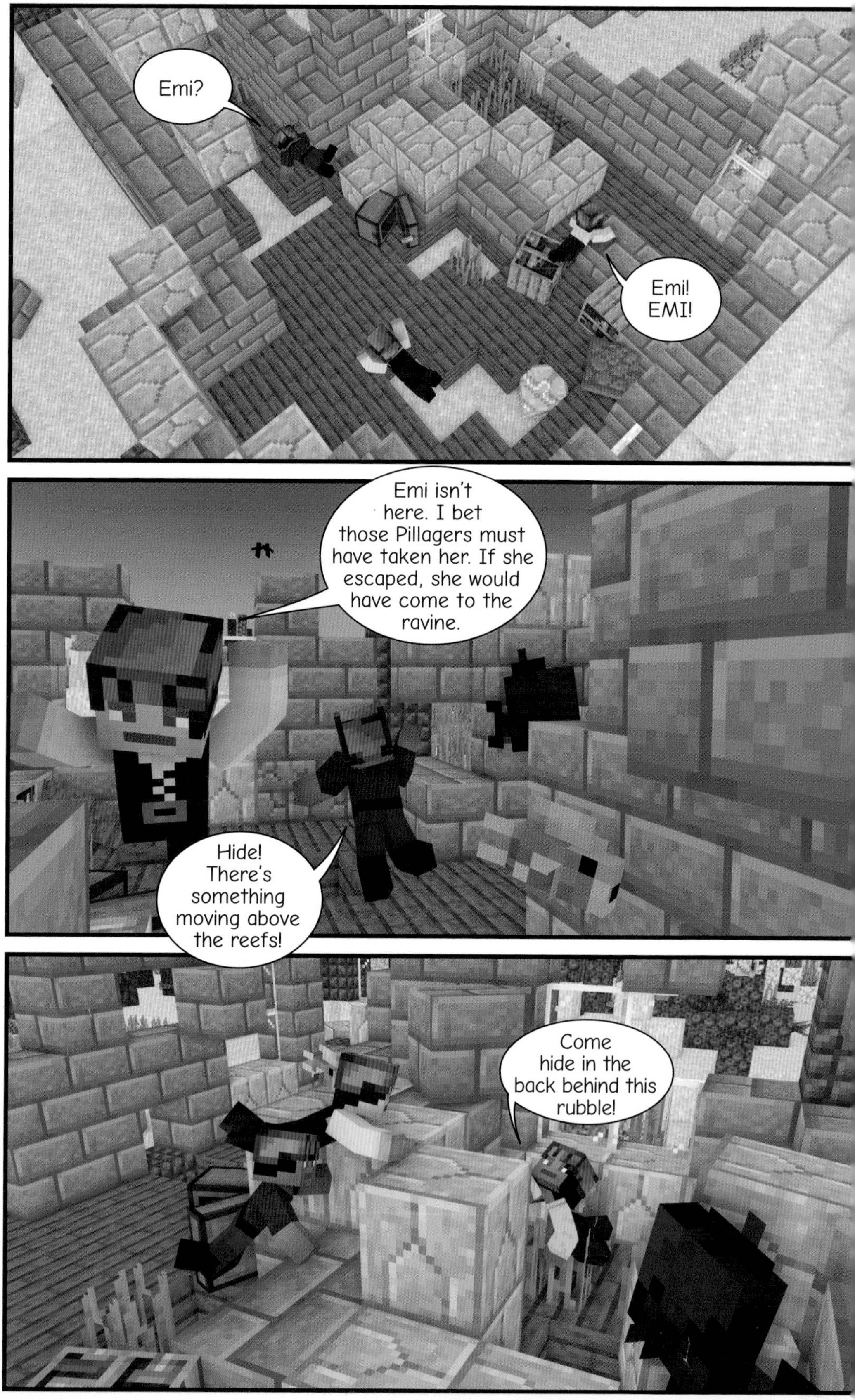
Emi?
Emi! EMI!
Emi isn't here. I bet those Pillagers must have taken her. If she escaped, she would have come to the ravine.
Hide! There's something moving above the reefs!
Come hide in the back behind this rubble!

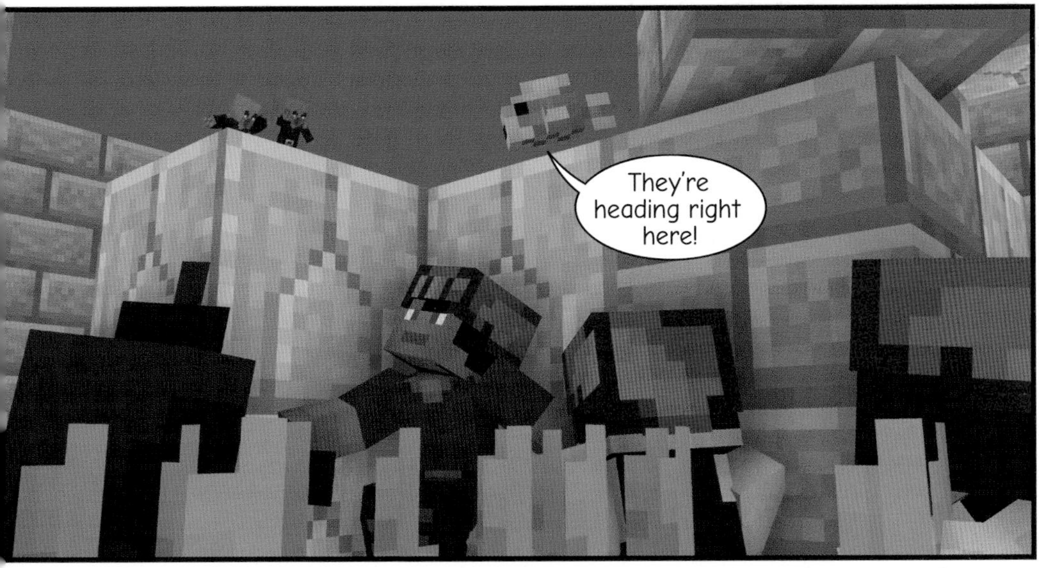
They're heading right here!

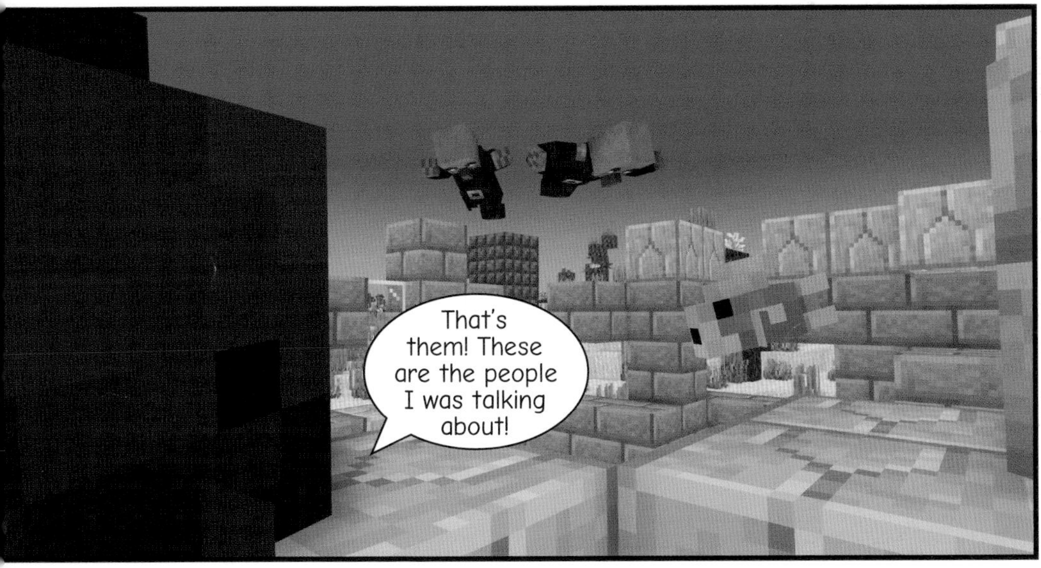
That's them! These are the people I was talking about!

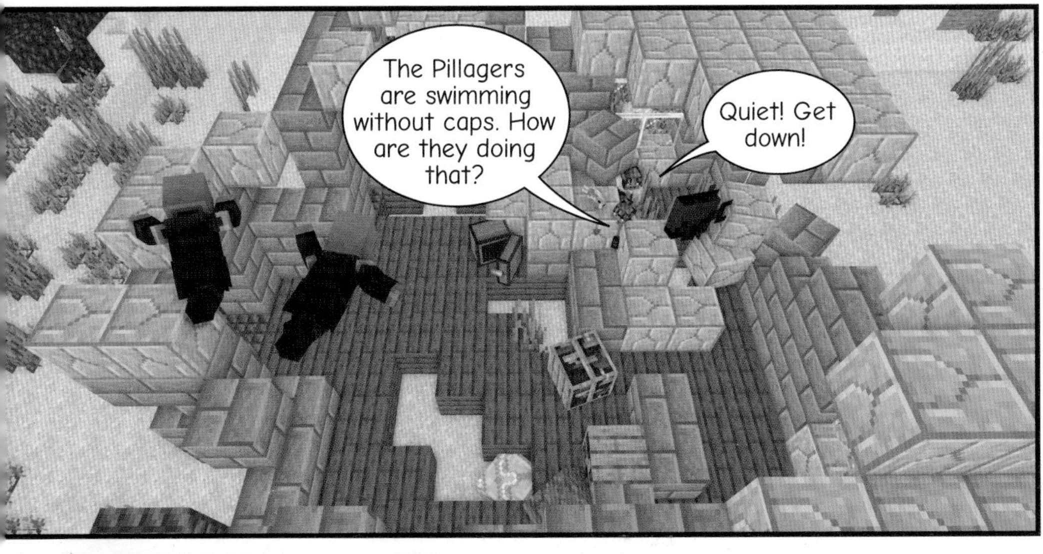
The Pillagers are swimming without caps. How are they doing that?
Quiet! Get down!

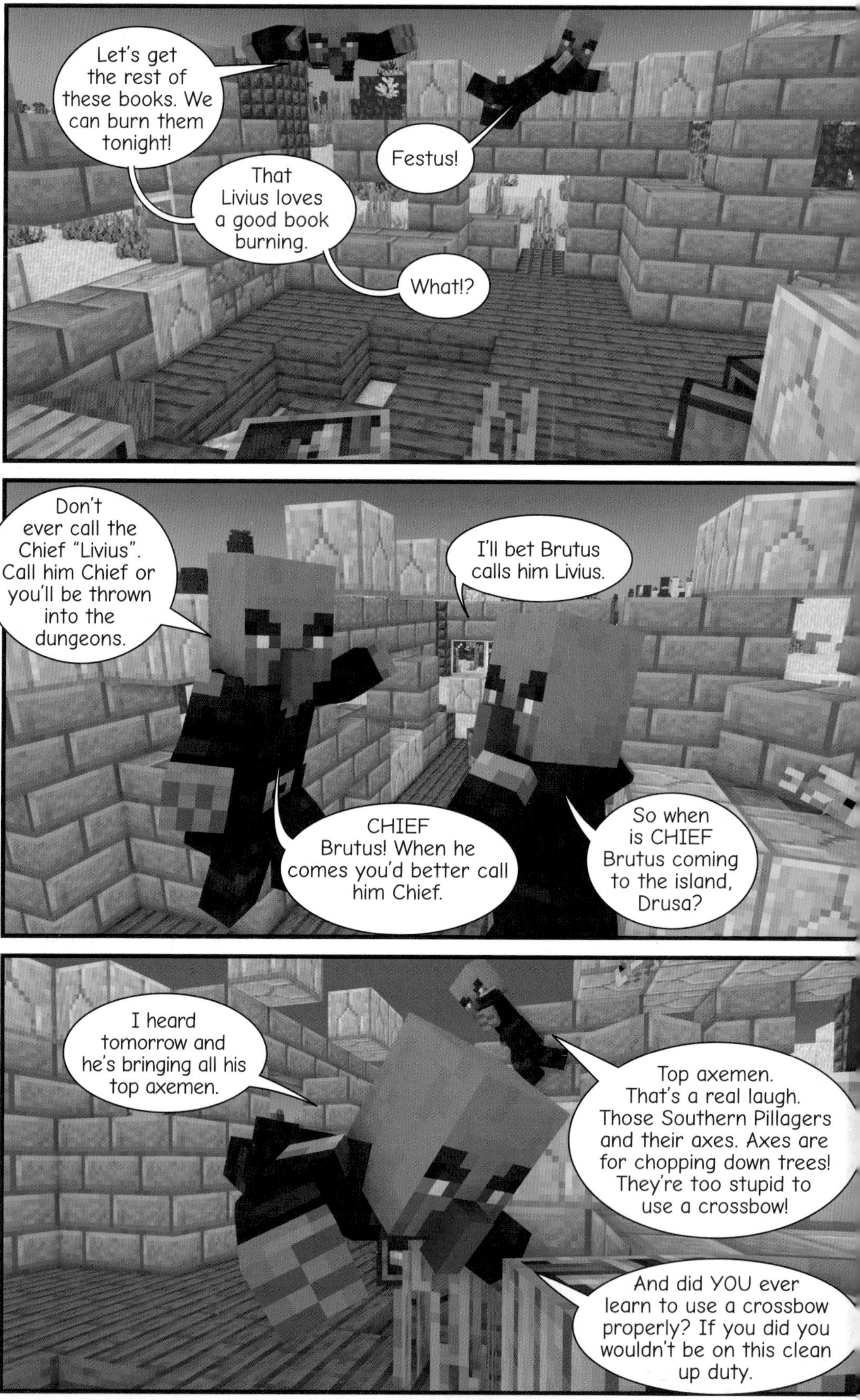
Let's get the rest of these books. We can burn them tonight!
Festus!
That Livius loves a good book burning.
What!?
Don't ever call the Chief "Livius". Call him Chief or you'll be thrown into the dungeons.
I'll bet Brutus calls him Livius.
CHIEF Brutus! When he comes you'd better call him Chief.
So when is CHIEF Brutus coming to the island, Drusa?
I heard tomorrow and he's bringing all his top axemen.
Top axemen. That's a real laugh. Those Southern Pillagers and their axes. Axes are for chopping down trees! They're too stupid to use a crossbow!
And did YOU ever learn to use a crossbow properly? If you did you wouldn't be on this clean up duty.

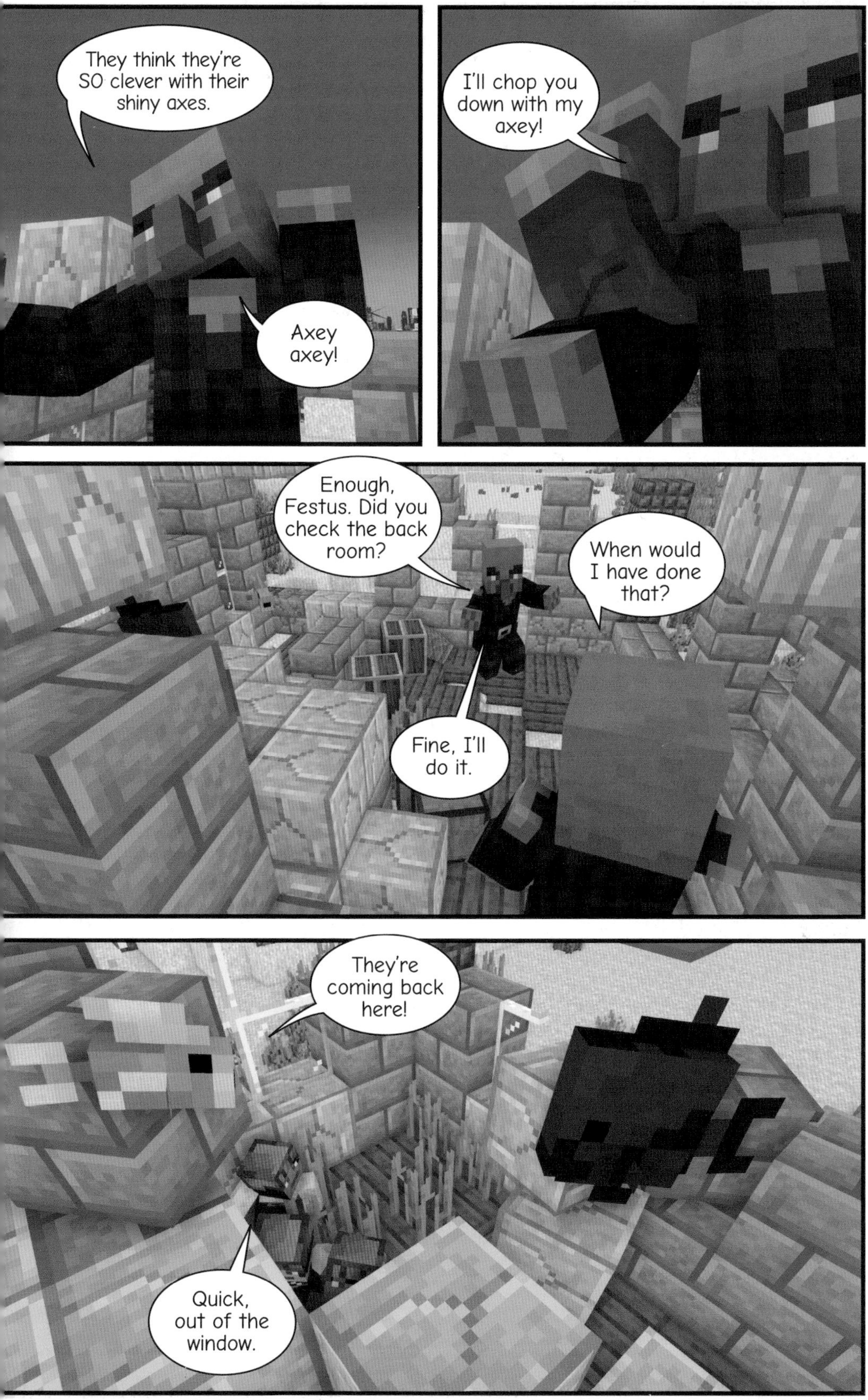

They think they're SO clever with their shiny axes.
Axey axey!
I'll chop you down with my axey!
Enough, Festus. Did you check the back room?
When would I have done that?
Fine, I'll do it.
They're coming back here!
Quick, out of the window.

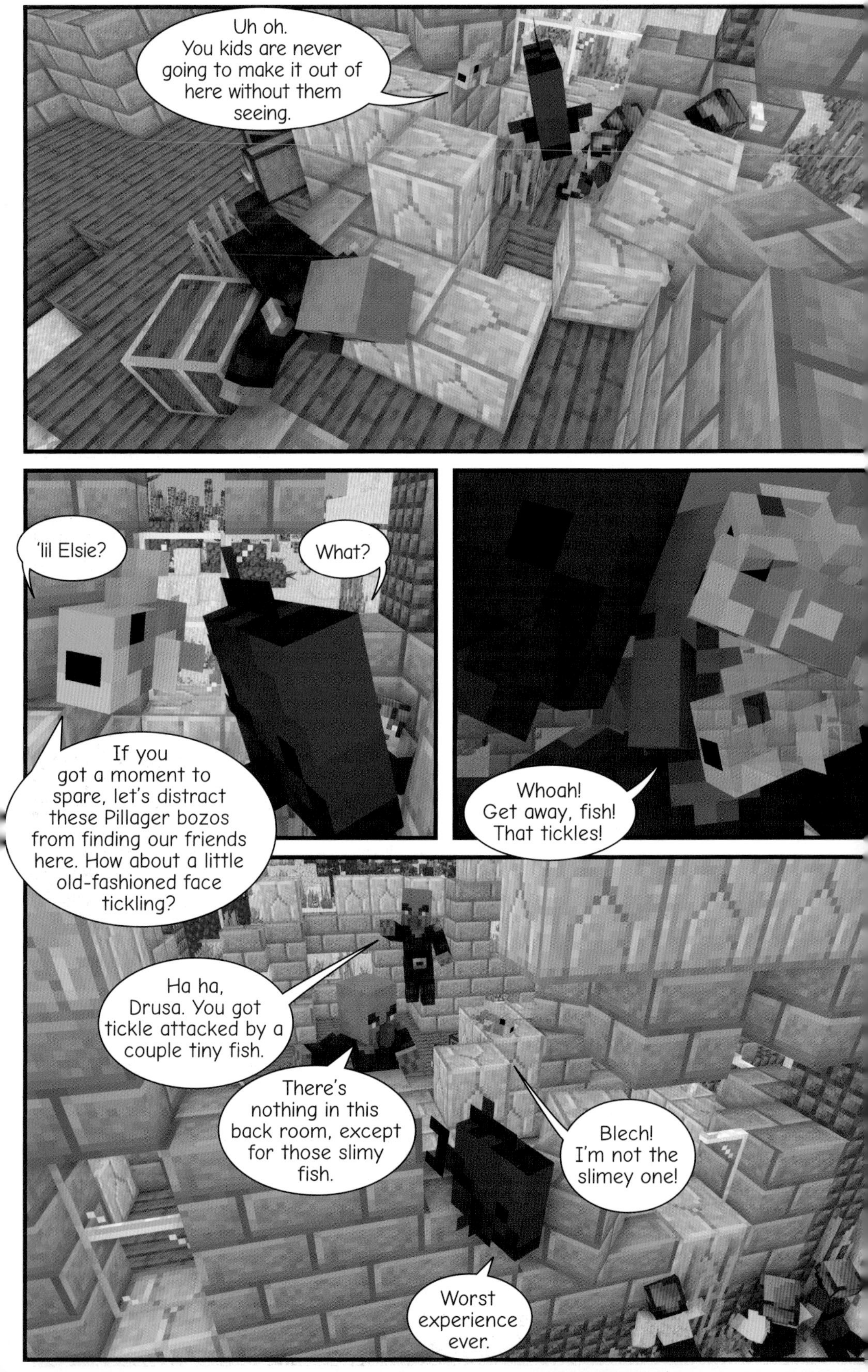
Uh oh. You kids are never going to make it out of here without them seeing.
'lil Elsie?
What?
If you got a moment to spare, let's distract these Pillager bozos from finding our friends here. How about a little old-fashioned face tickling?
Whoah! Get away, fish! That tickles!
Ha ha, Drusa. You got tickle attacked by a couple tiny fish.
There's nothing in this back room, except for those slimy fish.
Blech! I'm not the slimey one!
Worst experience ever.

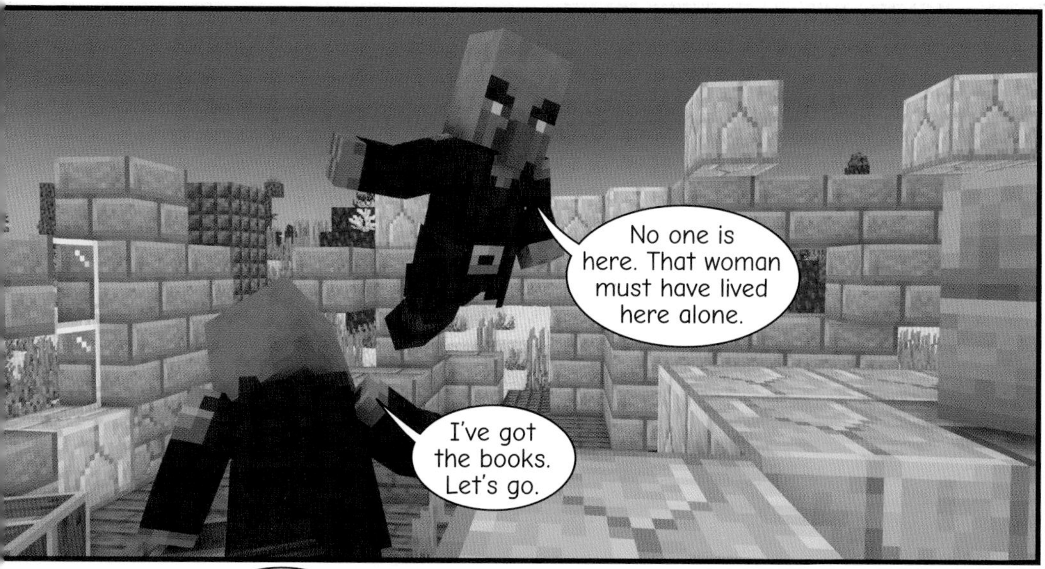
No one is here. That woman must have lived here alone.
I've got the books. Let's go.

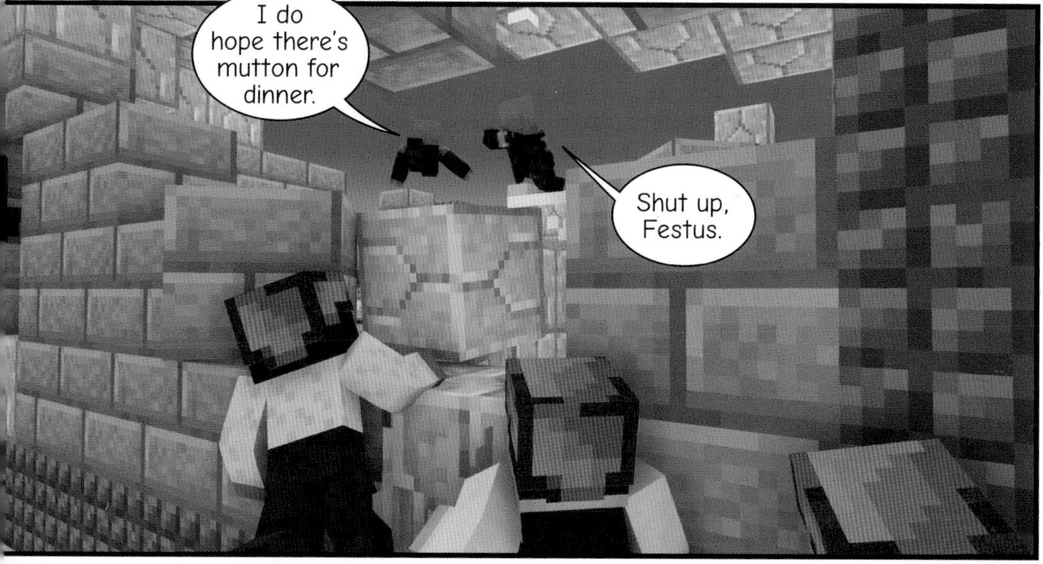
I do hope there's mutton for dinner.
Shut up, Festus.

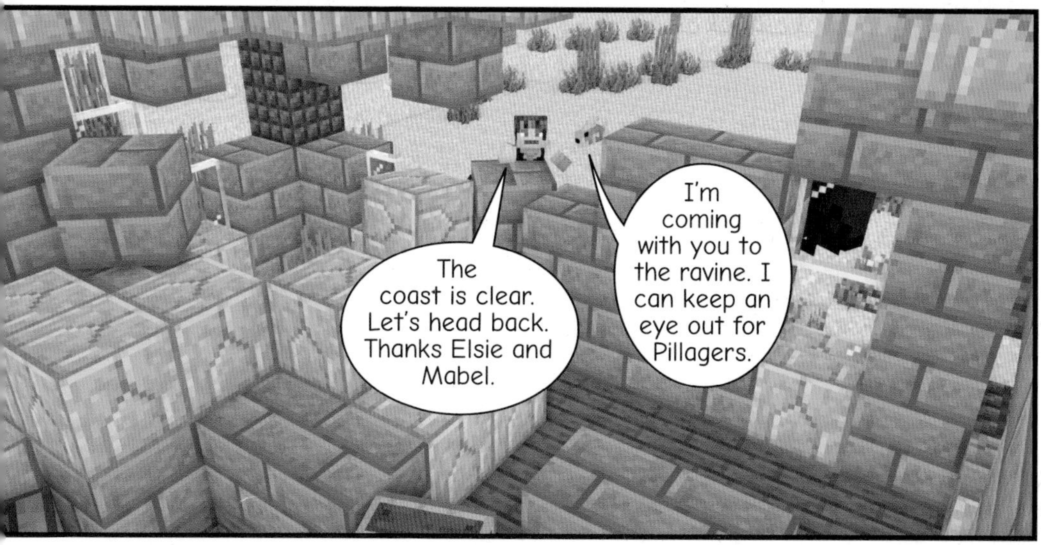
The coast is clear. Let's head back. Thanks Elsie and Mabel.
I'm coming with you to the ravine. I can keep an eye out for Pillagers.

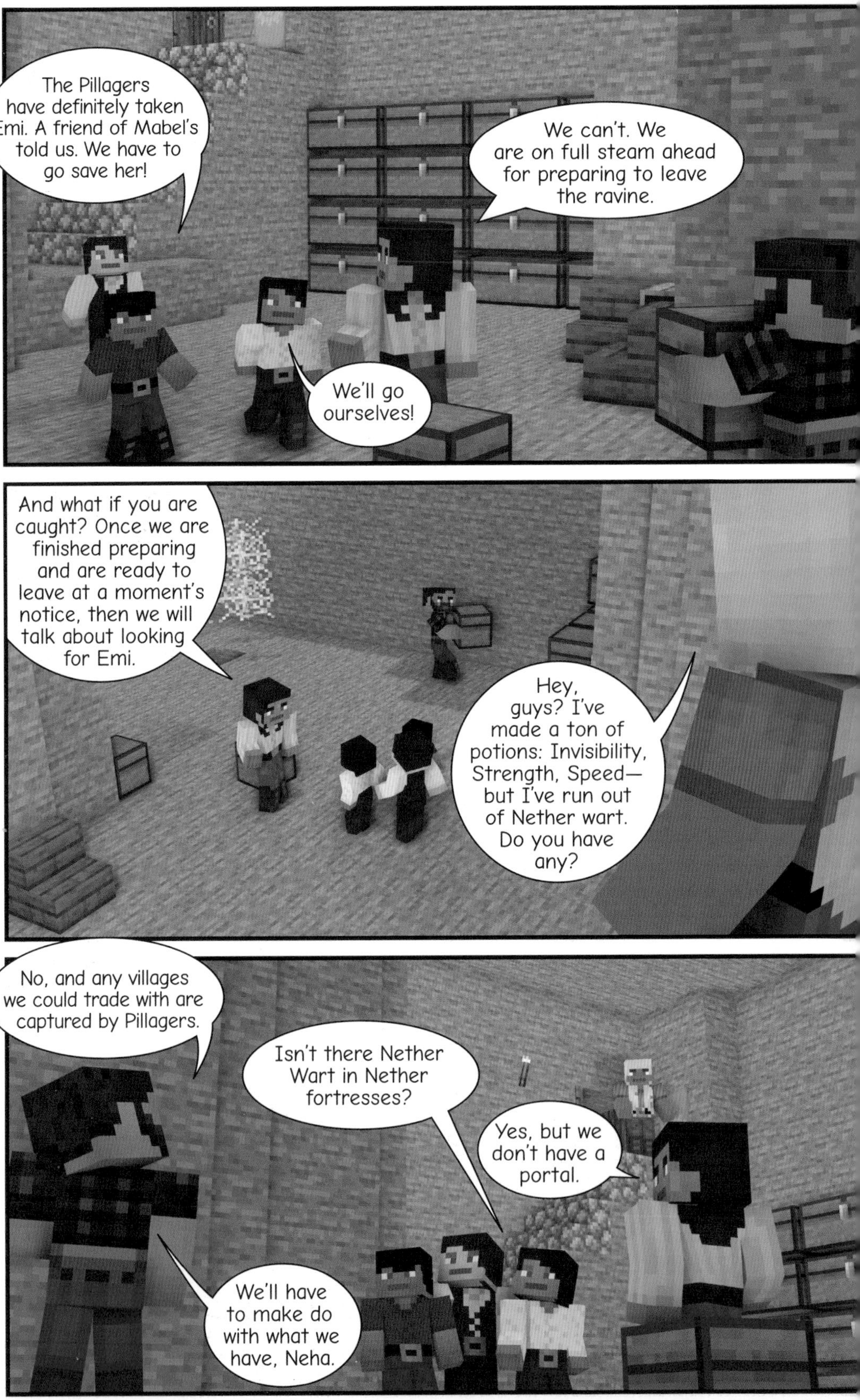
The Pillagers have definitely taken Emi. A friend of Mabel's told us. We have to go save her!
We can't. We are on full steam ahead for preparing to leave the ravine.
We'll go ourselves!
And what if you are caught? Once we are finished preparing and are ready to leave at a moment's notice, then we will talk about looking for Emi.
Hey, guys? I've made a ton of potions: Invisibility, Strength, Speed—but I've run out of Nether wart. Do you have any?
No, and any villages we could trade with are captured by Pillagers.
Isn't there Nether Wart in Nether fortresses?
Yes, but we don't have a portal.
We'll have to make do with what we have, Neha.

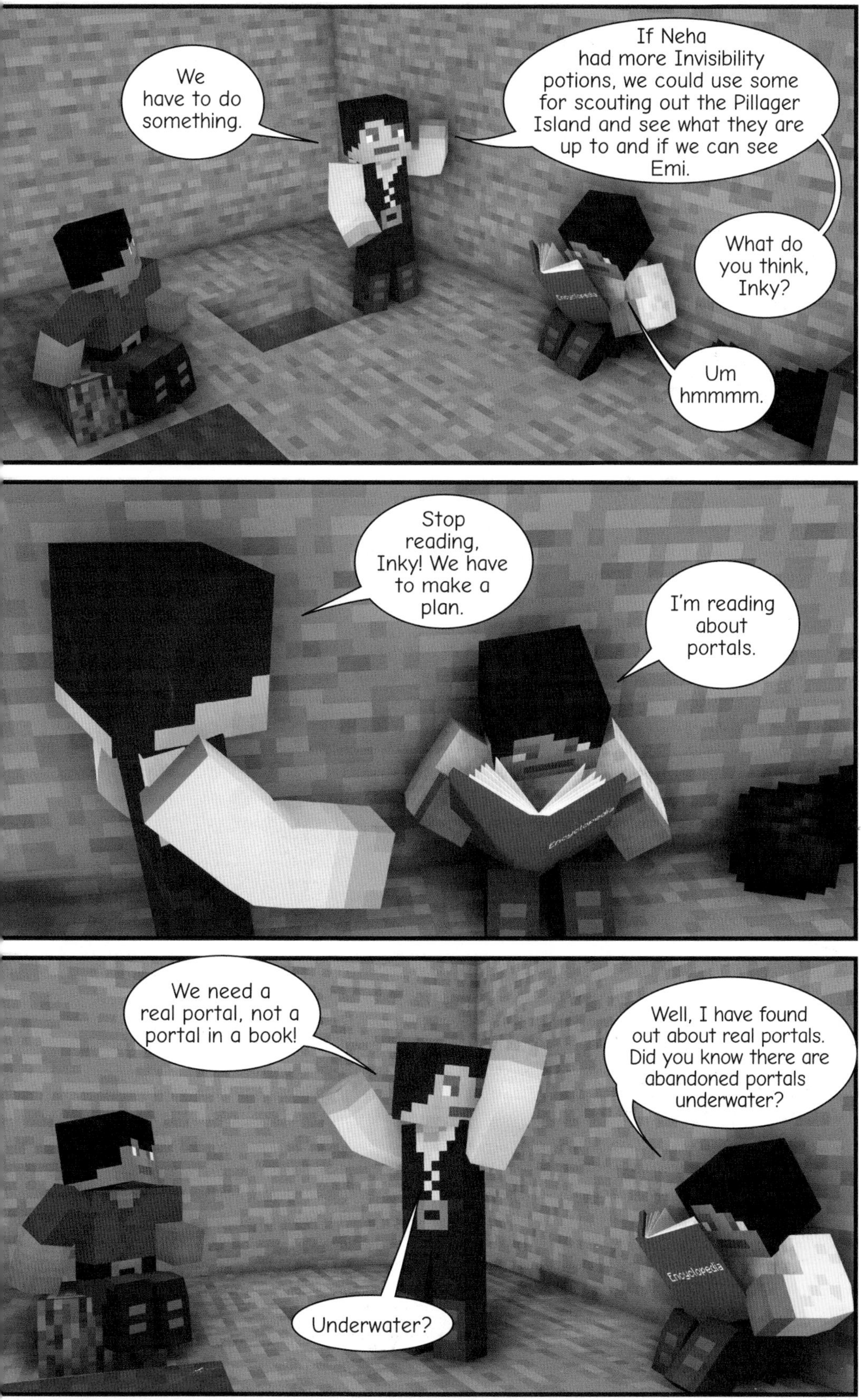
We have to do something.
If Neha had more Invisibility potions, we could use some for scouting out the Pillager Island and see what they are up to and if we can see Emi.
What do you think, Inky?
Um hmmmm.
Stop reading, Inky! We have to make a plan.
I'm reading about portals.
We need a real portal, not a portal in a book!
Well, I have found out about real portals. Did you know there are abandoned portals underwater?
Underwater?

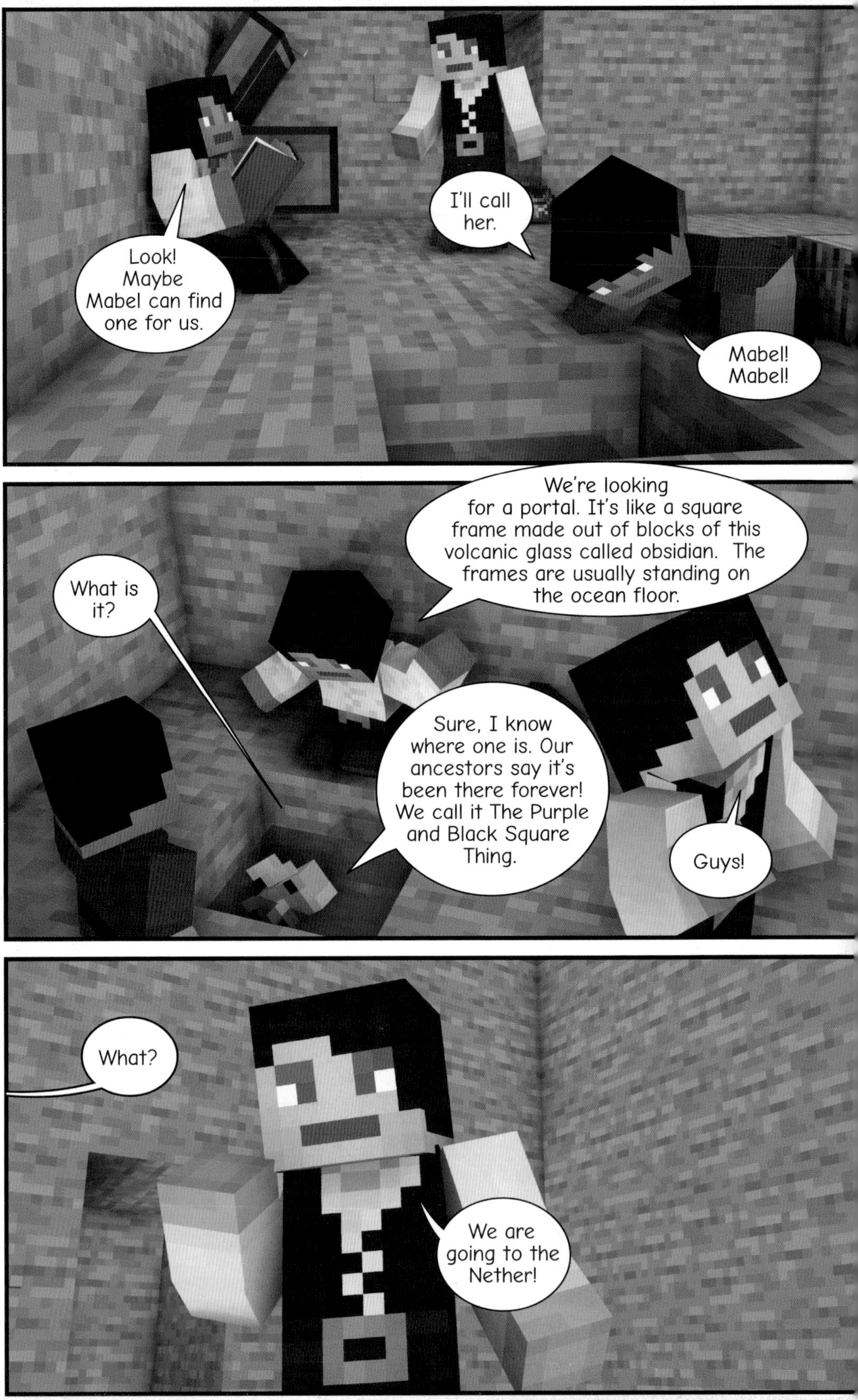
Look! Maybe Mabel can find one for us.
I'll call her.
Mabel! Mabel!
What is it?
We're looking for a portal. It's like a square frame made out of blocks of this volcanic glass called obsidian. The frames are usually standing on the ocean floor.
Sure, I know where one is. Our ancestors say it's been there forever! We call it The Purple and Black Square Thing.
Guys!
What?
We are going to the Nether!

Chapter 3
Netherbound

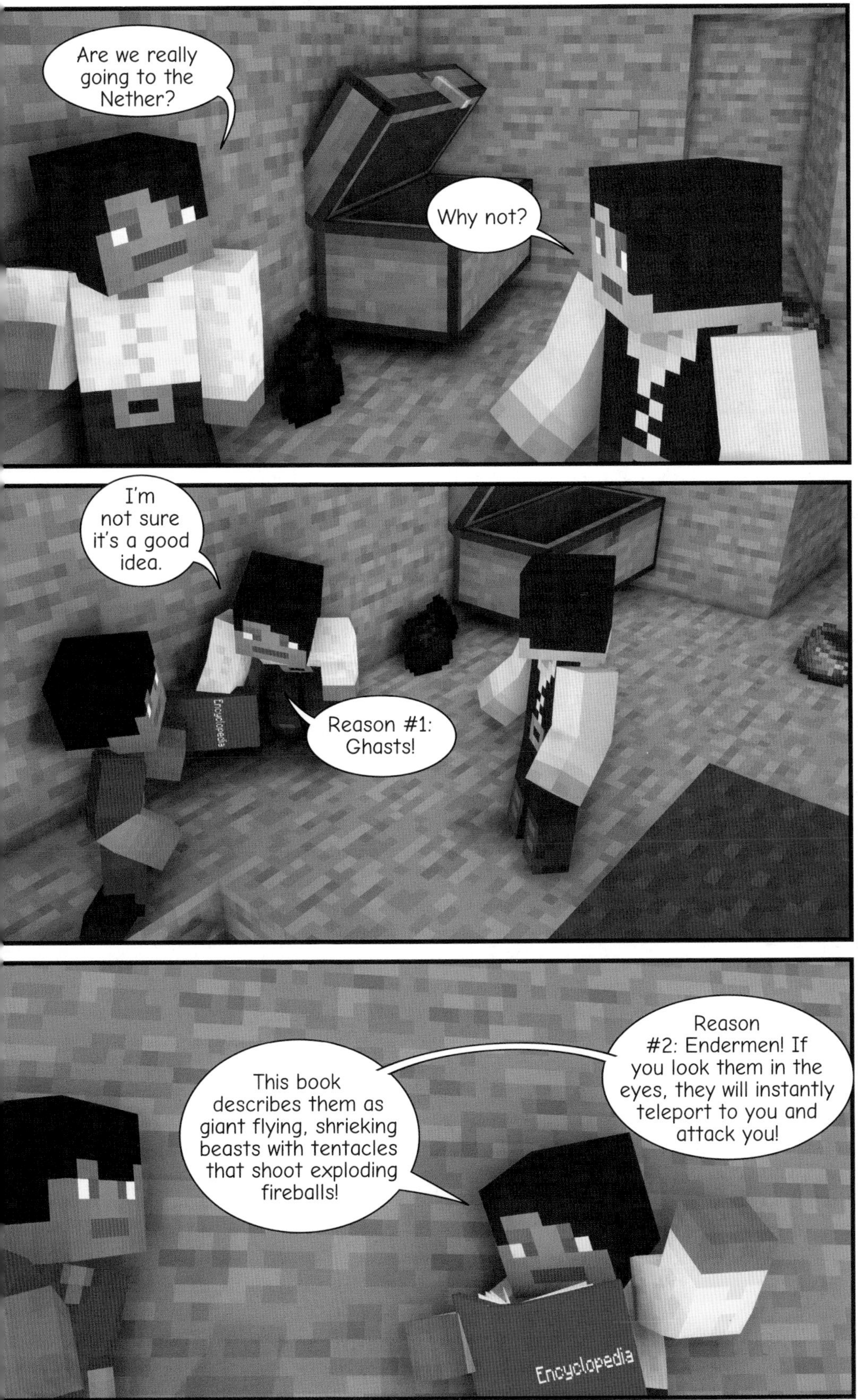
Are we really going to the Nether?
Why not?
I'm not sure it's a good idea.
Encyclopedia
Reason #1: Ghasts!
This book describes them as giant flying, shrieking beasts with tentacles that shoot exploding fireballs!
Reason #2: Endermen! If you look them in the eyes, they will instantly teleport to you and attack you!
Encyclopedia

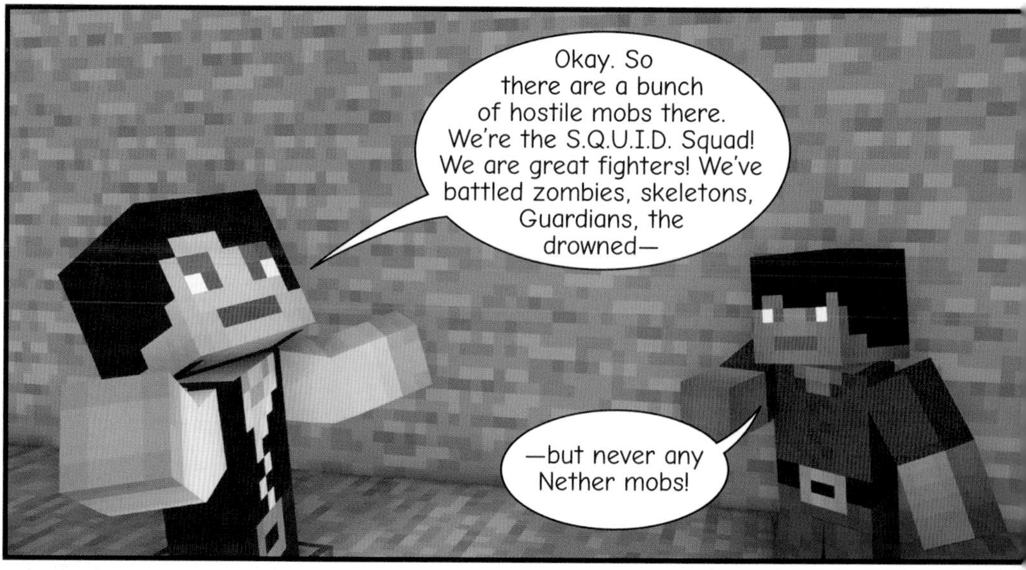
Okay. So there are a bunch of hostile mobs there. We're the S.Q.U.I.D. Squad! We are great fighters! We've battled zombies, skeletons, Guardians, the drowned—
—but never any Nether mobs!

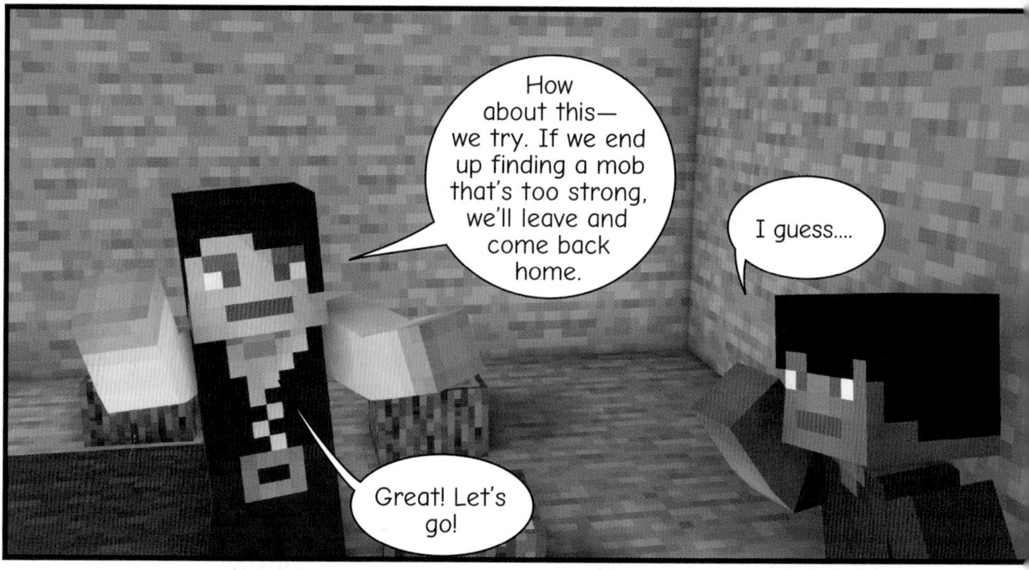
How about this—we try. If we end up finding a mob that's too strong, we'll leave and come back home.
I guess....
Great! Let's go!

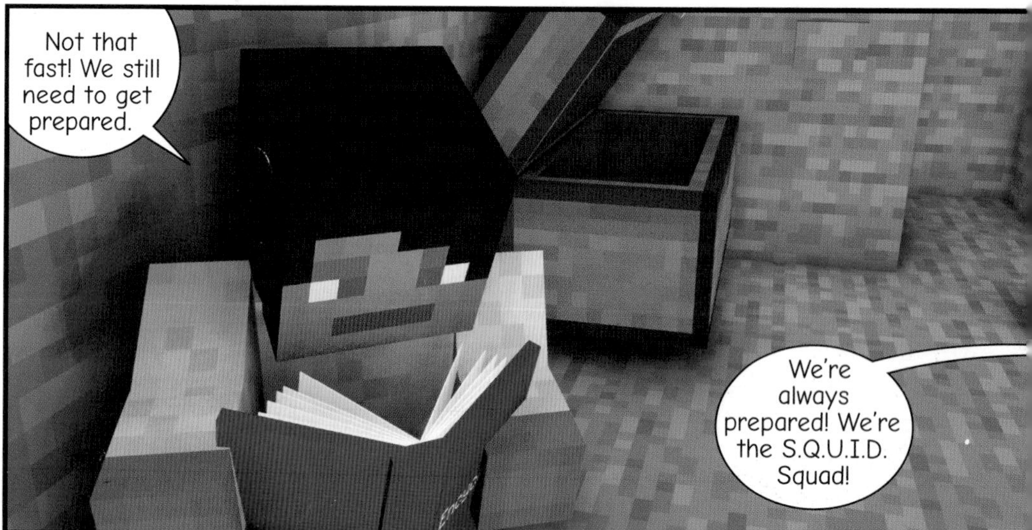
Not that fast! We still need to get prepared.
We're always prepared! We're the S.Q.U.I.D. Squad!

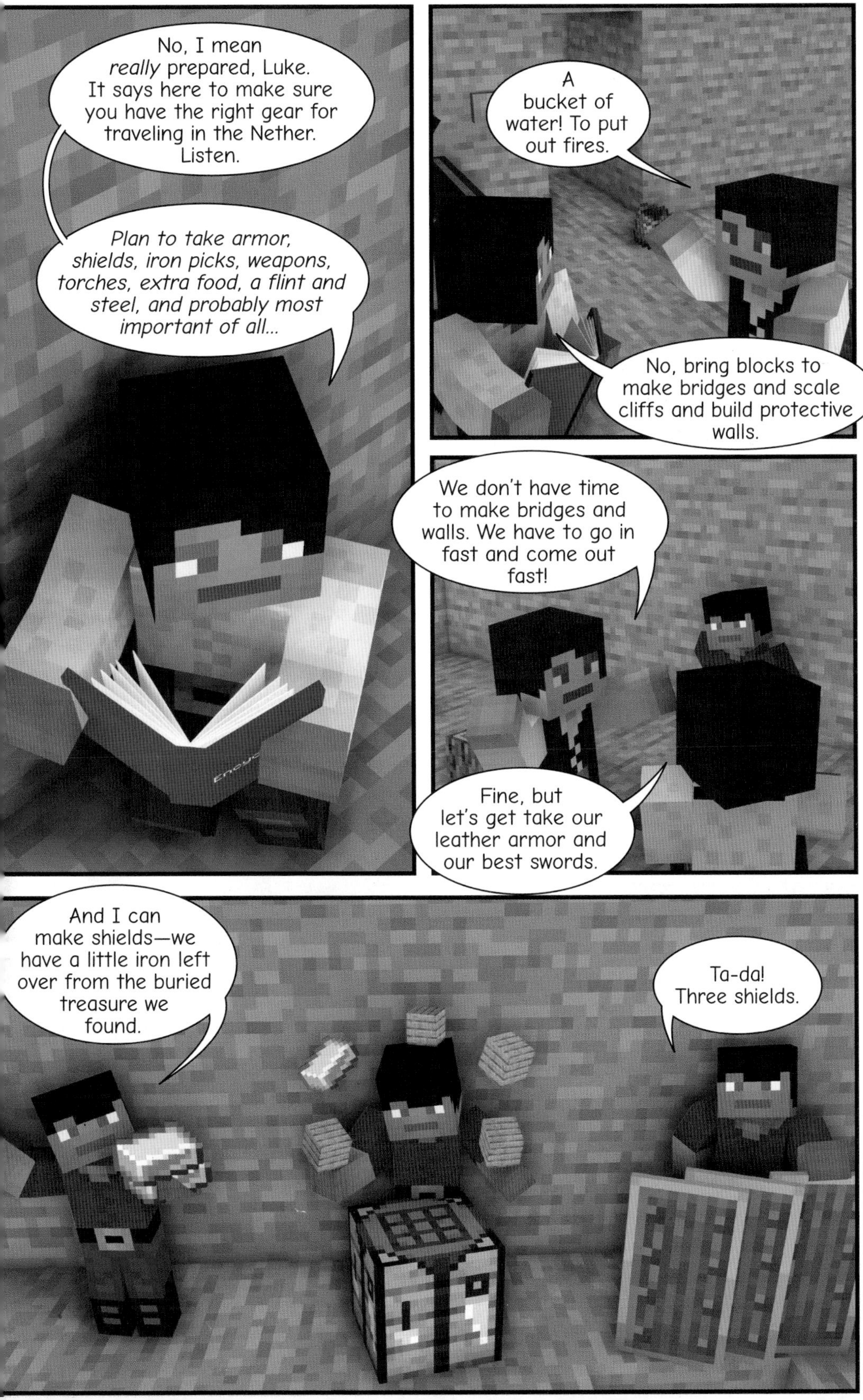
No, I mean *really* prepared, Luke. It says here to make sure you have the right gear for traveling in the Nether. Listen.
Plan to take armor, shields, iron picks, weapons, torches, extra food, a flint and steel, and probably most important of all...
A bucket of water! To put out fires.
No, bring blocks to make bridges and scale cliffs and build protective walls.
We don't have time to make bridges and walls. We have to go in fast and come out fast!
Fine, but let's get take our leather armor and our best swords.
And I can make shields—we have a little iron left over from the buried treasure we found.
Ta-da! Three shields.

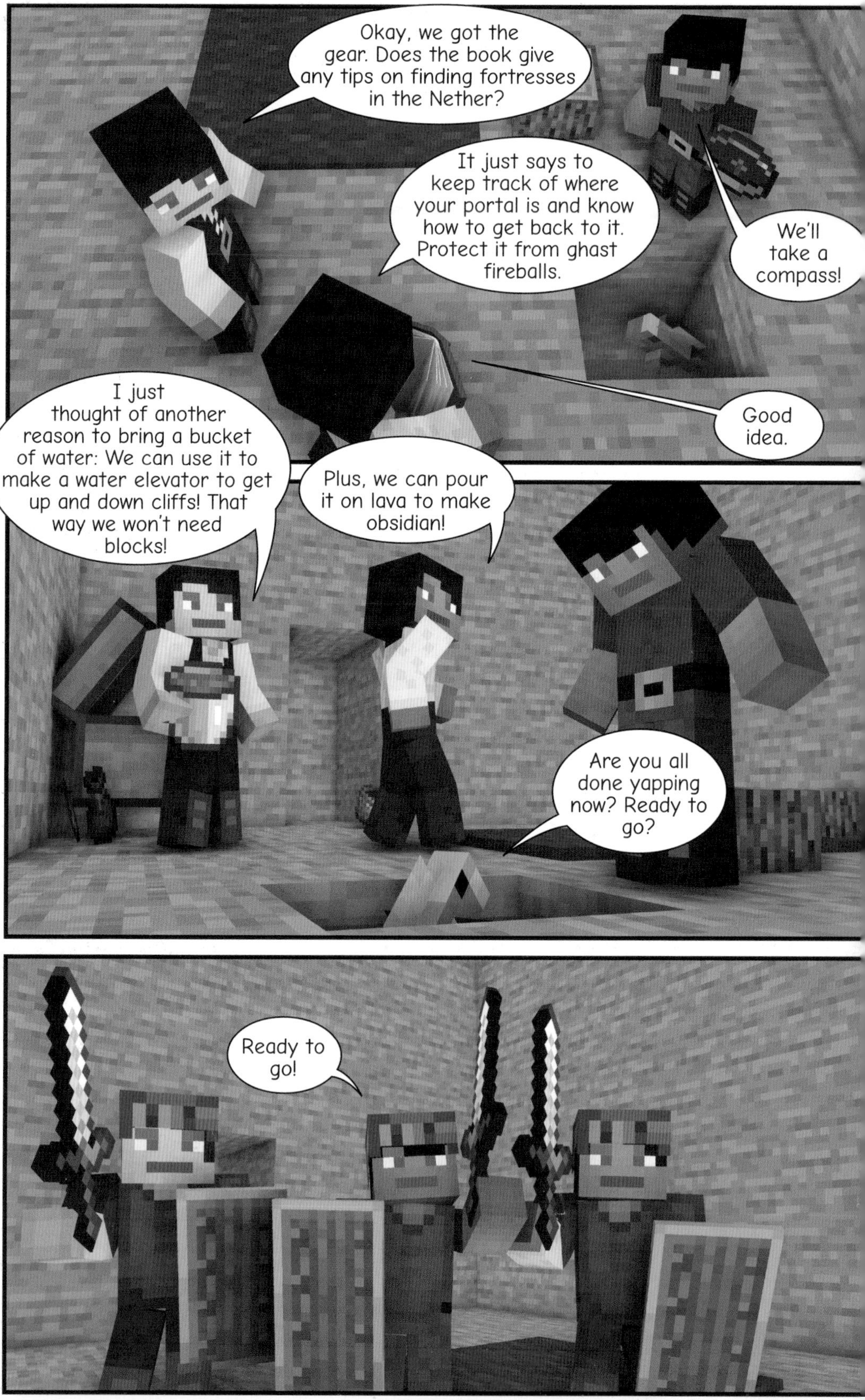

Okay, we got the gear. Does the book give any tips on finding fortresses in the Nether?
It just says to keep track of where your portal is and know how to get back to it. Protect it from ghast fireballs.
We'll take a compass!
Good idea.
I just thought of another reason to bring a bucket of water: We can use it to make a water elevator to get up and down cliffs! That way we won't need blocks!
Plus, we can pour it on lava to make obsidian!
Are you all done yapping now? Ready to go?
Ready to go!

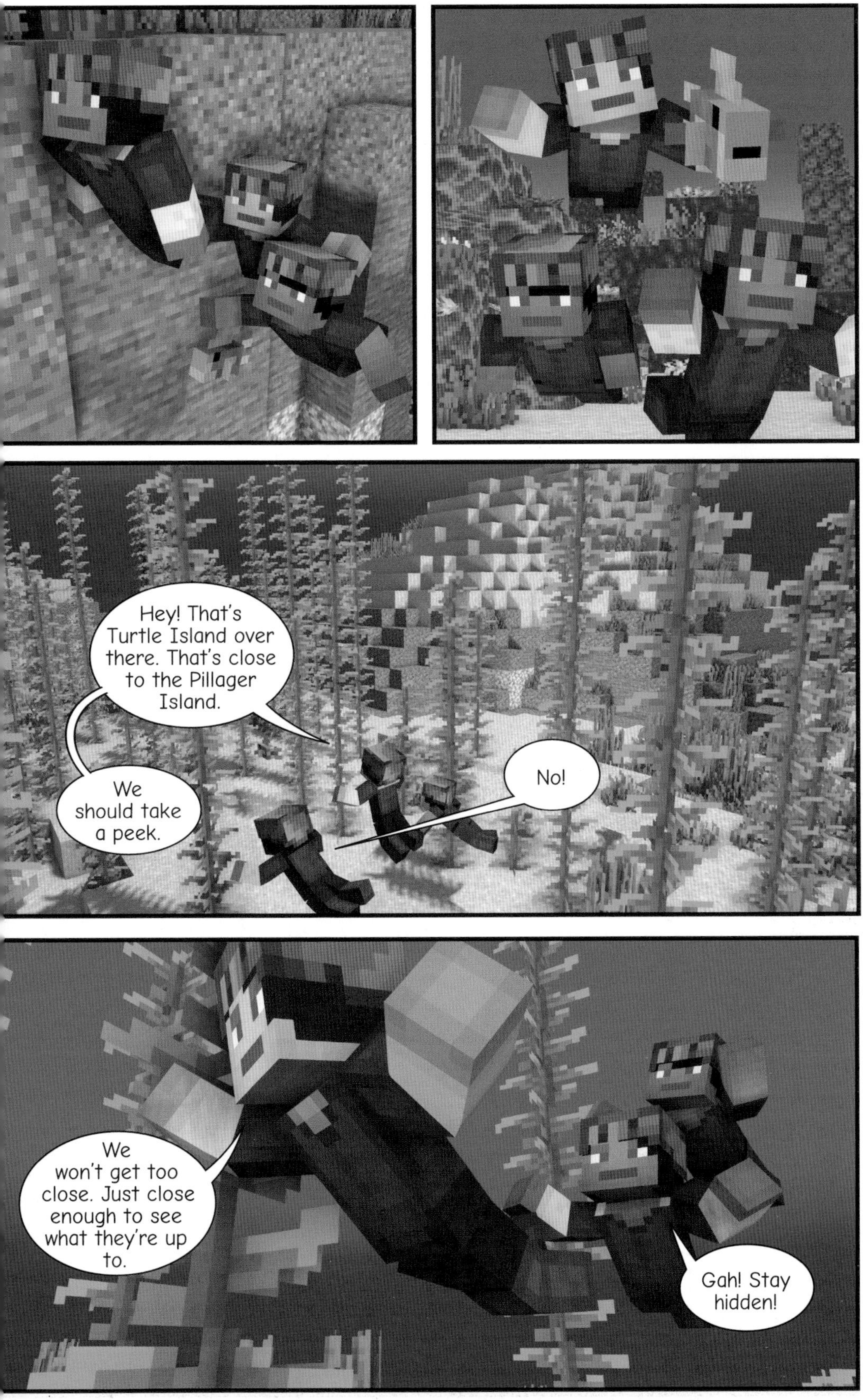
Hey! That's Turtle Island over there. That's close to the Pillager Island.
We should take a peek.
No!
We won't get too close. Just close enough to see what they're up to.
Gah! Stay hidden!

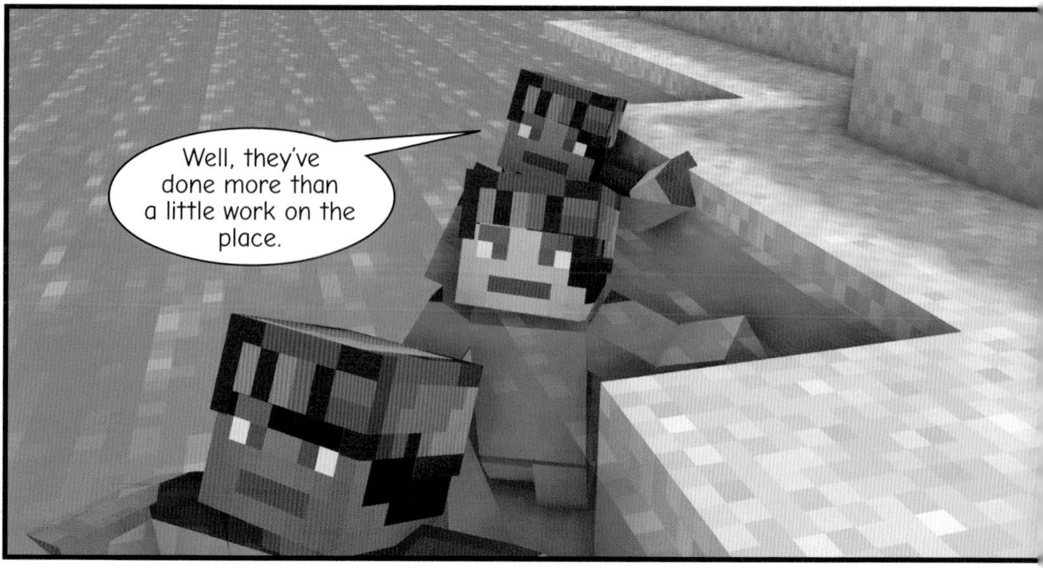
Well, they've done more than a little work on the place.

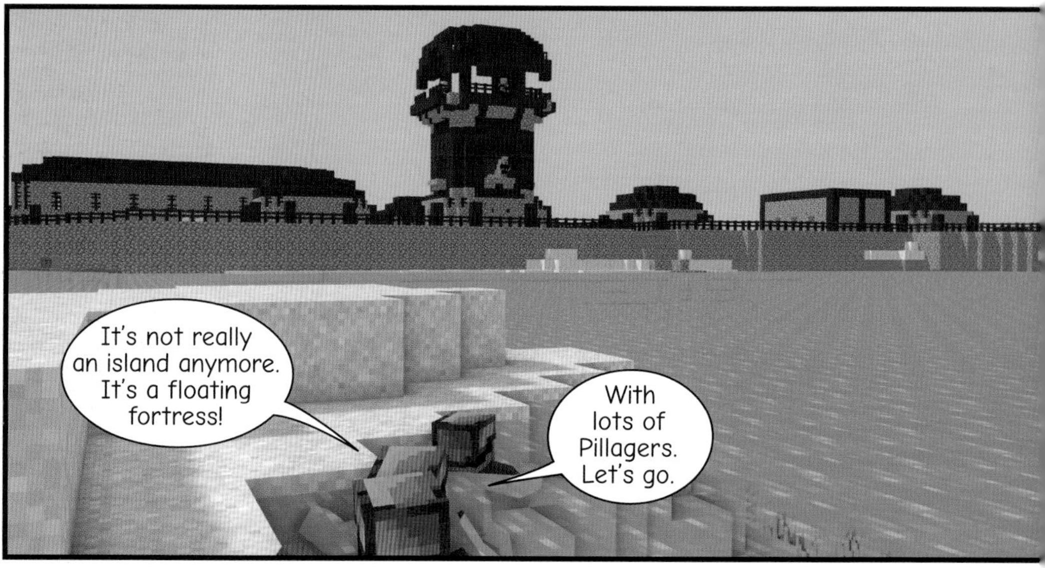
It's not really an island anymore. It's a floating fortress!
With lots of Pillagers. Let's go.

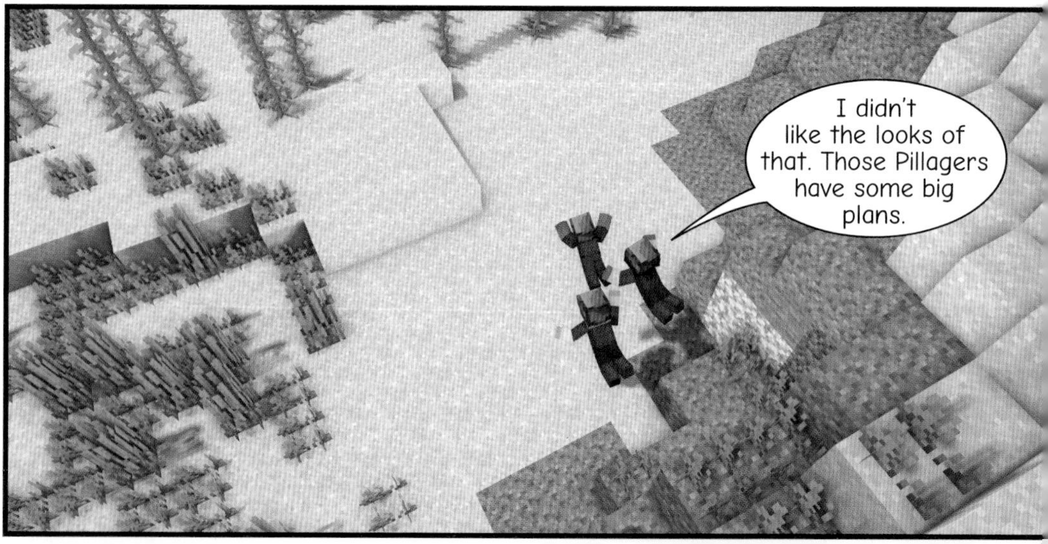
I didn't like the looks of that. Those Pillagers have some big plans.

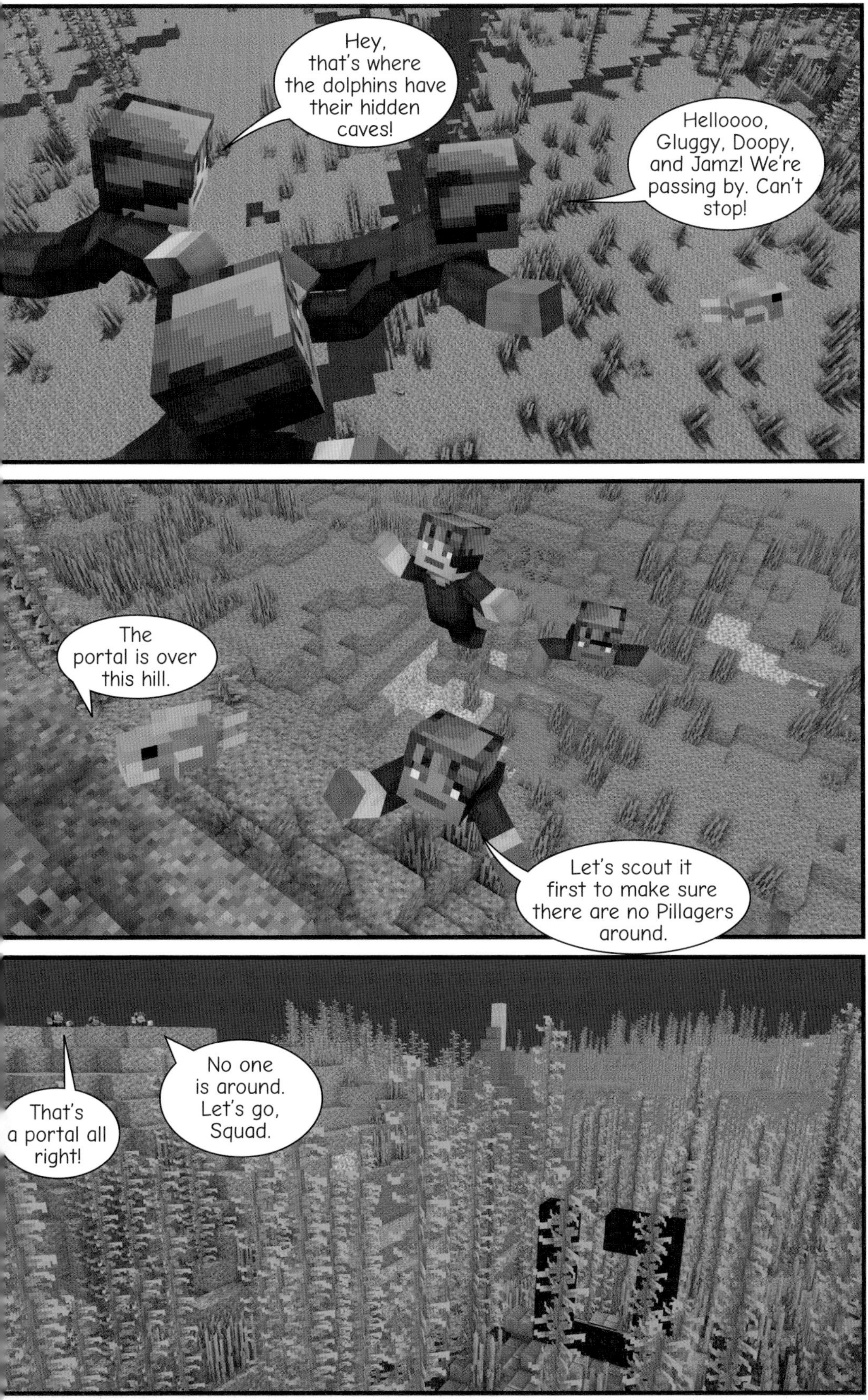
Hey, that's where the dolphins have their hidden caves!
Helloooo, Gluggy, Doopy, and Jamz! We're passing by. Can't stop!
The portal is over this hill.
Let's scout it first to make sure there are no Pillagers around.
That's a portal all right!
No one is around. Let's go, Squad.

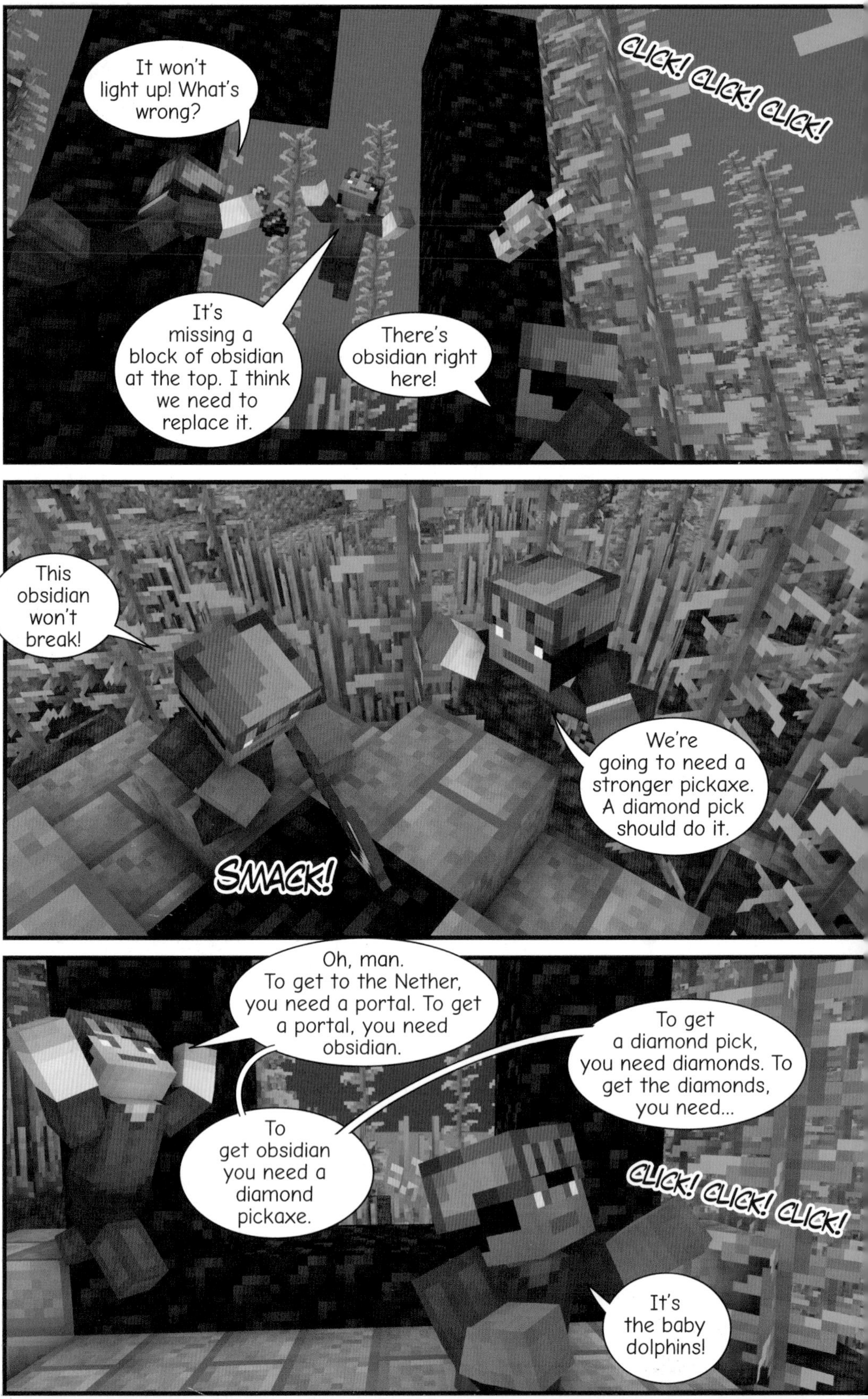
It won't light up! What's wrong?
CLICK! CLICK! CLICK!
It's missing a block of obsidian at the top. I think we need to replace it.
There's obsidian right here!
This obsidian won't break!
We're going to need a stronger pickaxe. A diamond pick should do it.
SMACK!
Oh, man. To get to the Nether, you need a portal. To get a portal, you need obsidian.
To get obsidian you need a diamond pickaxe.
To get a diamond pick, you need diamonds. To get the diamonds, you need...
CLICK! CLICK! CLICK!
It's the baby dolphins!

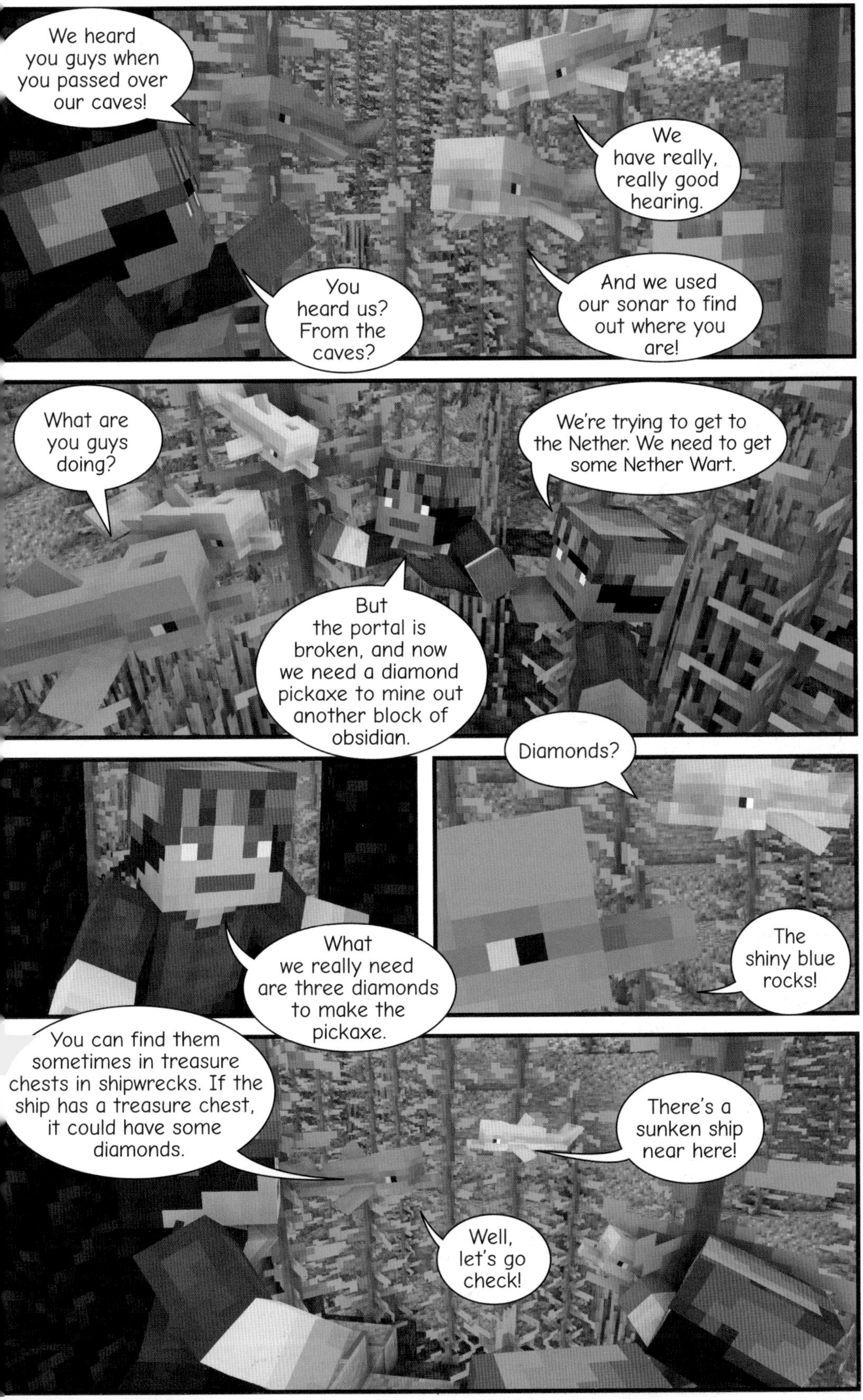
We heard you guys when you passed over our caves!
We have really, really good hearing.
You heard us? From the caves?
And we used our sonar to find out where you are!
What are you guys doing?
We're trying to get to the Nether. We need to get some Nether Wart.
But the portal is broken, and now we need a diamond pickaxe to mine out another block of obsidian.
Diamonds?
What we really need are three diamonds to make the pickaxe.
The shiny blue rocks!
You can find them sometimes in treasure chests in shipwrecks. If the ship has a treasure chest, it could have some diamonds.
There's a sunken ship near here!
Well, let's go check!

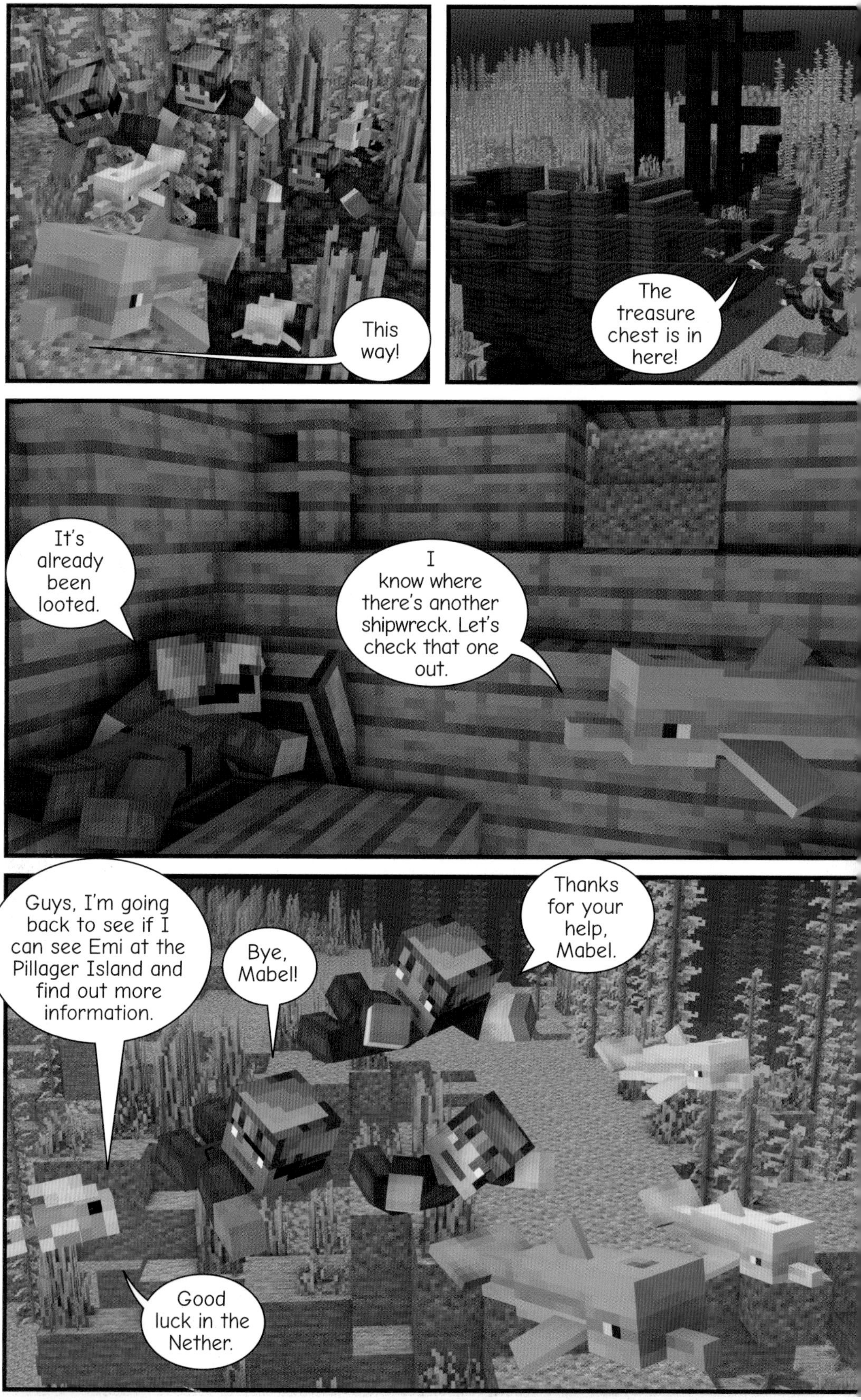
This way!
The treasure chest is in here!
It's already been looted.
I know where there's another shipwreck. Let's check that one out.
Guys, I'm going back to see if I can see Emi at the Pillager Island and find out more information.
Bye, Mabel!
Thanks for your help, Mabel.
Good luck in the Nether.

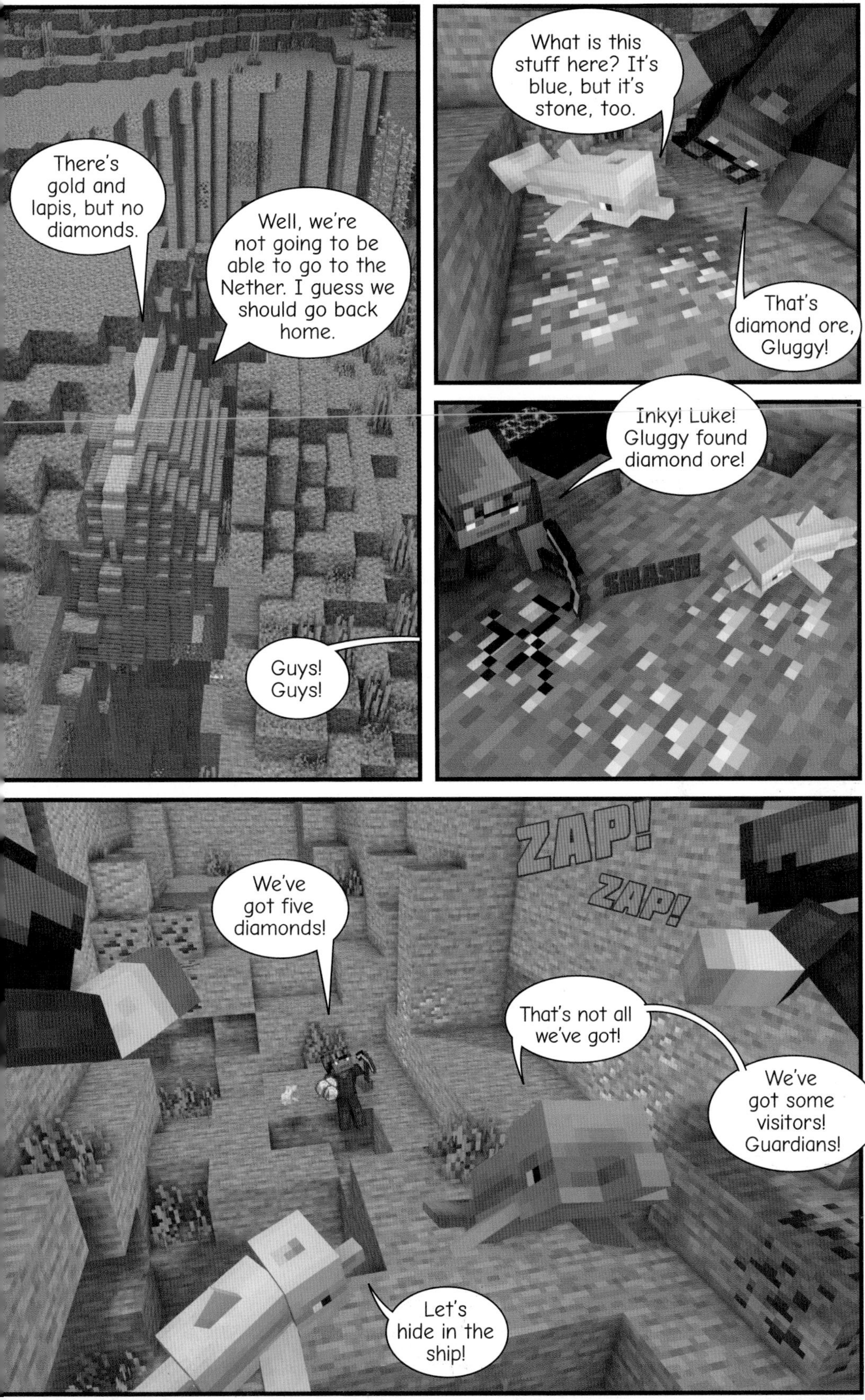
There's gold and lapis, but no diamonds.
Well, we're not going to be able to go to the Nether. I guess we should go back home.
Guys! Guys!
What is this stuff here? It's blue, but it's stone, too.
That's diamond ore, Gluggy!
Inky! Luke! Gluggy found diamond ore!
SMASH!
We've got five diamonds!
ZAP!
ZAP!
That's not all we've got!
We've got some visitors! Guardians!
Let's hide in the ship!

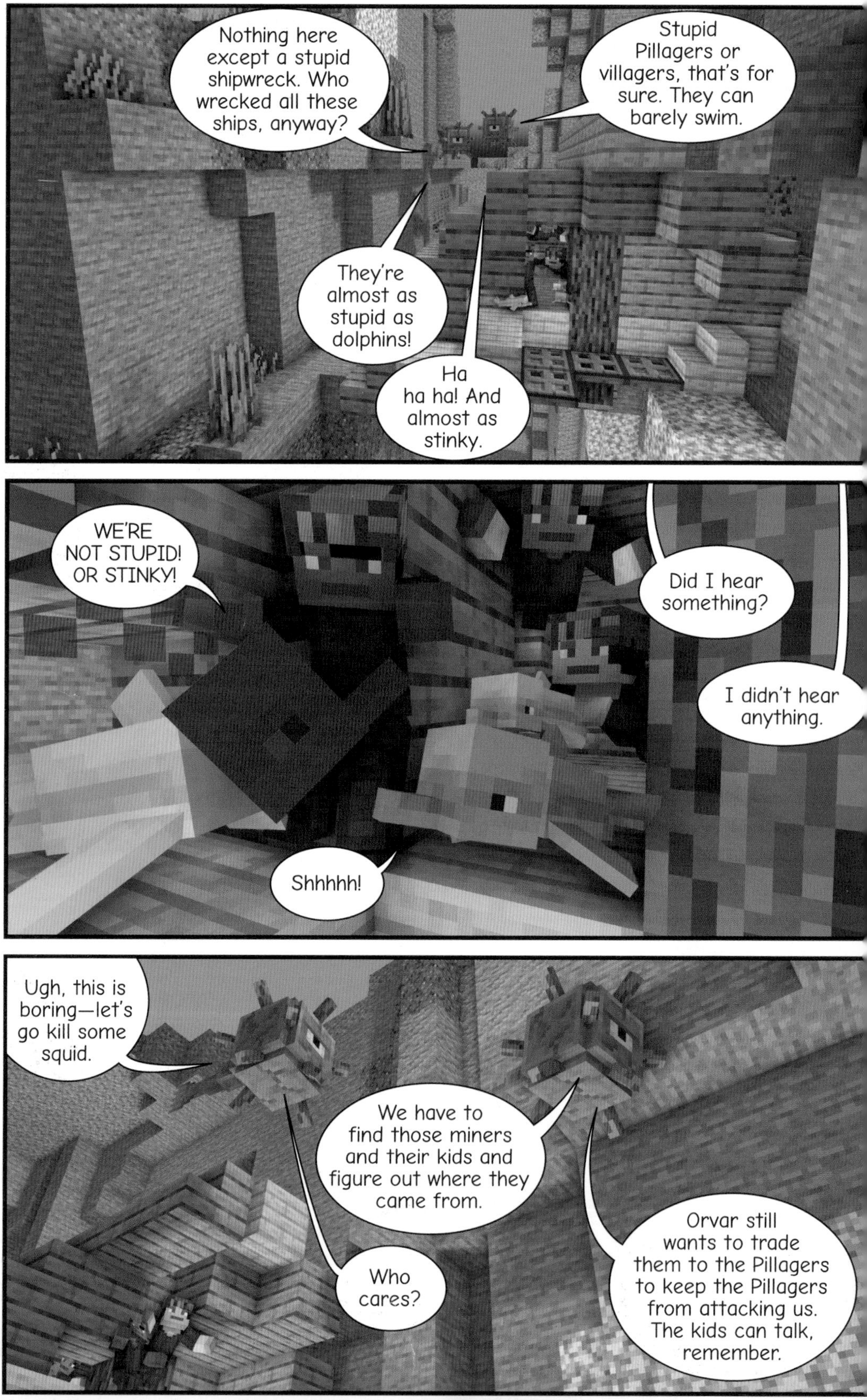
Nothing here except a stupid shipwreck. Who wrecked all these ships, anyway?
Stupid Pillagers or villagers, that's for sure. They can barely swim.
They're almost as stupid as dolphins!
Ha ha ha! And almost as stinky.
WE'RE NOT STUPID! OR STINKY!
Did I hear something?
I didn't hear anything.
Shhhhh!
Ugh, this is boring—let's go kill some squid.
We have to find those miners and their kids and figure out where they came from.
Who cares?
Orvar still wants to trade them to the Pillagers to keep the Pillagers from attacking us. The kids can talk, remember.

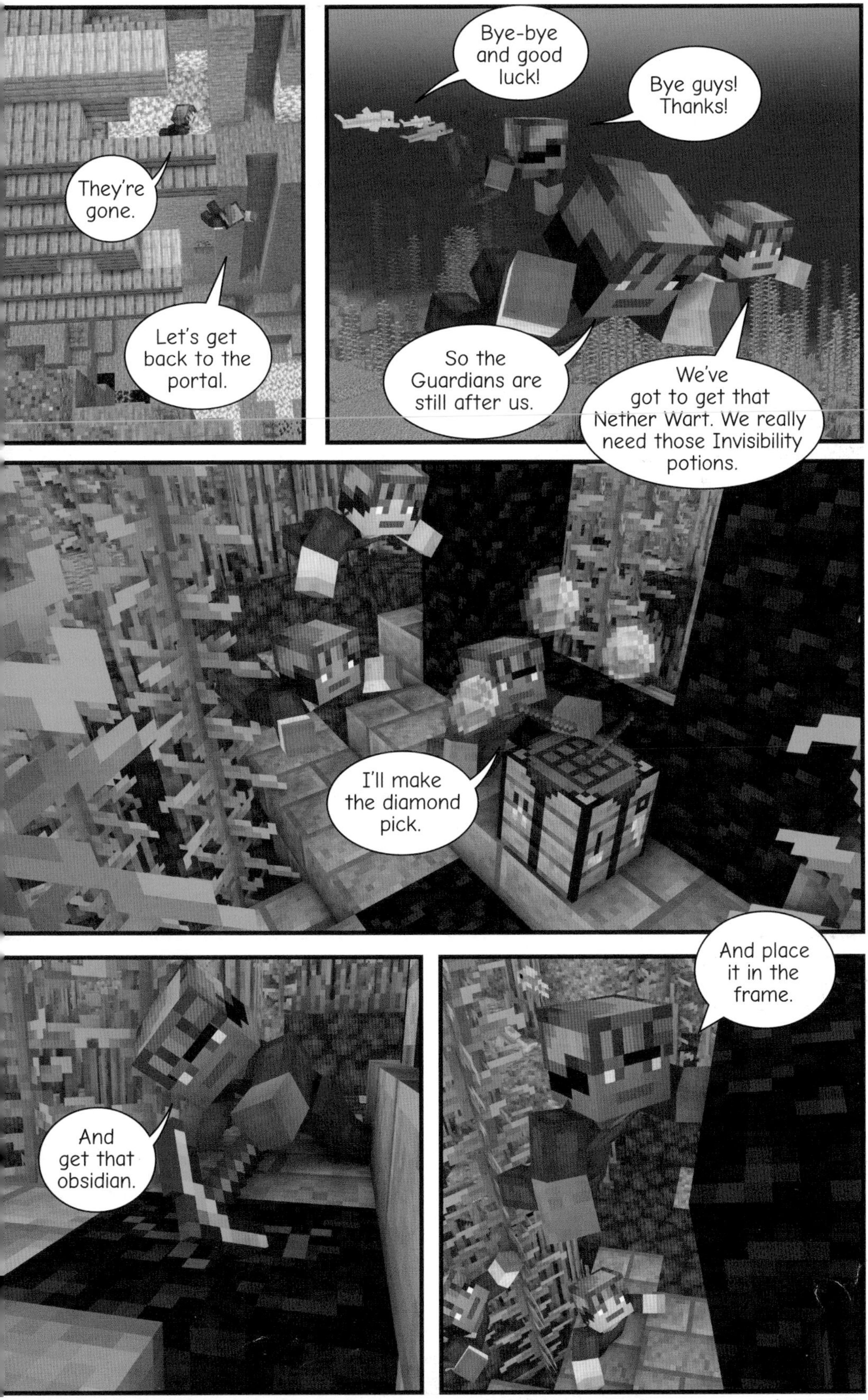
They're gone.
Let's get back to the portal.
Bye-bye and good luck!
Bye guys! Thanks!
So the Guardians are still after us.
We've got to get that Nether Wart. We really need those Invisibility potions.
I'll make the diamond pick.
And get that obsidian.
And place it in the frame.

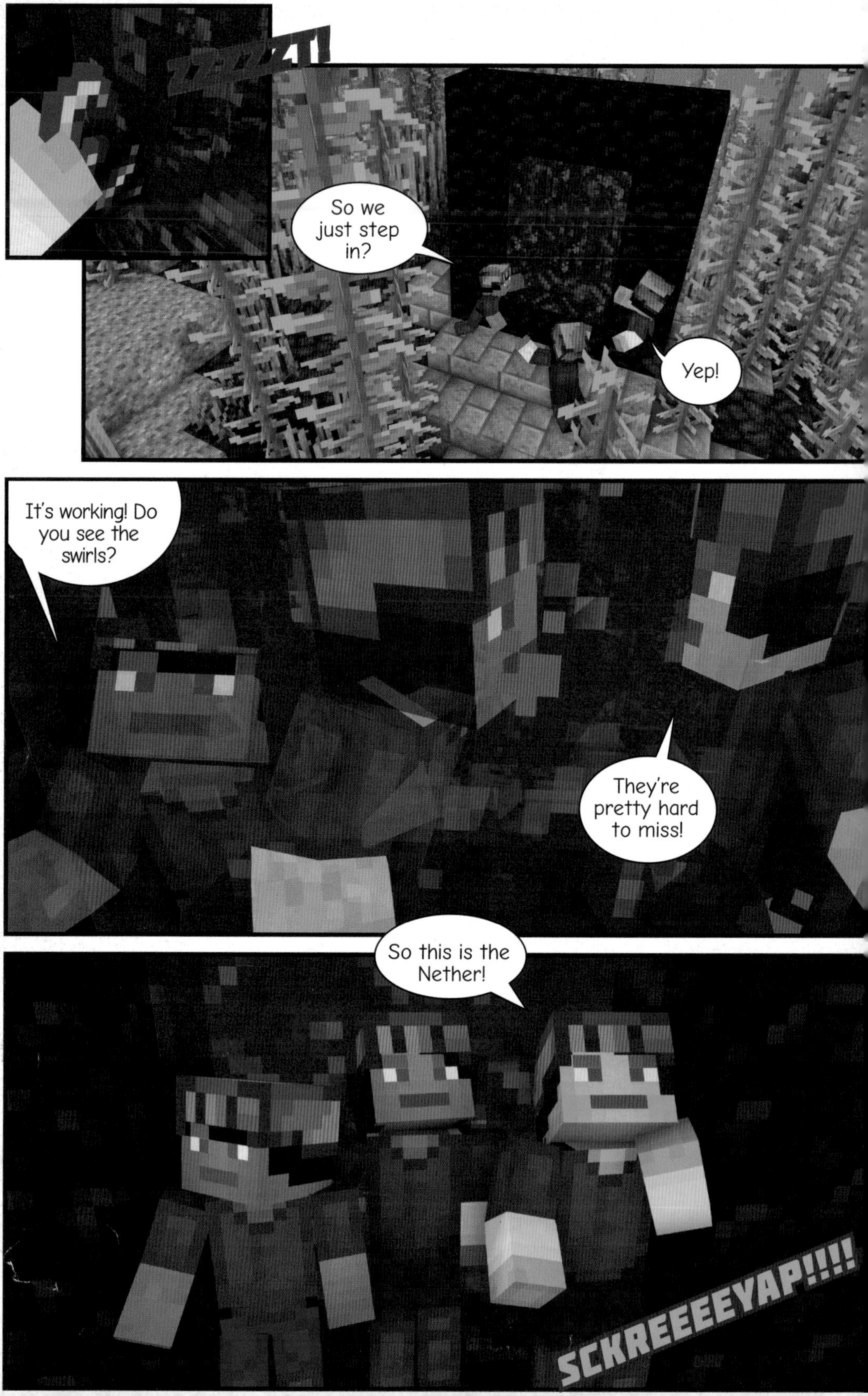
ZZZZZT!
So we just step in?
Yep!
It's working! Do you see the swirls?
They're pretty hard to miss!
So this is the Nether!
SCKREEEEEYAP!!!!

Chapter 4
Ghastly
Surprises

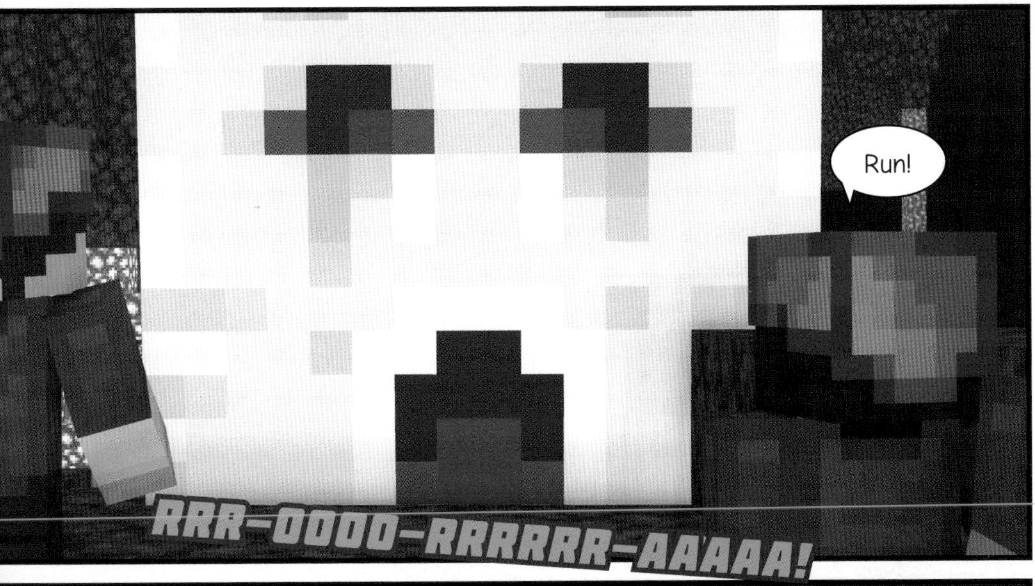
Run!
RRR-OOOO-RRRRRR-AAAAA!

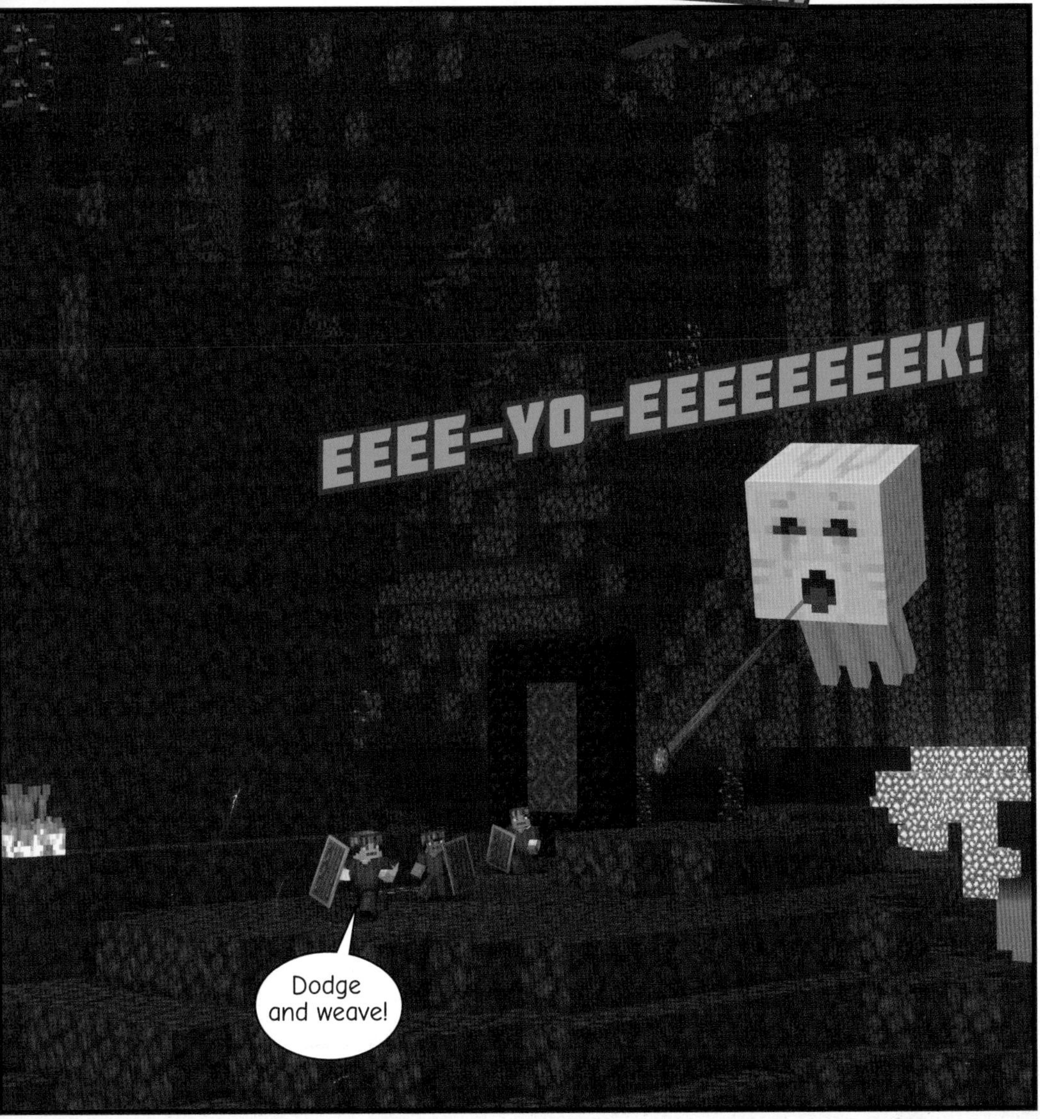
EEEE-YO-EEEEEEEEK!
Dodge and weave!

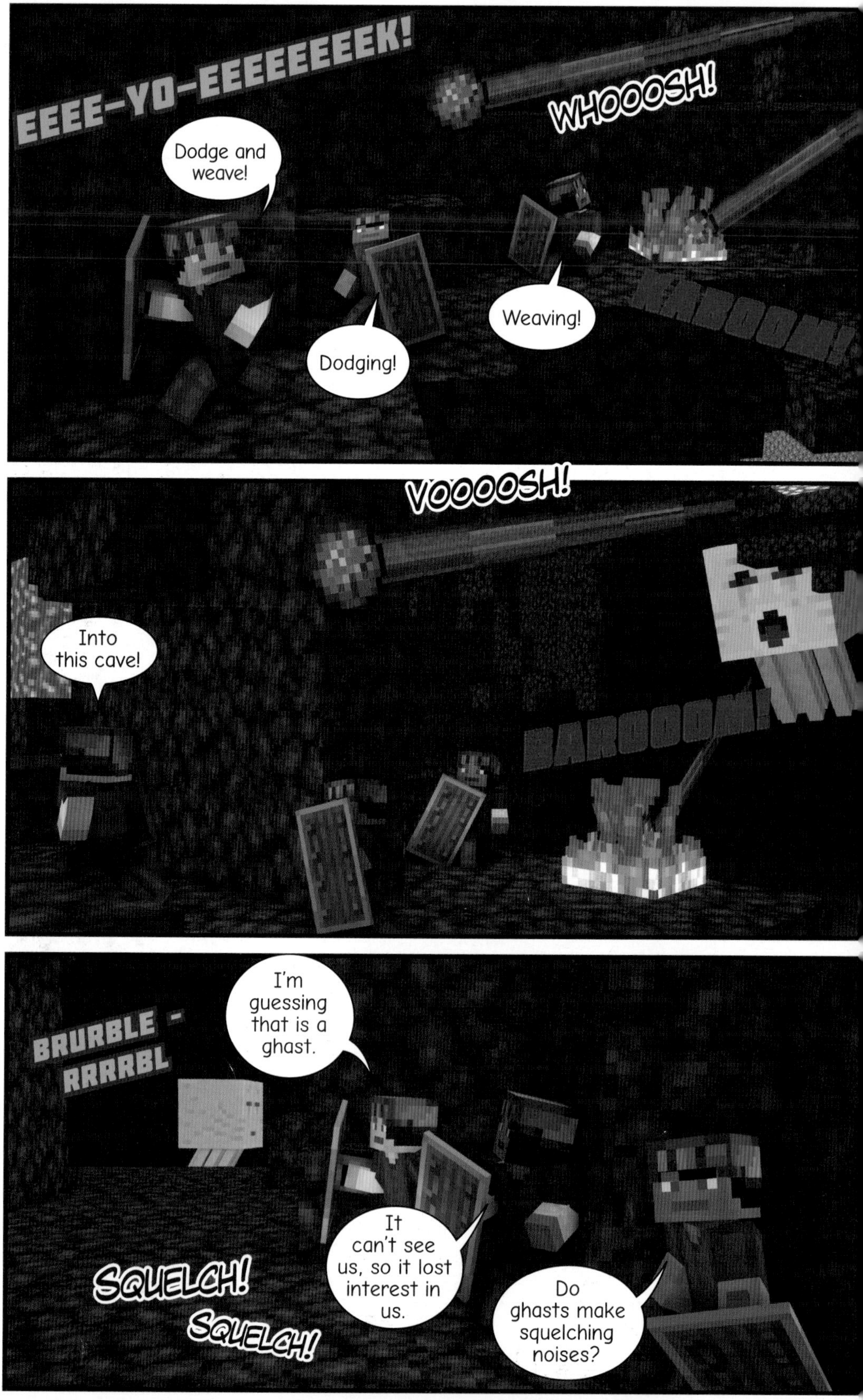
EEEE-YO-EEEEEEEEK!
WHOOOSH!
Dodge and weave!
Dodging!
Weaving!
KABOOM!
VOOOOSH!
Into this cave!
BAROOOM!
BRURBLE - RRRRBL
I'm guessing that is a ghast.
It can't see us, so it lost interest in us.
SQUELCH!
SQUELCH!
Do ghasts make squelching noises?

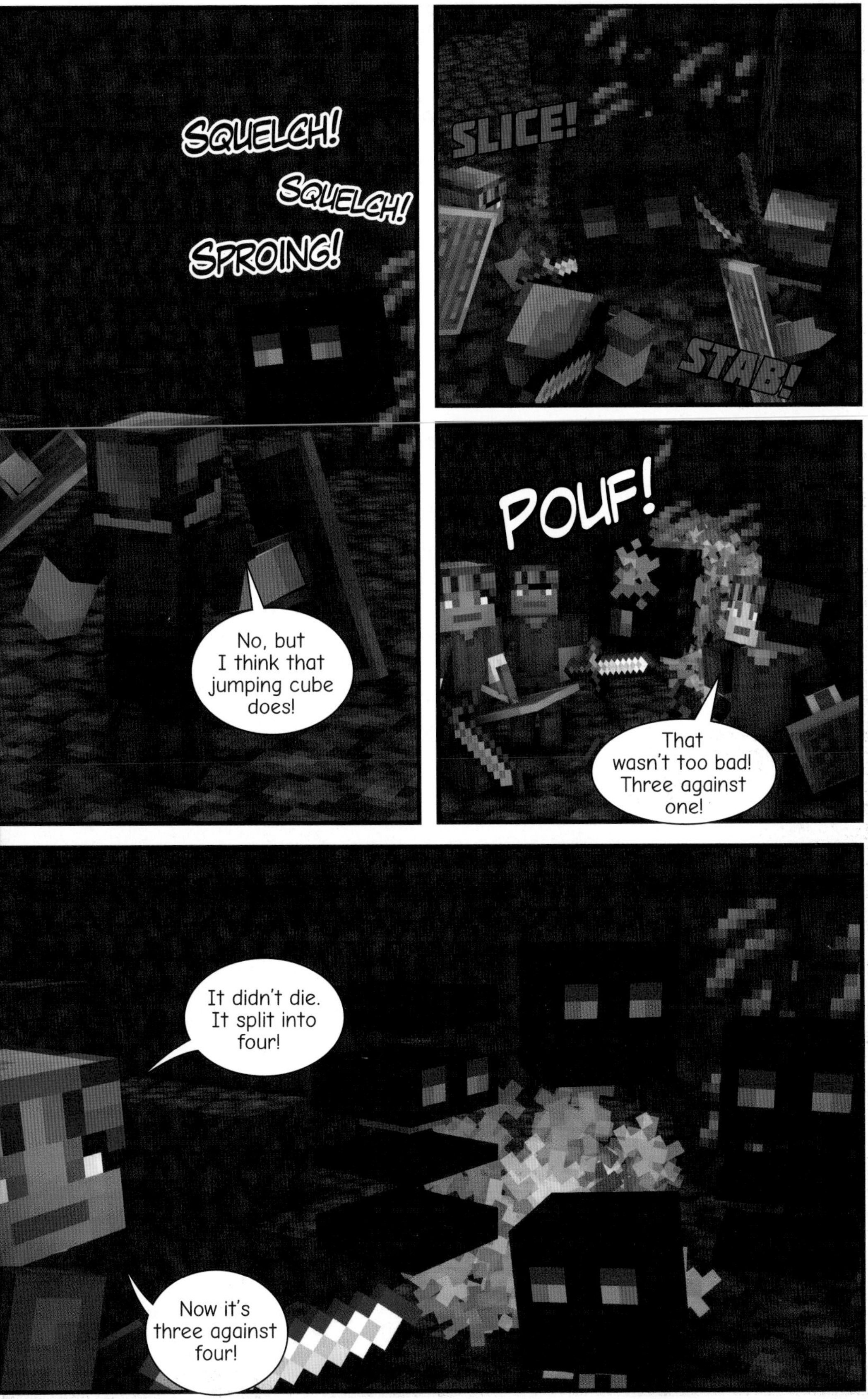
SQUELCH!
SQUELCH!
SPROING!
SLICE!
STAB!
No, but I think that jumping cube does!
POUF!
That wasn't too bad! Three against one!
It didn't die. It split into four!
Now it's three against four!

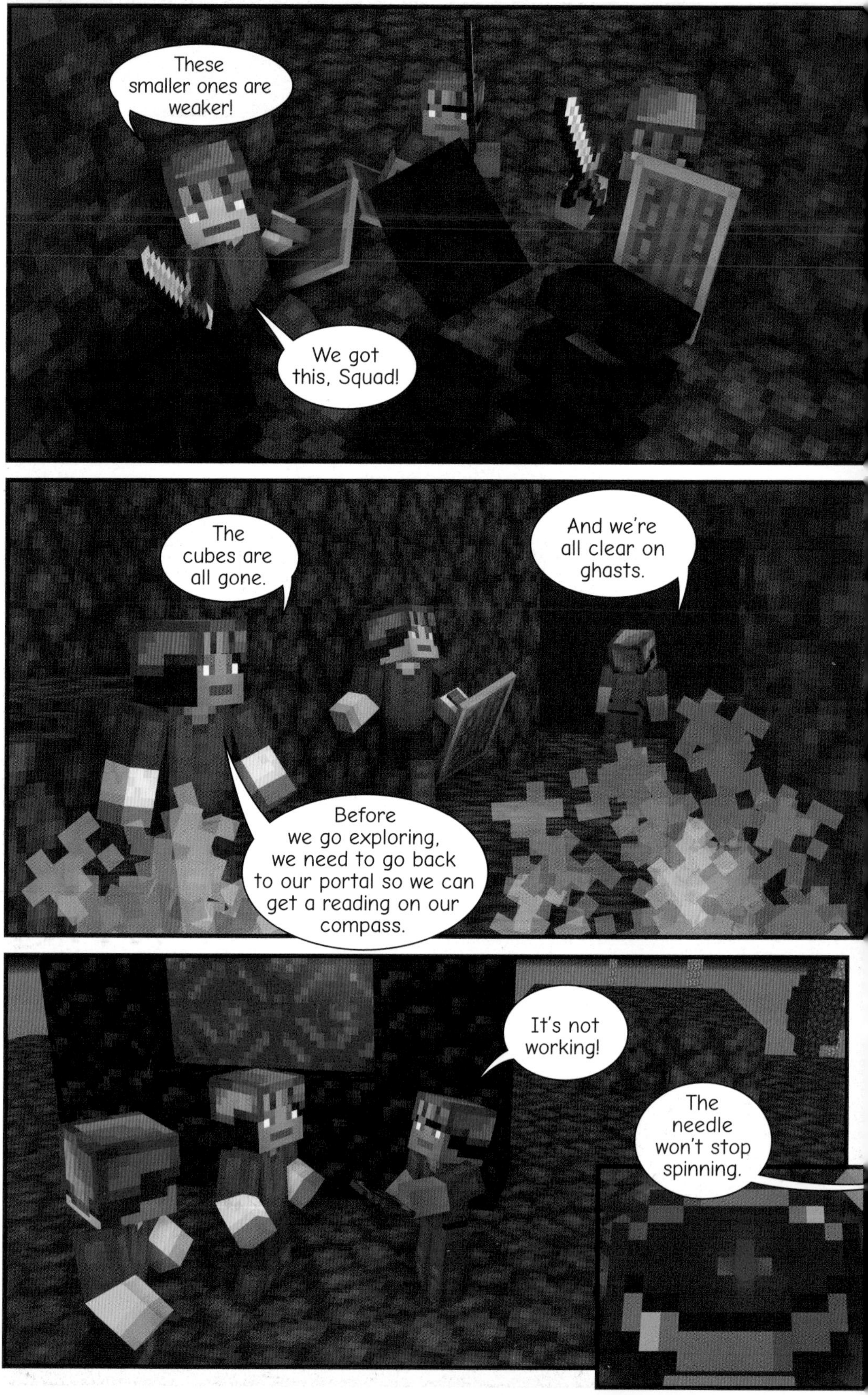
These smaller ones are weaker!
We got this, Squad!
The cubes are all gone.
And we're all clear on ghasts.
Before we go exploring, we need to go back to our portal so we can get a reading on our compass.
It's not working!
The needle won't stop spinning.

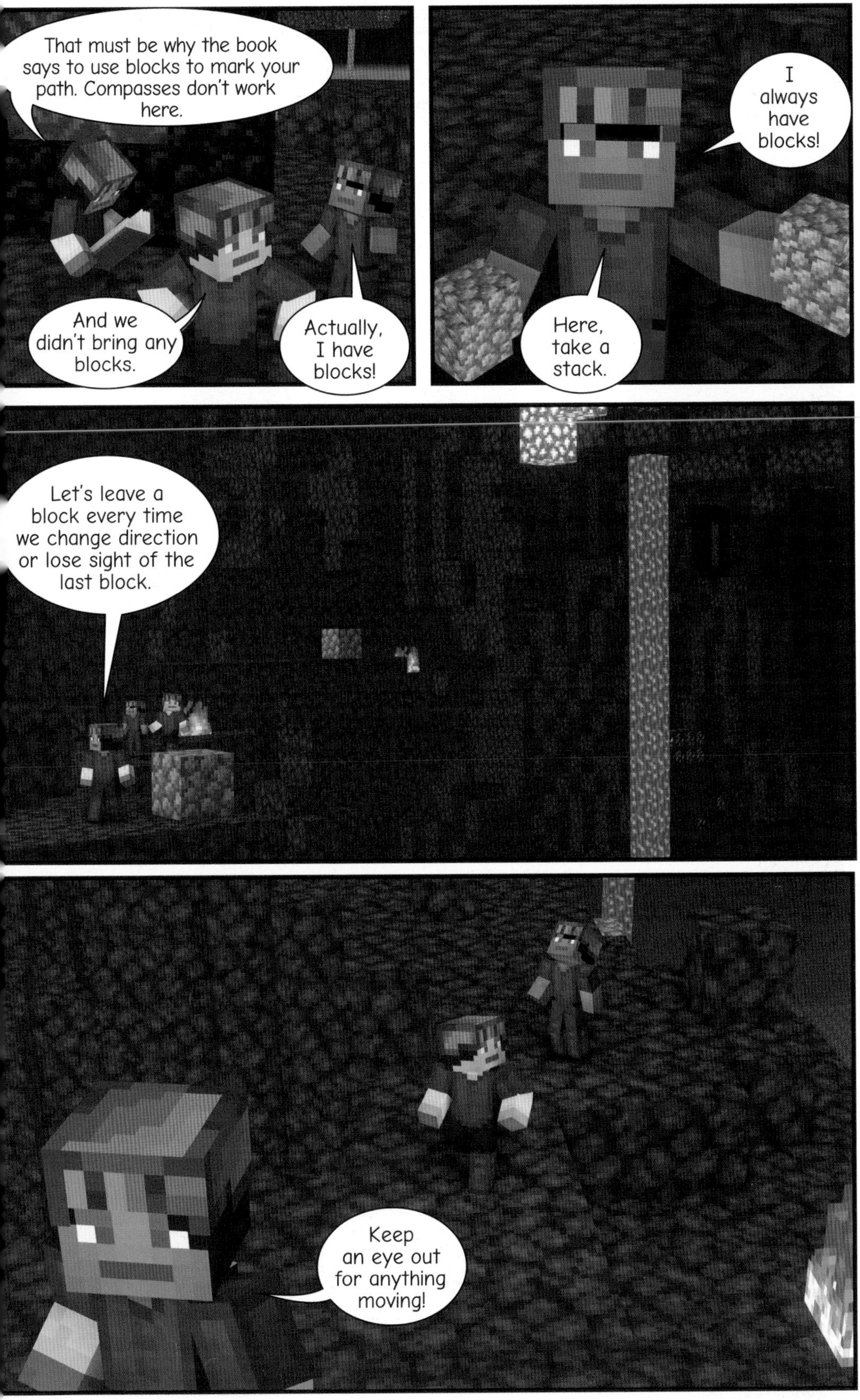
That must be why the book says to use blocks to mark your path. Compasses don't work here.
And we didn't bring any blocks.
Actually, I have blocks!
I always have blocks!
Here, take a stack.
Let's leave a block every time we change direction or lose sight of the last block.
Keep an eye out for anything moving!

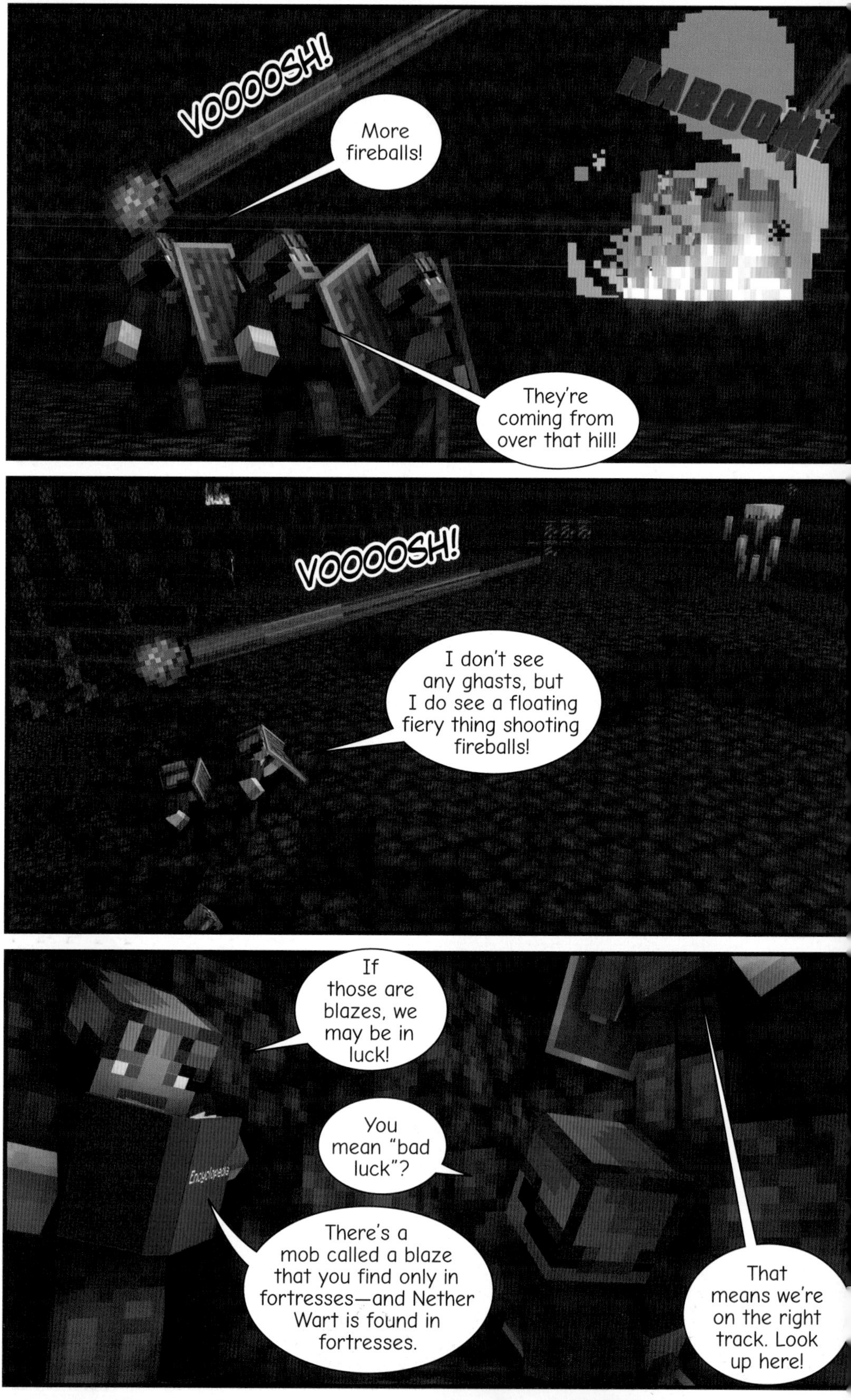
VOOOOSH!
More fireballs!
KABOOM!
They're coming from over that hill!
VOOOOSH!
I don't see any ghasts, but I do see a floating fiery thing shooting fireballs!
If those are blazes, we may be in luck!
You mean "bad luck"?
Encyclopedia
There's a mob called a blaze that you find only in fortresses—and Nether Wart is found in fortresses.
That means we're on the right track. Look up here!

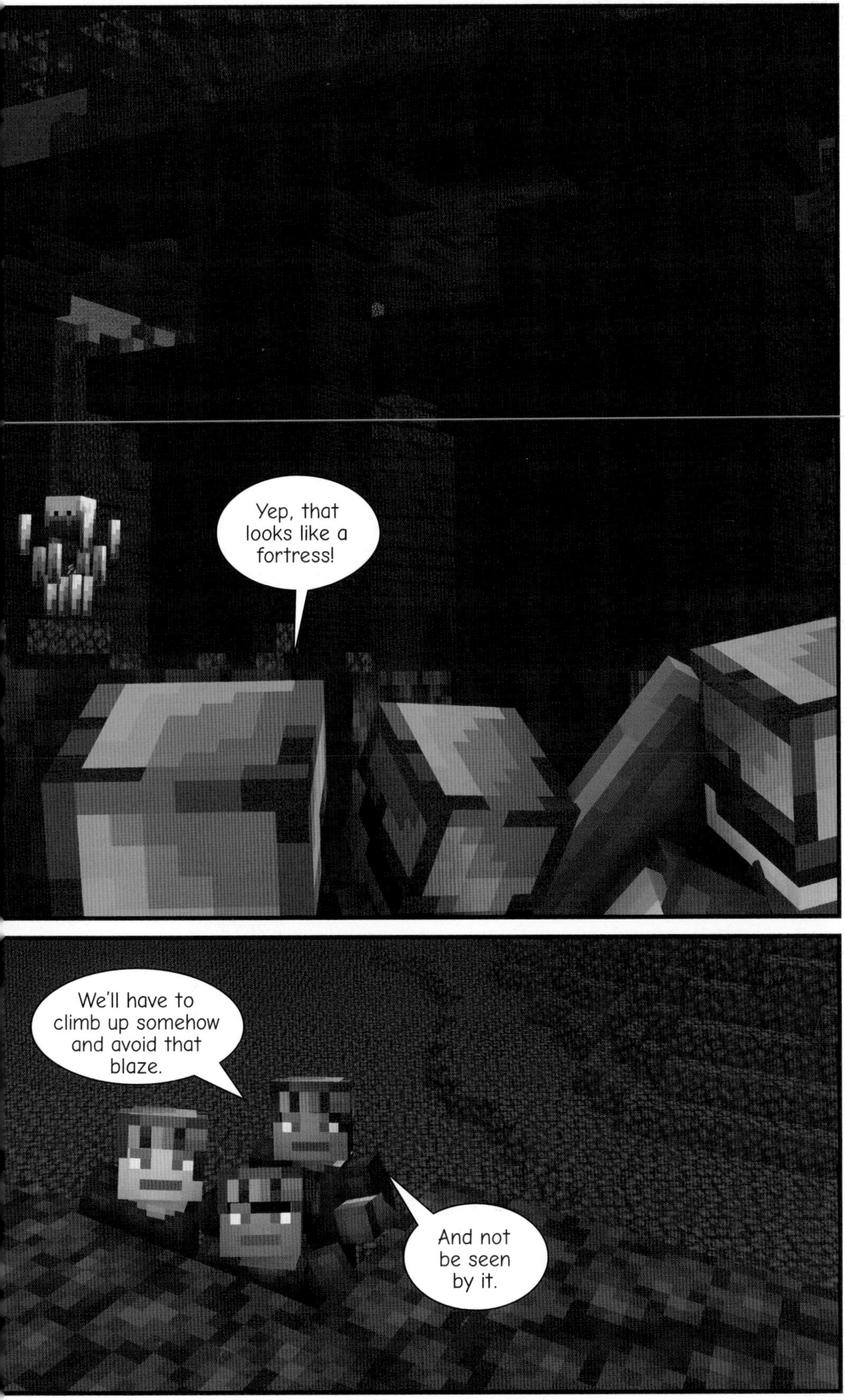
Yep, that looks like a fortress!
We'll have to climb up somehow and avoid that blaze.
And not be seen by it.

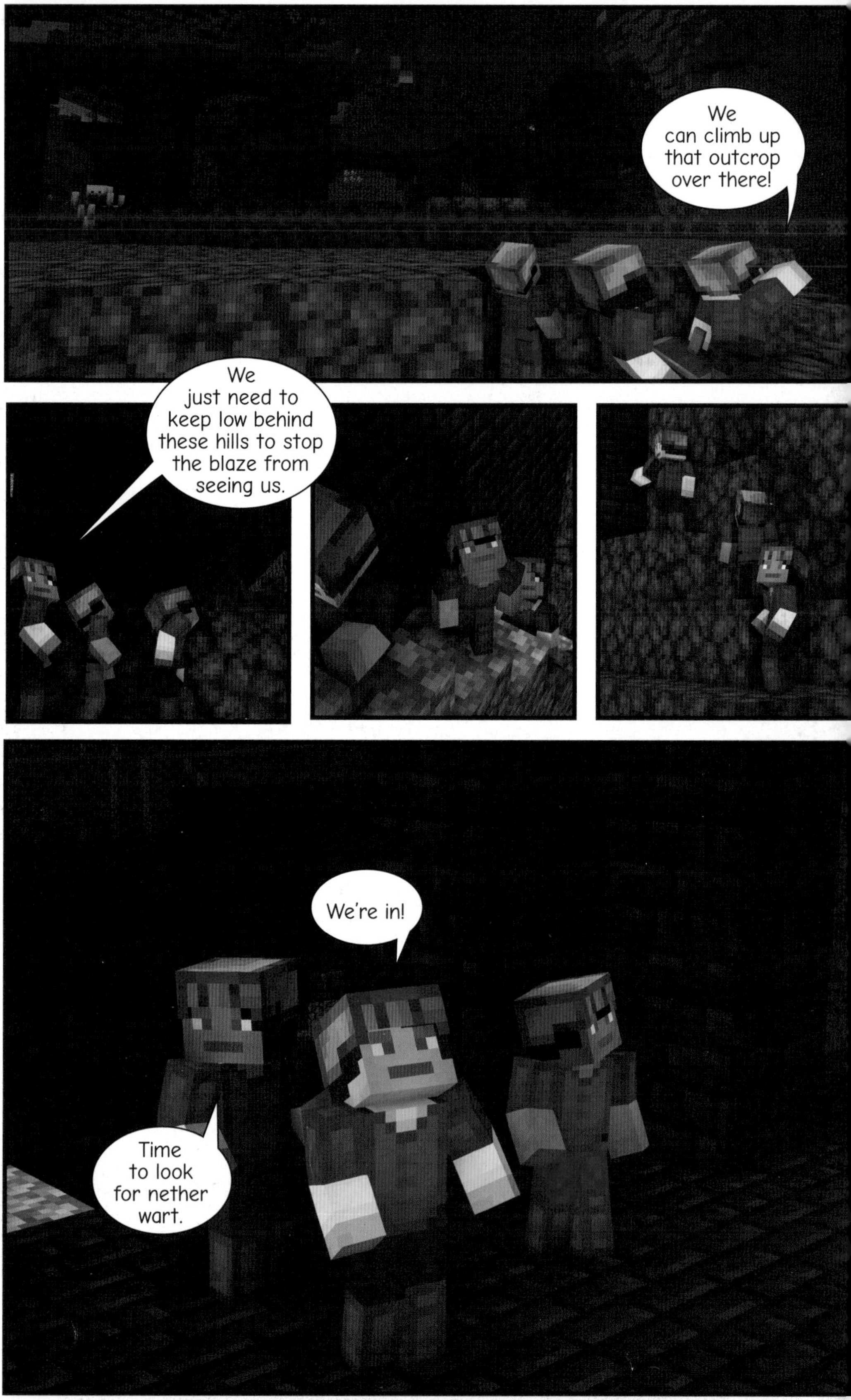
We can climb up that outcrop over there!
We just need to keep low behind these hills to stop the blaze from seeing us.
We're in!
Time to look for nether wart.

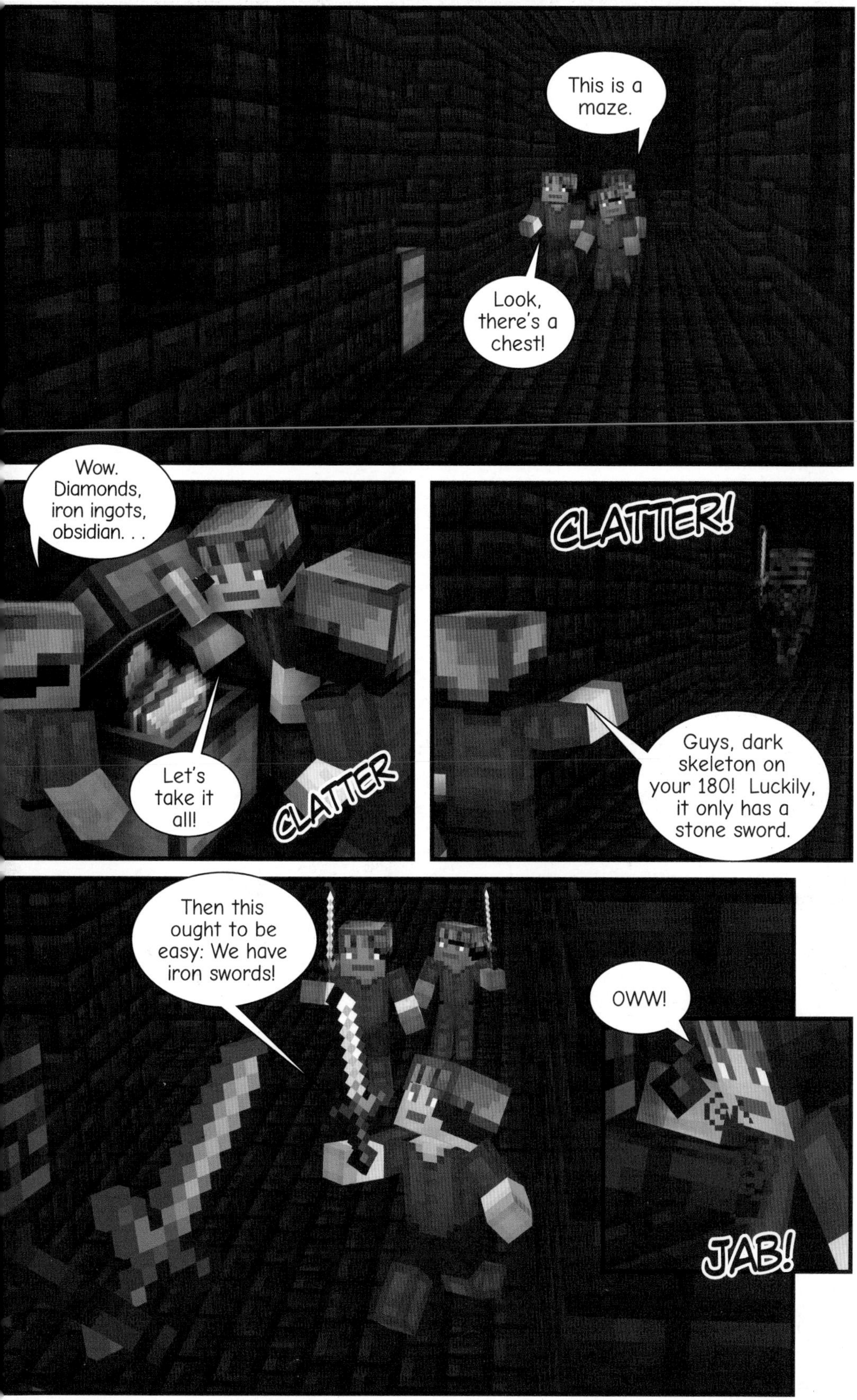
This is a maze.
Look, there's a chest!
Wow. Diamonds, iron ingots, obsidian. . .
Let's take it all!
CLATTER
CLATTER!
Guys, dark skeleton on your 180! Luckily, it only has a stone sword.
Then this ought to be easy: We have iron swords!
OWW!
JAB!

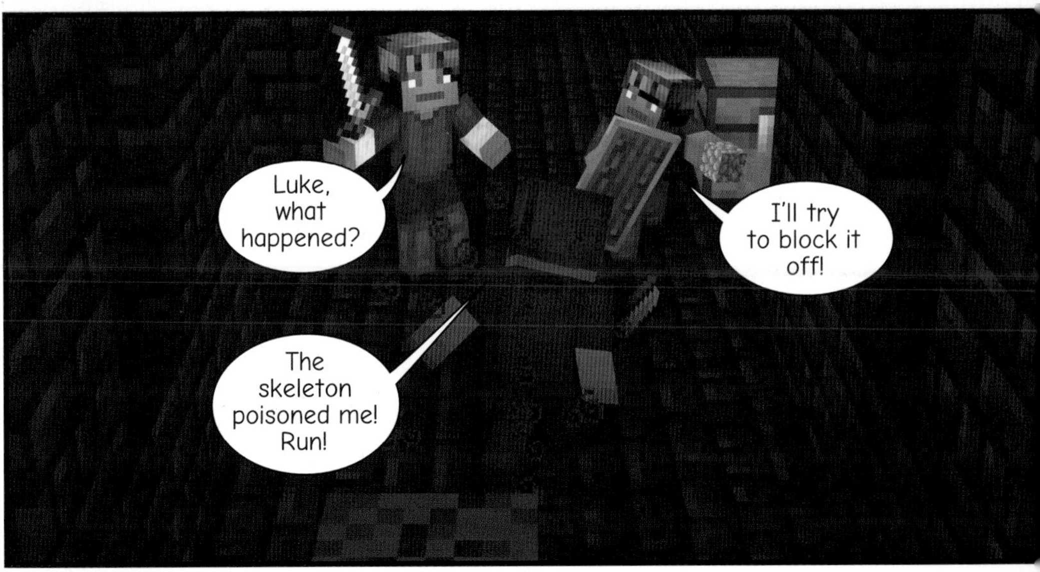
Luke, what happened?
I'll try to block it off!
The skeleton poisoned me! Run!

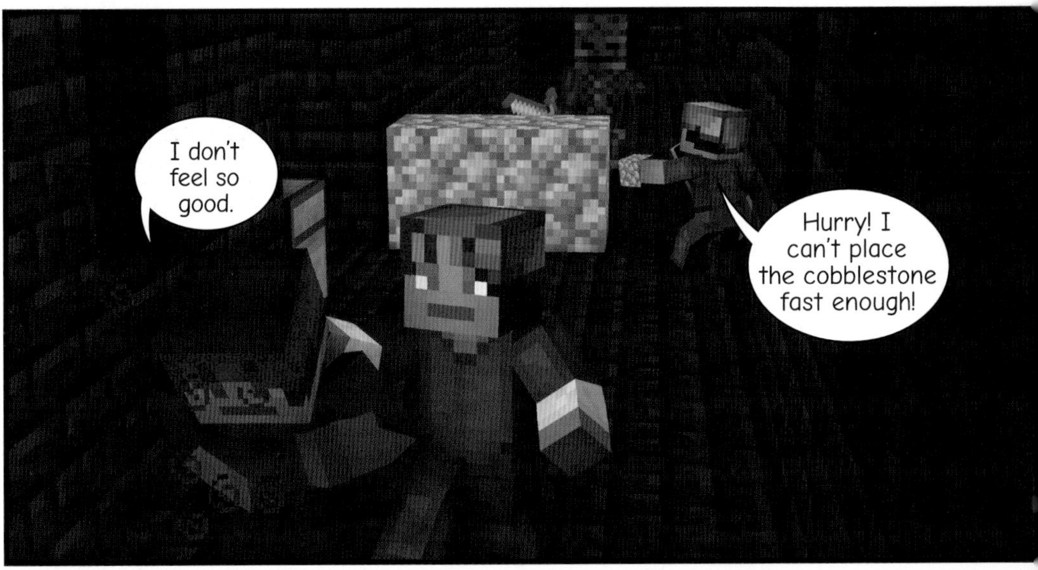
I don't feel so good.
Hurry! I can't place the cobblestone fast enough!

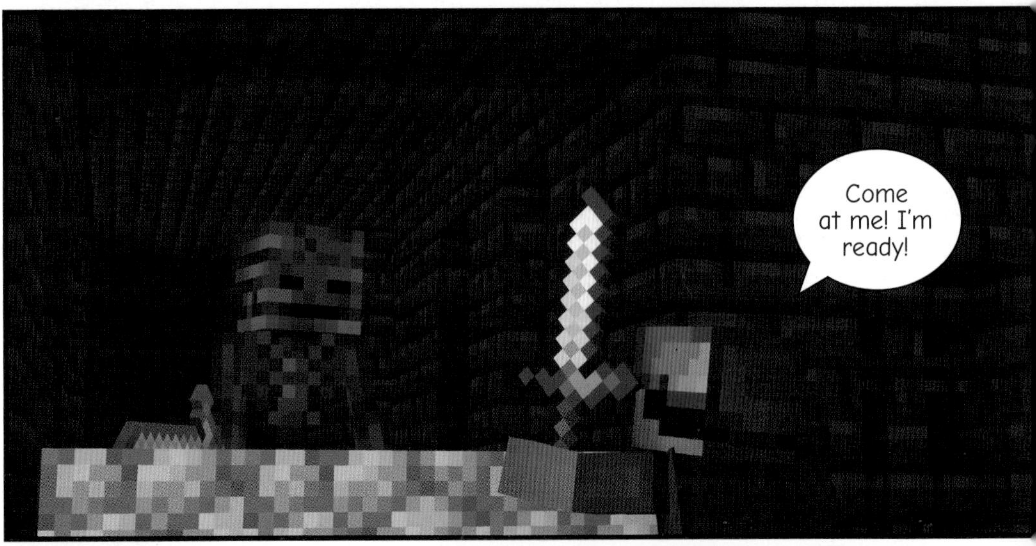
Come at me! I'm ready!

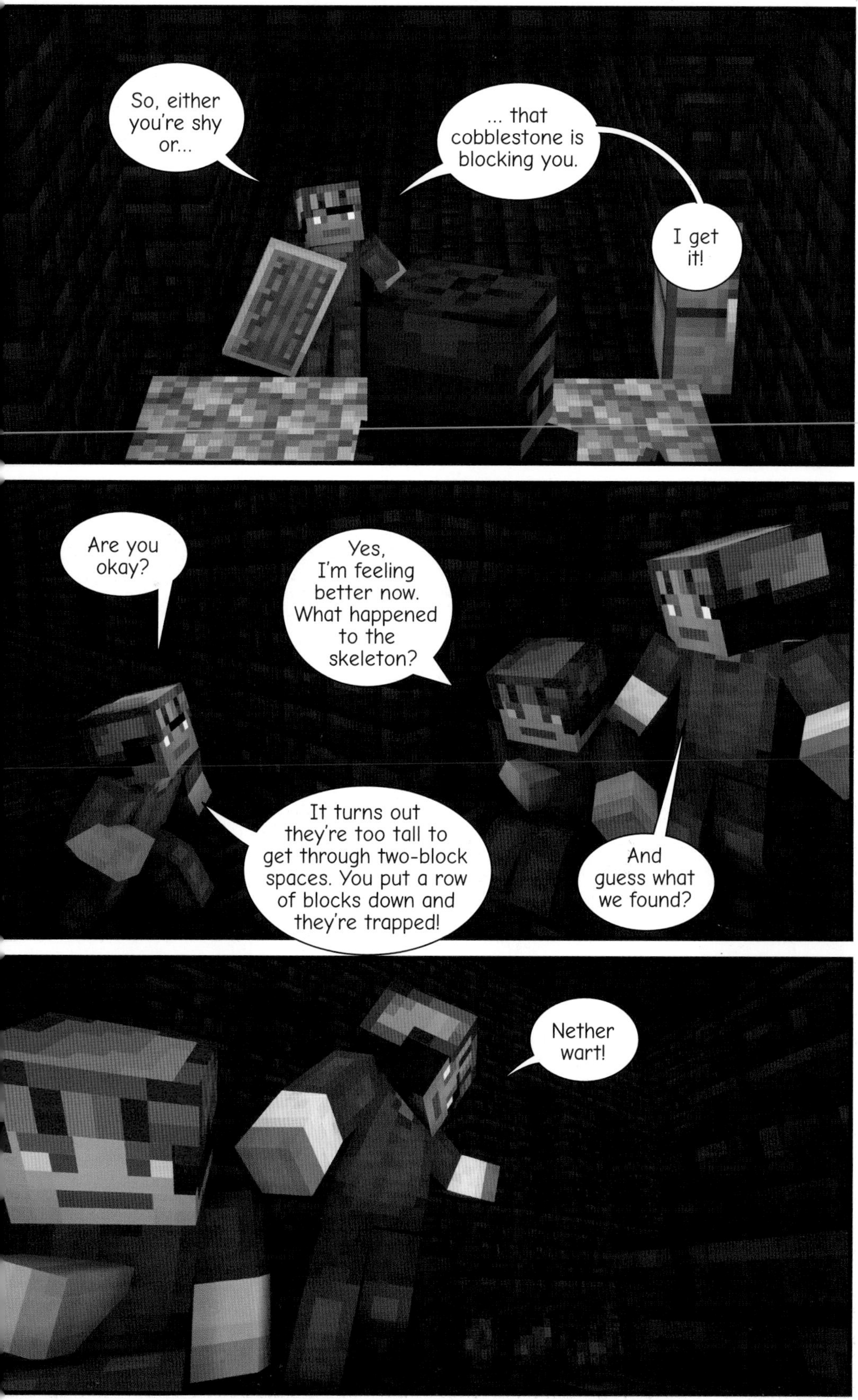
So, either you're shy or...
... that cobblestone is blocking you.
I get it!
Are you okay?
Yes, I'm feeling better now. What happened to the skeleton?
It turns out they're too tall to get through two-block spaces. You put a row of blocks down and they're trapped!
And guess what we found?
Nether wart!

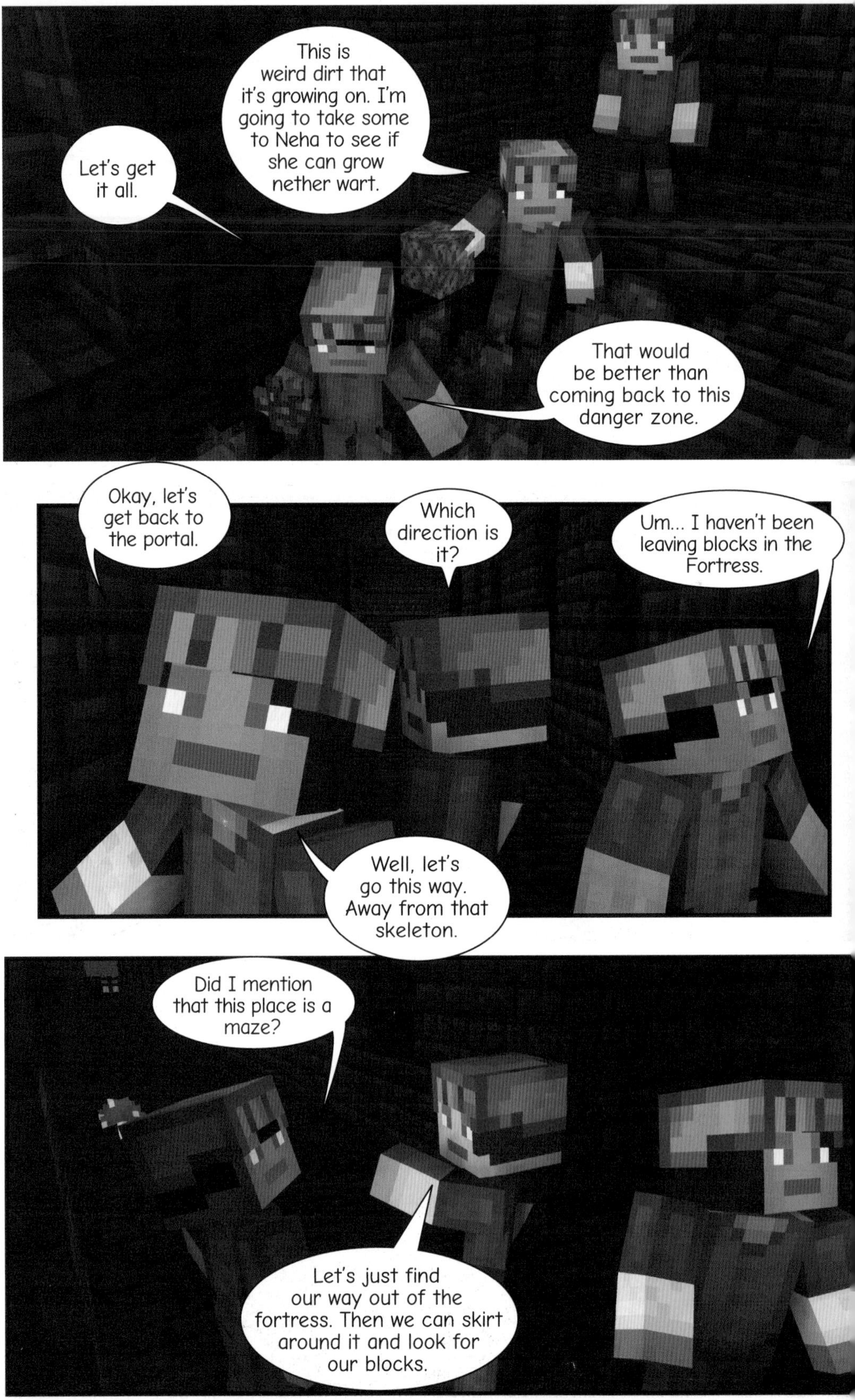
Let's get it all.
This is weird dirt that it's growing on. I'm going to take some to Neha to see if she can grow nether wart.
That would be better than coming back to this danger zone.
Okay, let's get back to the portal.
Which direction is it?
Um... I haven't been leaving blocks in the Fortress.
Well, let's go this way. Away from that skeleton.
Did I mention that this place is a maze?
Let's just find our way out of the fortress. Then we can skirt around it and look for our blocks.

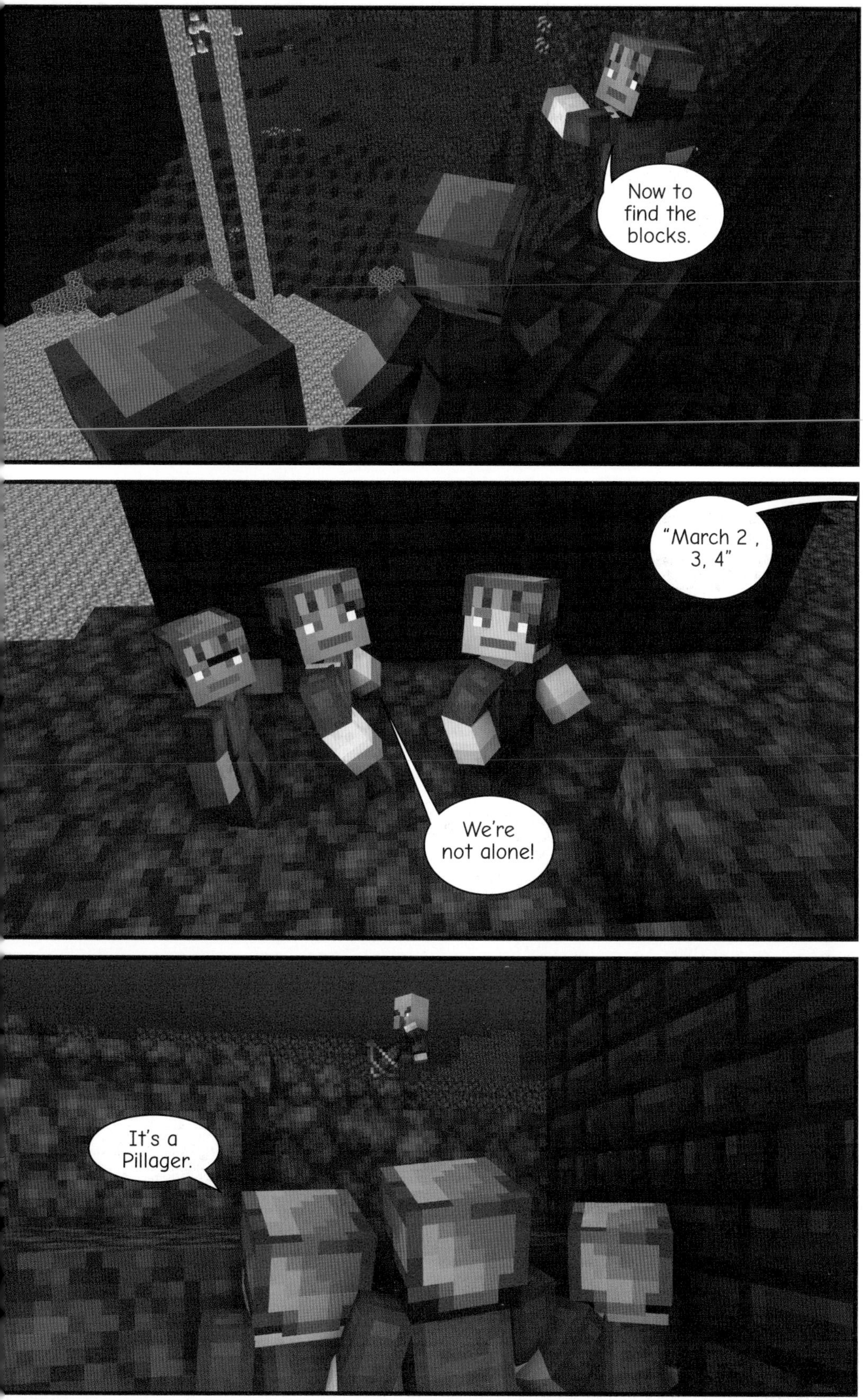
Now to find the blocks.
"March 2 , 3, 4"
We're not alone!
It's a Pillager.

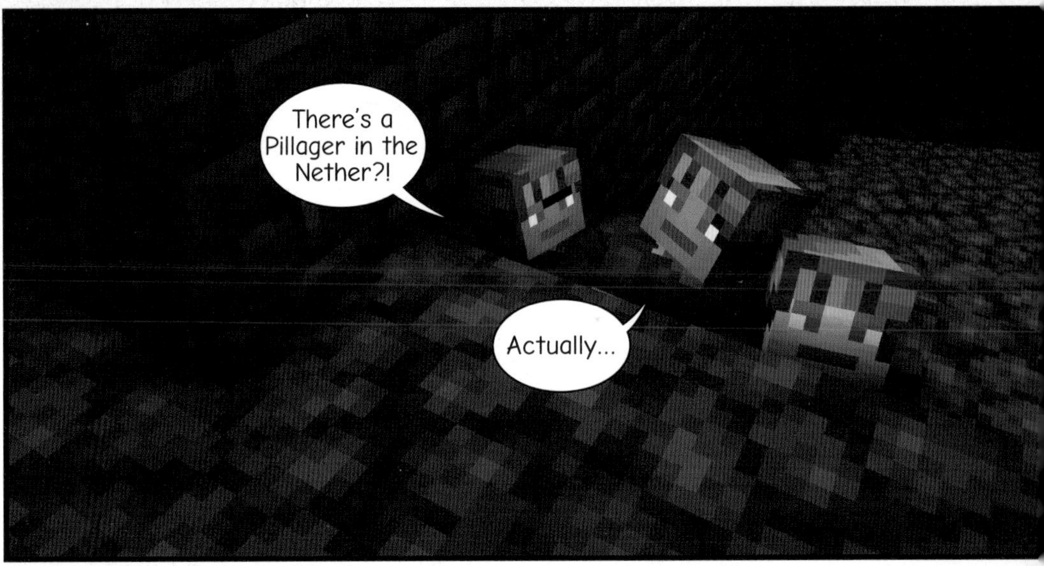
There's a Pillager in the Nether?!
Actually...

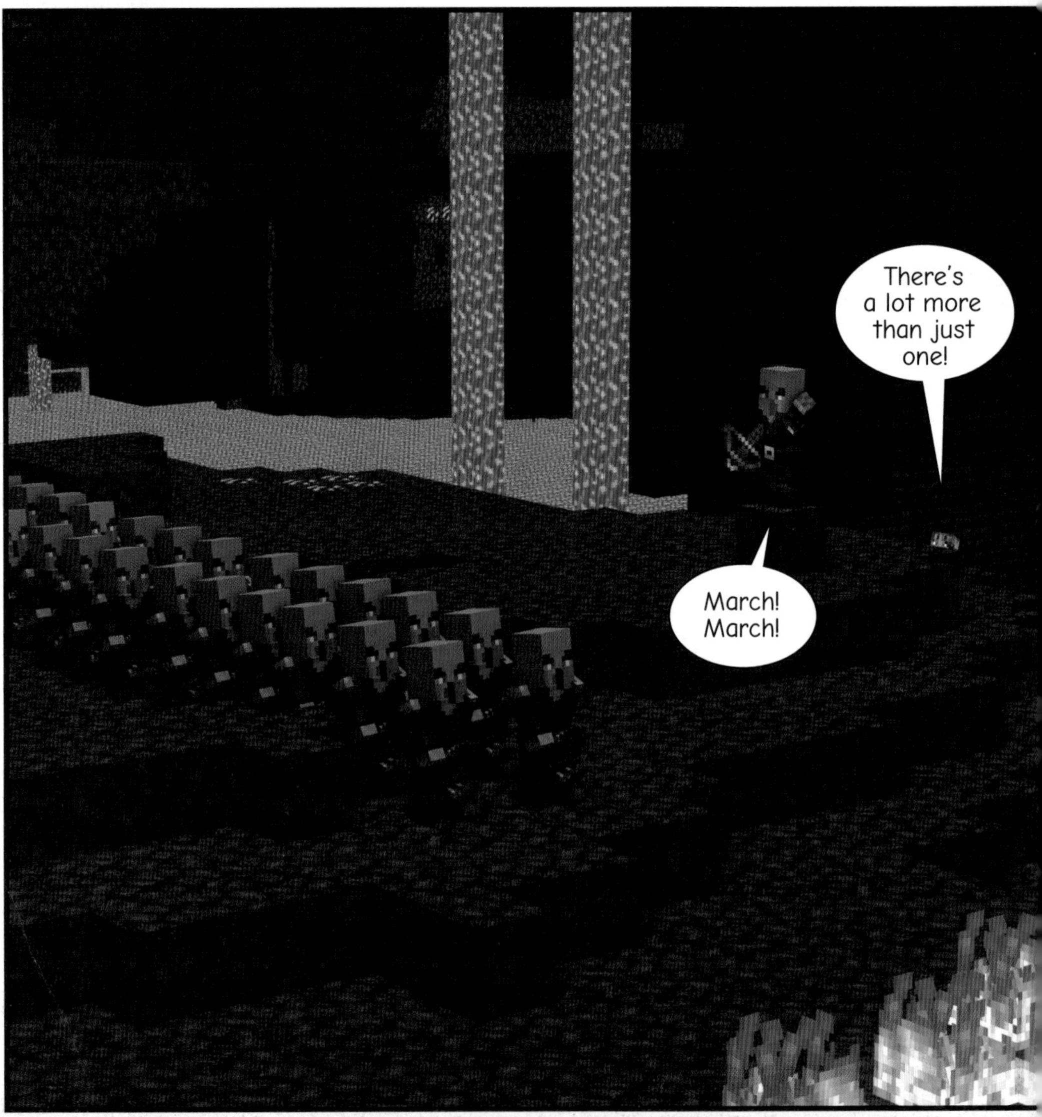
There's a lot more than just one!
March! March!

Chapter 5
Villagers
in Peril

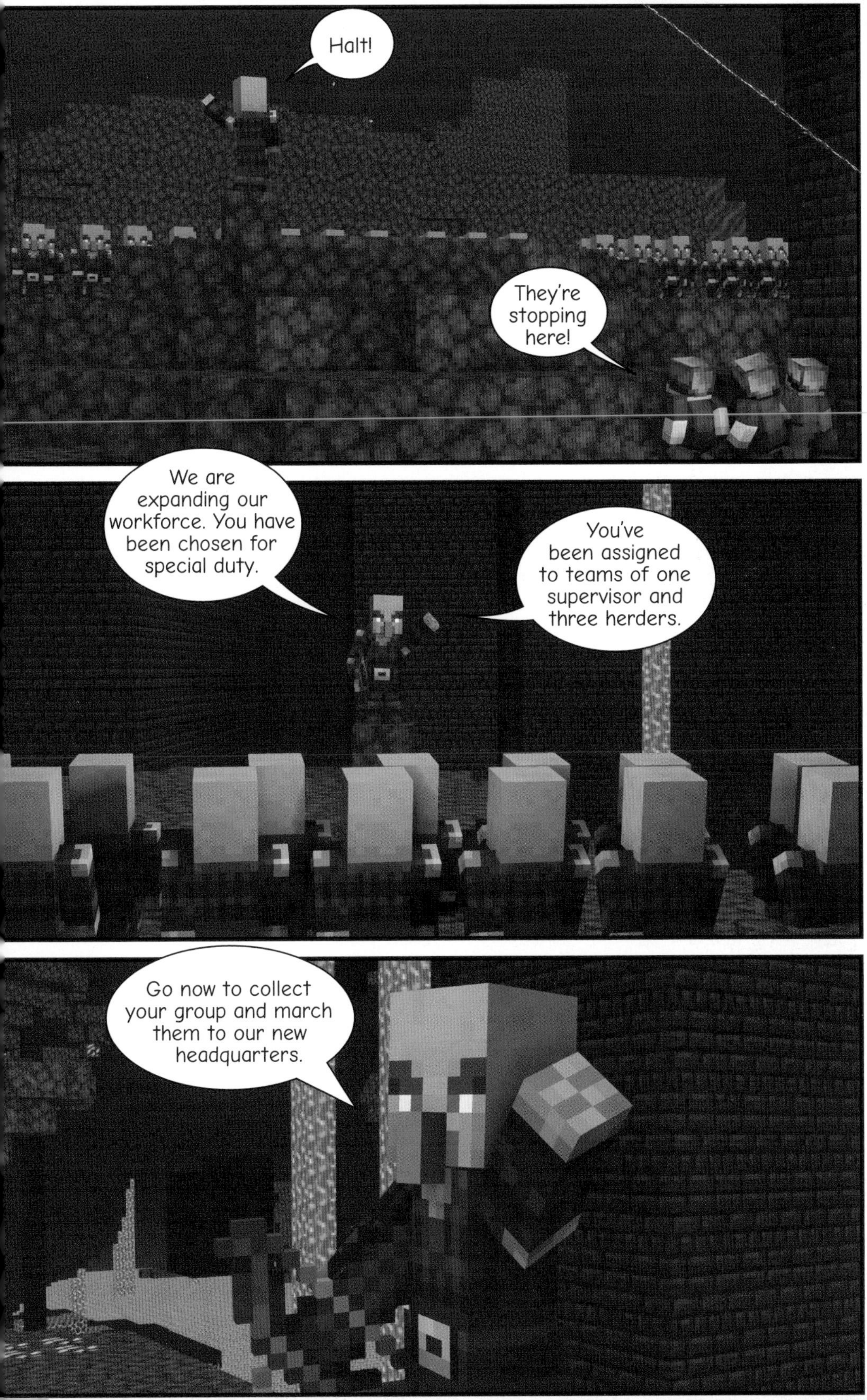
Halt!
They're stopping here!
We are expanding our workforce. You have been chosen for special duty.
You've been assigned to teams of one supervisor and three herders.
Go now to collect your group and march them to our new headquarters.

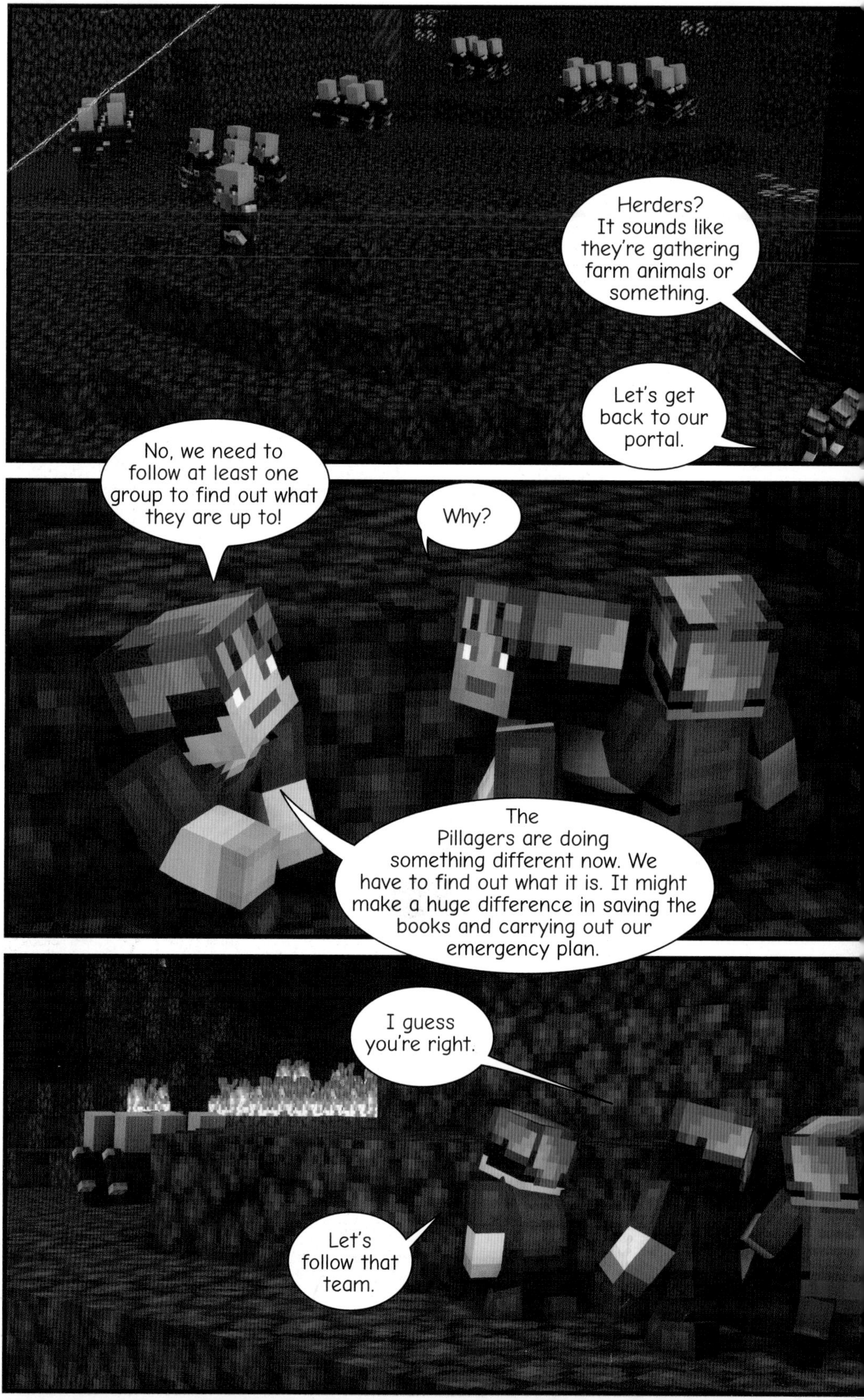
Herders? It sounds like they're gathering farm animals or something.
Let's get back to our portal.
No, we need to follow at least one group to find out what they are up to!
Why?
The Pillagers are doing something different now. We have to find out what it is. It might make a huge difference in saving the books and carrying out our emergency plan.
I guess you're right.
Let's follow that team.

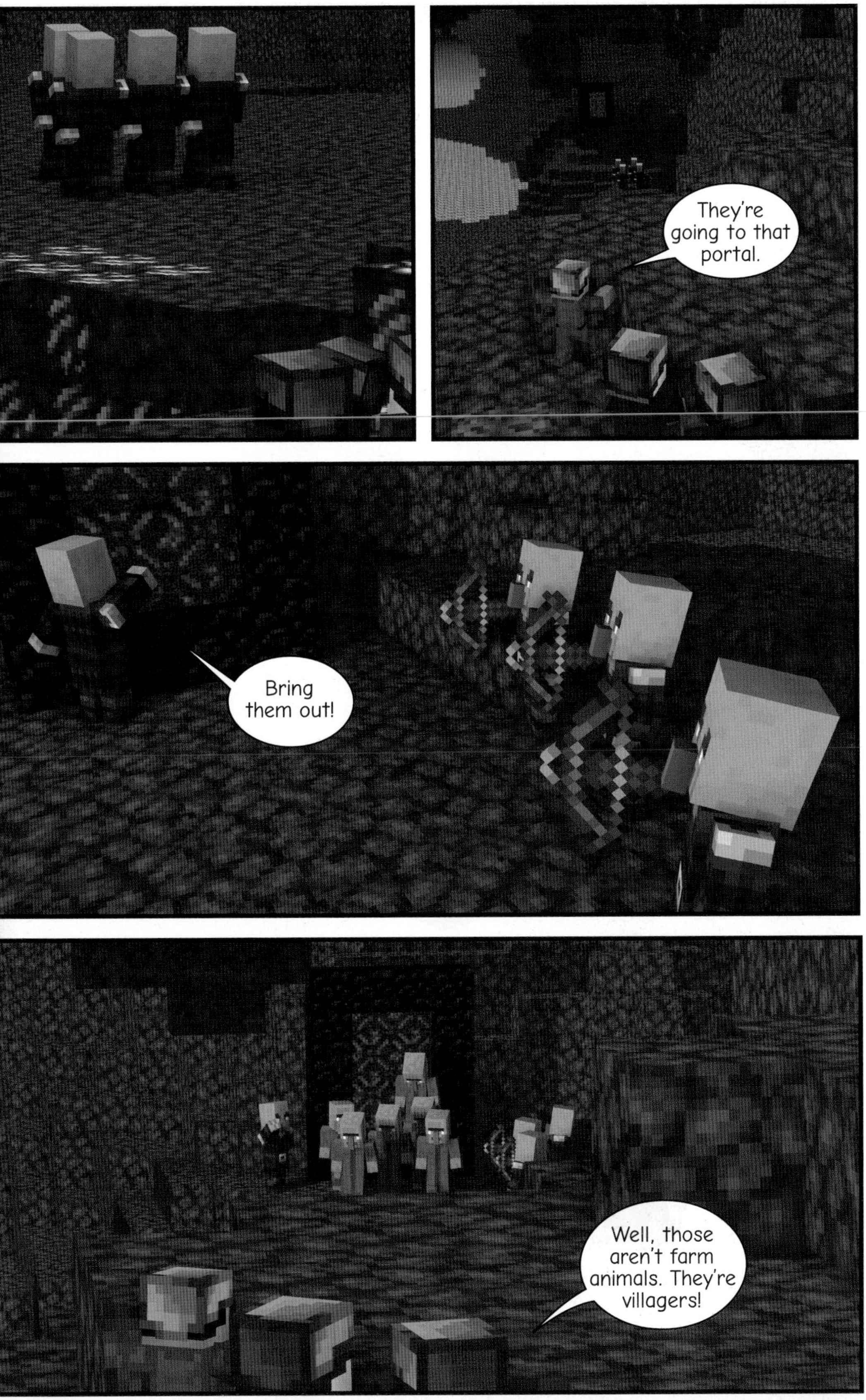
They're going to that portal.
Bring them out!
Well, those aren't farm animals. They're villagers!

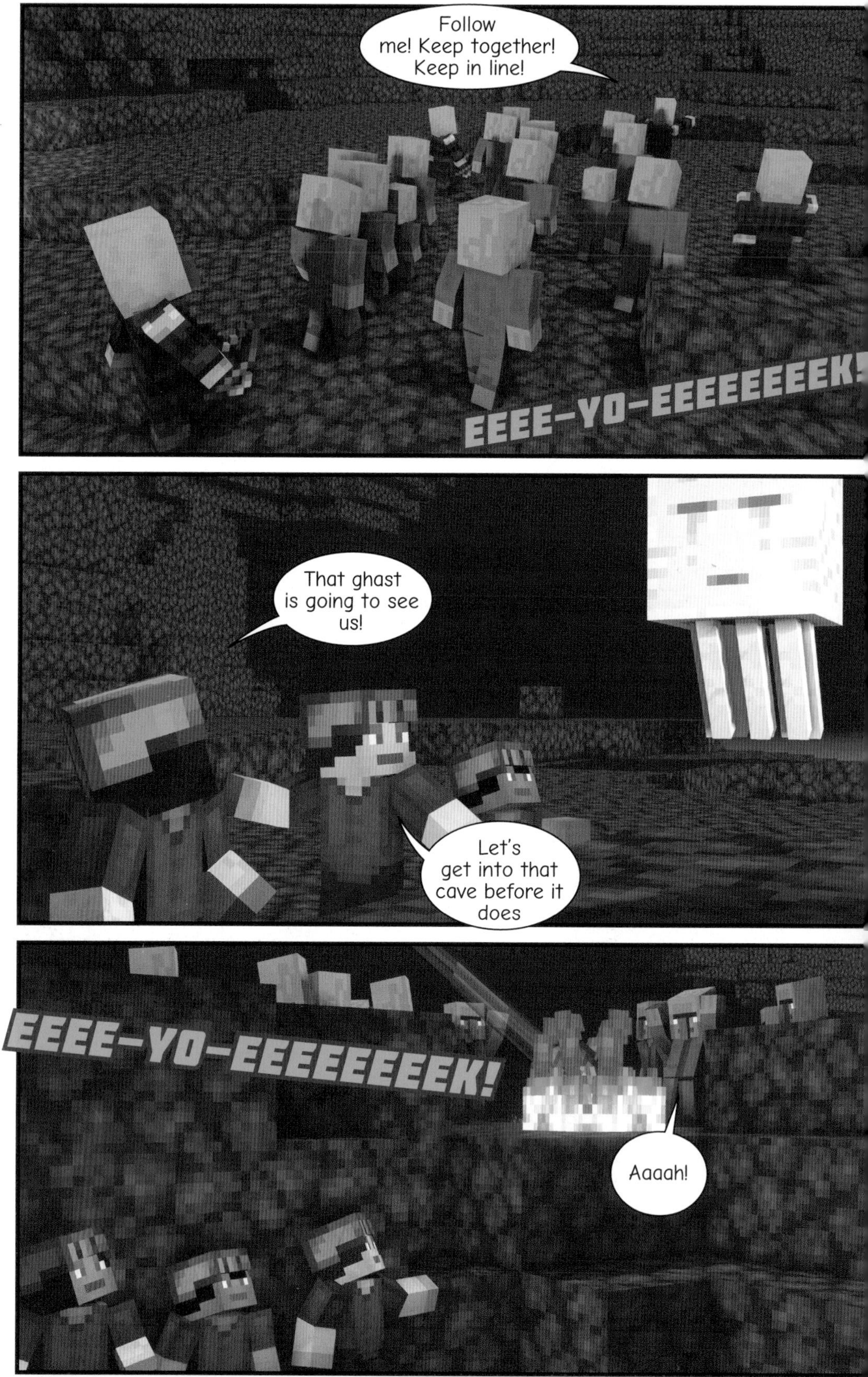
Follow me! Keep together! Keep in line!
EEEE-YO-EEEEEEEK!
That ghast is going to see us!
Let's get into that cave before it does
EEEE-YO-EEEEEEEEK!
Aaaah!

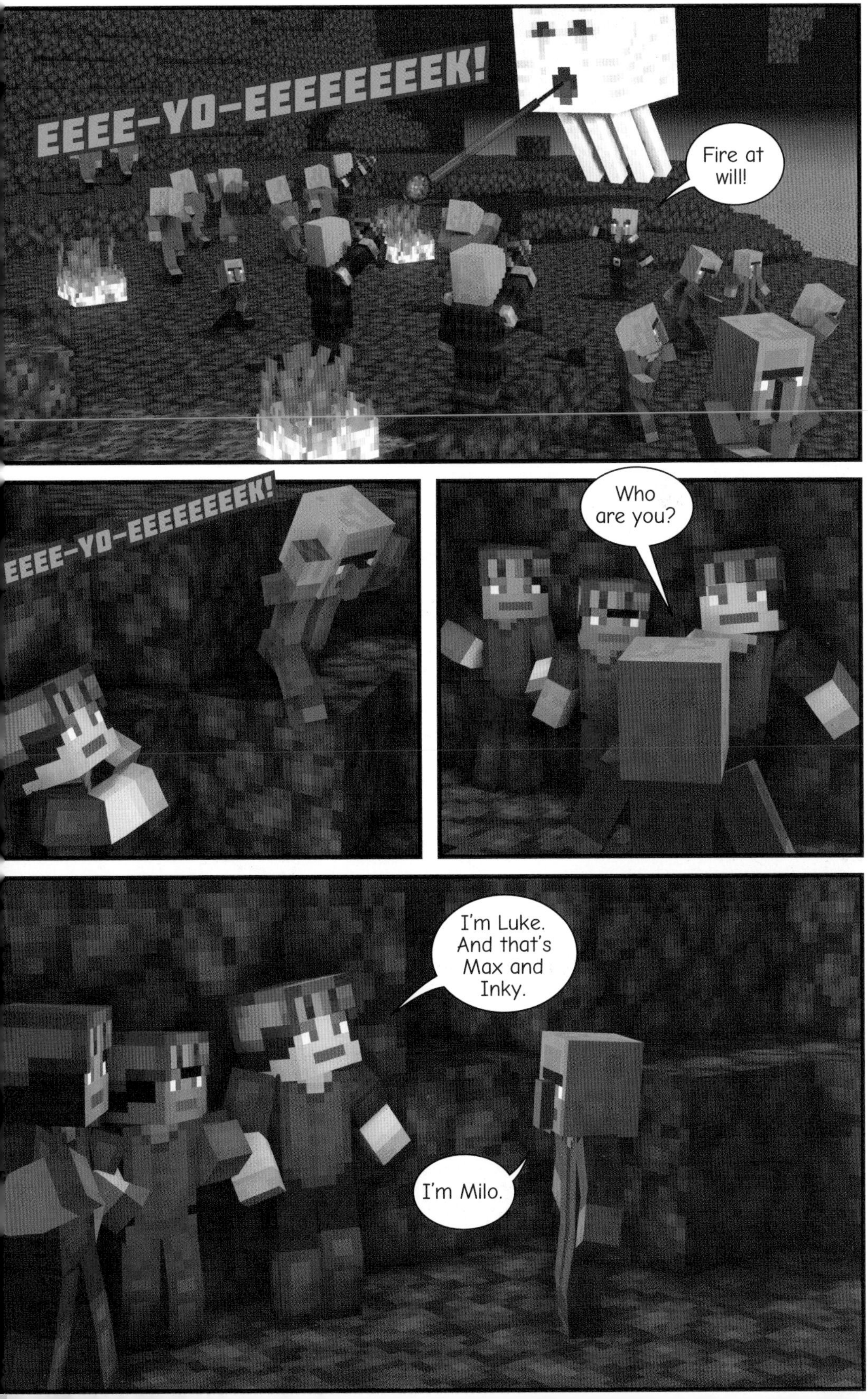
EEEE-YO-EEEEEEEEK!
Fire at will!
EEEE-YO-EEEEEEEEK!
Who are you?
I'm Luke. And that's Max and Inky.
I'm Milo.

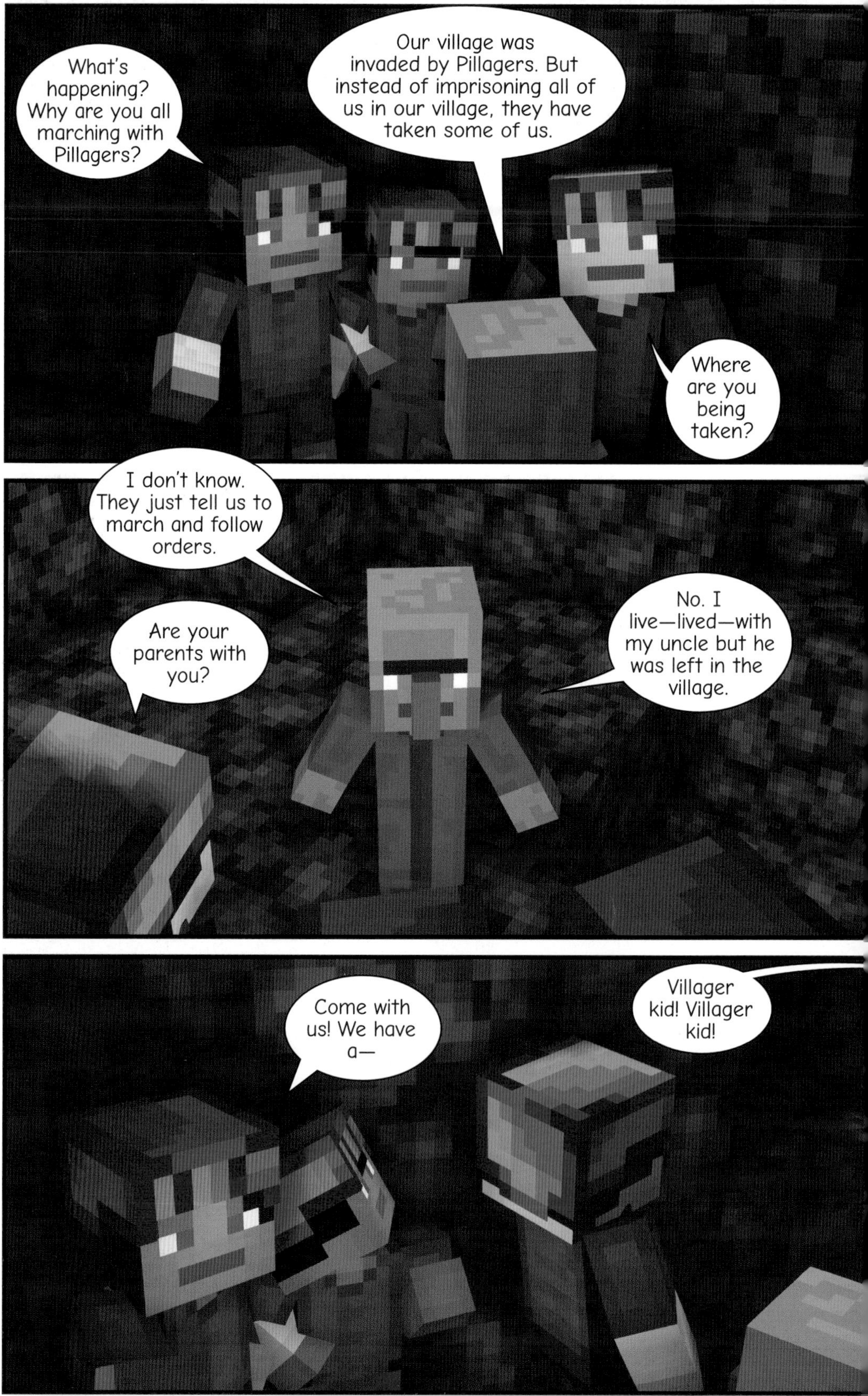
What's happening? Why are you all marching with Pillagers?
Our village was invaded by Pillagers. But instead of imprisoning all of us in our village, they have taken some of us.
Where are you being taken?
I don't know. They just tell us to march and follow orders.
Are your parents with you?
No. I live—lived—with my uncle but he was left in the village.
Come with us! We have a—
Villager kid! Villager kid!

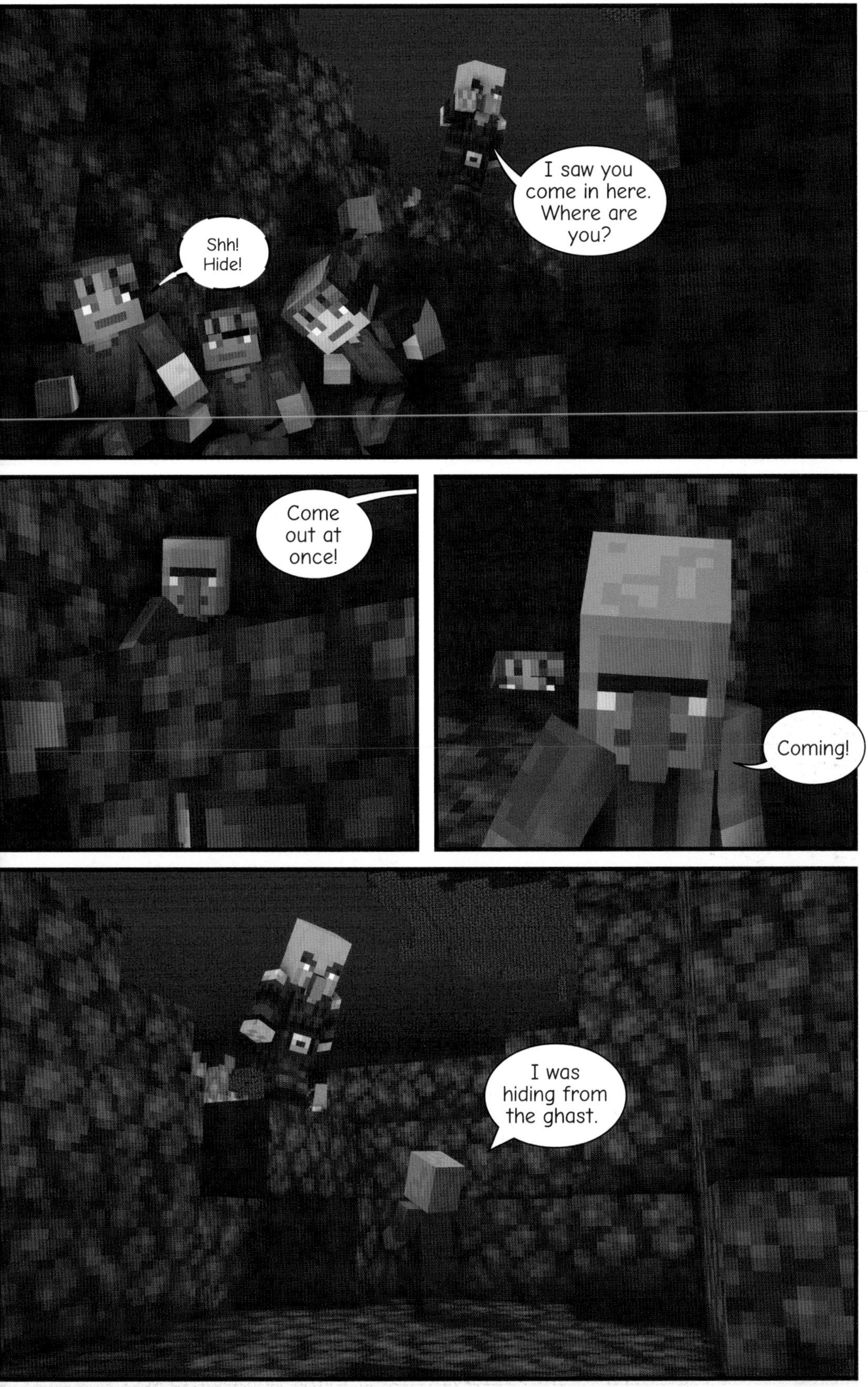
I saw you come in here. Where are you?
Shh! Hide!
Come out at once!
Coming!
I was hiding from the ghast.

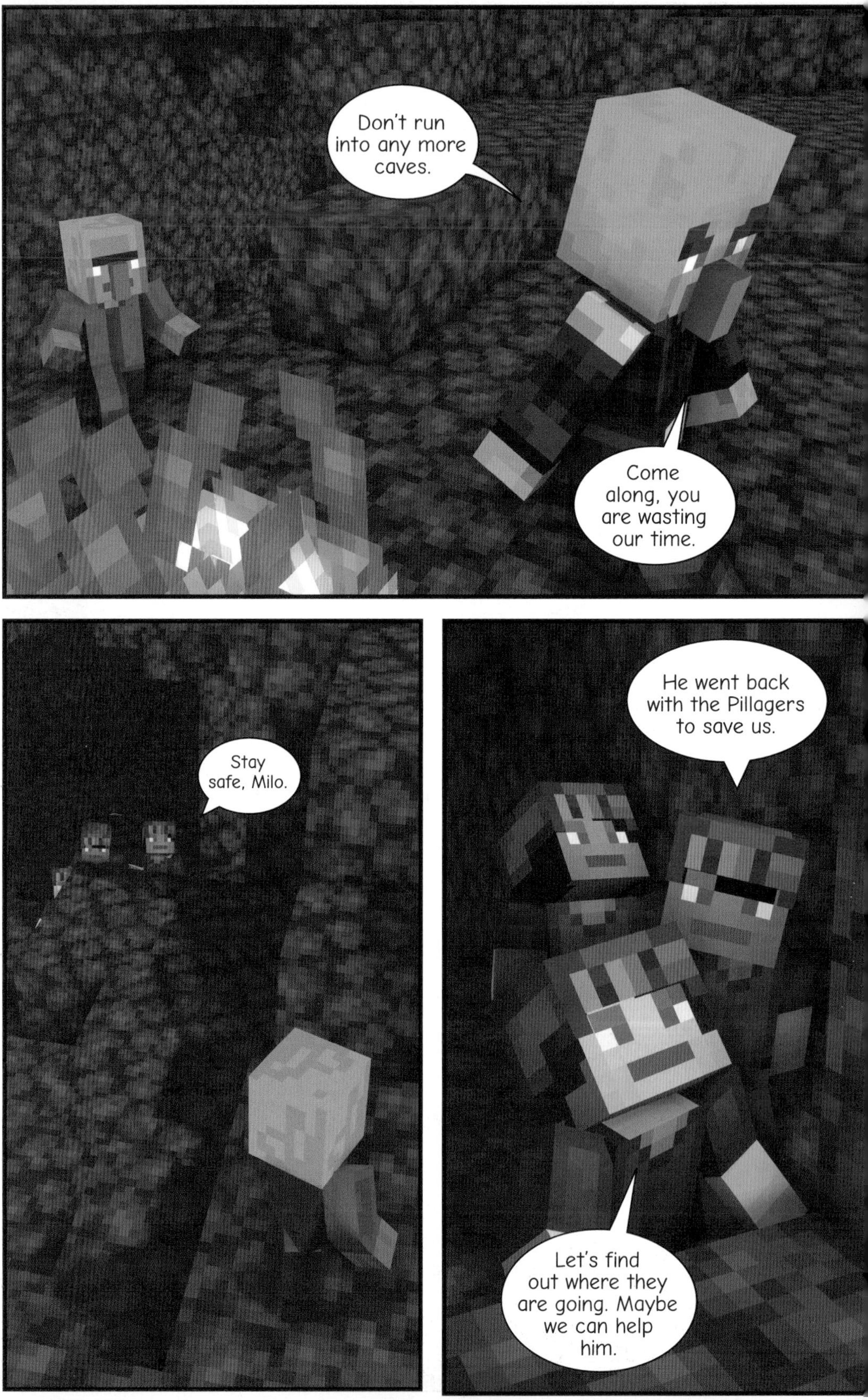
Don't run into any more caves.
Come along, you are wasting our time.
Stay safe, Milo.
He went back with the Pillagers to save us.
Let's find out where they are going. Maybe we can help him.

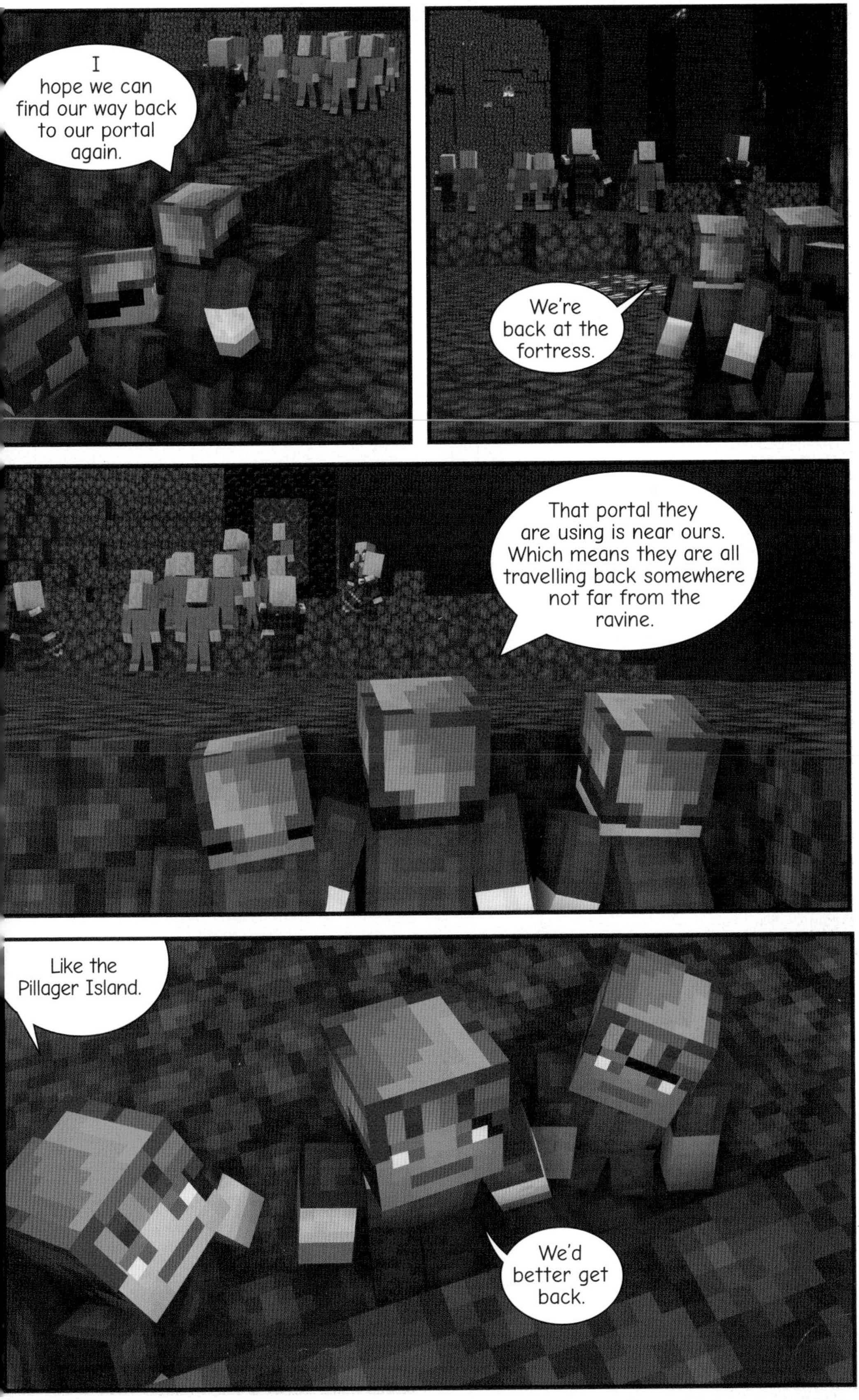
I hope we can find our way back to our portal again.
We're back at the fortress.
That portal they are using is near ours. Which means they are all travelling back somewhere not far from the ravine.
Like the Pillager Island.
We'd better get back.

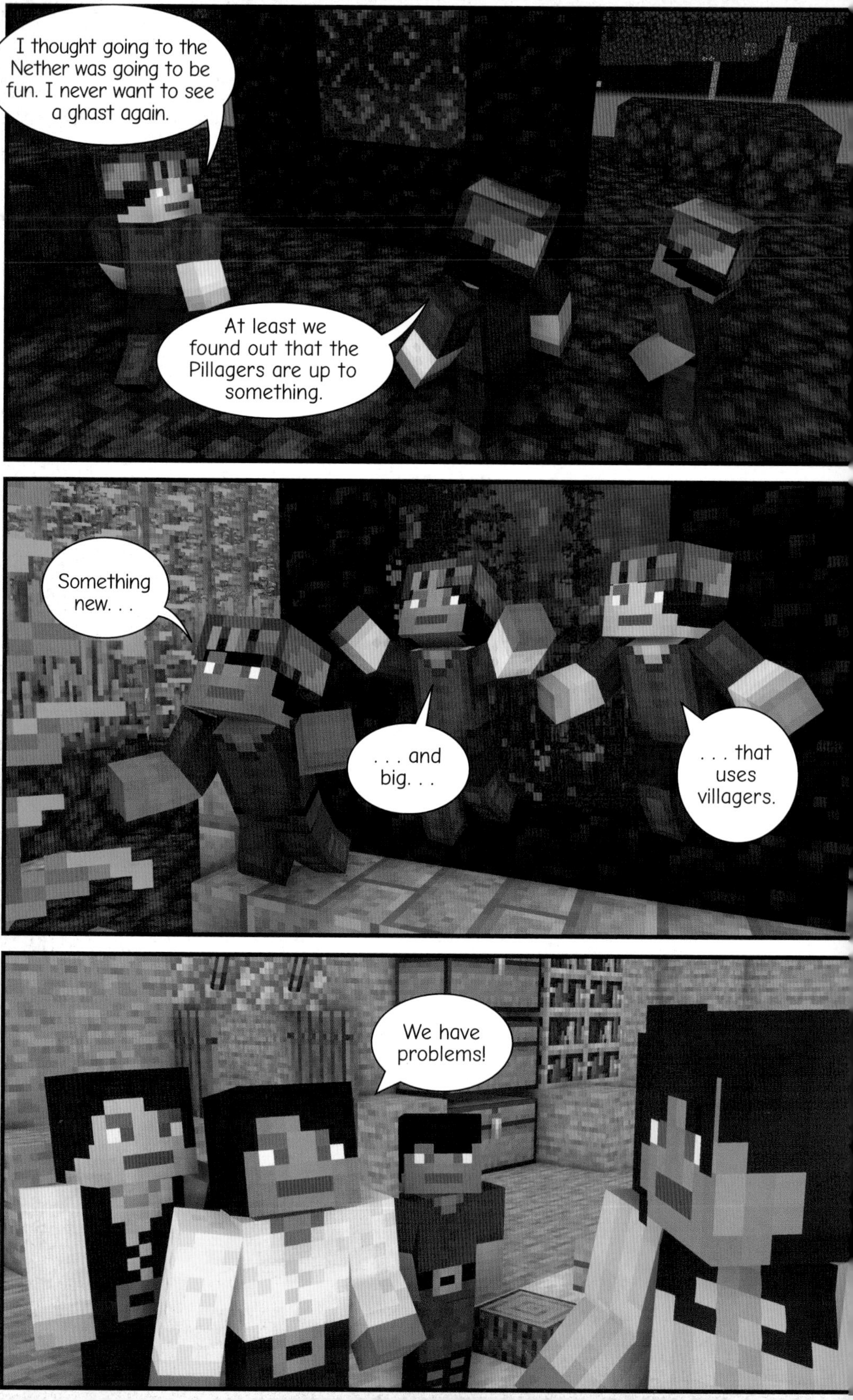
I thought going to the Nether was going to be fun. I never want to see a ghast again.
At least we found out that the Pillagers are up to something.
Something new. . .
. . . and big. . .
. . . that uses villagers.
We have problems!

Chapter 6
Scouting
Pillager Island

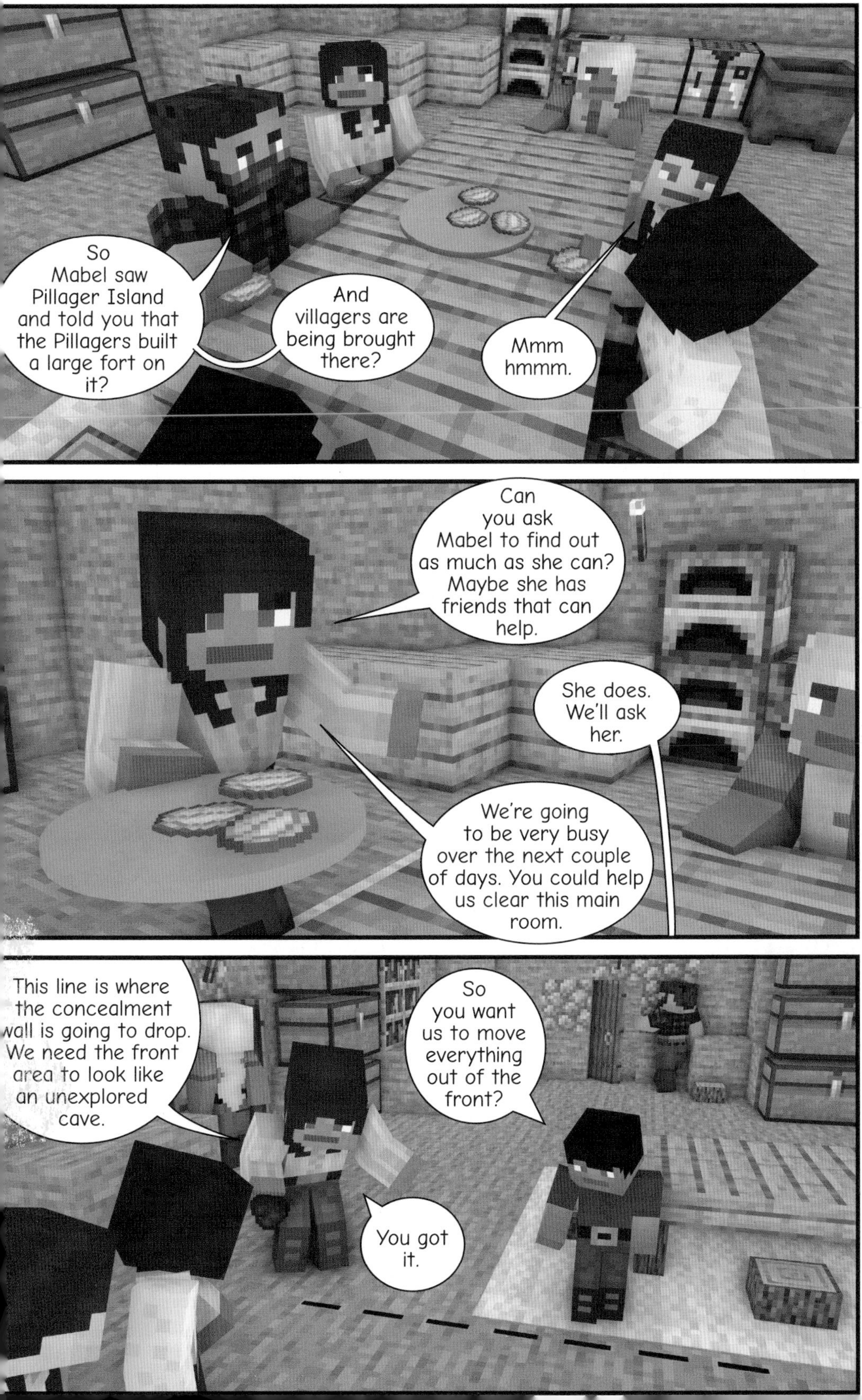
So Mabel saw Pillager Island and told you that the Pillagers built a large fort on it?
And villagers are being brought there?
Mmm hmmm.
Can you ask Mabel to find out as much as she can? Maybe she has friends that can help.
She does. We'll ask her.
We're going to be very busy over the next couple of days. You could help us clear this main room.
This line is where the concealment wall is going to drop. We need the front area to look like an unexplored cave.
So you want us to move everything out of the front?
You got it.

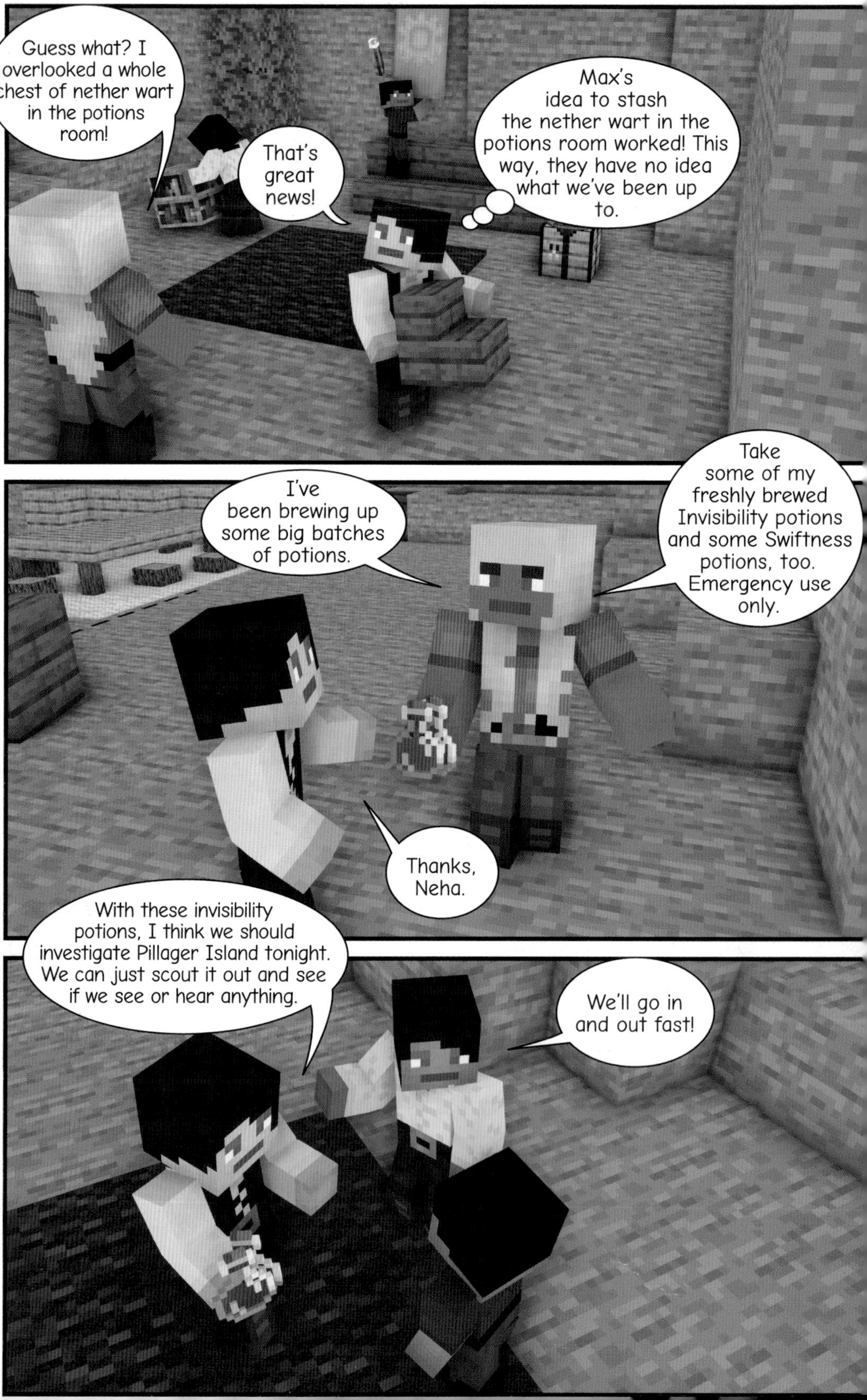
Guess what? I overlooked a whole chest of nether wart in the potions room!
That's great news!
Max's idea to stash the nether wart in the potions room worked! This way, they have no idea what we've been up to.
I've been brewing up some big batches of potions.
Take some of my freshly brewed Invisibility potions and some Swiftness potions, too. Emergency use only.
Thanks, Neha.
With these invisibility potions, I think we should investigate Pillager Island tonight. We can just scout it out and see if we see or hear anything.
We'll go in and out fast!

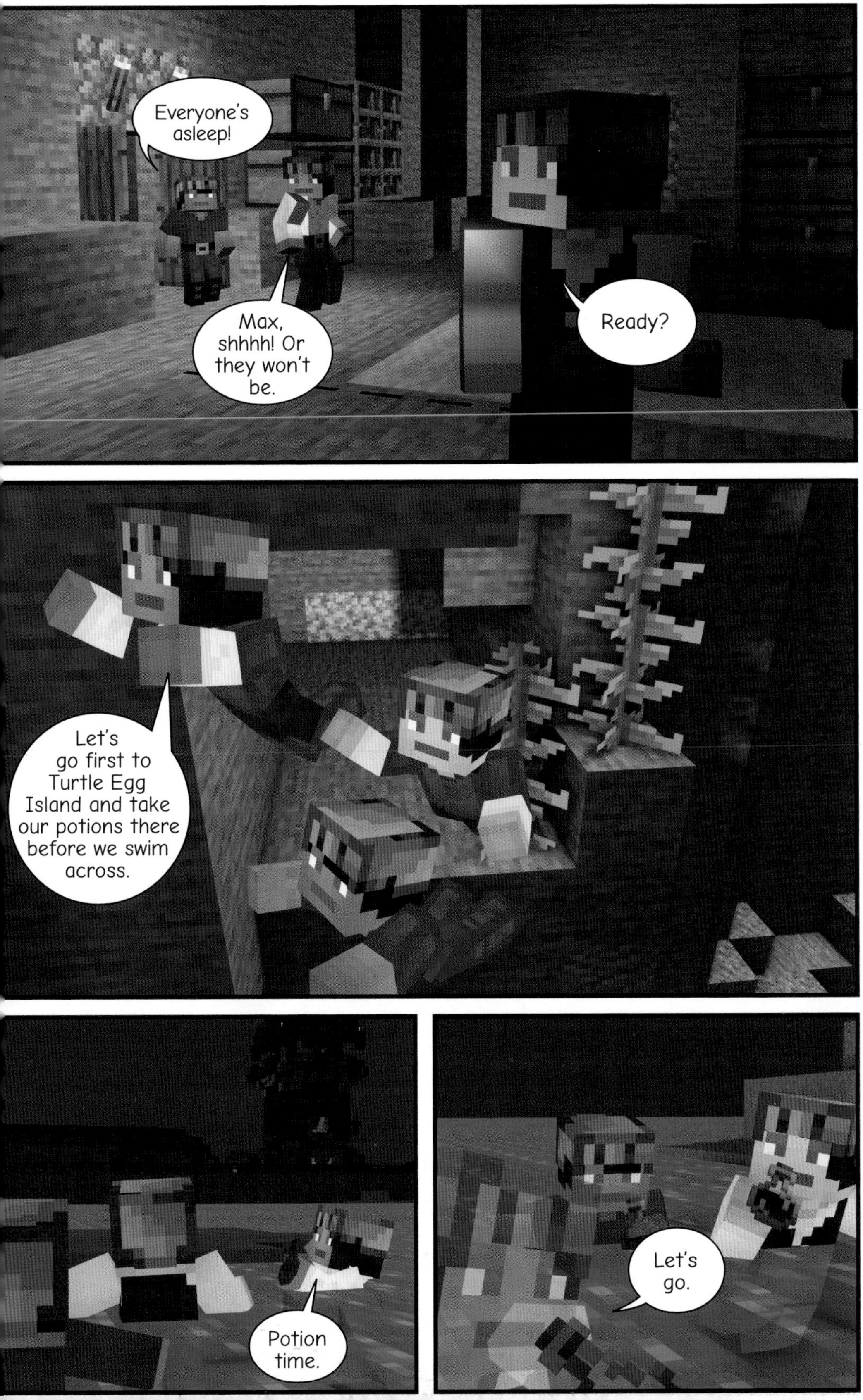

Everyone's asleep!
Max, shhhh! Or they won't be.
Ready?
Let's go first to Turtle Egg Island and take our potions there before we swim across.
Potion time.
Let's go.

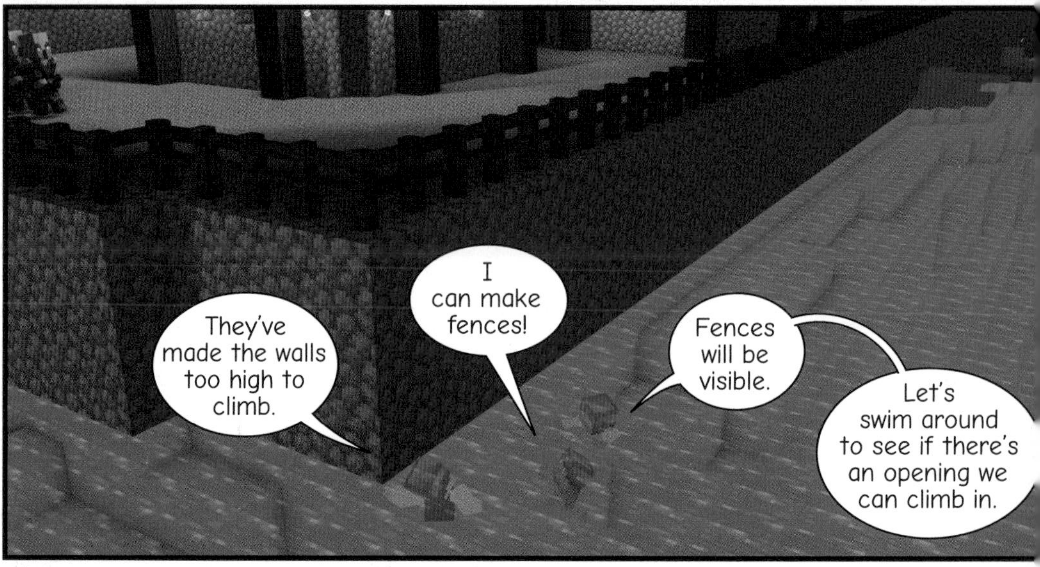
They've made the walls too high to climb.
I can make fences!
Fences will be visible.
Let's swim around to see if there's an opening we can climb in.

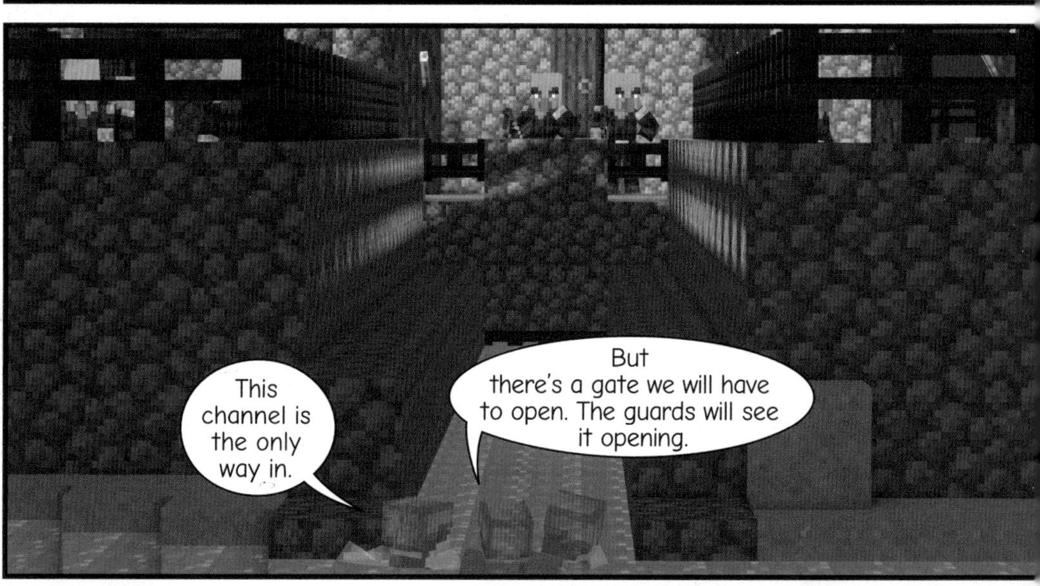
This channel is the only way in.
But there's a gate we will have to open. The guards will see it opening.

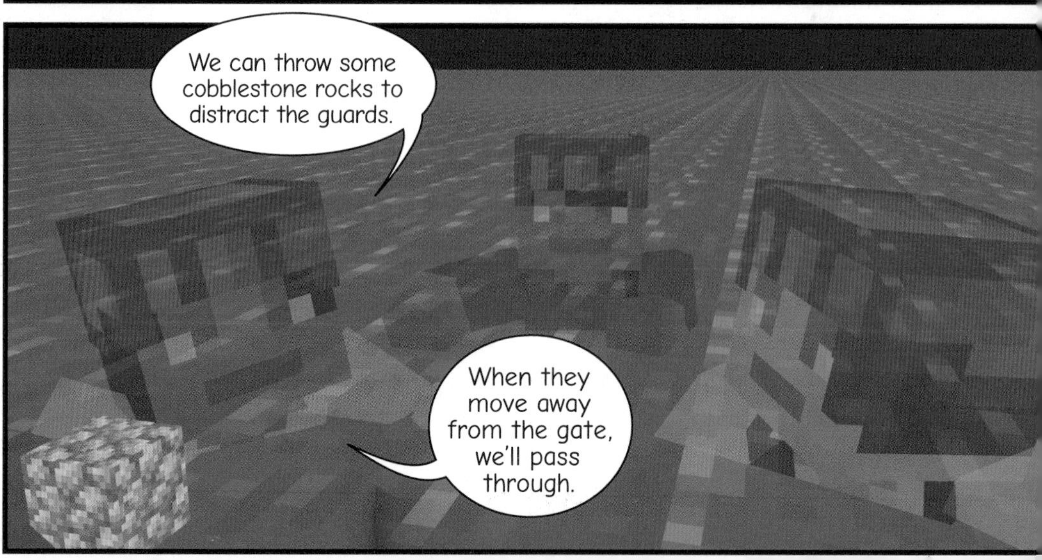
We can throw some cobblestone rocks to distract the guards.
When they move away from the gate, we'll pass through.

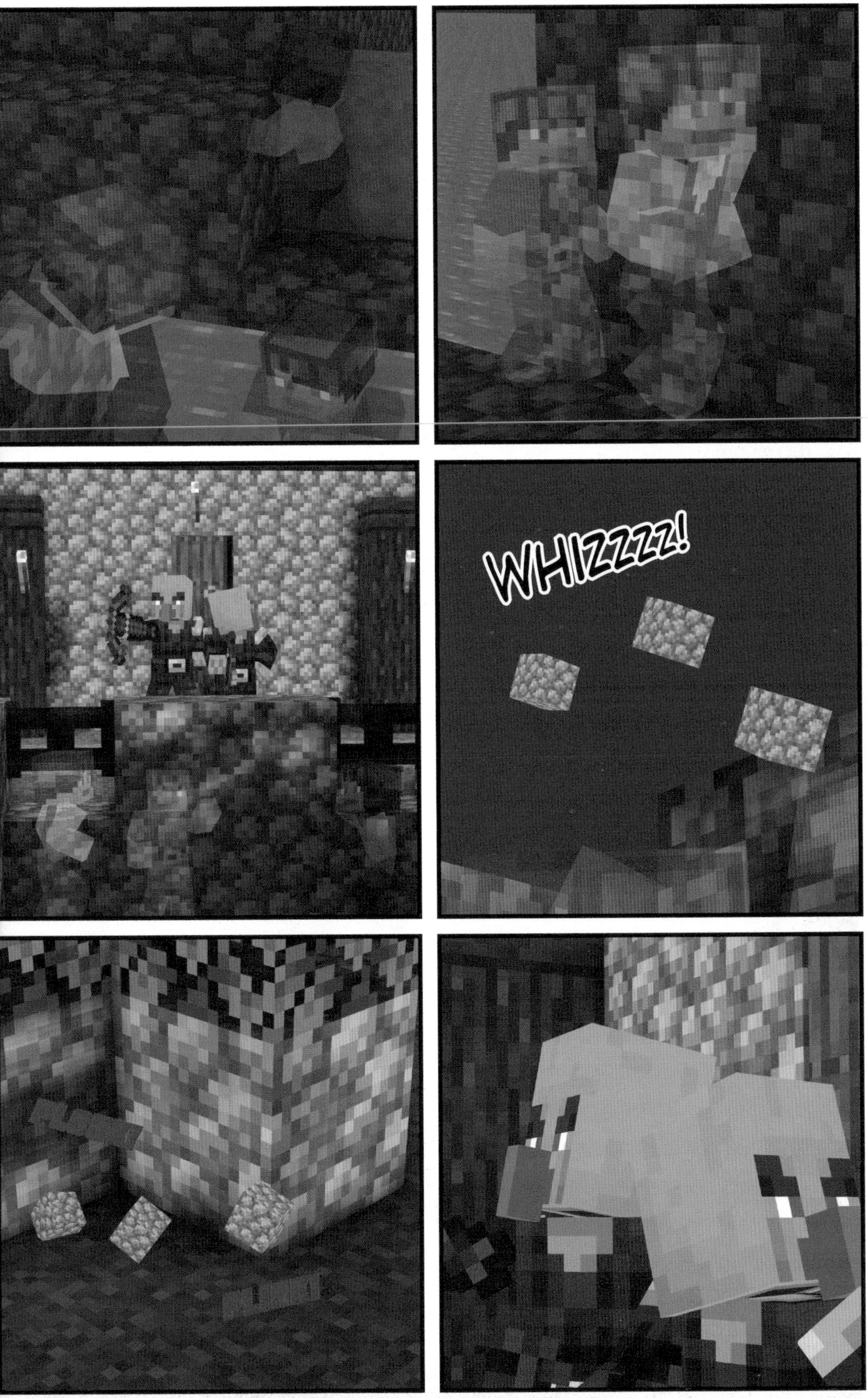
WHIZZZZ!

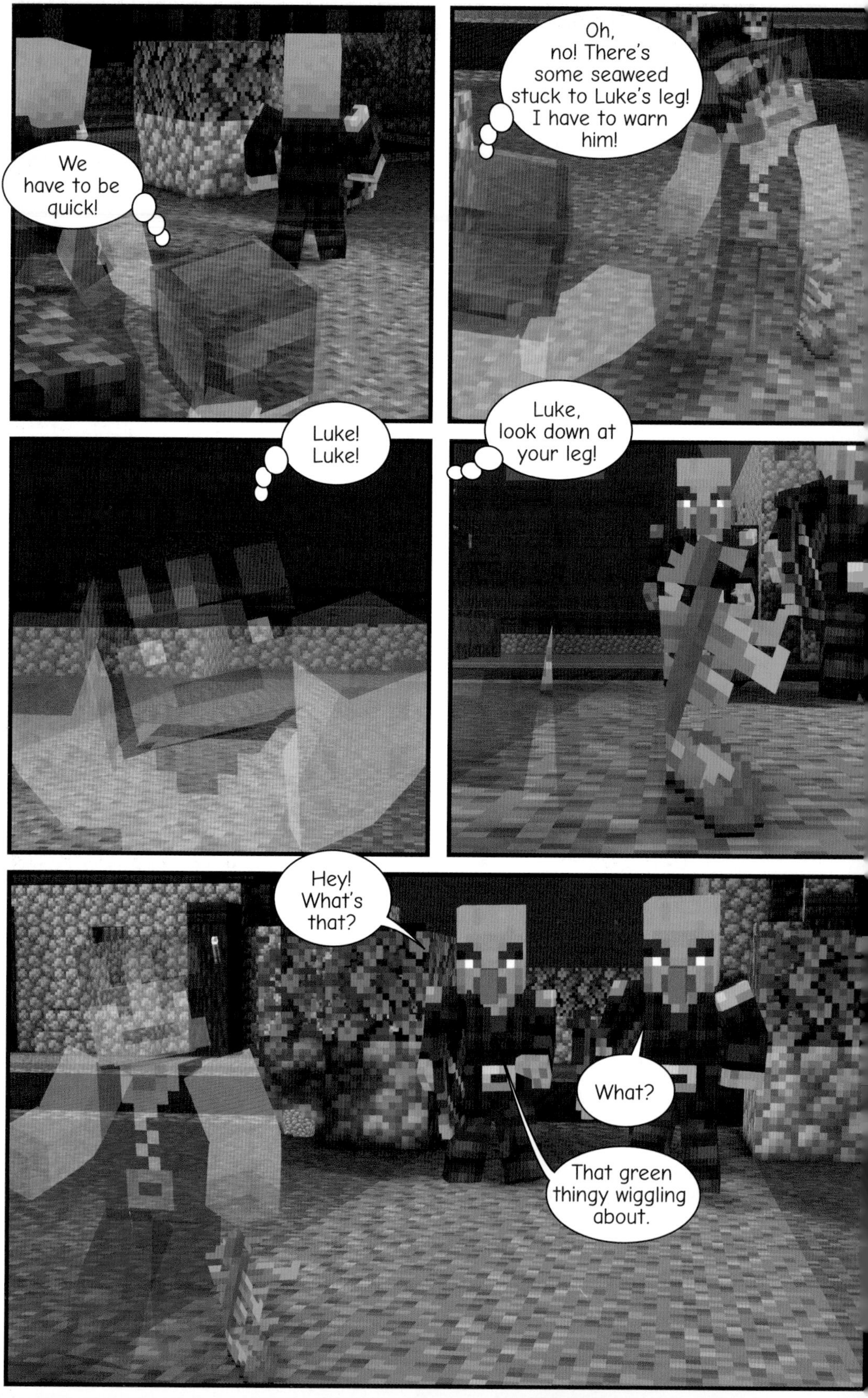
We have to be quick!
Oh, no! There's some seaweed stuck to Luke's leg! I have to warn him!
Luke! Luke!
Luke, look down at your leg!
Hey! What's that?
What?
That green thingy wiggling about.

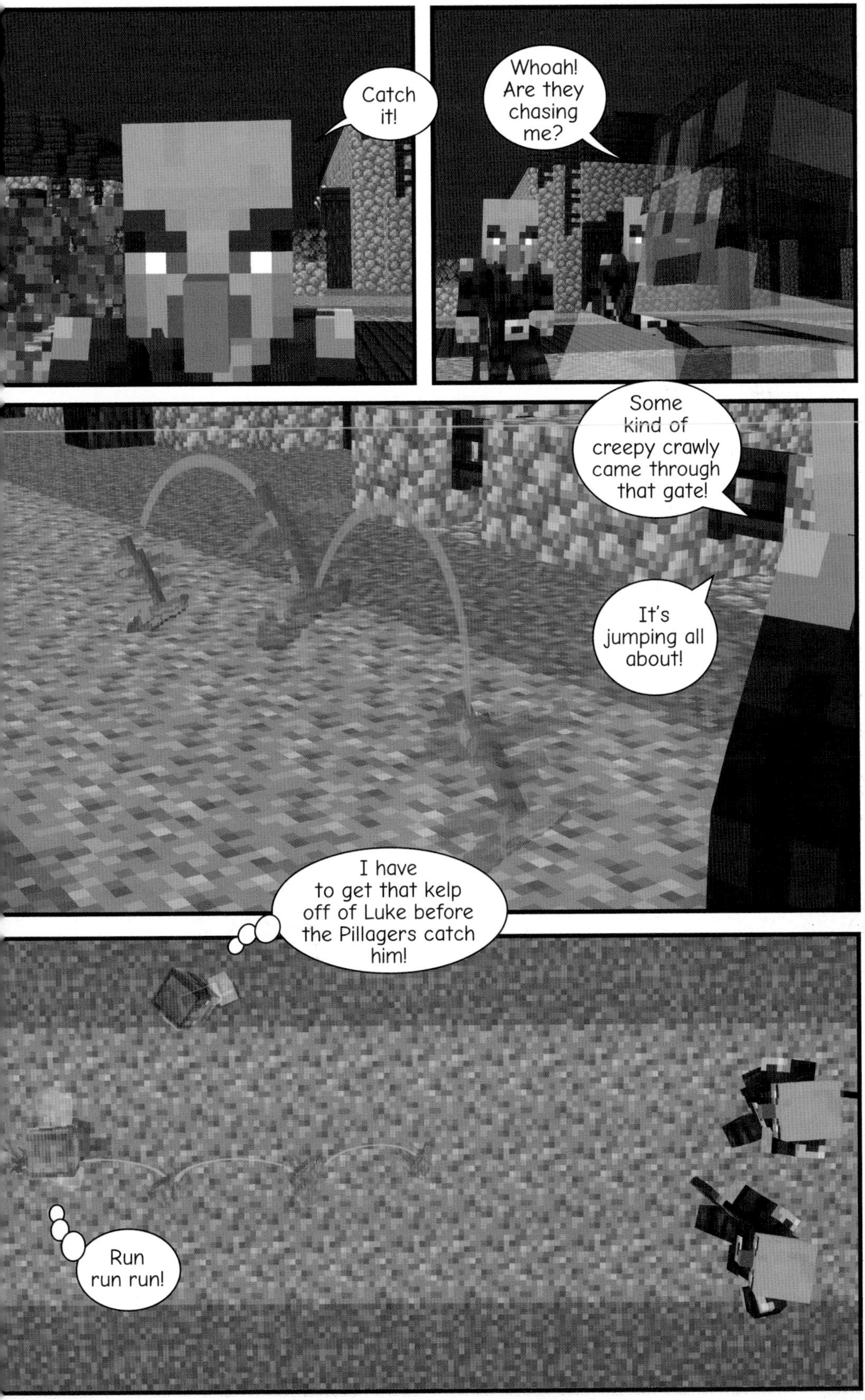
Catch it!
Whoah! Are they chasing me?
Some kind of creepy crawly came through that gate!
It's jumping all about!
I have to get that kelp off of Luke before the Pillagers catch him!
Run run run!

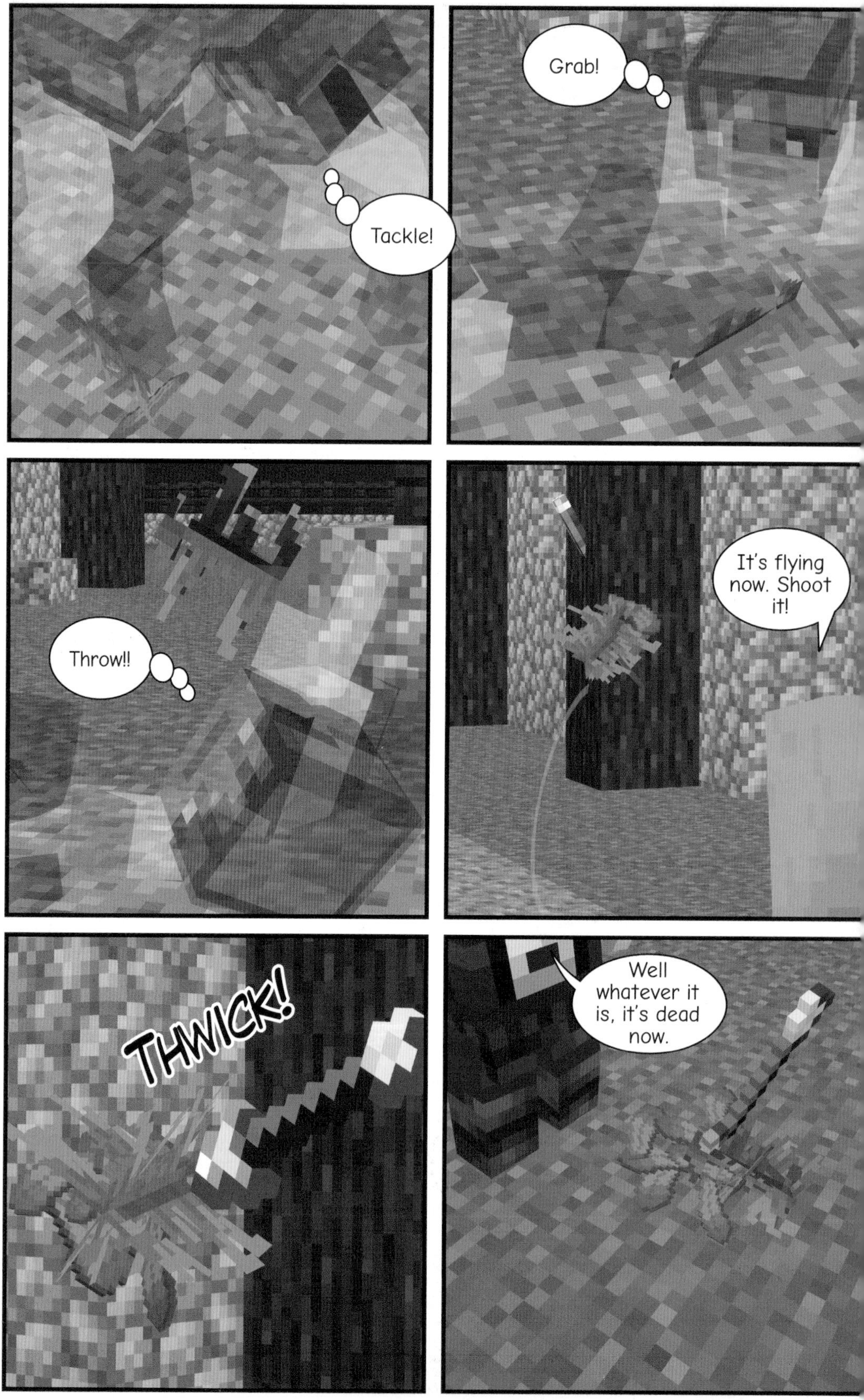
Tackle!
Grab!
Throw!!
It's flying now. Shoot it!
THWICK!
Well whatever it is, it's dead now.

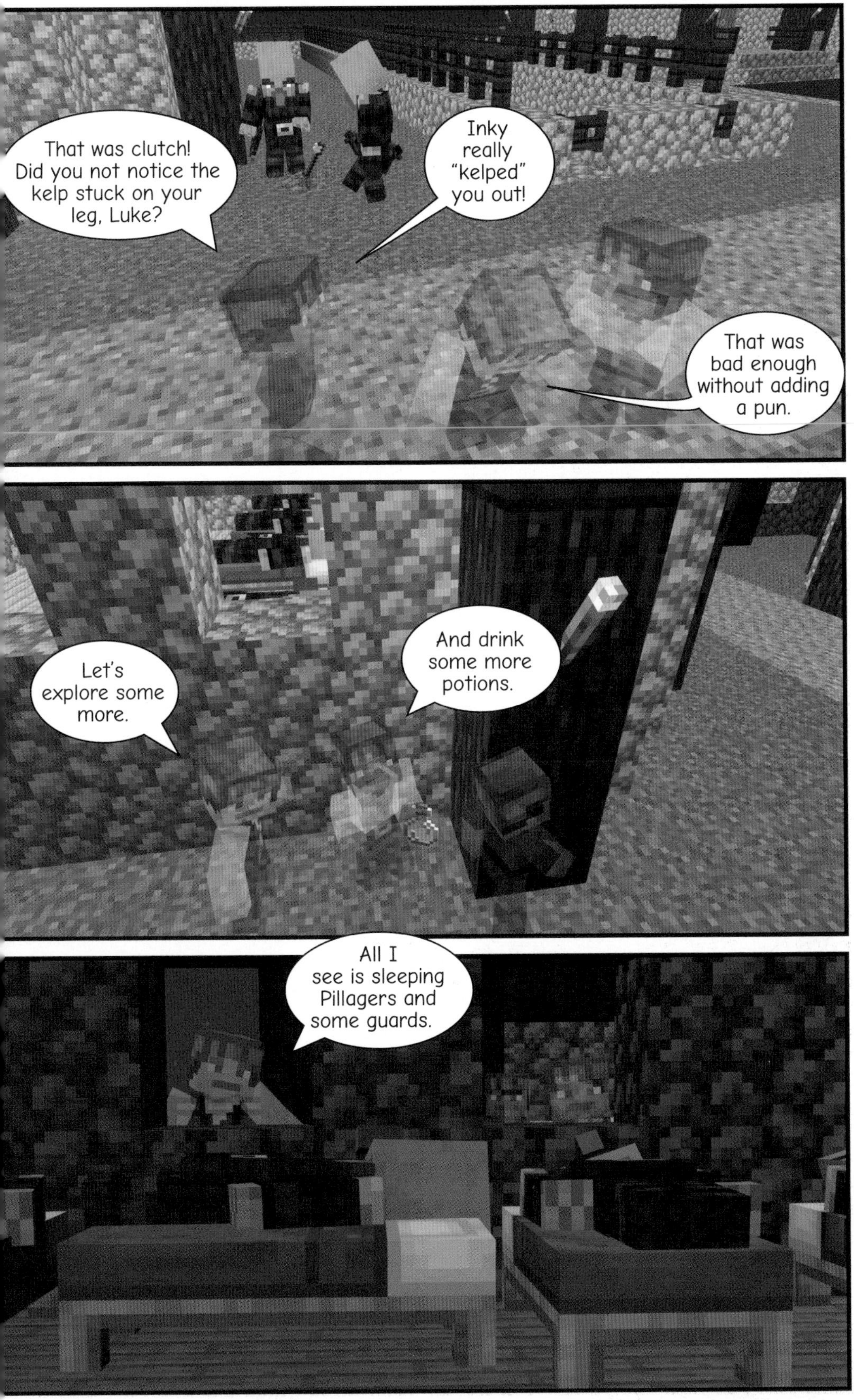
That was clutch! Did you not notice the kelp stuck on your leg, Luke?
Inky really "kelped" you out!
That was bad enough without adding a pun.
Let's explore some more.
And drink some more potions.
All I see is sleeping Pillagers and some guards.

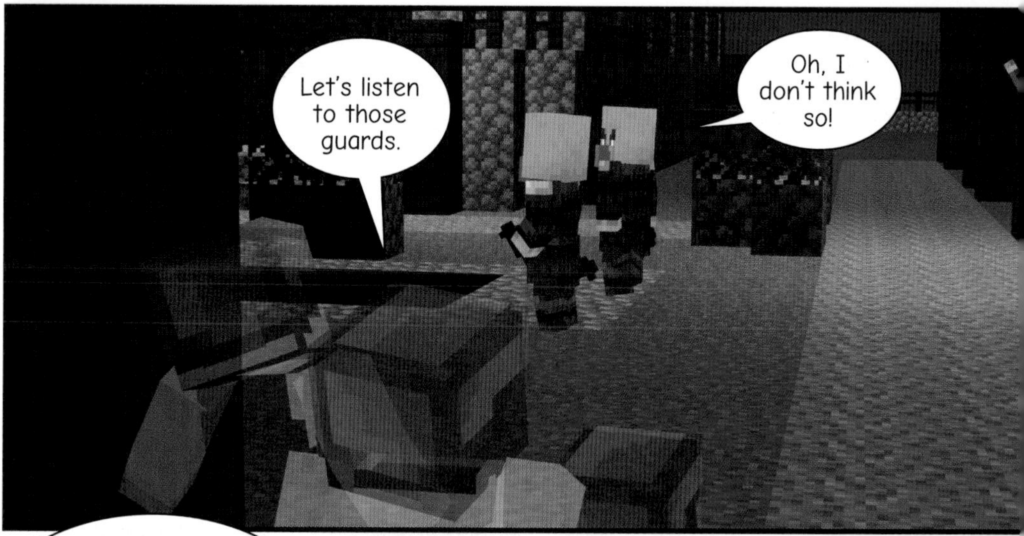
Let's listen to those guards.
Oh, I don't think so!

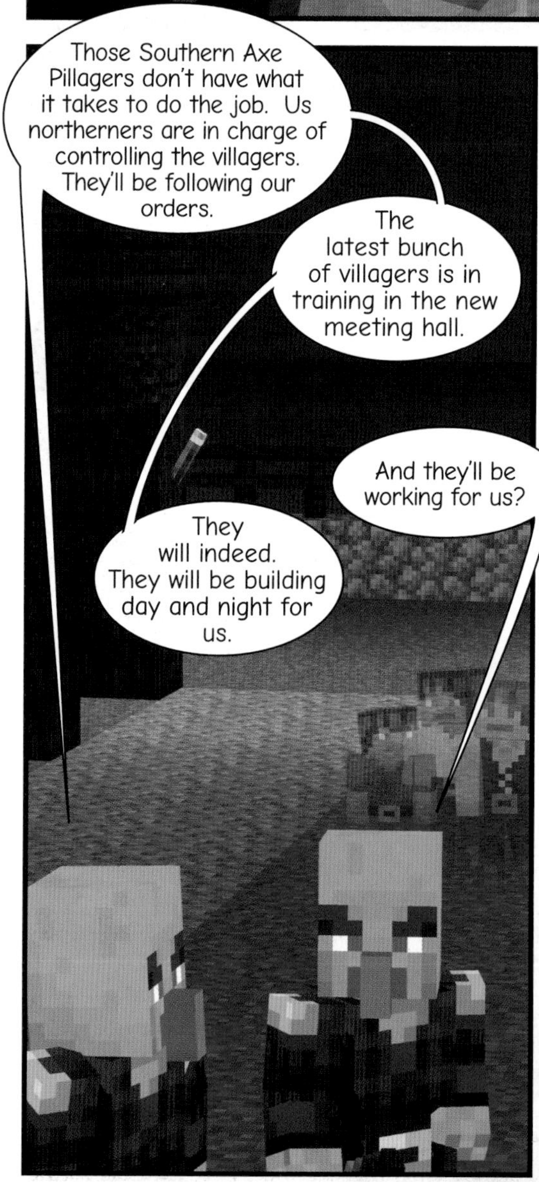
Those Southern Axe Pillagers don't have what it takes to do the job. Us northerners are in charge of controlling the villagers. They'll be following our orders.
The latest bunch of villagers is in training in the new meeting hall.
And they'll be working for us?
They will indeed. They will be building day and night for us.

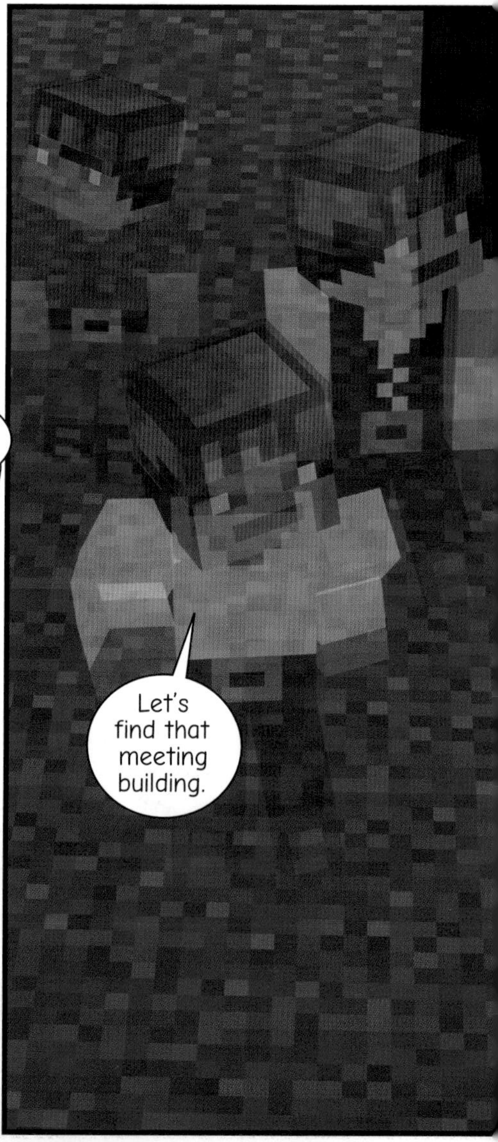
Let's find that meeting building.

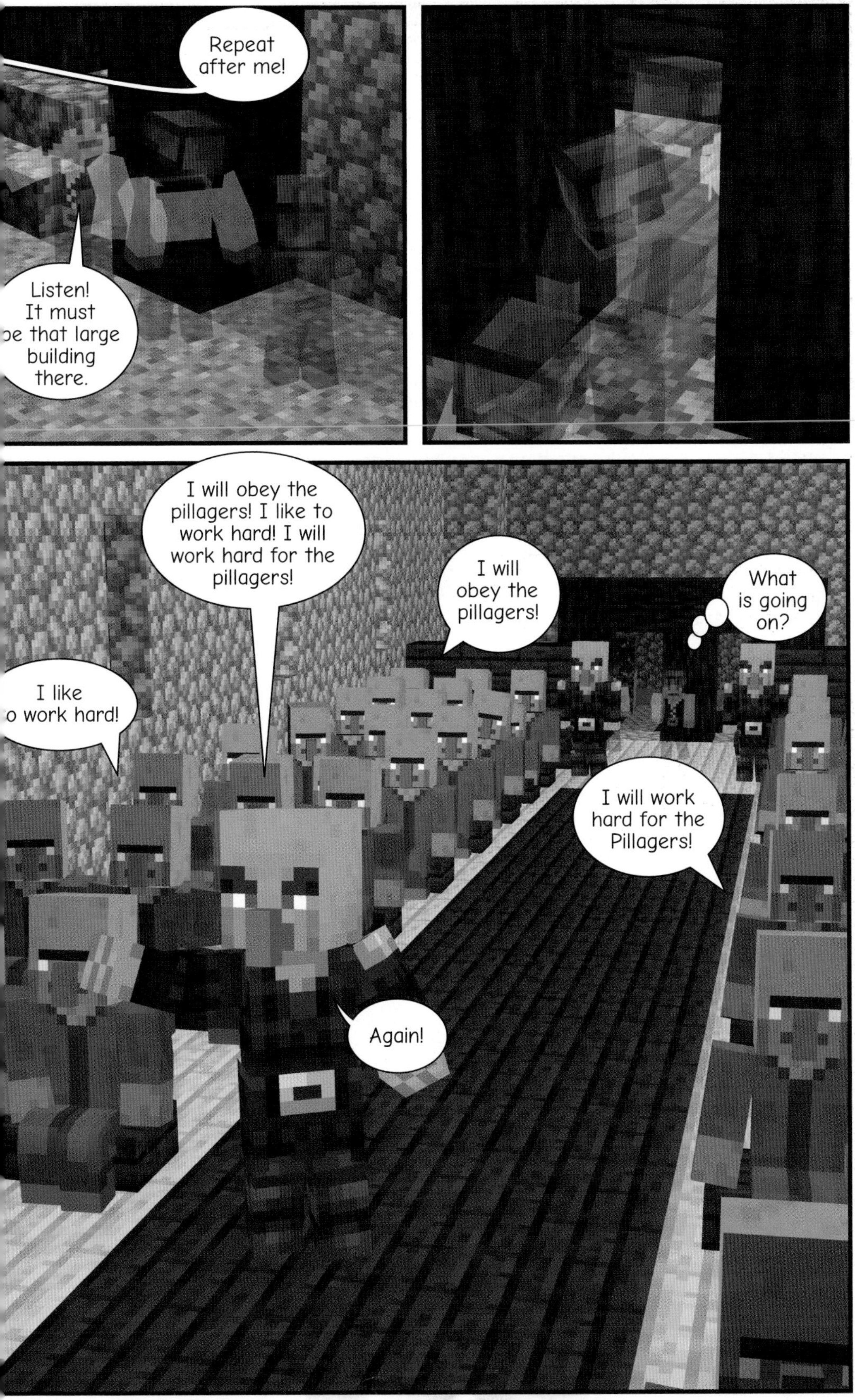

Repeat after me!
Listen! It must be that large building there.
I will obey the pillagers! I like to work hard! I will work hard for the pillagers!
I will obey the pillagers!
What is going on?
I like to work hard!
I will work hard for the Pillagers!
Again!

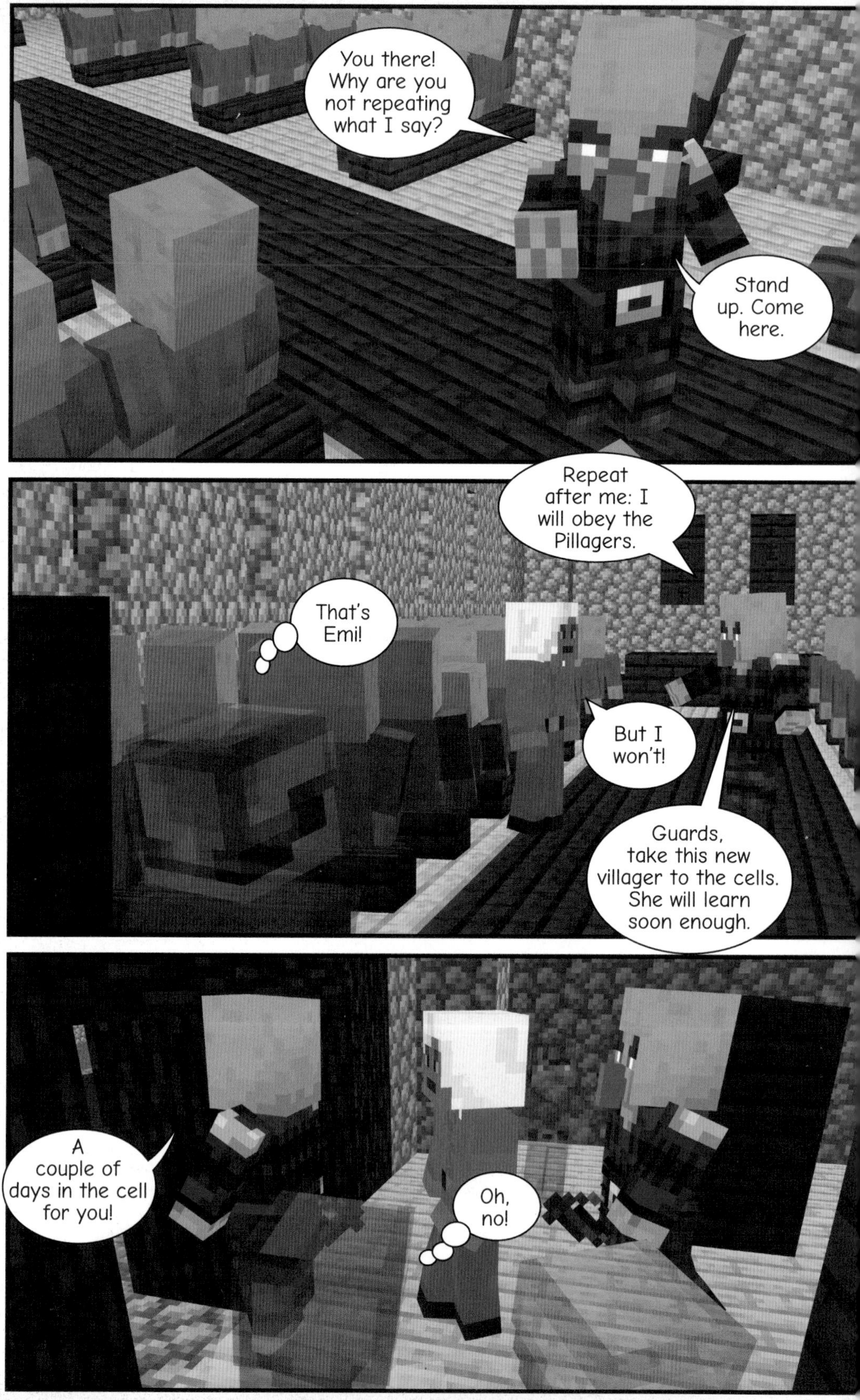
You there! Why are you not repeating what I say?
Stand up. Come here.
Repeat after me: I will obey the Pillagers.
That's Emi!
But I won't!
Guards, take this new villager to the cells. She will learn soon enough.
A couple of days in the cell for you!
Oh, no!

Chapter 7
Operation
Villager Kids

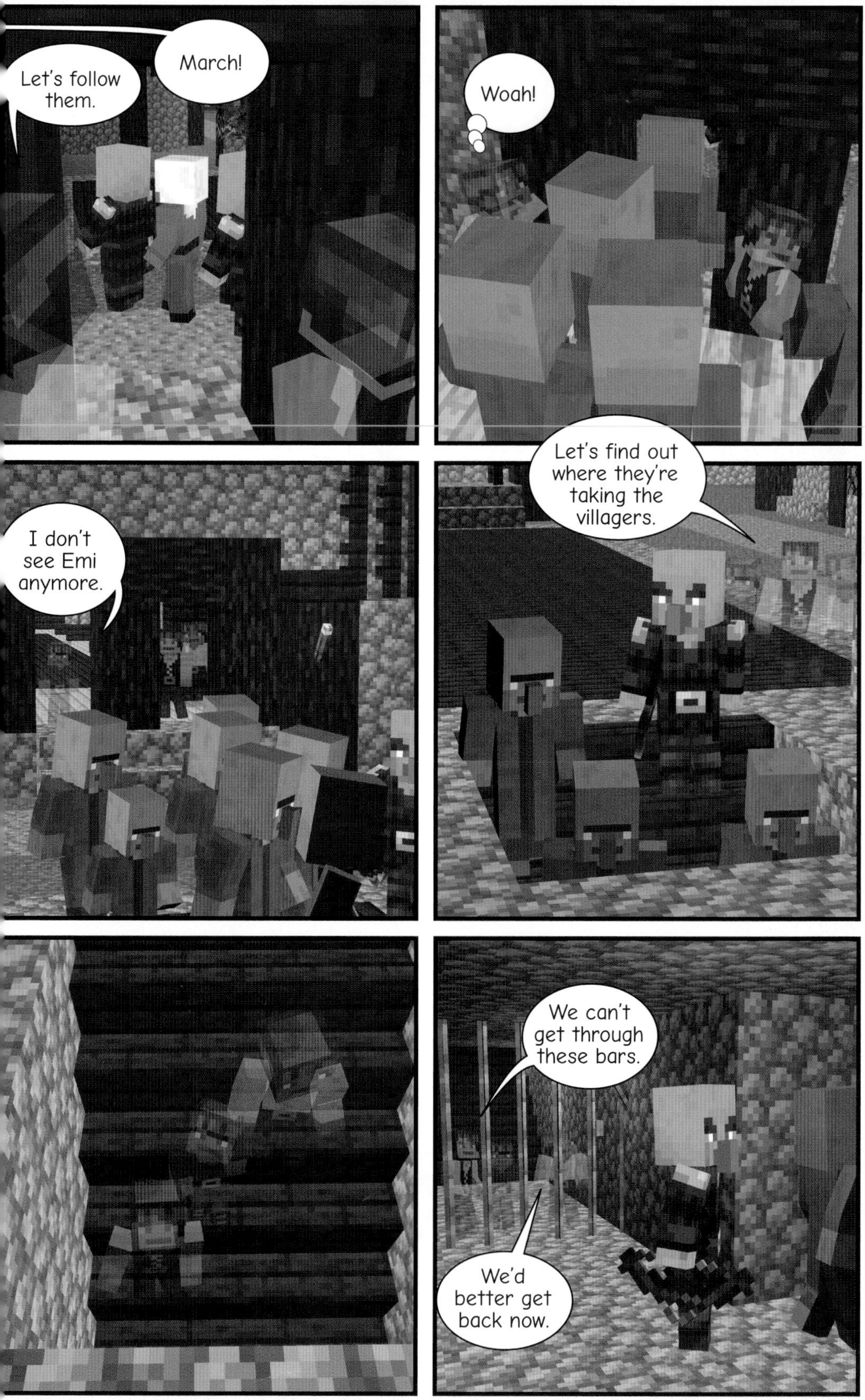
March!
Let's follow them.
Woah!
I don't see Emi anymore.
Let's find out where they're taking the villagers.
We can't get through these bars.
We'd better get back now.

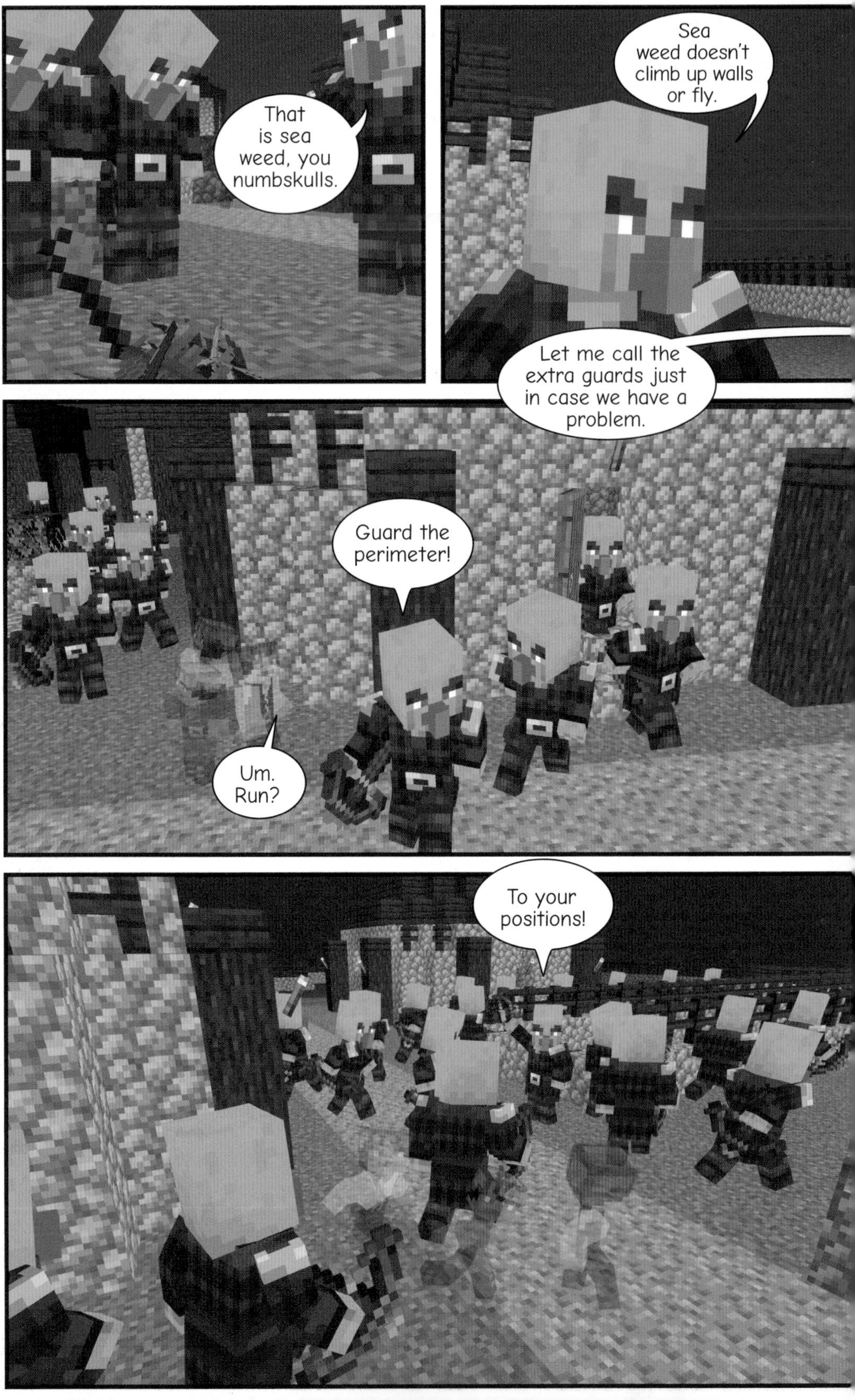
That is sea weed, you numbskulls.
Sea weed doesn't climb up walls or fly.
Let me call the extra guards just in case we have a problem.
Guard the perimeter!
Um. Run?
To your positions!

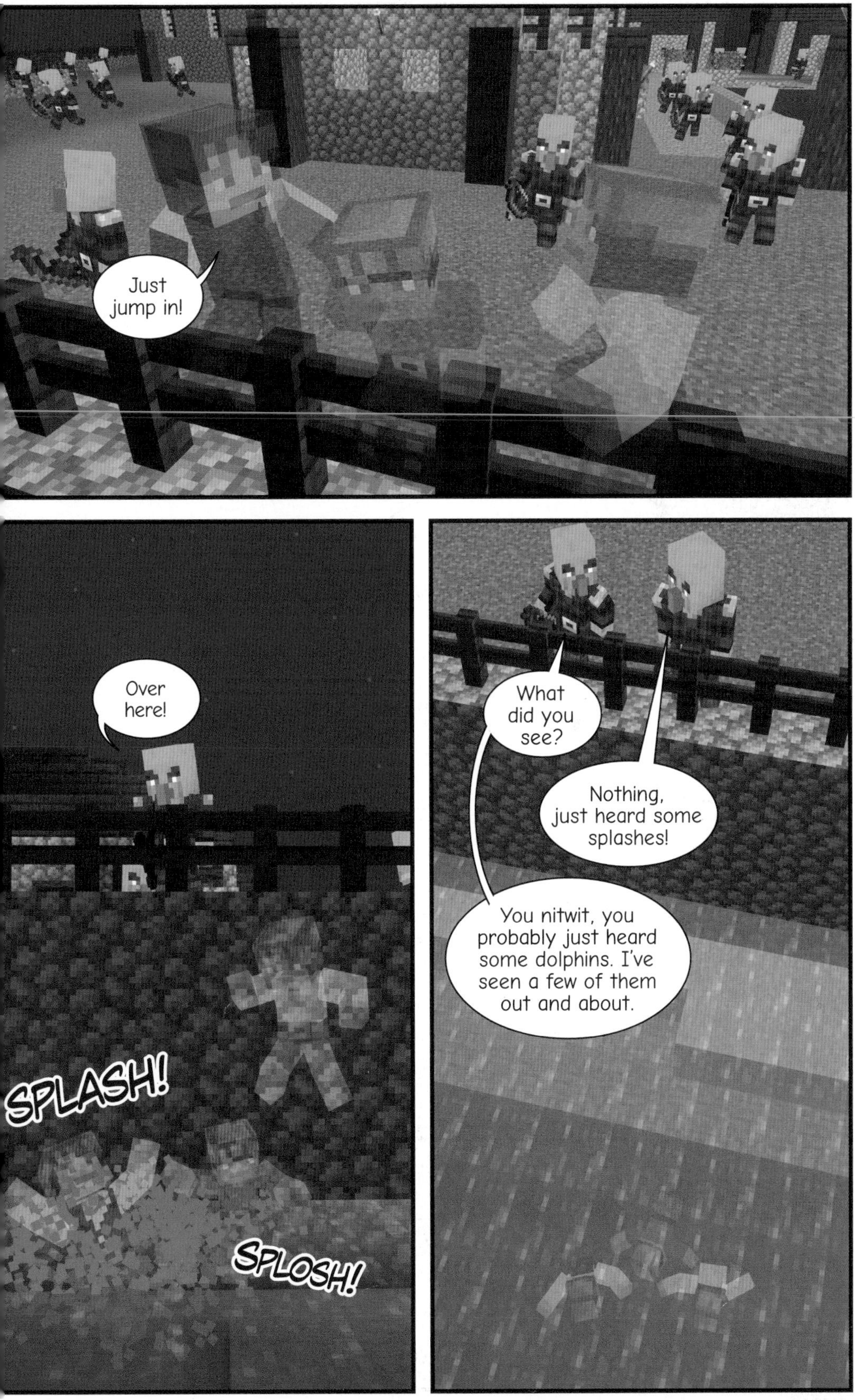
Just jump in!
Over here!
SPLASH!
SPLOSH!
What did you see?
Nothing, just heard some splashes!
You nitwit, you probably just heard some dolphins. I've seen a few of them out and about.

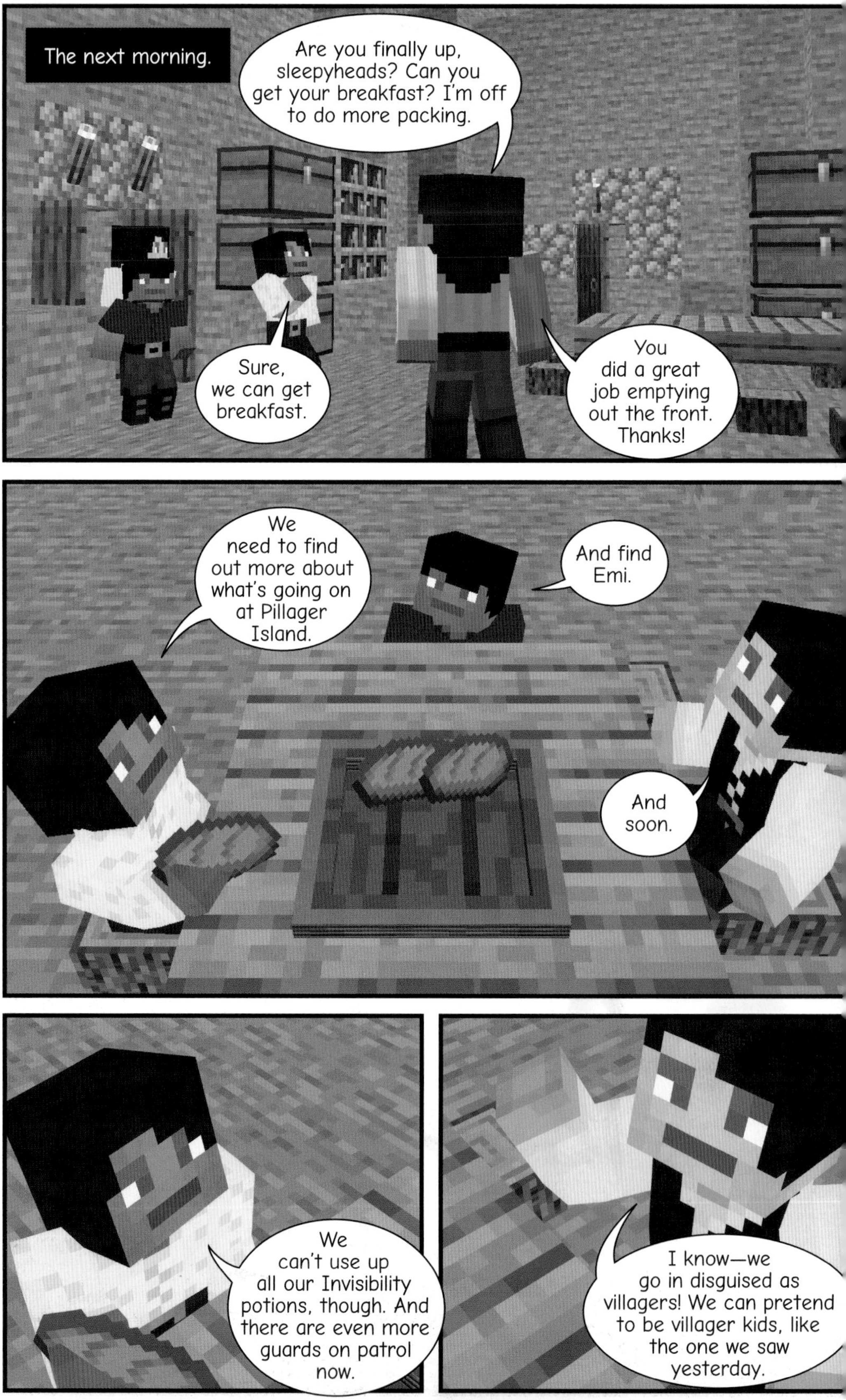
The next morning.
Are you finally up, sleepyheads? Can you get your breakfast? I'm off to do more packing.
Sure, we can get breakfast.
You did a great job emptying out the front. Thanks!
We need to find out more about what's going on at Pillager Island.
And find Emi.
And soon.
We can't use up all our Invisibility potions, though. And there are even more guards on patrol now.
I know—we go in disguised as villagers! We can pretend to be villager kids, like the one we saw yesterday.

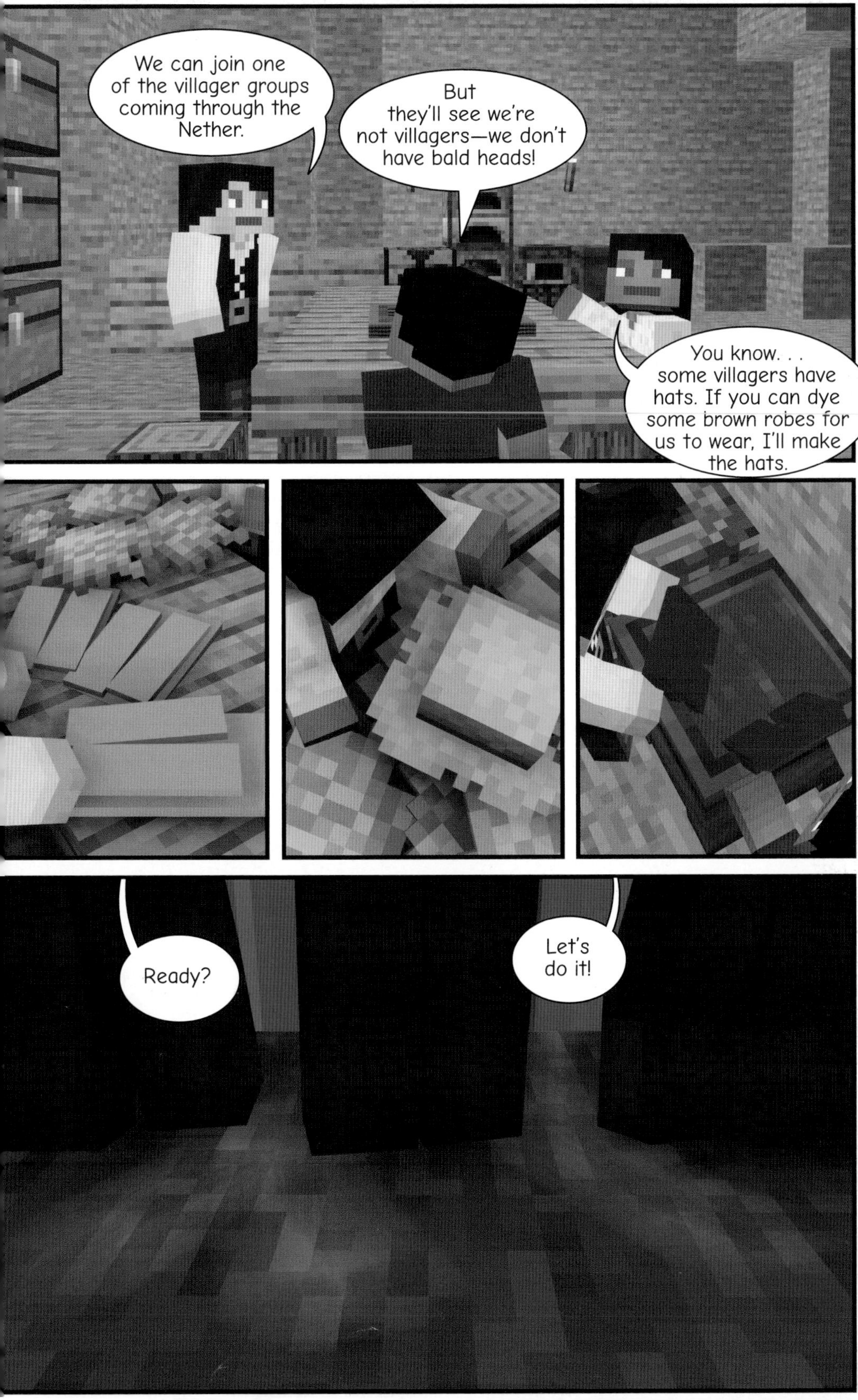
We can join one of the villager groups coming through the Nether.
But they'll see we're not villagers—we don't have bald heads!
You know. . . some villagers have hats. If you can dye some brown robes for us to wear, I'll make the hats.
Ready?
Let's do it!

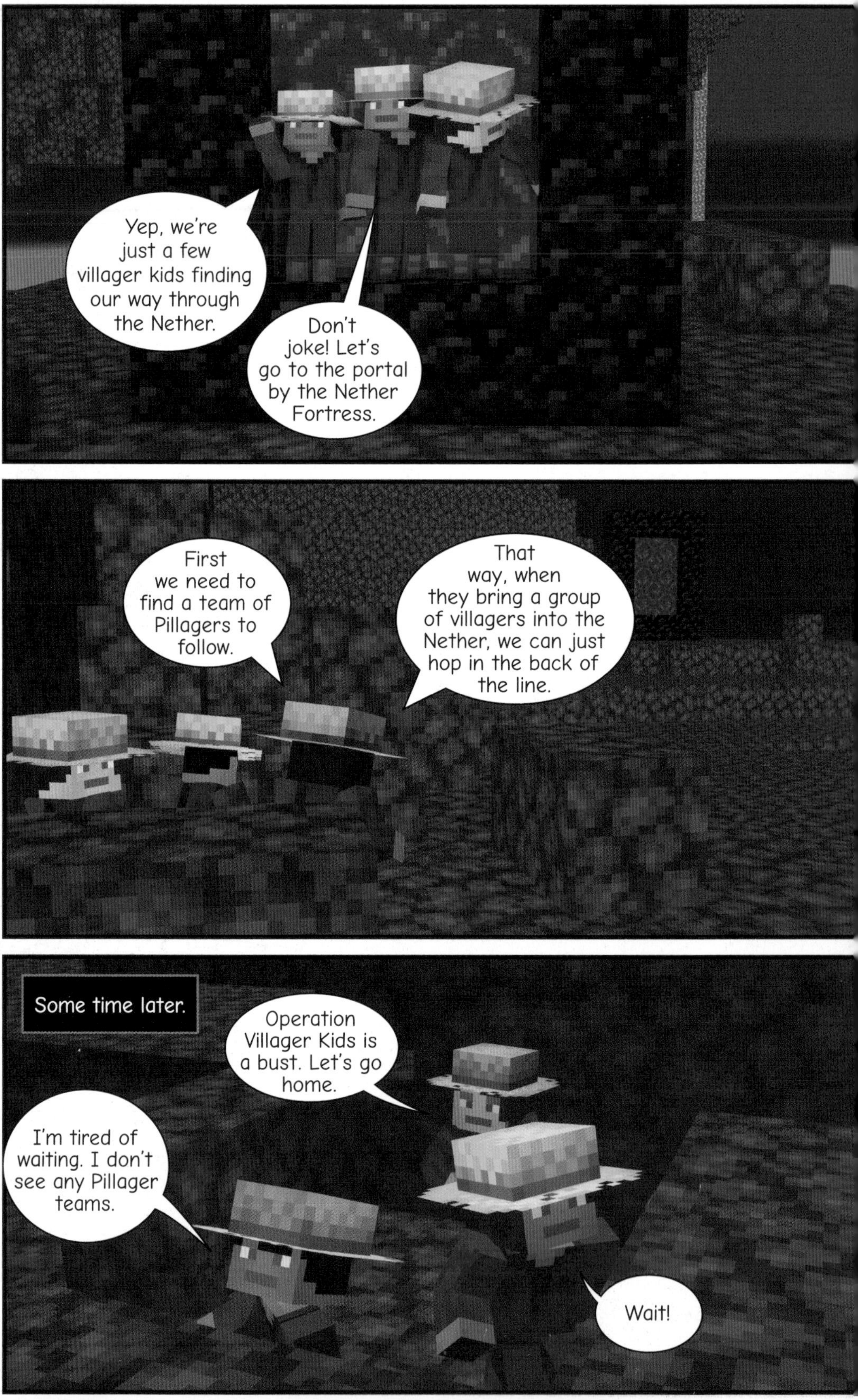
Yep, we're just a few villager kids finding our way through the Nether.
Don't joke! Let's go to the portal by the Nether Fortress.
First we need to find a team of Pillagers to follow.
That way, when they bring a group of villagers into the Nether, we can just hop in the back of the line.
Some time later.
Operation Villager Kids is a bust. Let's go home.
I'm tired of waiting. I don't see any Pillager teams.
Wait!

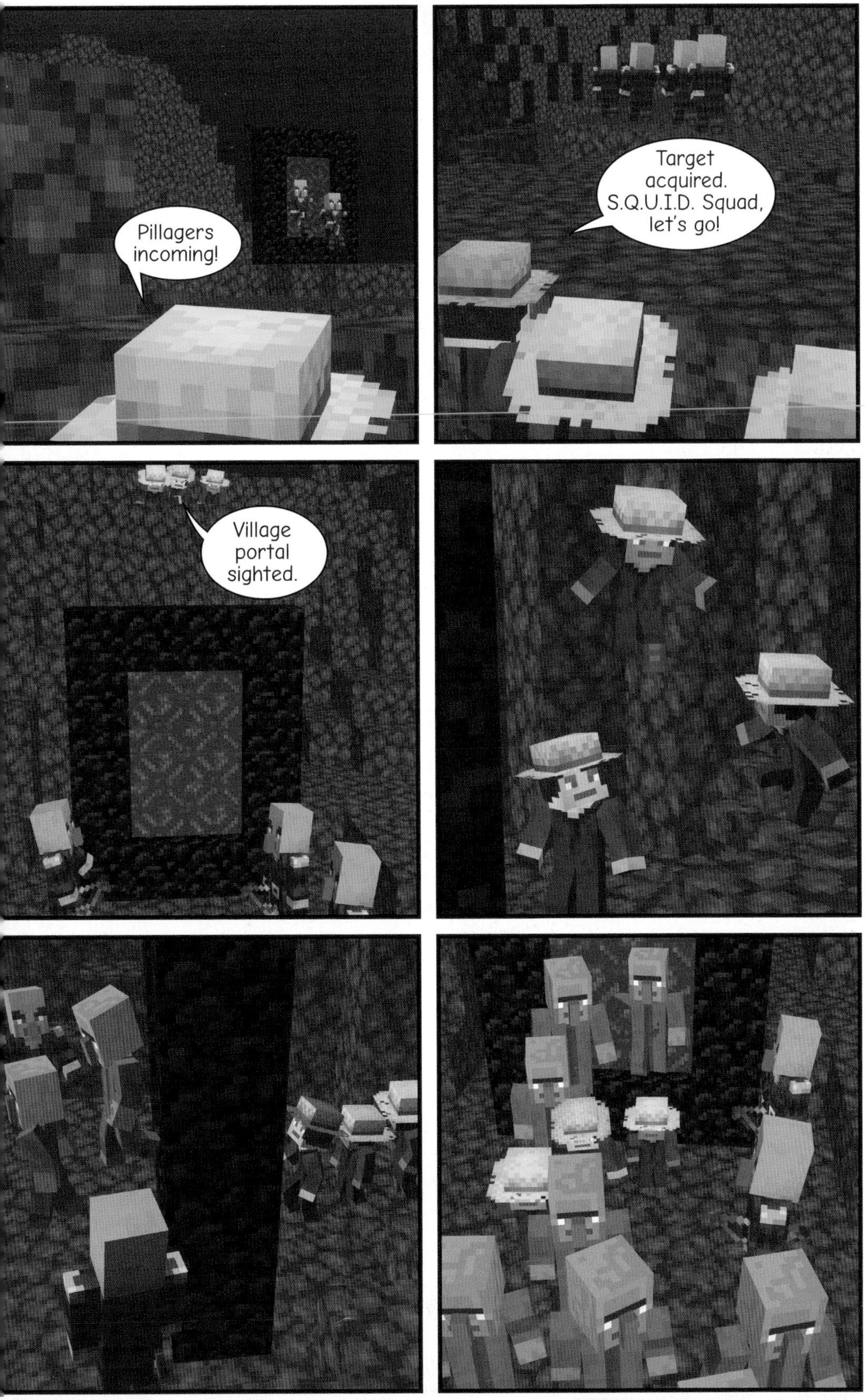
Pillagers incoming!
Target acquired. S.Q.U.I.D. Squad, let's go!
Village portal sighted.

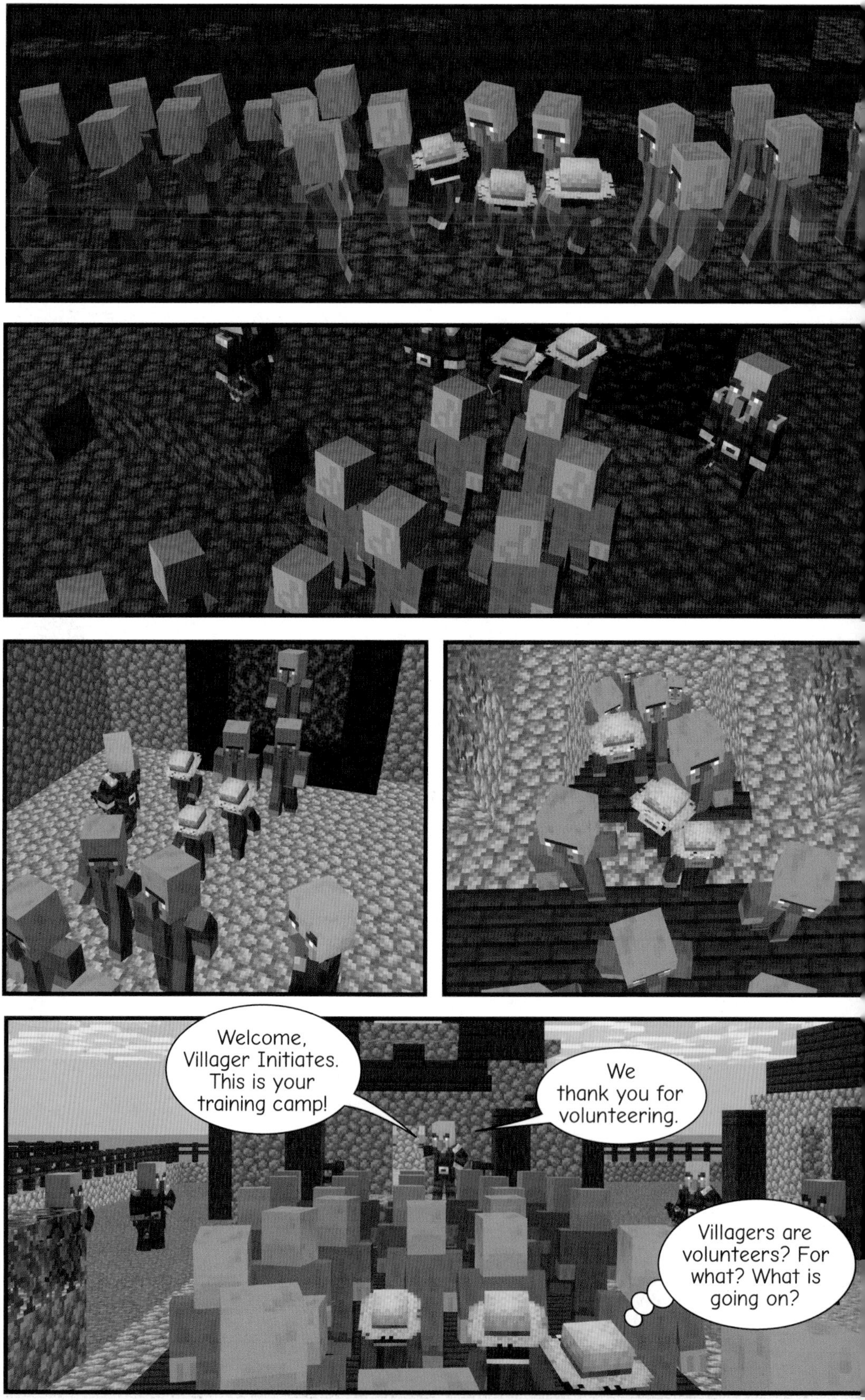
Welcome, Villager Initiates. This is your training camp!
We thank you for volunteering.
Villagers are volunteers? For what? What is going on?

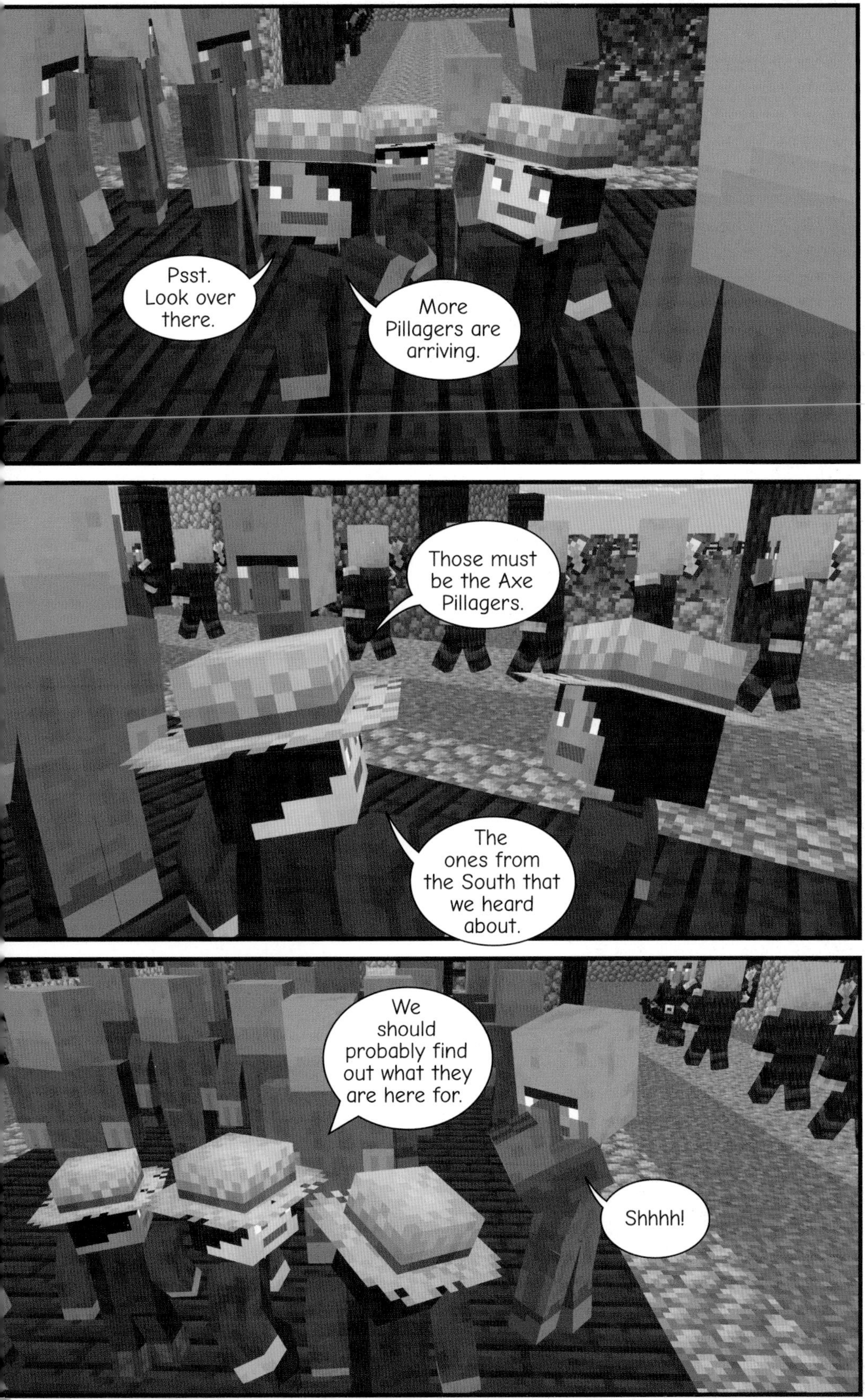
Psst. Look over there.
More Pillagers are arriving.
Those must be the Axe Pillagers.
The ones from the South that we heard about.
We should probably find out what they are here for.
Shhhh!

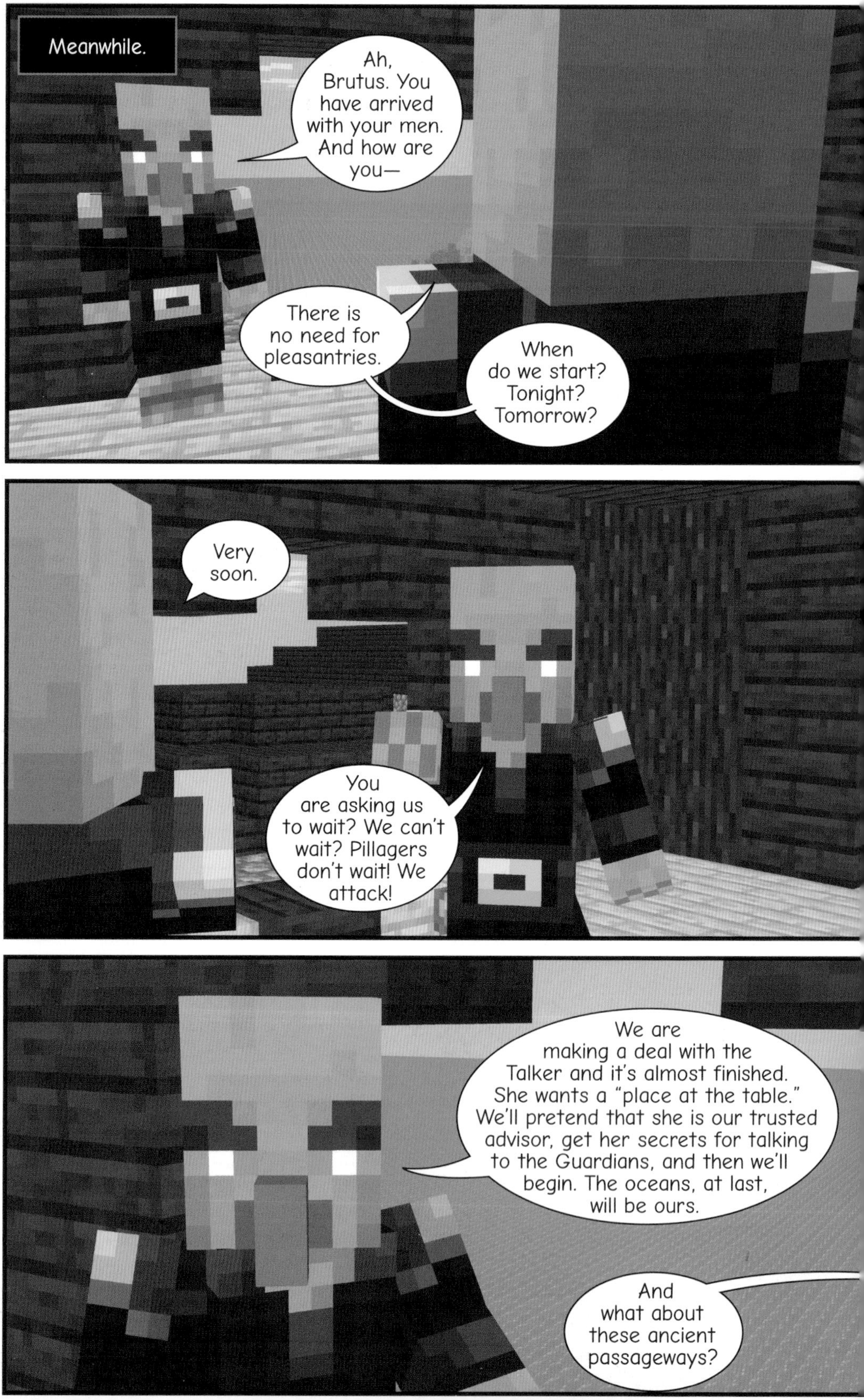
Meanwhile.
Ah, Brutus. You have arrived with your men. And how are you—
There is no need for pleasantries.
When do we start? Tonight? Tomorrow?
Very soon.
You are asking us to wait? We can't wait? Pillagers don't wait! We attack!
We are making a deal with the Talker and it's almost finished. She wants a "place at the table." We'll pretend that she is our trusted advisor, get her secrets for talking to the Guardians, and then we'll begin. The oceans, at last, will be ours.
And what about these ancient passageways?

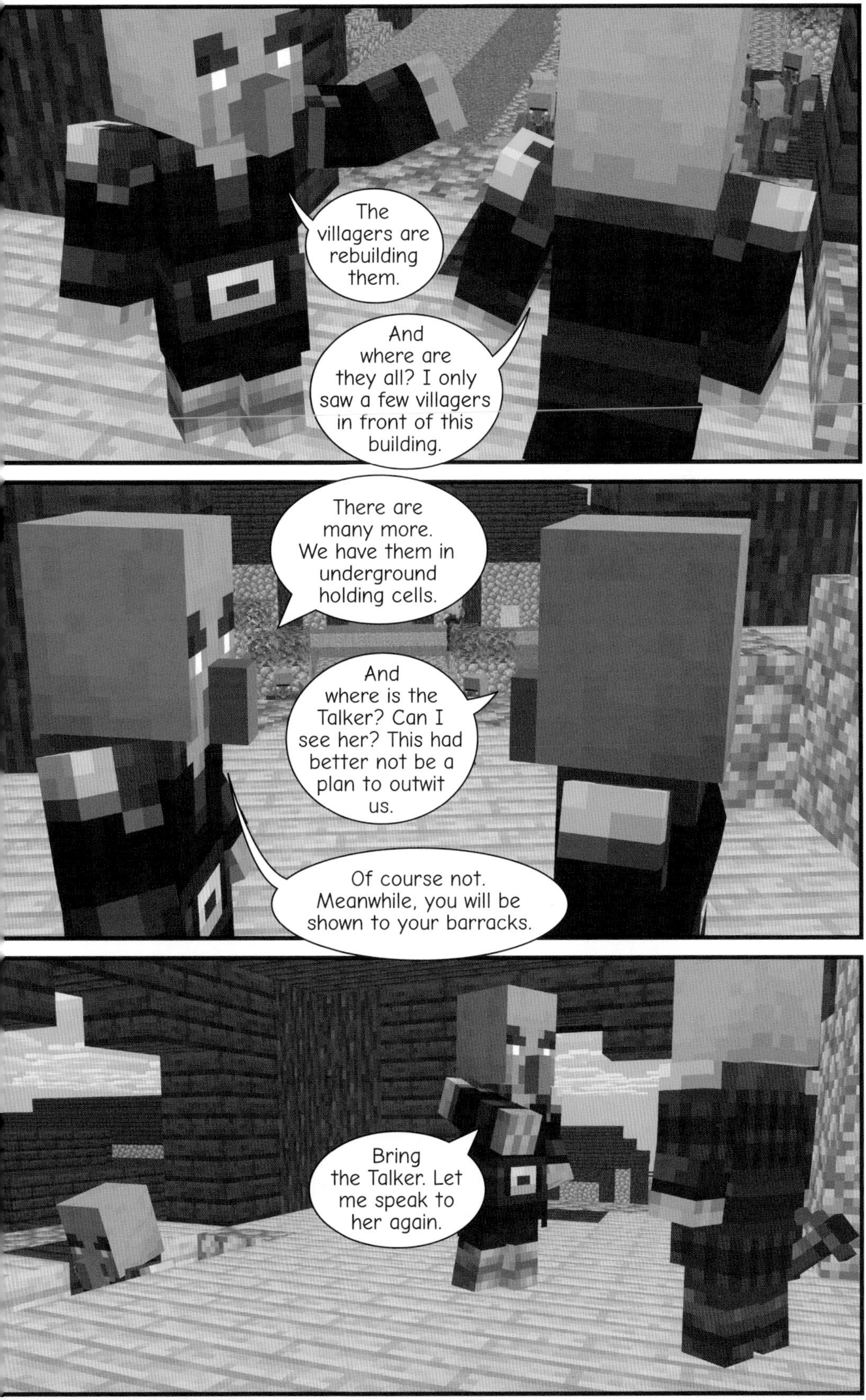
The villagers are rebuilding them.
And where are they all? I only saw a few villagers in front of this building.
There are many more. We have them in underground holding cells.
And where is the Talker? Can I see her? This had better not be a plan to outwit us.
Of course not. Meanwhile, you will be shown to your barracks.
Bring the Talker. Let me speak to her again.

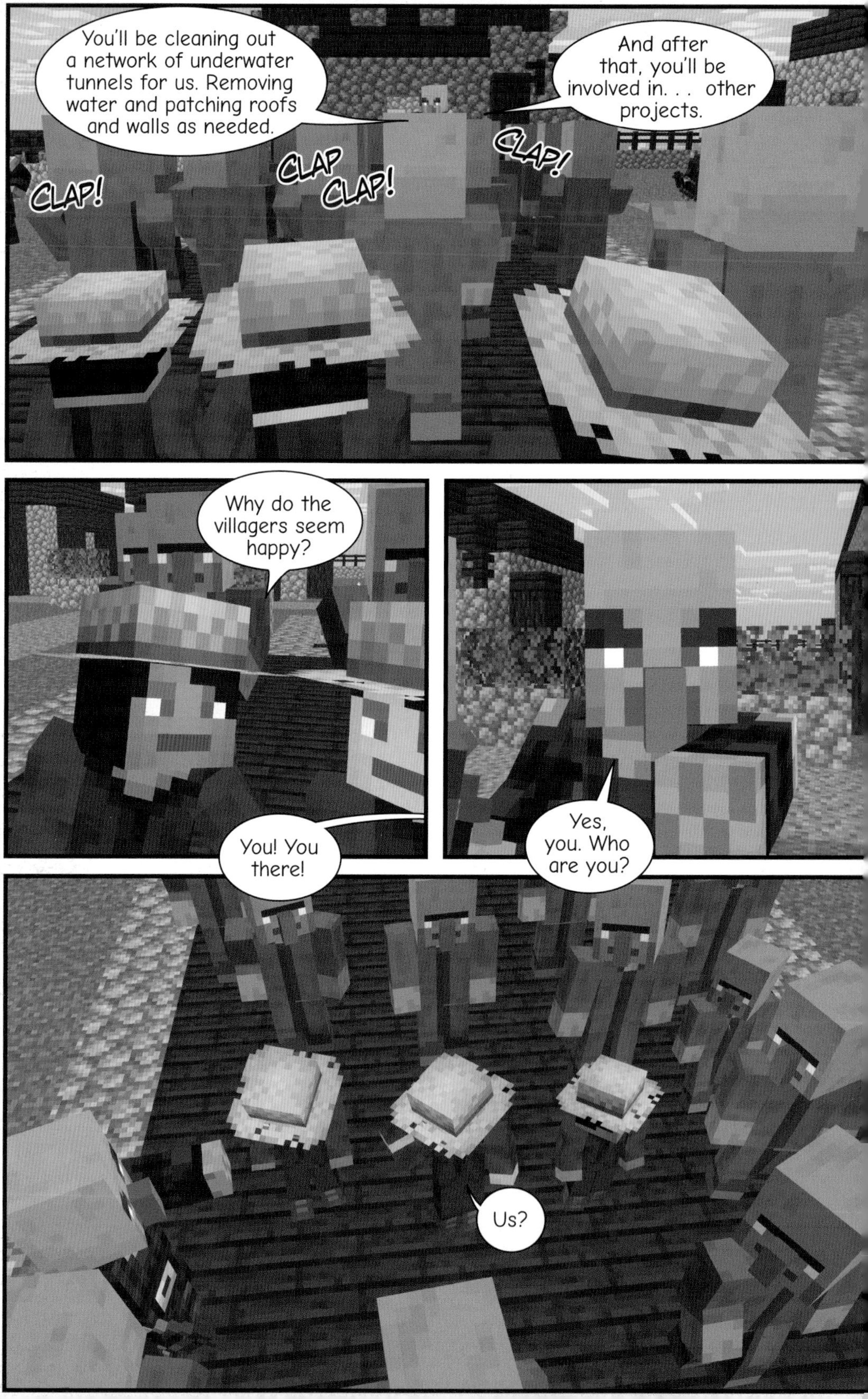
You'll be cleaning out a network of underwater tunnels for us. Removing water and patching roofs and walls as needed.
And after that, you'll be involved in. . . other projects.
CLAP!
CLAP CLAP!
CLAP!
Why do the villagers seem happy?
You! You there!
Yes, you. Who are you?
Us?

Chapter 8
Flooded Tunnels

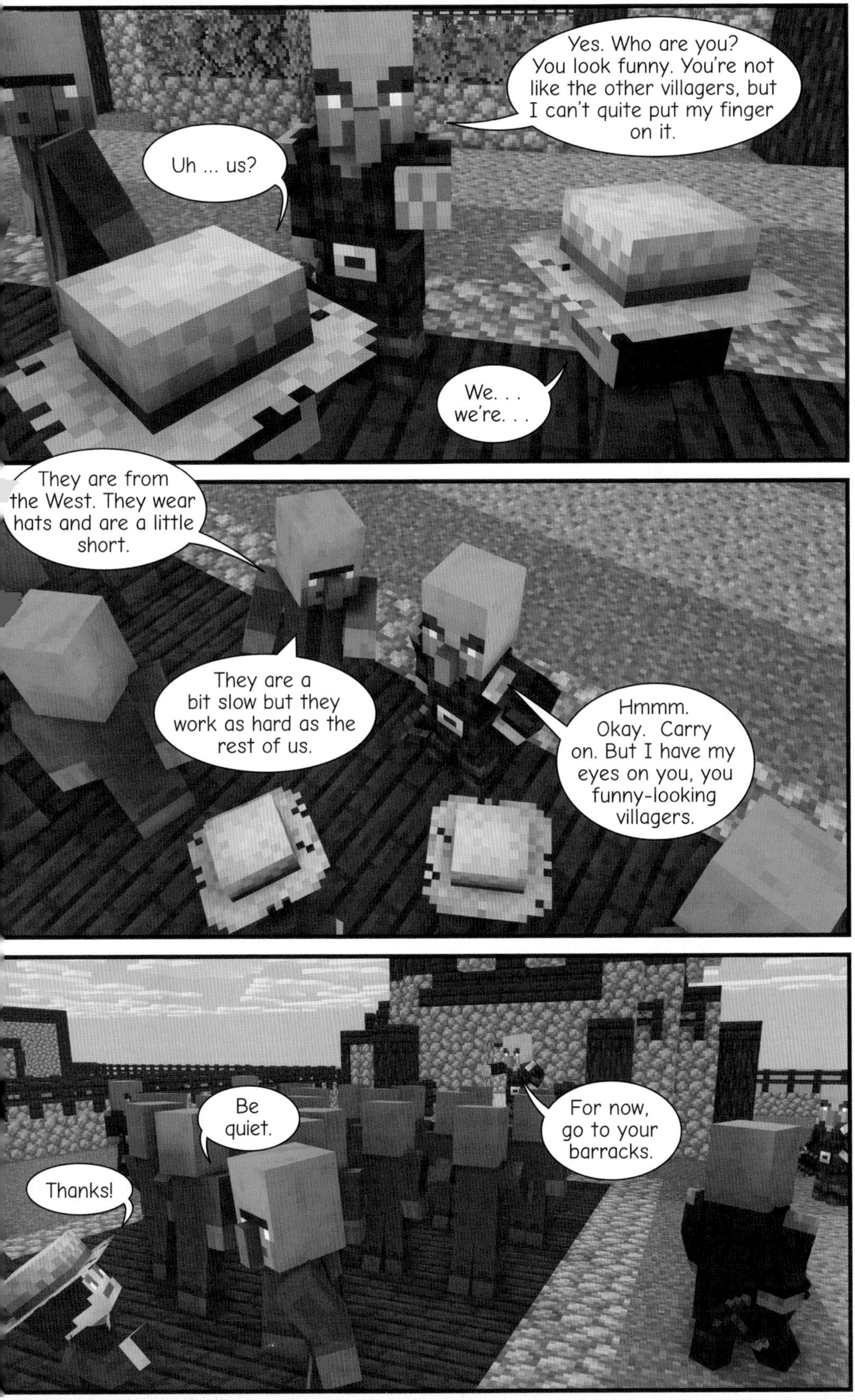
Yes. Who are you? You look funny. You're not like the other villagers, but I can't quite put my finger on it.
Uh ... us?
We. . . we're. . .
They are from the West. They wear hats and are a little short.
They are a bit slow but they work as hard as the rest of us.
Hmmm. Okay. Carry on. But I have my eyes on you, you funny-looking villagers.
Be quiet.
For now, go to your barracks.
Thanks!

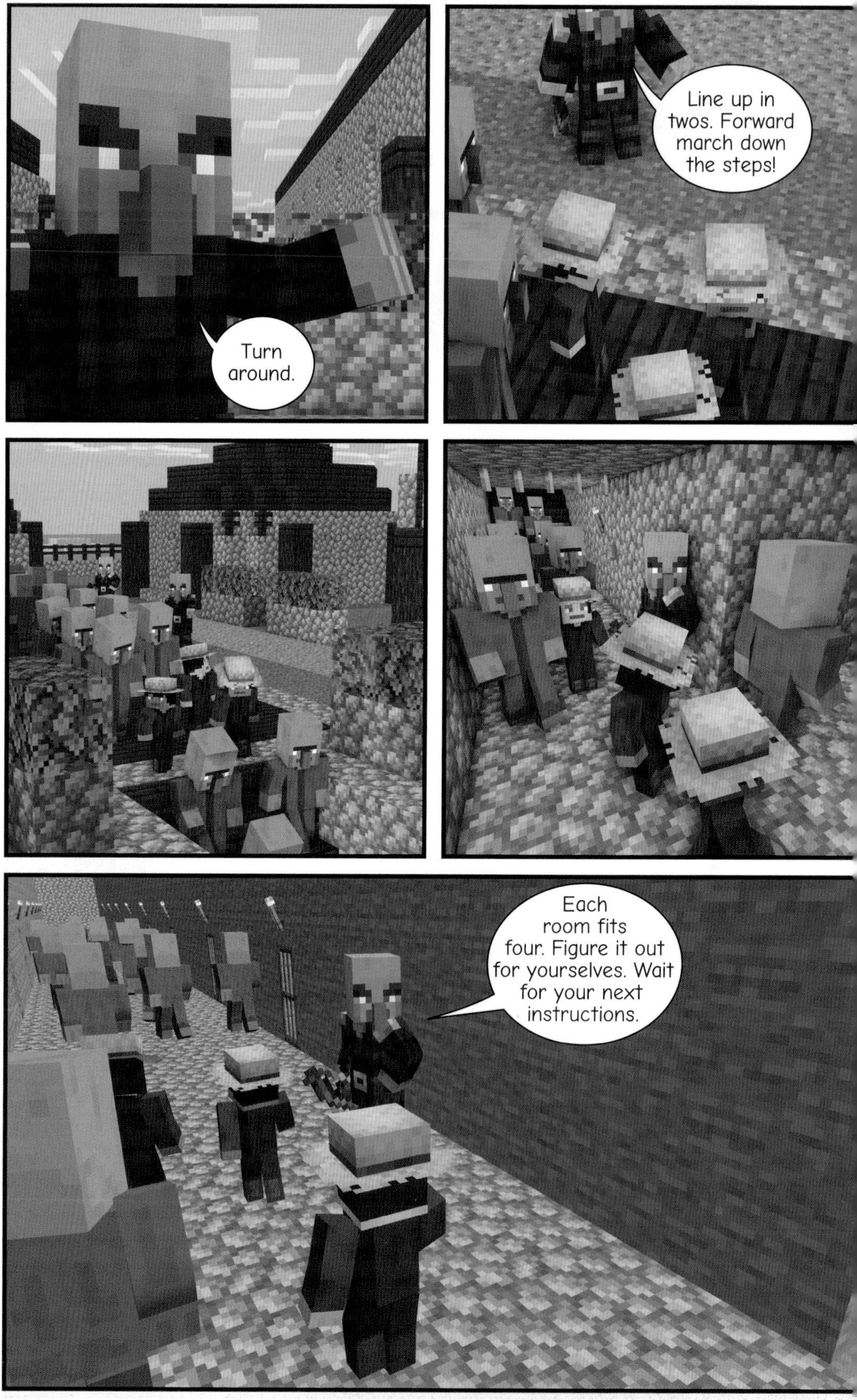
Turn around.
Line up in twos. Forward march down the steps!
Each room fits four. Figure it out for yourselves. Wait for your next instructions.

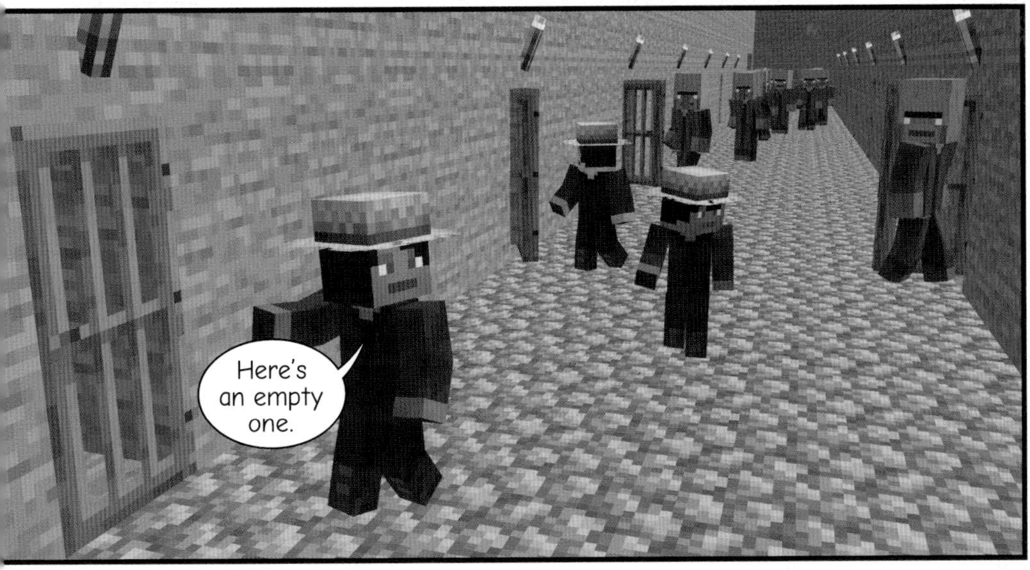
Here's
an empty
one.

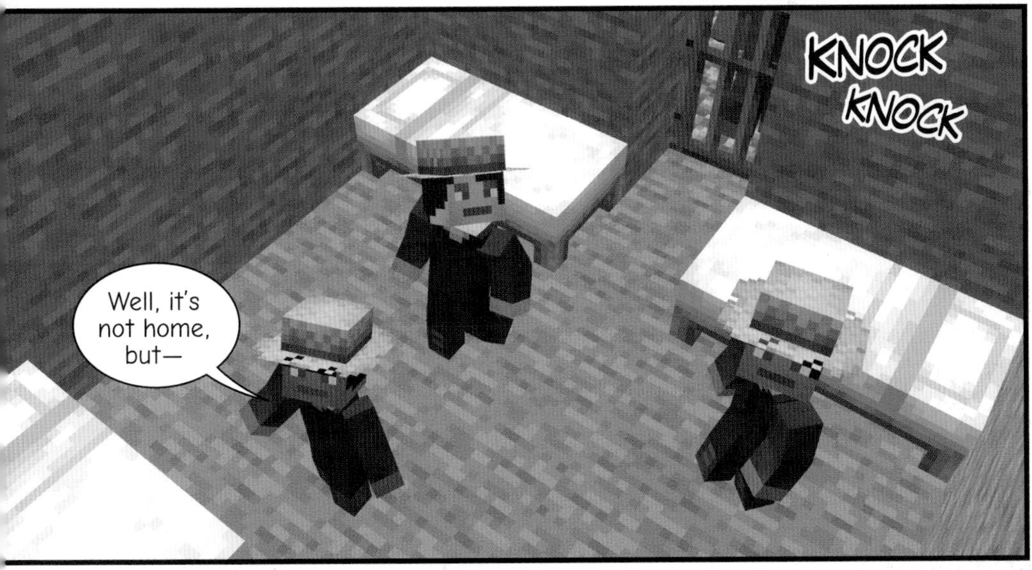
KNOCK
KNOCK
Well, it's
not home,
but—

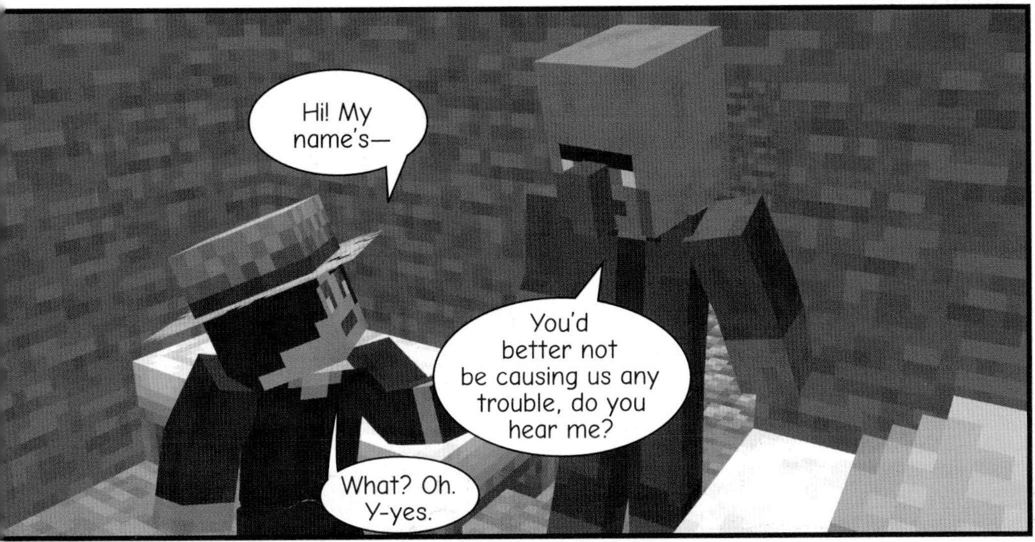
Hi! My
name's—
You'd
better not
be causing us any
trouble, do you
hear me?
What? Oh.
Y-yes.

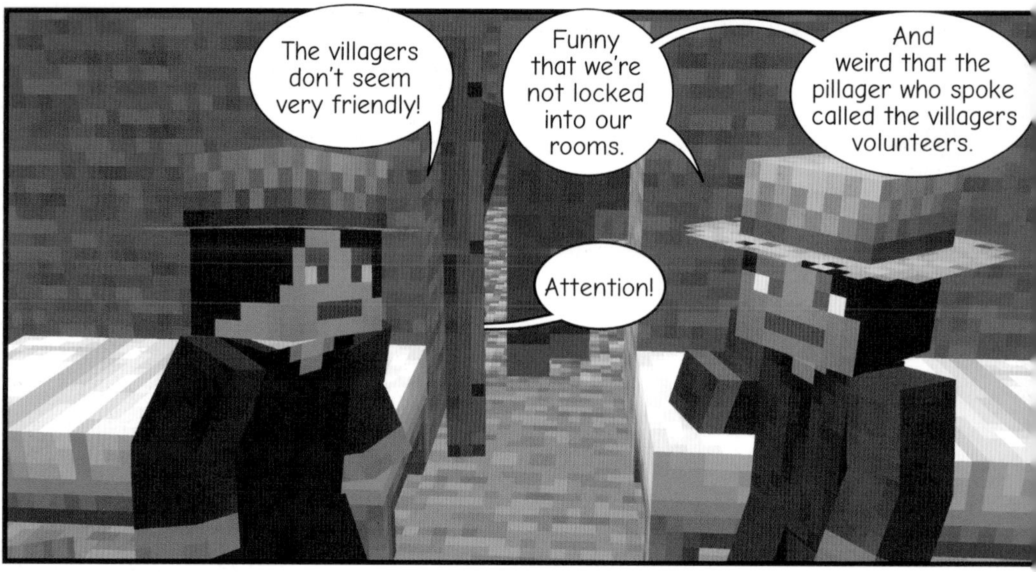
The villagers don't seem very friendly!
Funny that we're not locked into our rooms.
And weird that the pillager who spoke called the villagers volunteers.
Attention!

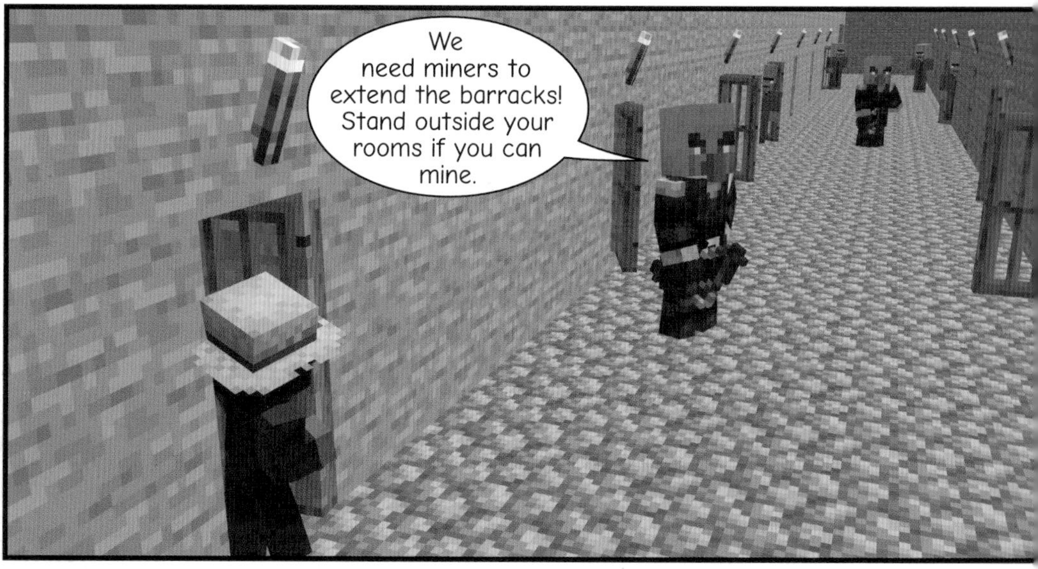
We need miners to extend the barracks! Stand outside your rooms if you can mine.

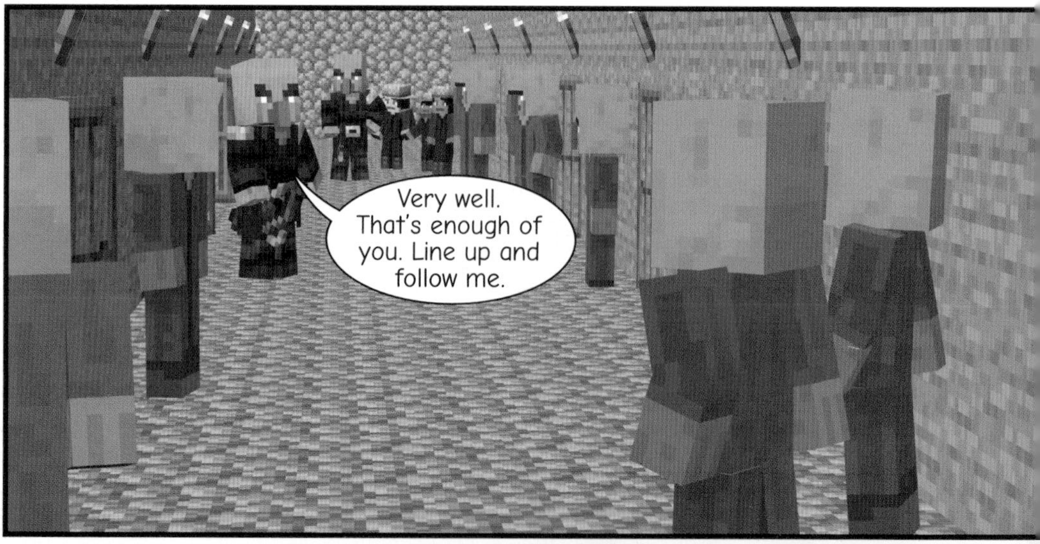
Very well. That's enough of you. Line up and follow me.

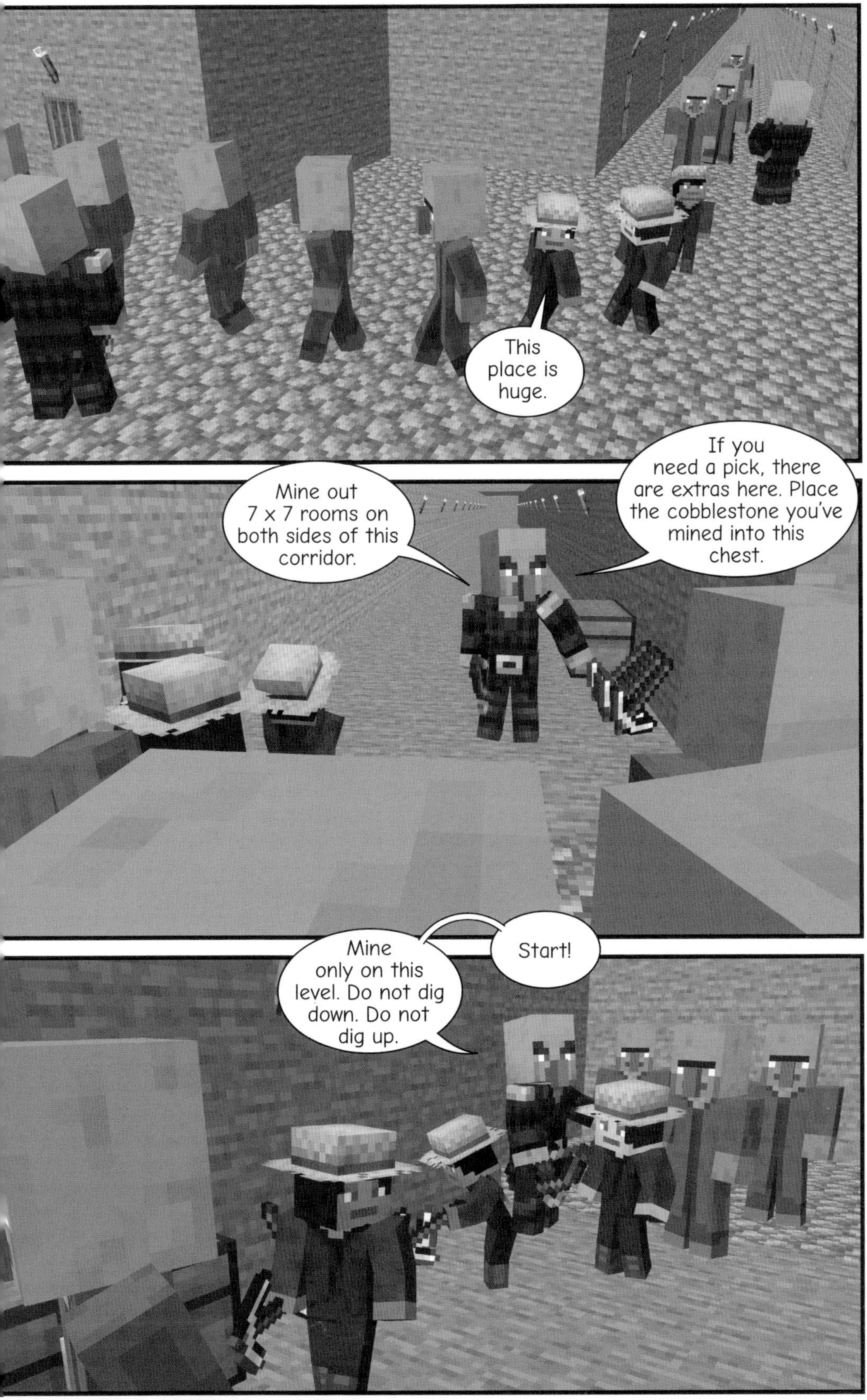
This place is huge.
Mine out 7 x 7 rooms on both sides of this corridor.
If you need a pick, there are extras here. Place the cobblestone you've mined into this chest.
Mine only on this level. Do not dig down. Do not dig up.
Start!

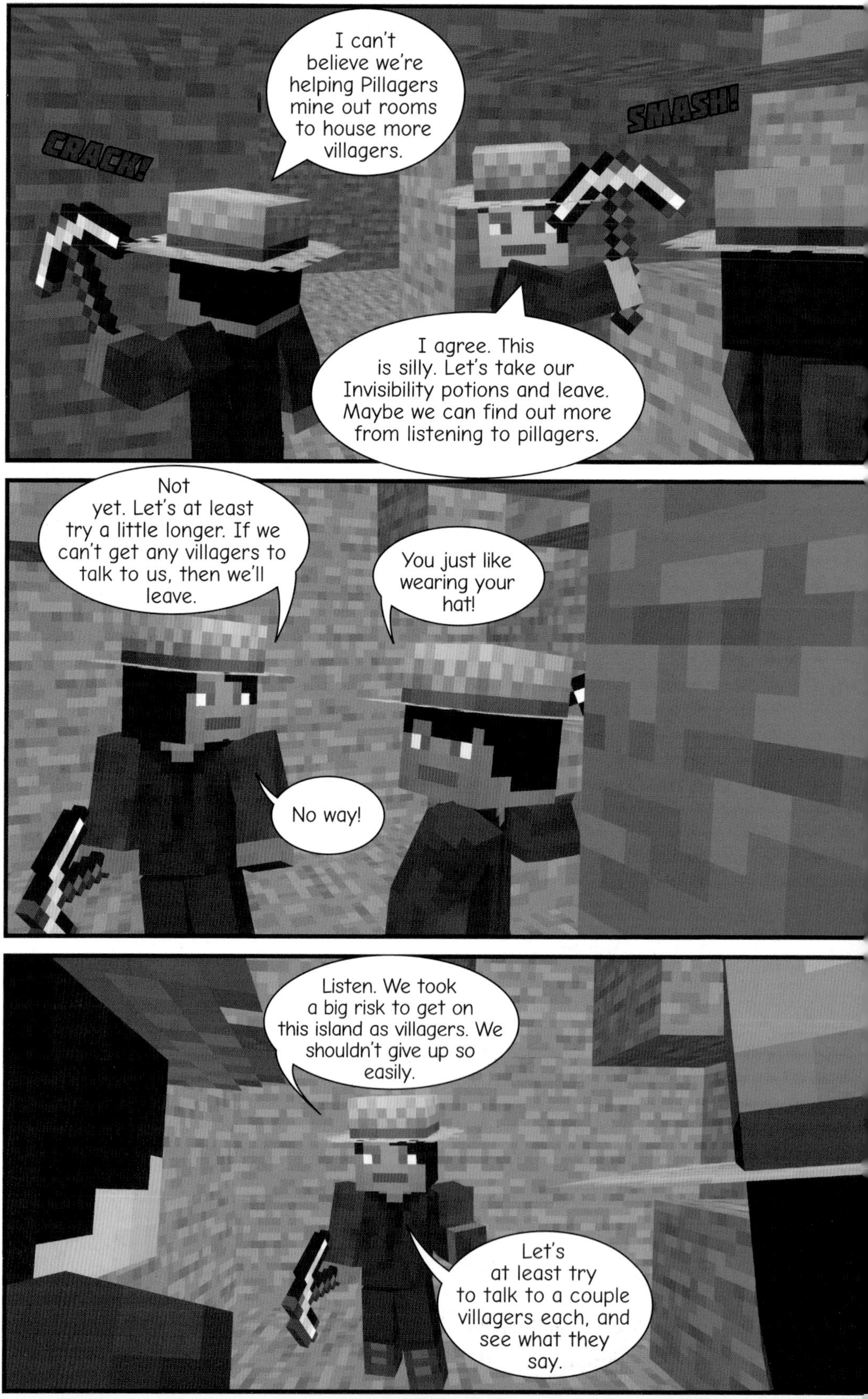
I can't believe we're helping Pillagers mine out rooms to house more villagers.
CRACK!
SMASH!
I agree. This is silly. Let's take our Invisibility potions and leave. Maybe we can find out more from listening to pillagers.
Not yet. Let's at least try a little longer. If we can't get any villagers to talk to us, then we'll leave.
You just like wearing your hat!
No way!
Listen. We took a big risk to get on this island as villagers. We shouldn't give up so easily.
Let's at least try to talk to a couple villagers each, and see what they say.

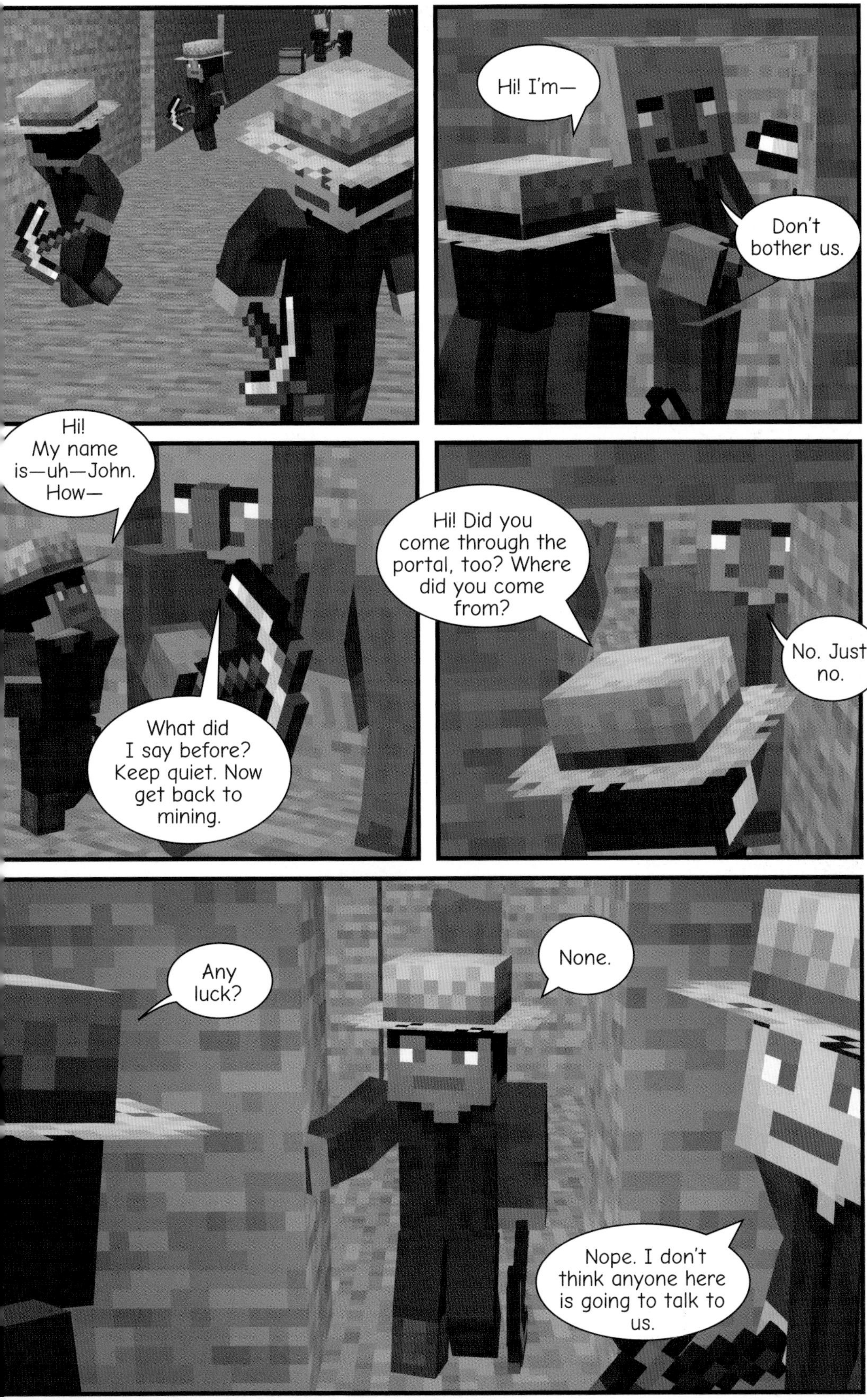
Hi! I'm—
Don't bother us.
Hi! My name is—uh—John. How—
What did I say before? Keep quiet. Now get back to mining.
Hi! Did you come through the portal, too? Where did you come from?
No. Just no.
Any luck?
None.
Nope. I don't think anyone here is going to talk to us.

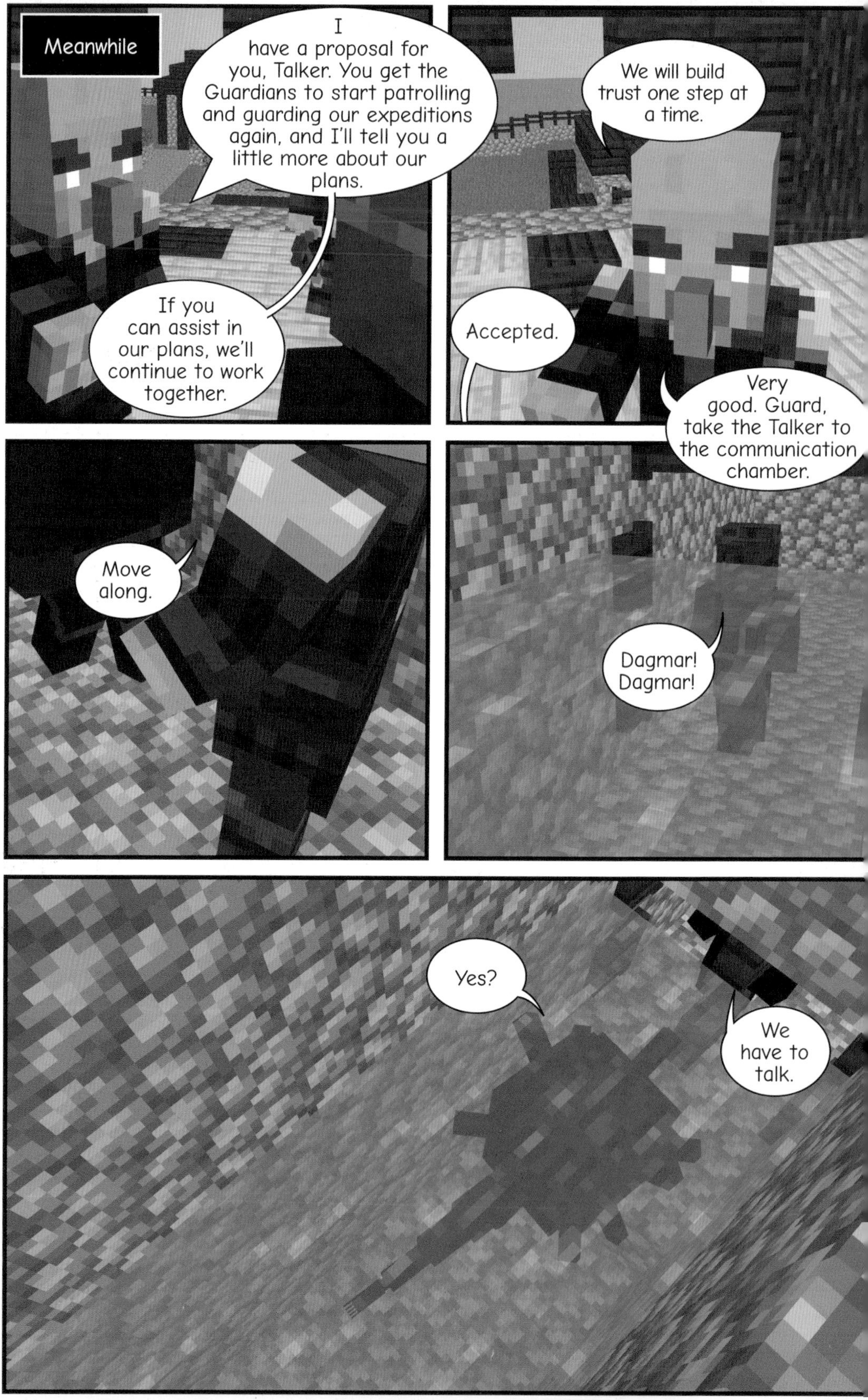
Meanwhile
I have a proposal for you, Talker. You get the Guardians to start patrolling and guarding our expeditions again, and I'll tell you a little more about our plans.
If you can assist in our plans, we'll continue to work together.
We will build trust one step at a time.
Accepted.
Very good. Guard, take the Talker to the communication chamber.
Move along.
Dagmar! Dagmar!
Yes?
We have to talk.

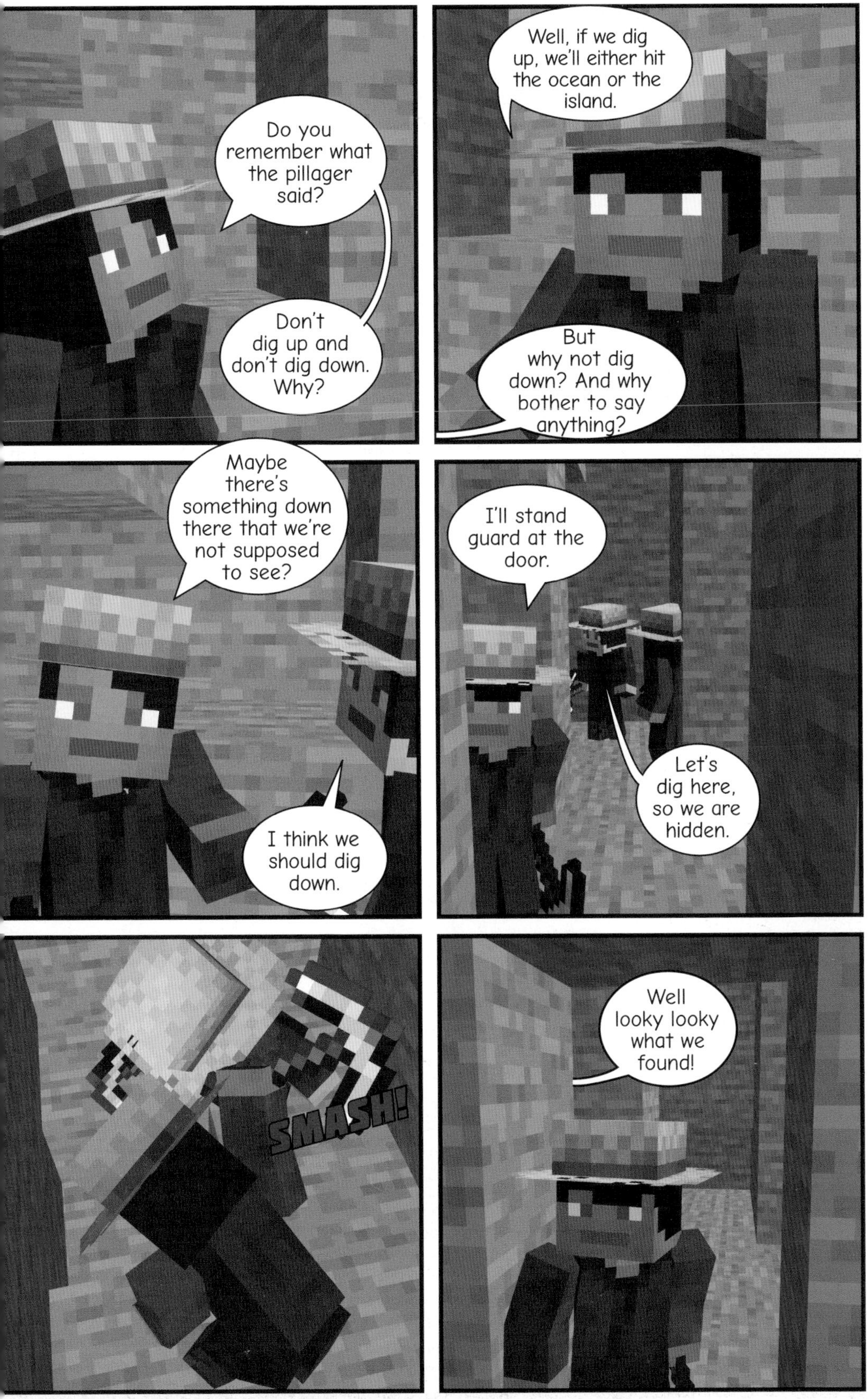
Do you remember what the pillager said?
Don't dig up and don't dig down. Why?
Well, if we dig up, we'll either hit the ocean or the island.
But why not dig down? And why bother to say anything?
Maybe there's something down there that we're not supposed to see?
I think we should dig down.
I'll stand guard at the door.
Let's dig here, so we are hidden.
SMASH!
Well looky looky what we found!

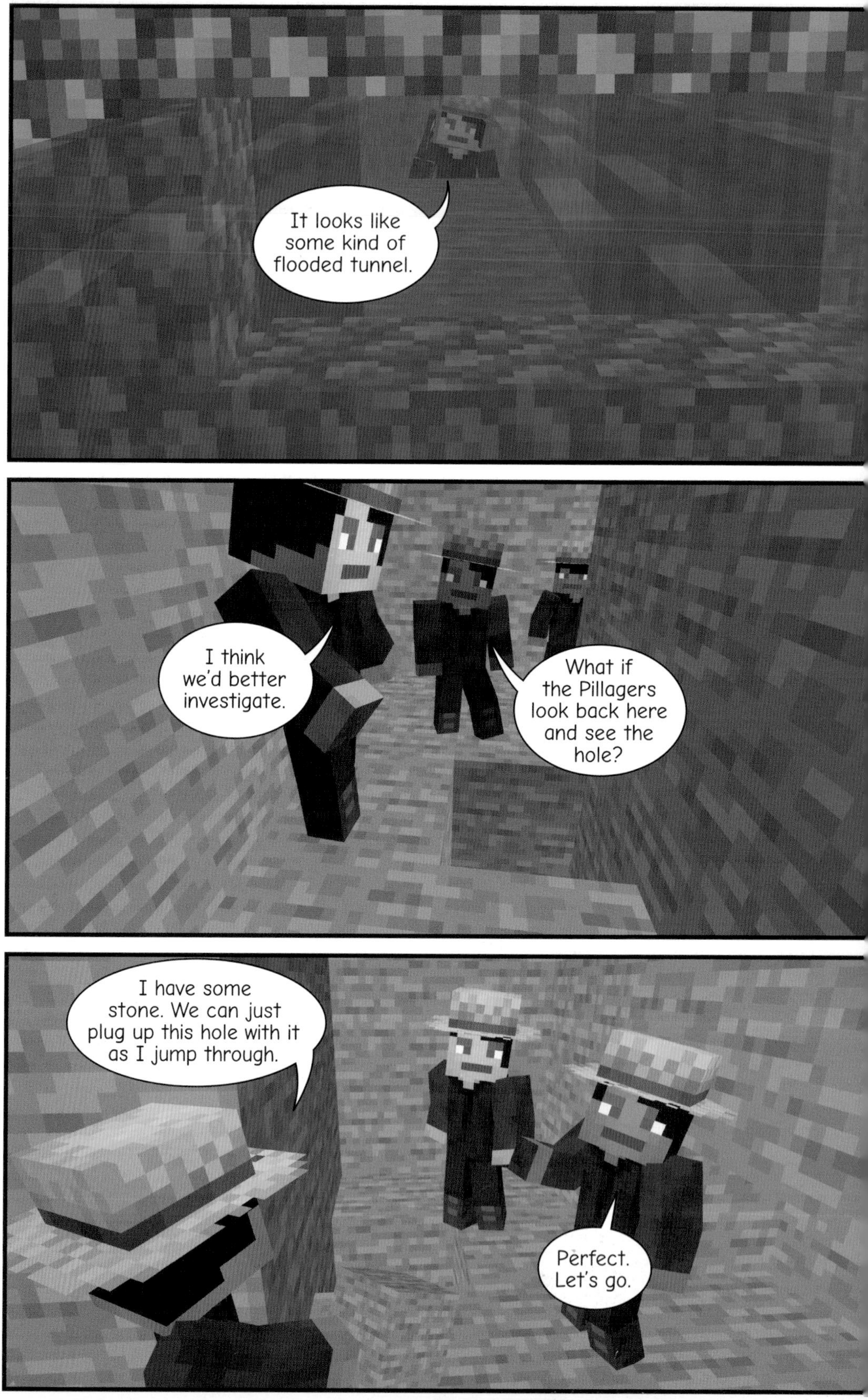
It looks like some kind of flooded tunnel.
I think we'd better investigate.
What if the Pillagers look back here and see the hole?
I have some stone. We can just plug up this hole with it as I jump through.
Perfect. Let's go.

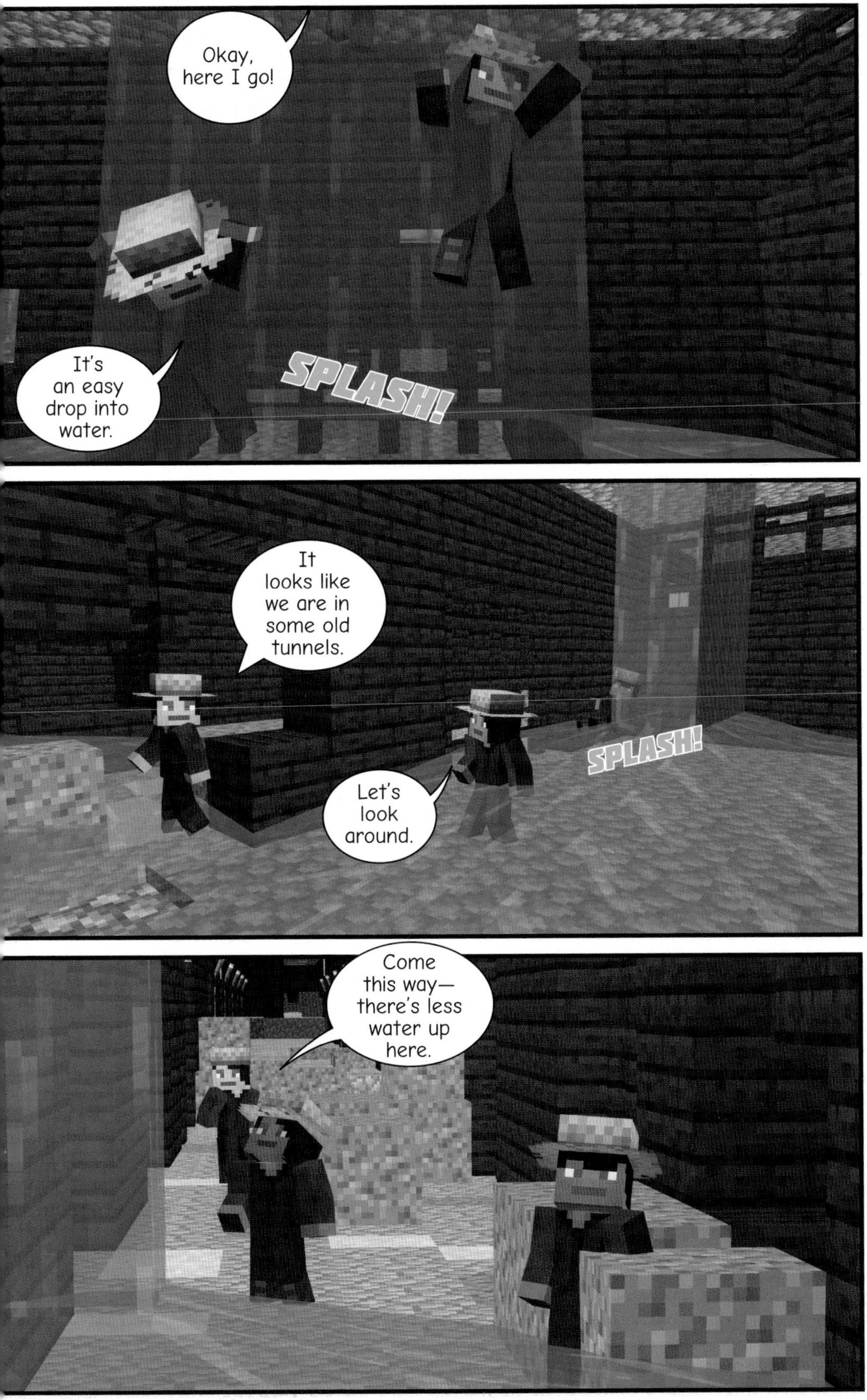
Okay, here I go!
It's an easy drop into water.
SPLASH!
It looks like we are in some old tunnels.
Let's look around.
SPLASH!
Come this way—there's less water up here.

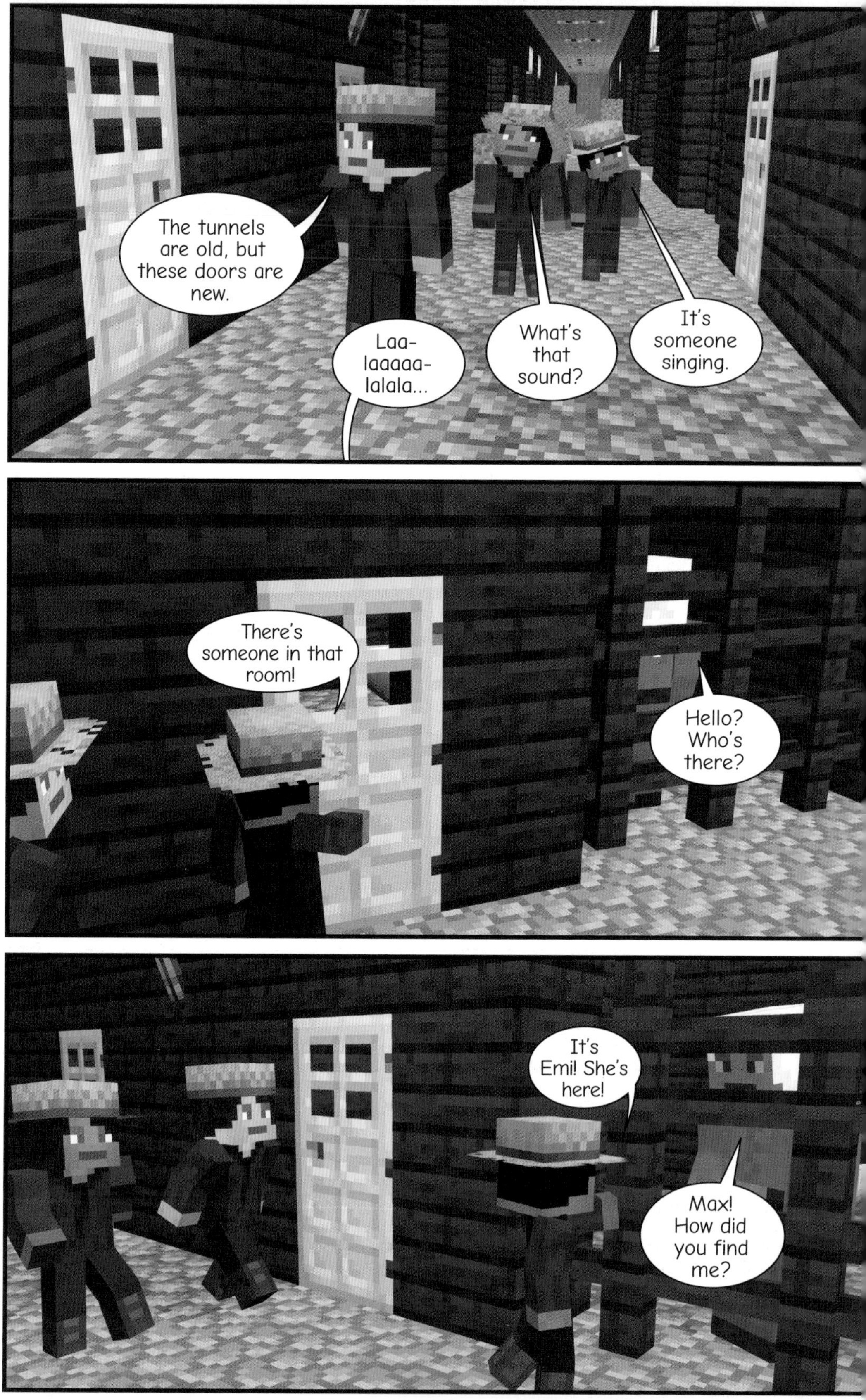
The tunnels are old, but these doors are new.
Laa-laaaaa-lalala...
What's that sound?
It's someone singing.
There's someone in that room!
Hello? Who's there?
It's Emi! She's here!
Max! How did you find me?

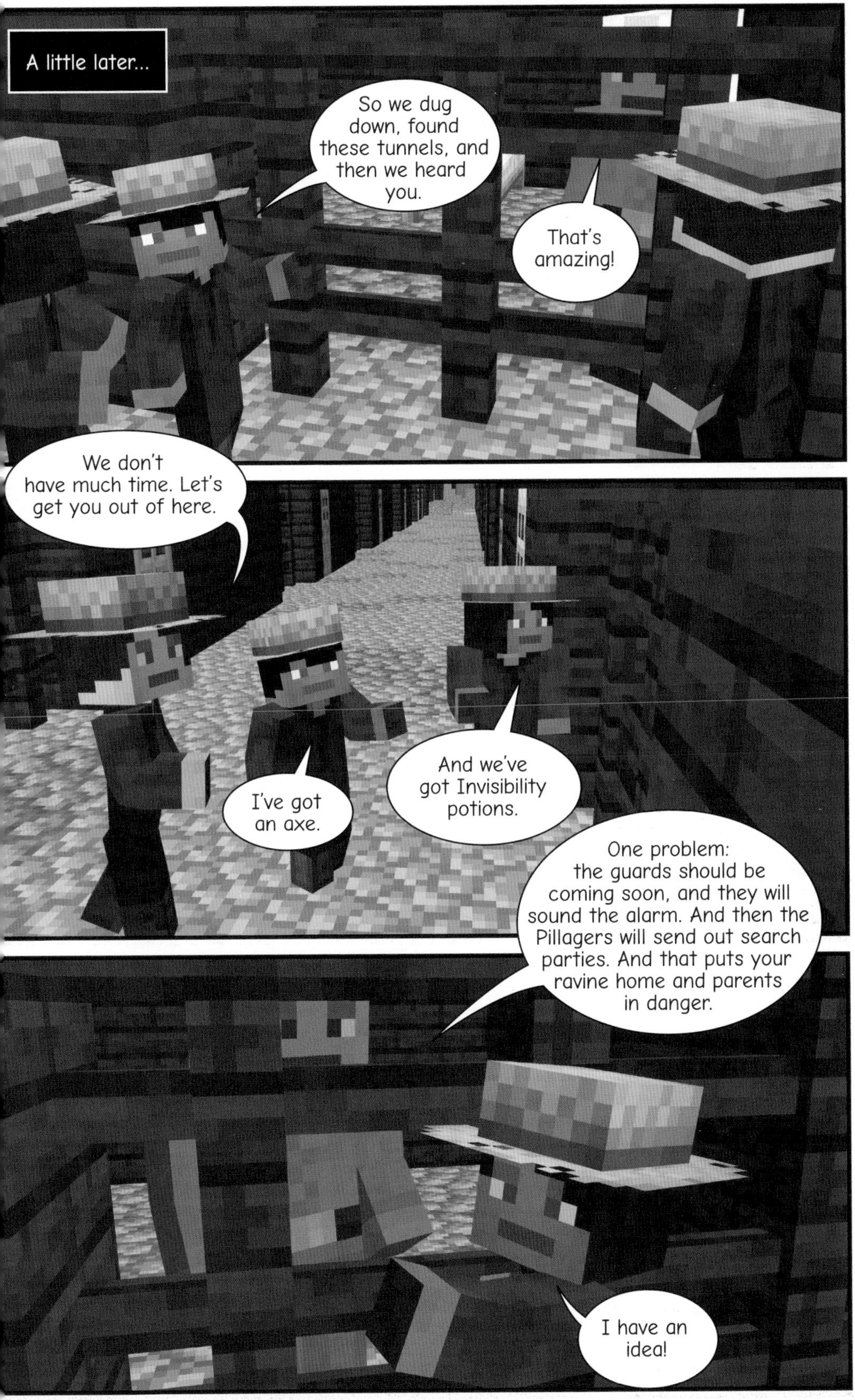
A little later...
So we dug down, found these tunnels, and then we heard you.
That's amazing!
We don't have much time. Let's get you out of here.
I've got an axe.
And we've got Invisibility potions.
One problem: the guards should be coming soon, and they will sound the alarm. And then the Pillagers will send out search parties. And that puts your ravine home and parents in danger.
I have an idea!

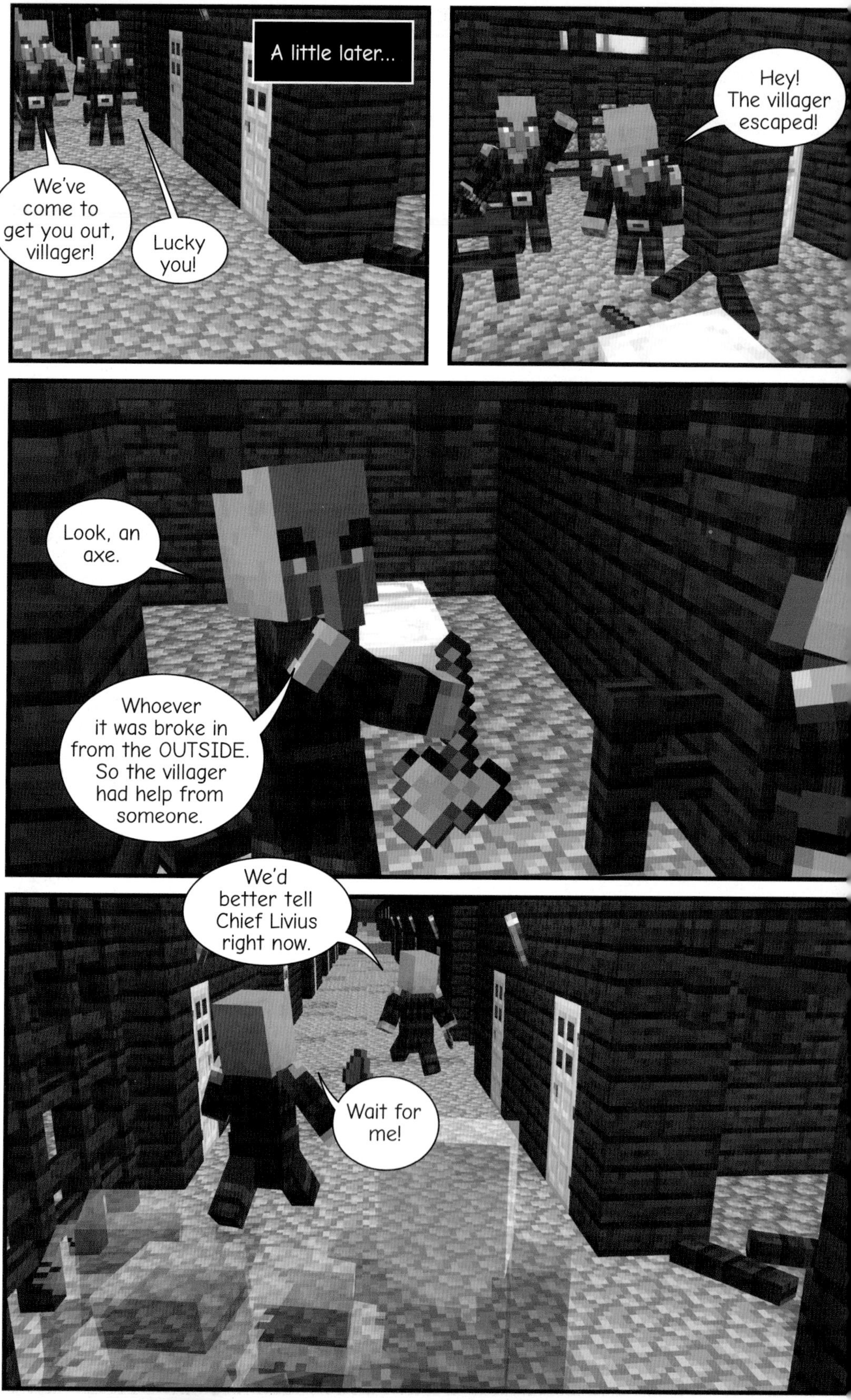
A little later...
We've come to get you out, villager!
Lucky you!
Hey! The villager escaped!
Look, an axe.
Whoever it was broke in from the OUTSIDE. So the villager had help from someone.
We'd better tell Chief Livius right now.
Wait for me!

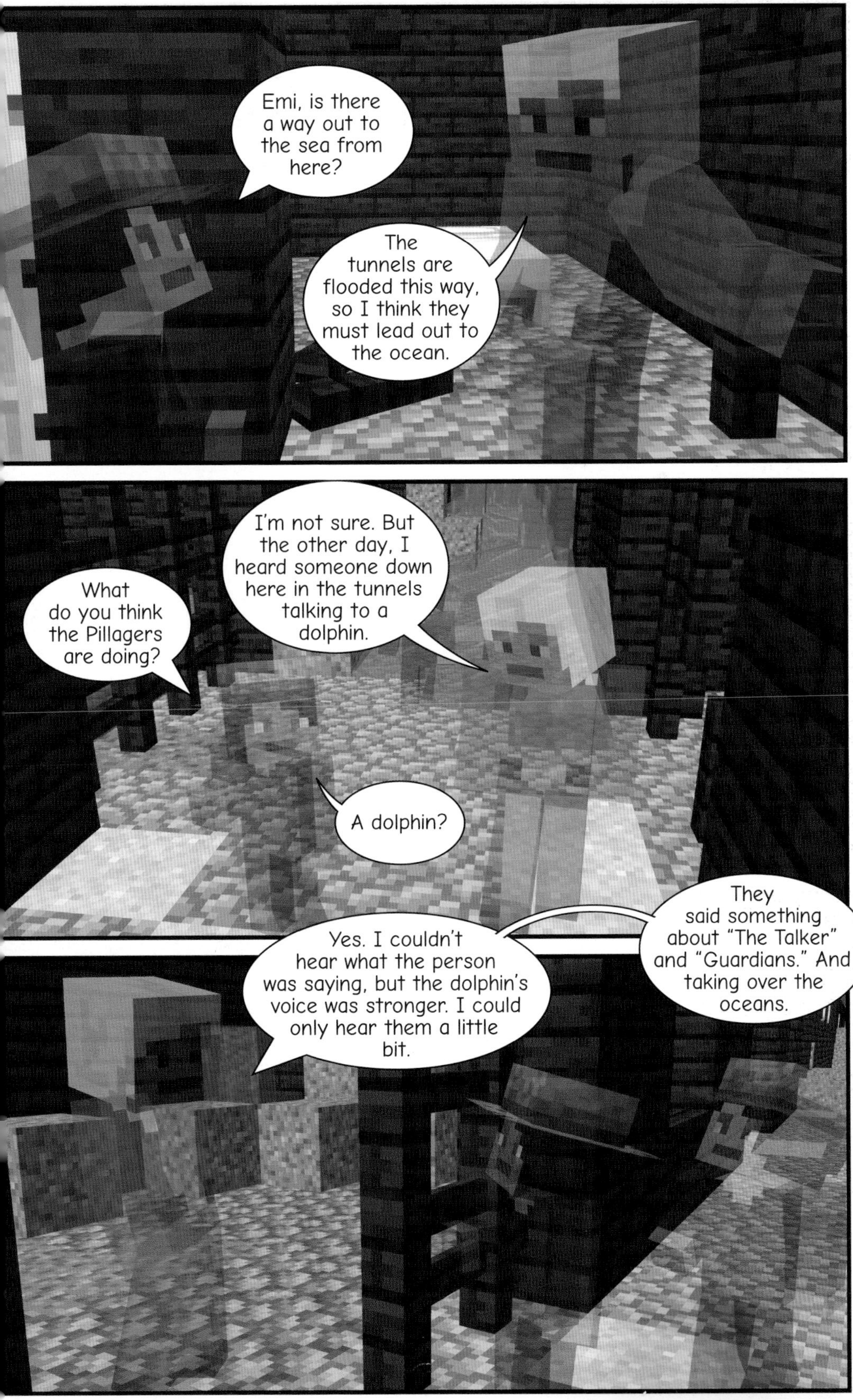
Emi, is there a way out to the sea from here?
The tunnels are flooded this way, so I think they must lead out to the ocean.
What do you think the Pillagers are doing?
I'm not sure. But the other day, I heard someone down here in the tunnels talking to a dolphin.
A dolphin?
Yes. I couldn't hear what the person was saying, but the dolphin's voice was stronger. I could only hear them a little bit.
They said something about "The Talker" and "Guardians." And taking over the oceans.

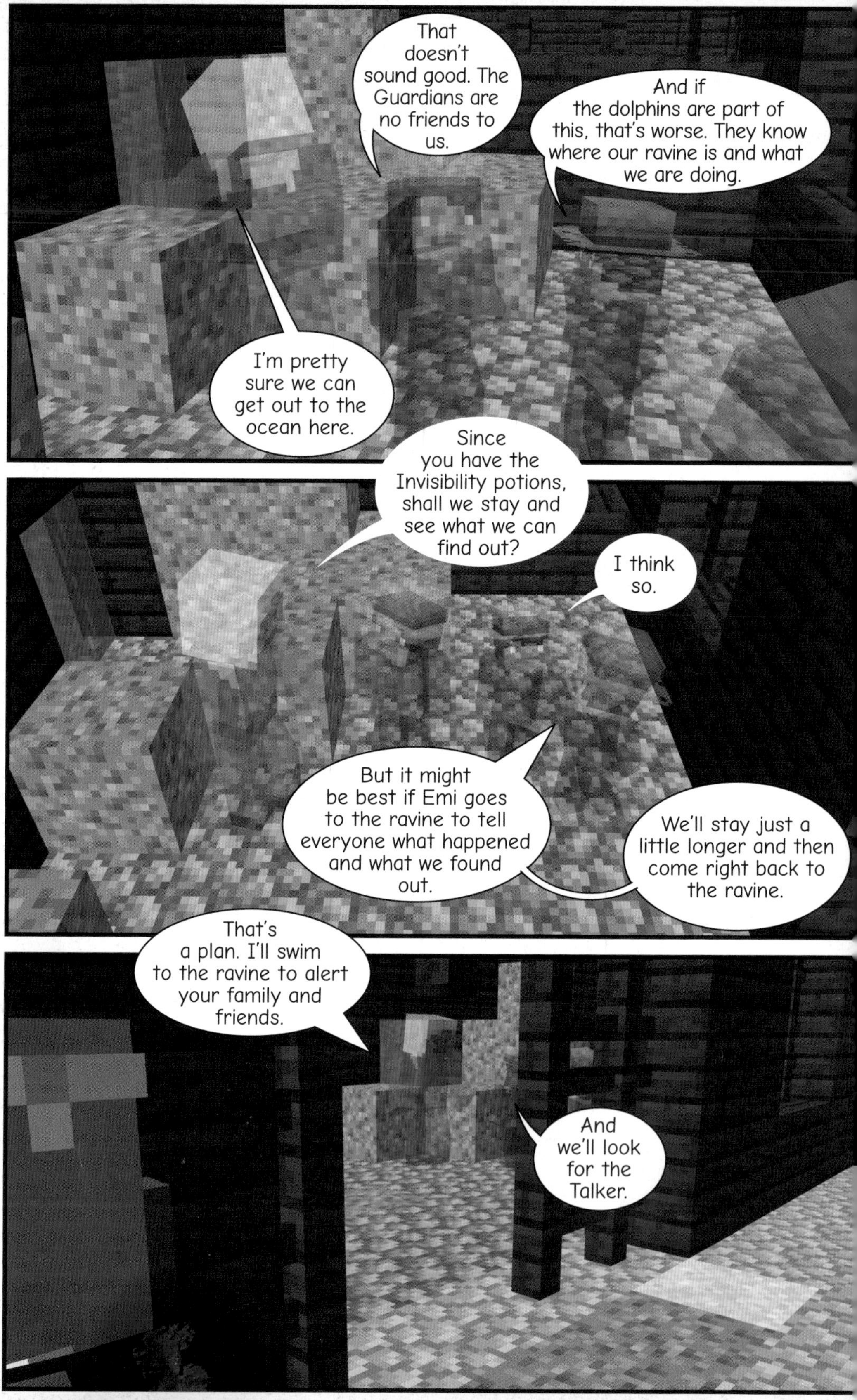
That doesn't sound good. The Guardians are no friends to us.
And if the dolphins are part of this, that's worse. They know where our ravine is and what we are doing.
I'm pretty sure we can get out to the ocean here.
Since you have the Invisibility potions, shall we stay and see what we can find out?
I think so.
But it might be best if Emi goes to the ravine to tell everyone what happened and what we found out.
We'll stay just a little longer and then come right back to the ravine.
That's a plan. I'll swim to the ravine to alert your family and friends.
And we'll look for the Talker.

Chapter 9
"Diabolical, Chief."

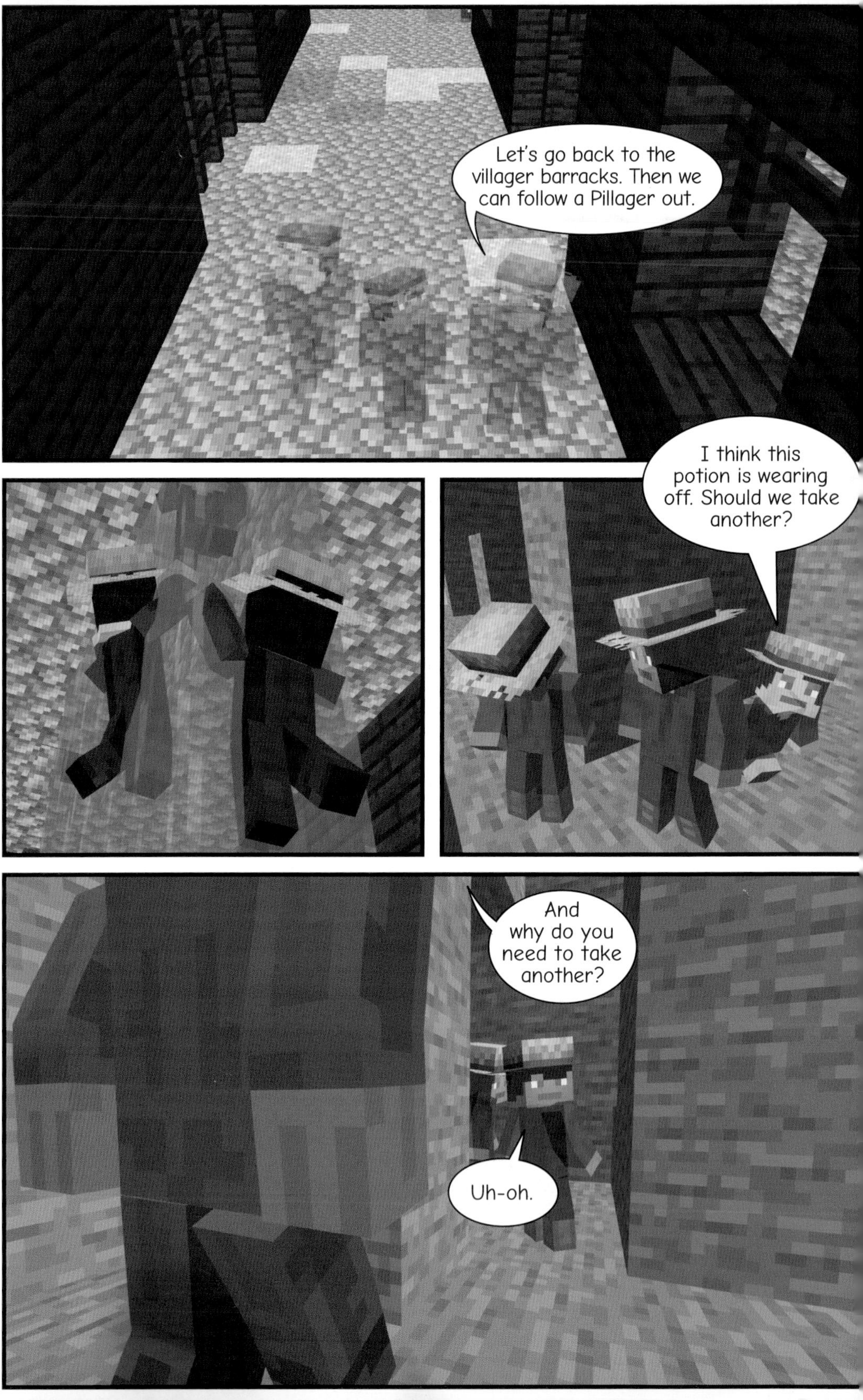
Let's go back to the villager barracks. Then we can follow a Pillager out.
I think this potion is wearing off. Should we take another?
And why do you need to take another?
Uh-oh.

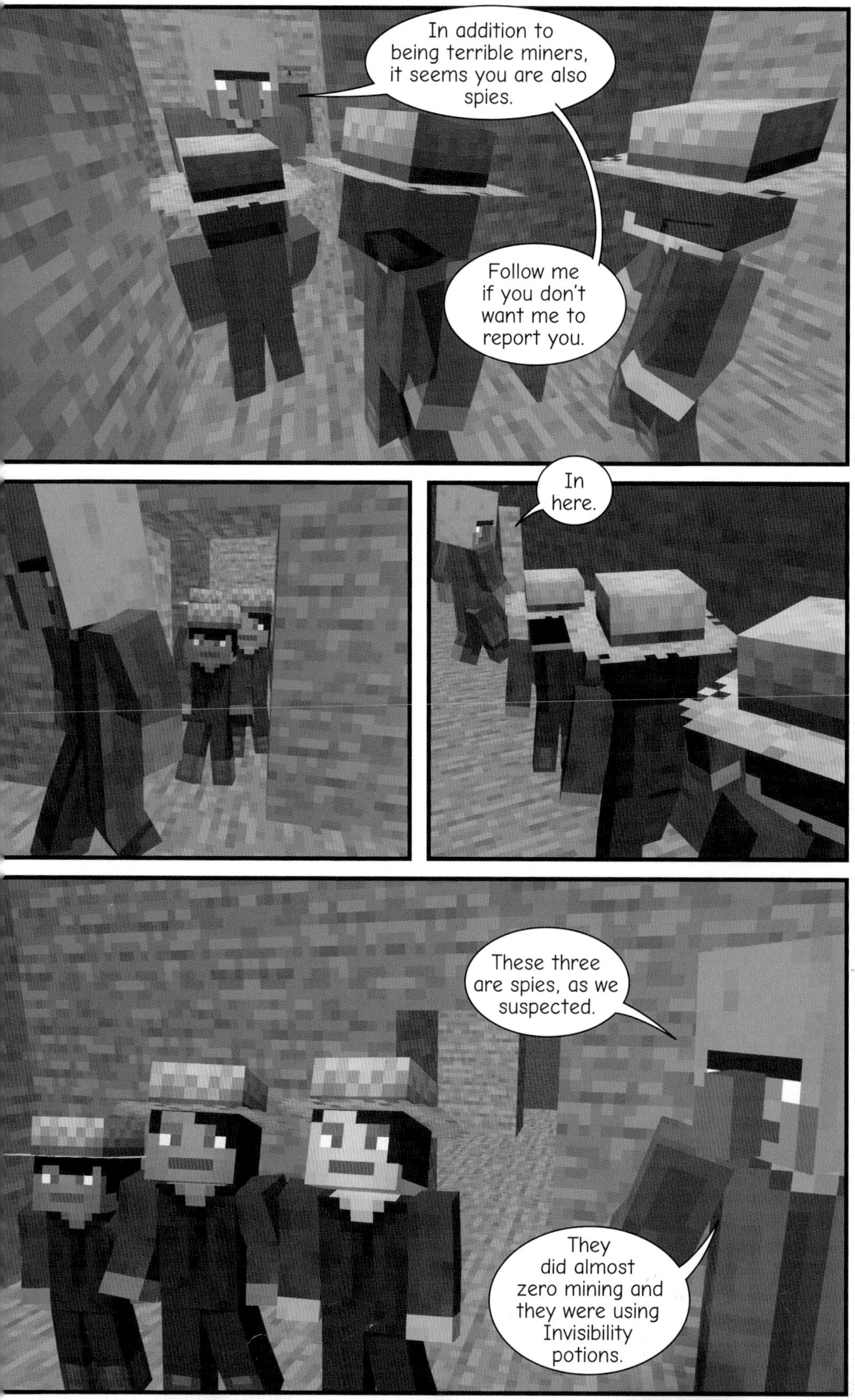
In addition to being terrible miners, it seems you are also spies.
Follow me if you don't want me to report you.
In here.
These three are spies, as we suspected.
They did almost zero mining and they were using Invisibility potions.

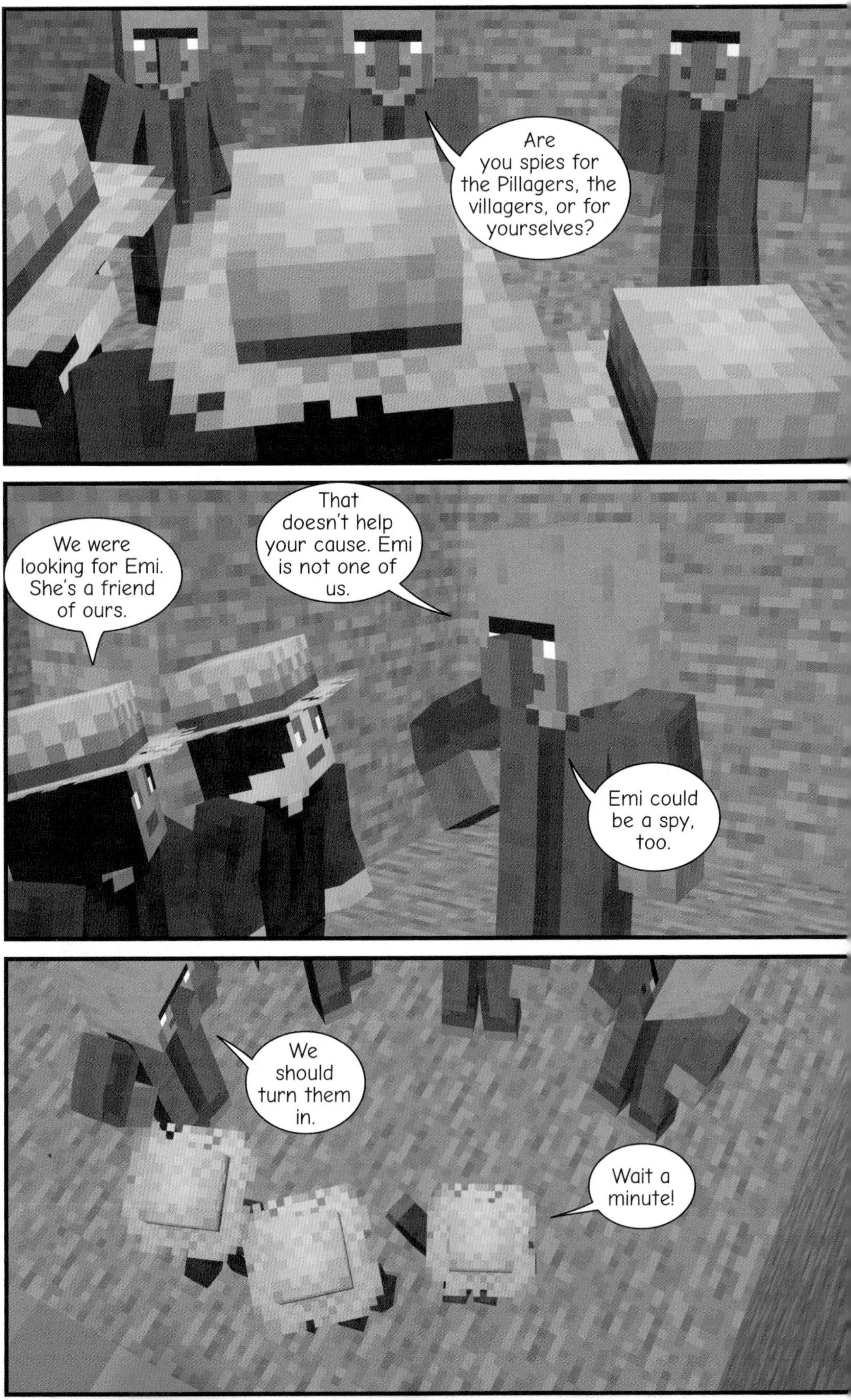
Are you spies for the Pillagers, the villagers, or for yourselves?
We were looking for Emi. She's a friend of ours.
That doesn't help your cause. Emi is not one of us.
Emi could be a spy, too.
We should turn them in.
Wait a minute!

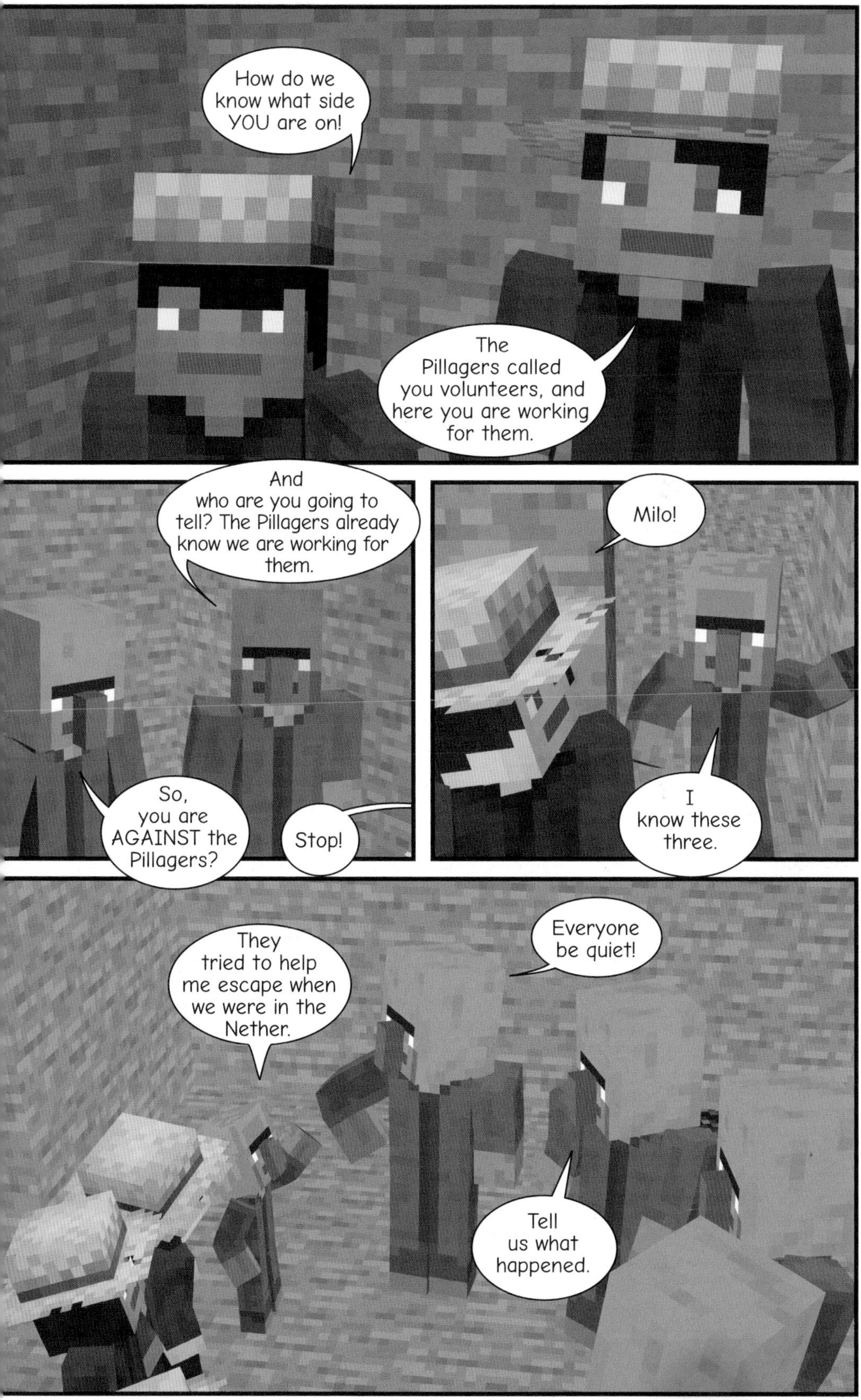
How do we know what side YOU are on!
The Pillagers called you volunteers, and here you are working for them.
And who are you going to tell? The Pillagers already know we are working for them.
So, you are AGAINST the Pillagers?
Stop!
Milo!
I know these three.
They tried to help me escape when we were in the Nether.
Everyone be quiet!
Tell us what happened.

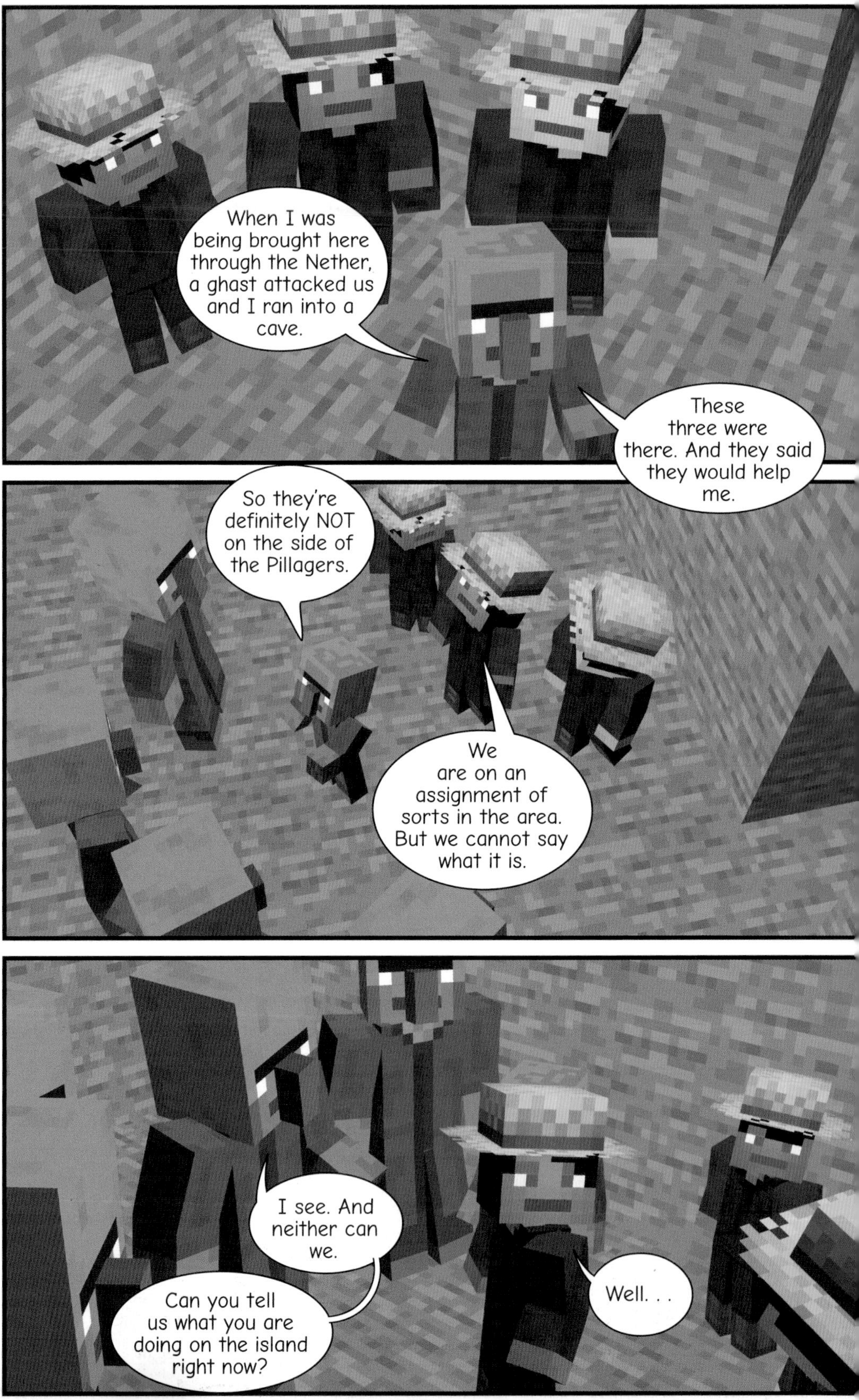
When I was being brought here through the Nether, a ghast attacked us and I ran into a cave.
These three were there. And they said they would help me.
So they're definitely NOT on the side of the Pillagers.
We are on an assignment of sorts in the area. But we cannot say what it is.
I see. And neither can we.
Can you tell us what you are doing on the island right now?
Well. . .

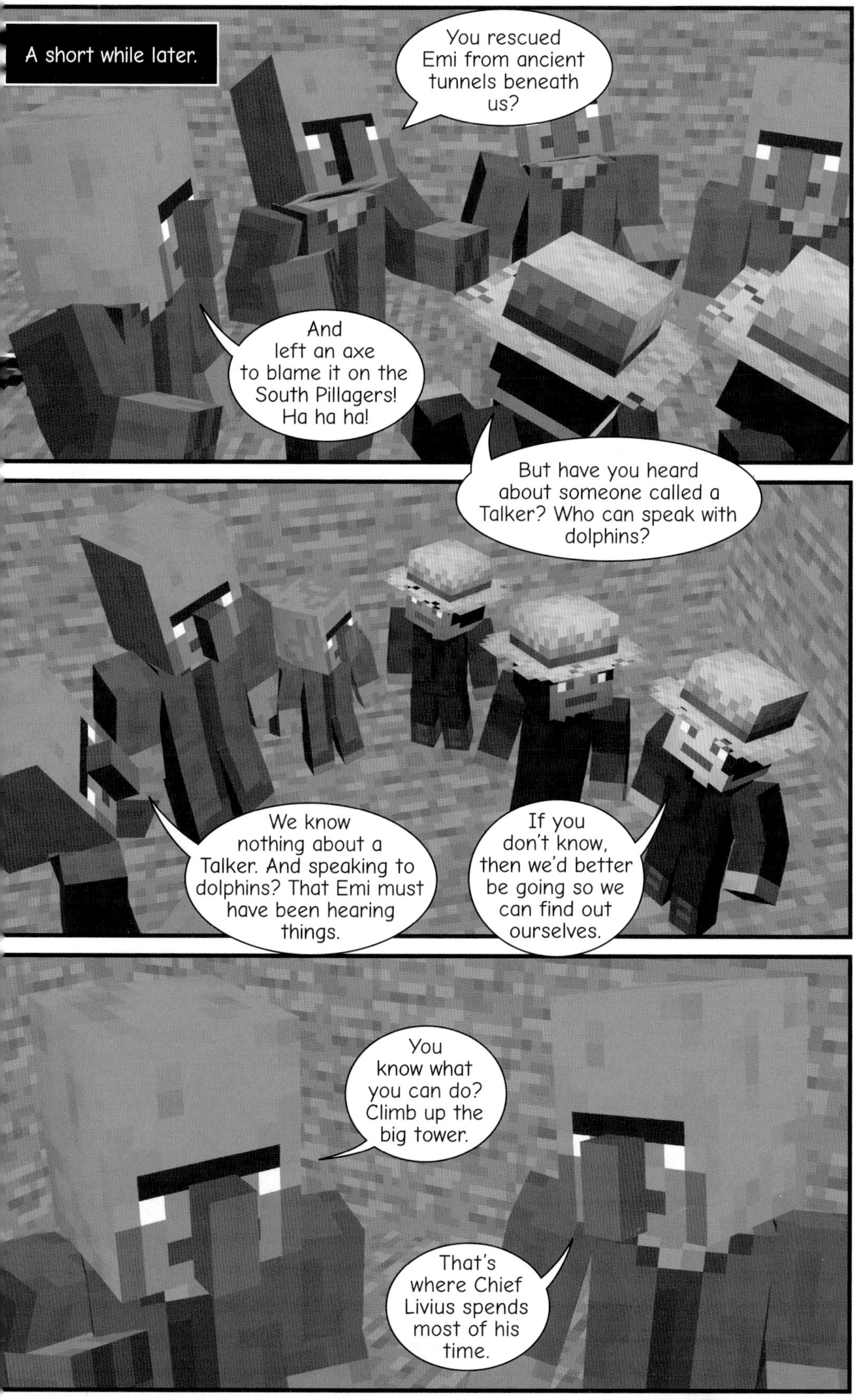
A short while later.
You rescued Emi from ancient tunnels beneath us?
And left an axe to blame it on the South Pillagers! Ha ha ha!
But have you heard about someone called a Talker? Who can speak with dolphins?
We know nothing about a Talker. And speaking to dolphins? That Emi must have been hearing things.
If you don't know, then we'd better be going so we can find out ourselves.
You know what you can do? Climb up the big tower.
That's where Chief Livius spends most of his time.

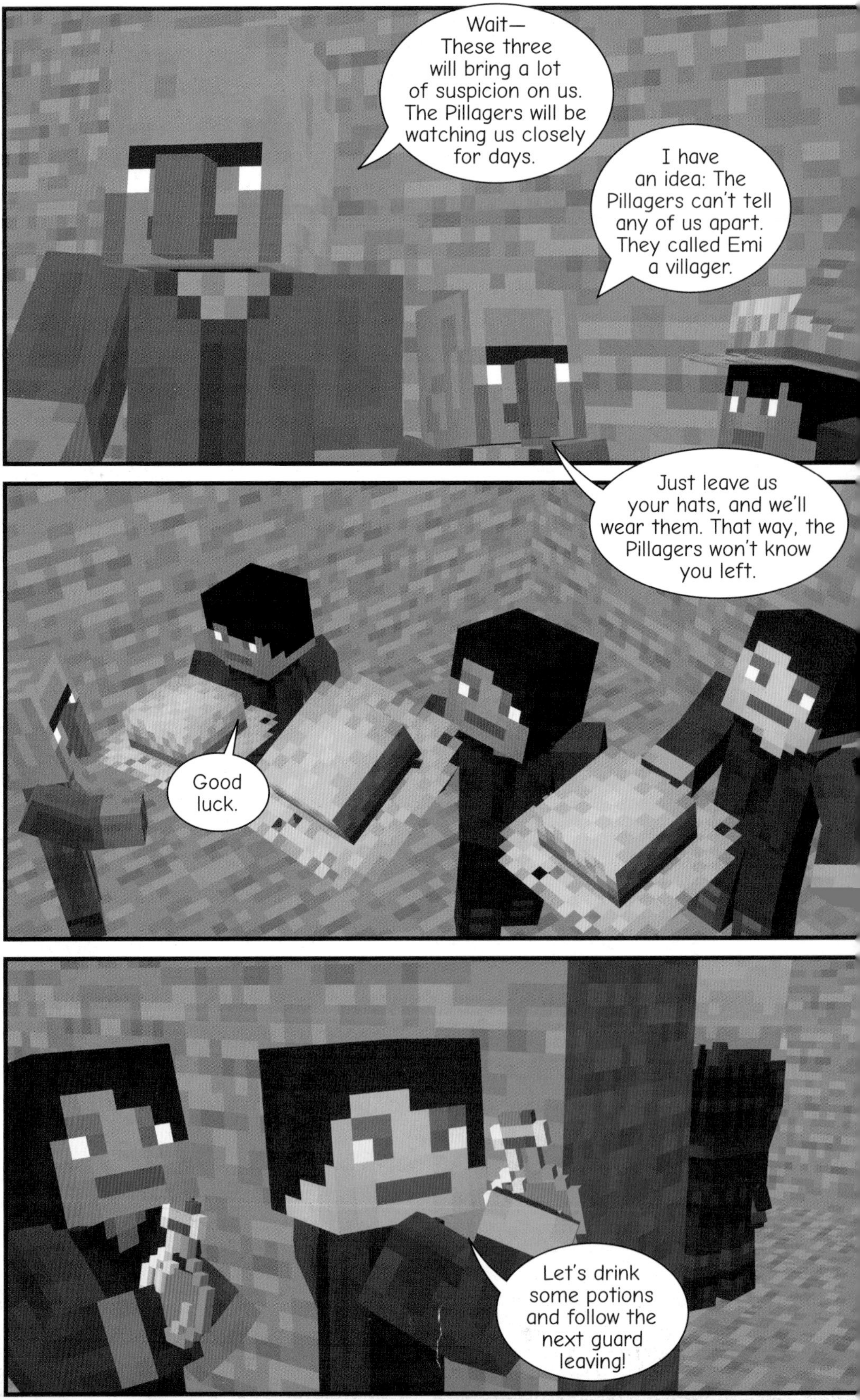
Wait—
These three will bring a lot of suspicion on us. The Pillagers will be watching us closely for days.
I have an idea: The Pillagers can't tell any of us apart. They called Emi a villager.
Just leave us your hats, and we'll wear them. That way, the Pillagers won't know you left.
Good luck.
Let's drink some potions and follow the next guard leaving!

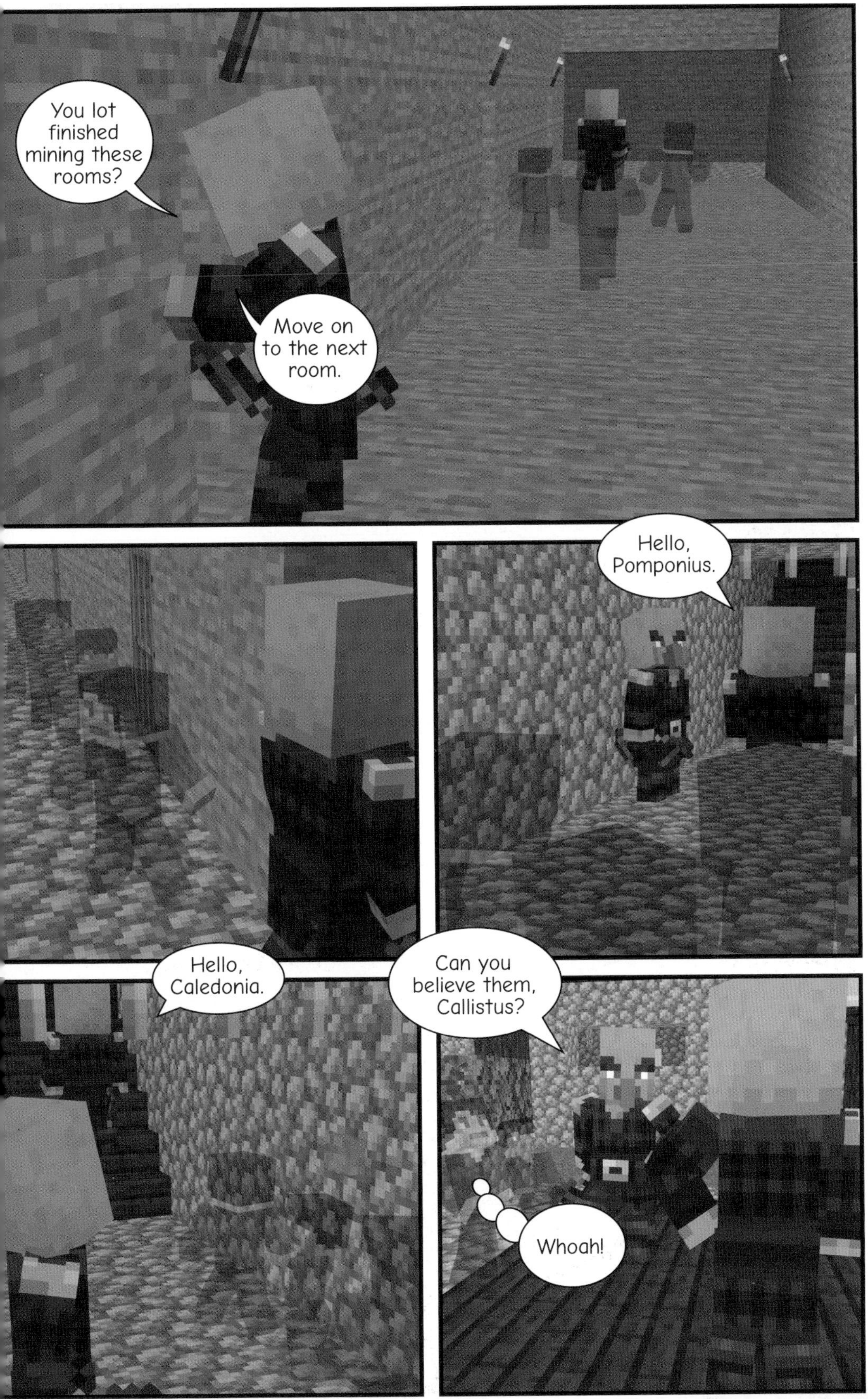
You lot finished mining these rooms?
Move on to the next room.
Hello, Pomponius.
Hello, Caledonia.
Can you believe them, Callistus?
Whoah!

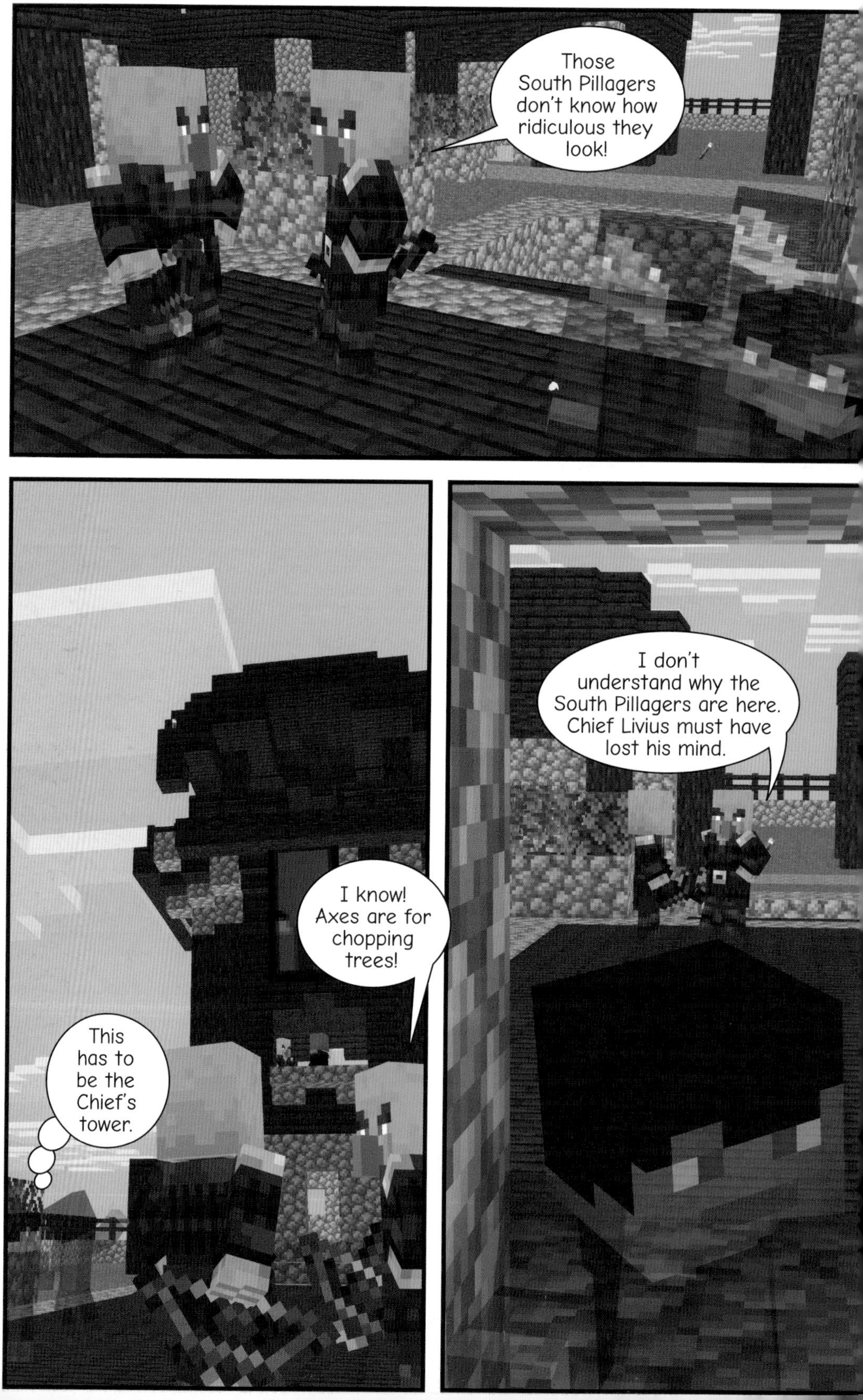
Those South Pillagers don't know how ridiculous they look!
This has to be the Chief's tower.
I know! Axes are for chopping trees!
I don't understand why the South Pillagers are here. Chief Livius must have lost his mind.

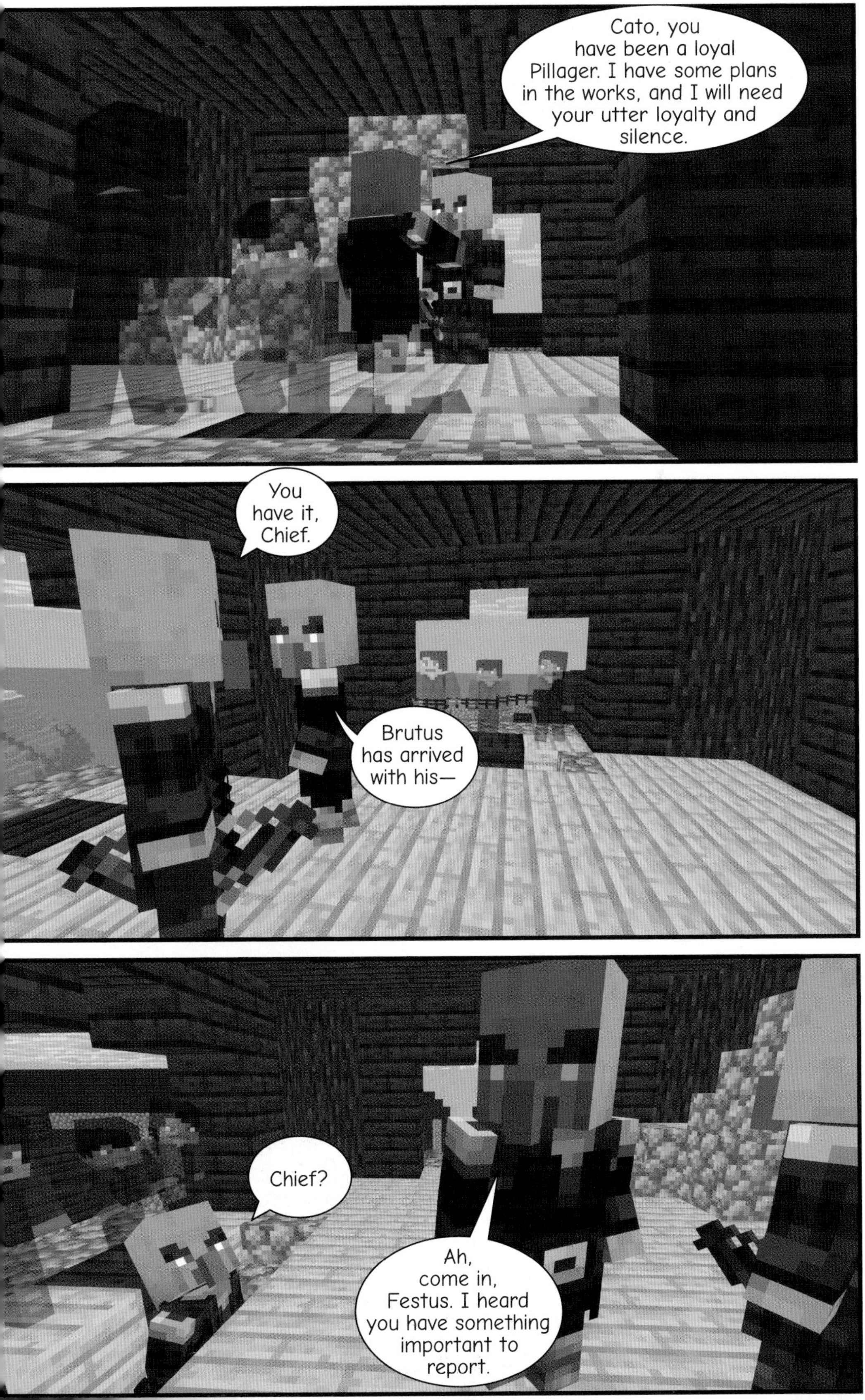
Cato, you have been a loyal Pillager. I have some plans in the works, and I will need your utter loyalty and silence.
You have it, Chief.
Brutus has arrived with his—
Chief?
Ah, come in, Festus. I heard you have something important to report.

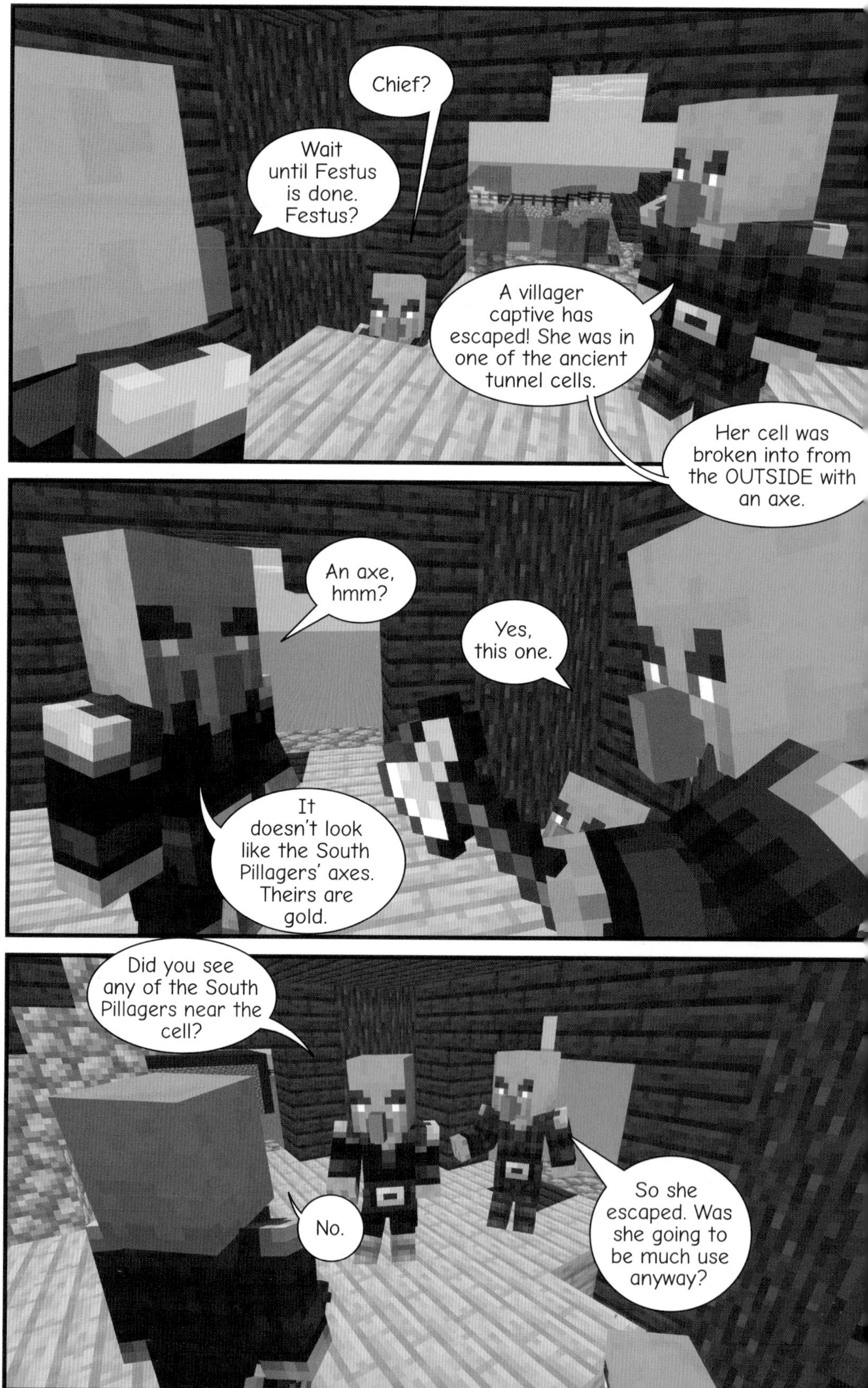
Chief?
Wait until Festus is done. Festus?
A villager captive has escaped! She was in one of the ancient tunnel cells.
Her cell was broken into from the OUTSIDE with an axe.
An axe, hmm?
Yes, this one.
It doesn't look like the South Pillagers' axes. Theirs are gold.
Did you see any of the South Pillagers near the cell?
No.
So she escaped. Was she going to be much use anyway?

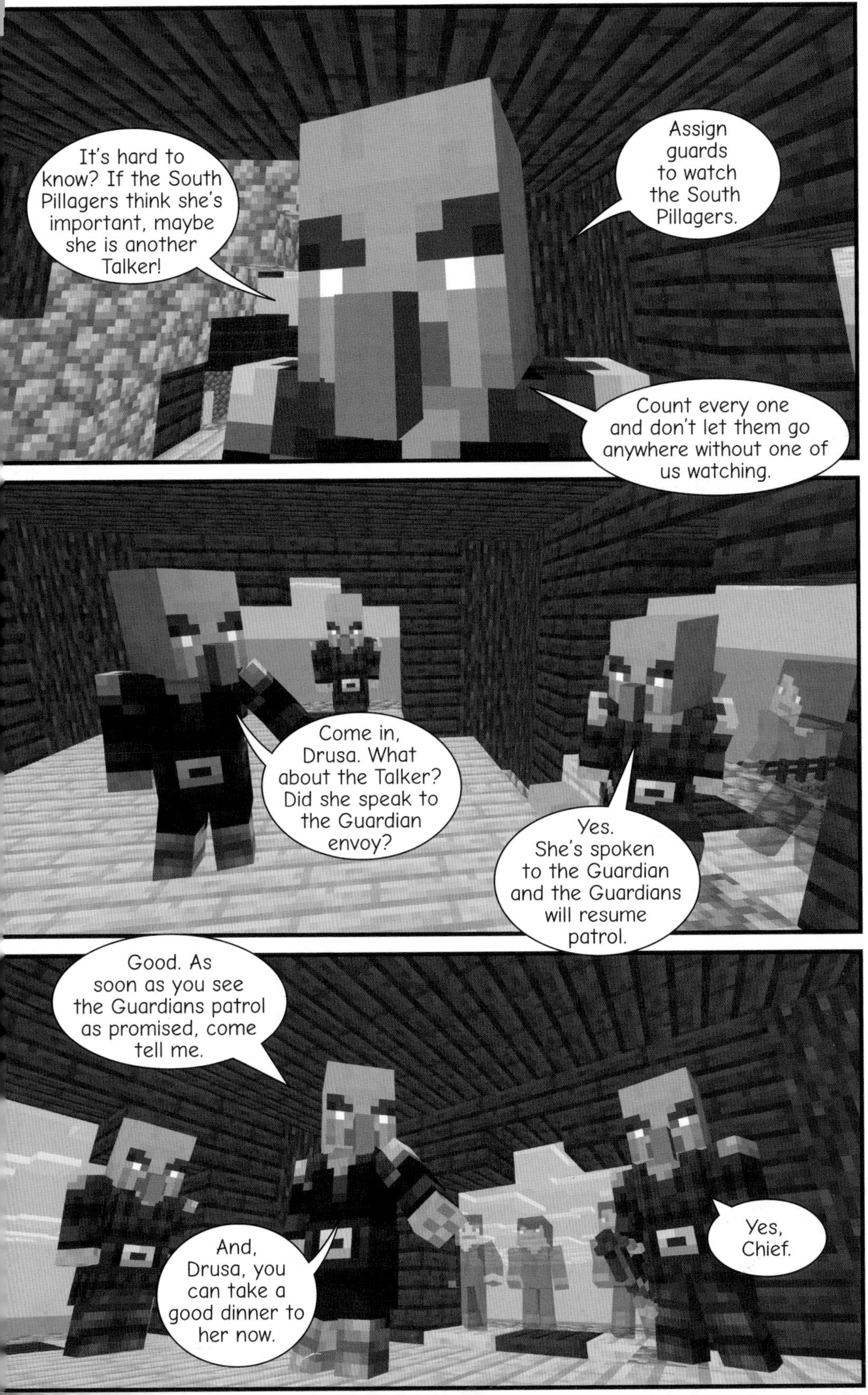
It's hard to know? If the South Pillagers think she's important, maybe she is another Talker!
Assign guards to watch the South Pillagers.
Count every one and don't let them go anywhere without one of us watching.
Come in, Drusa. What about the Talker? Did she speak to the Guardian envoy?
Yes. She's spoken to the Guardian and the Guardians will resume patrol.
Good. As soon as you see the Guardians patrol as promised, come tell me.
And, Drusa, you can take a good dinner to her now.
Yes, Chief.

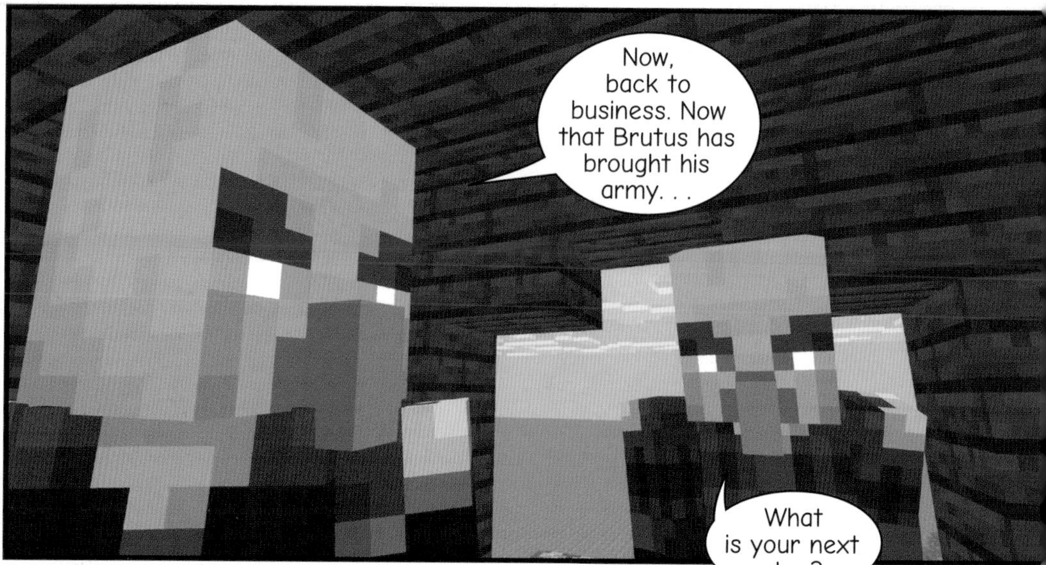
Now, back to business. Now that Brutus has brought his army. . .
What is your next step?

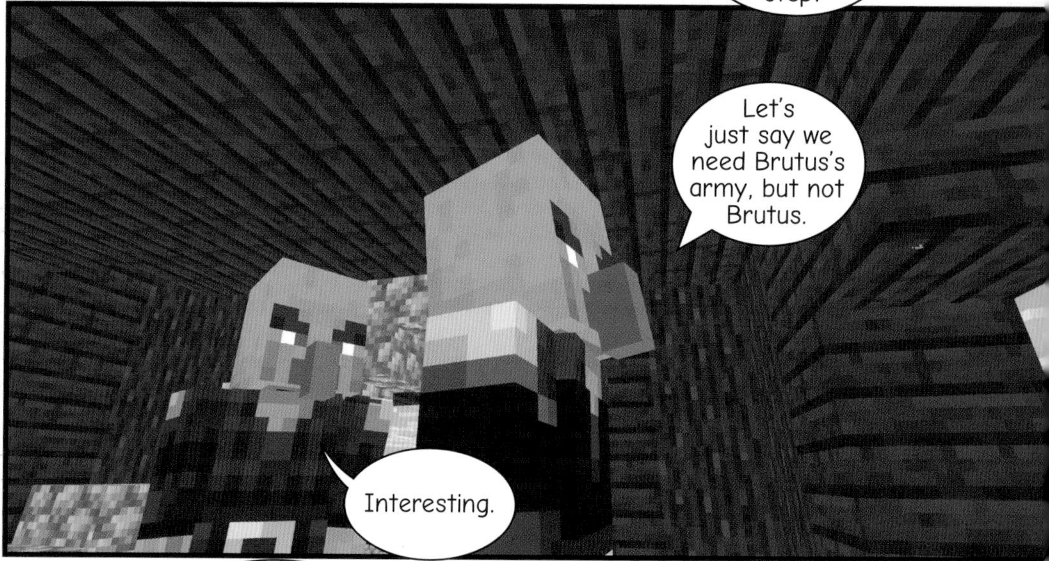
Let's just say we need Brutus's army, but not Brutus.
Interesting.

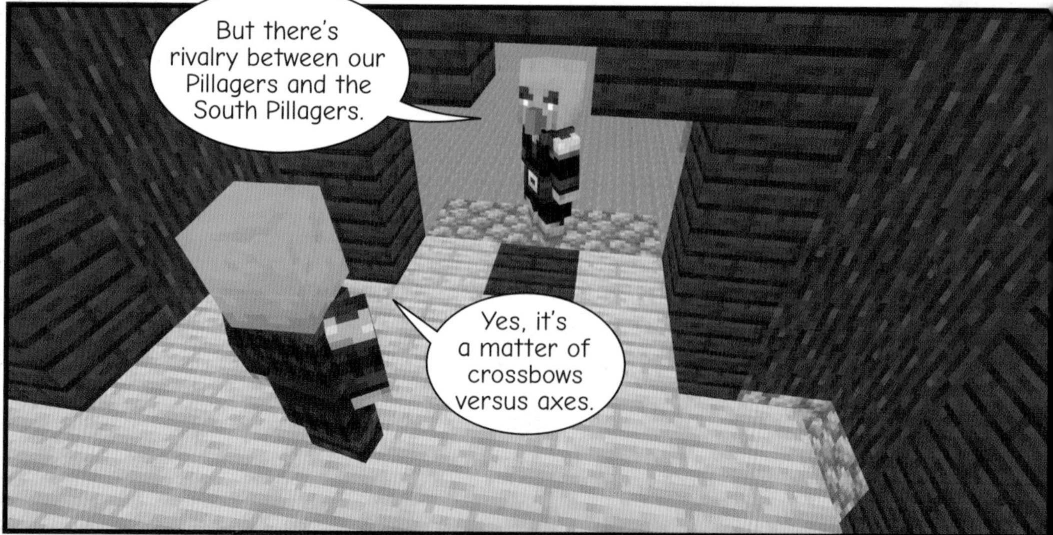
But there's rivalry between our Pillagers and the South Pillagers.
Yes, it's a matter of crossbows versus axes.

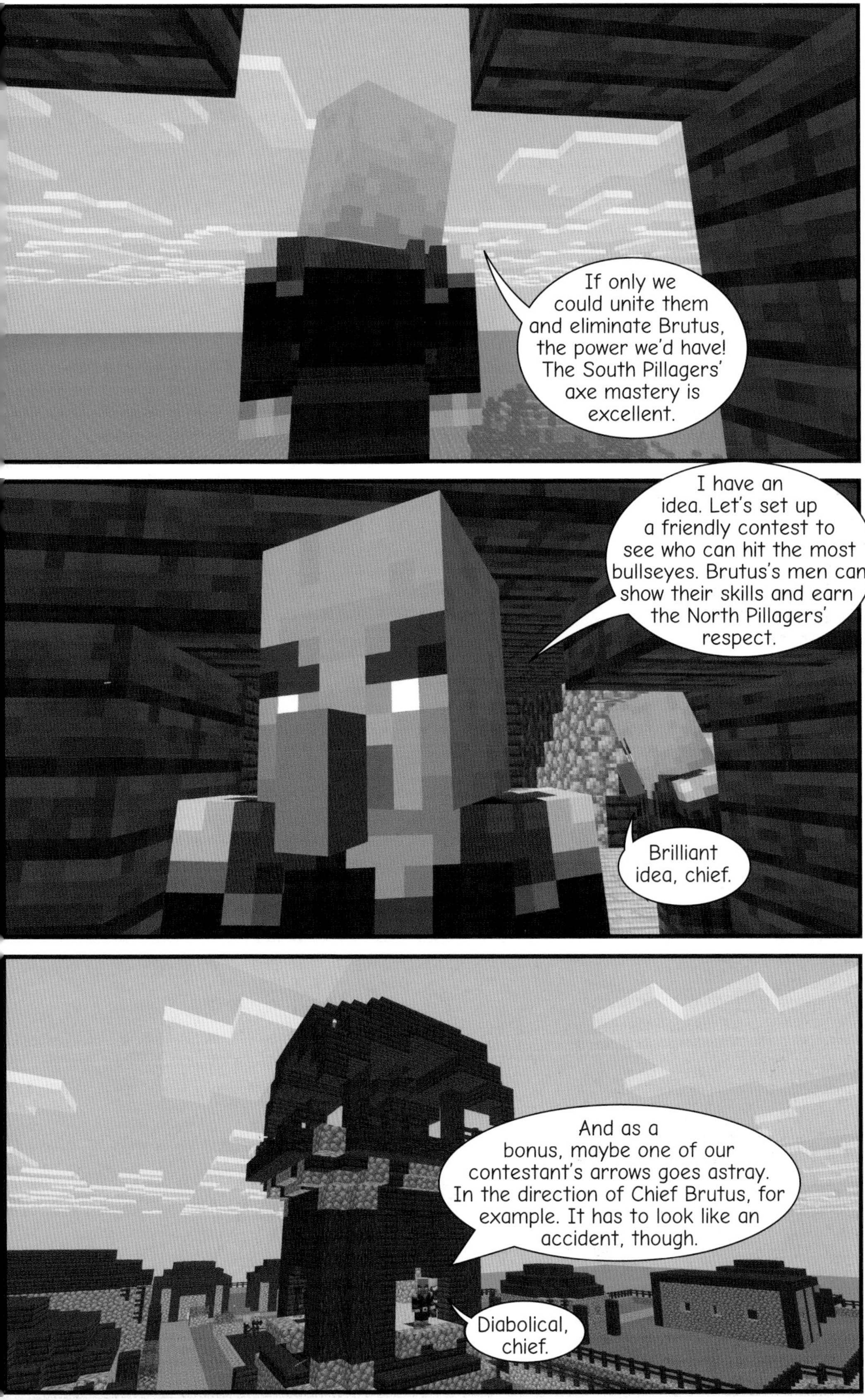
If only we could unite them and eliminate Brutus, the power we'd have! The South Pillagers' axe mastery is excellent.
I have an idea. Let's set up a friendly contest to see who can hit the most bullseyes. Brutus's men can show their skills and earn the North Pillagers' respect.
Brilliant idea, chief.
And as a bonus, maybe one of our contestant's arrows goes astray. In the direction of Chief Brutus, for example. It has to look like an accident, though.
Diabolical, chief.

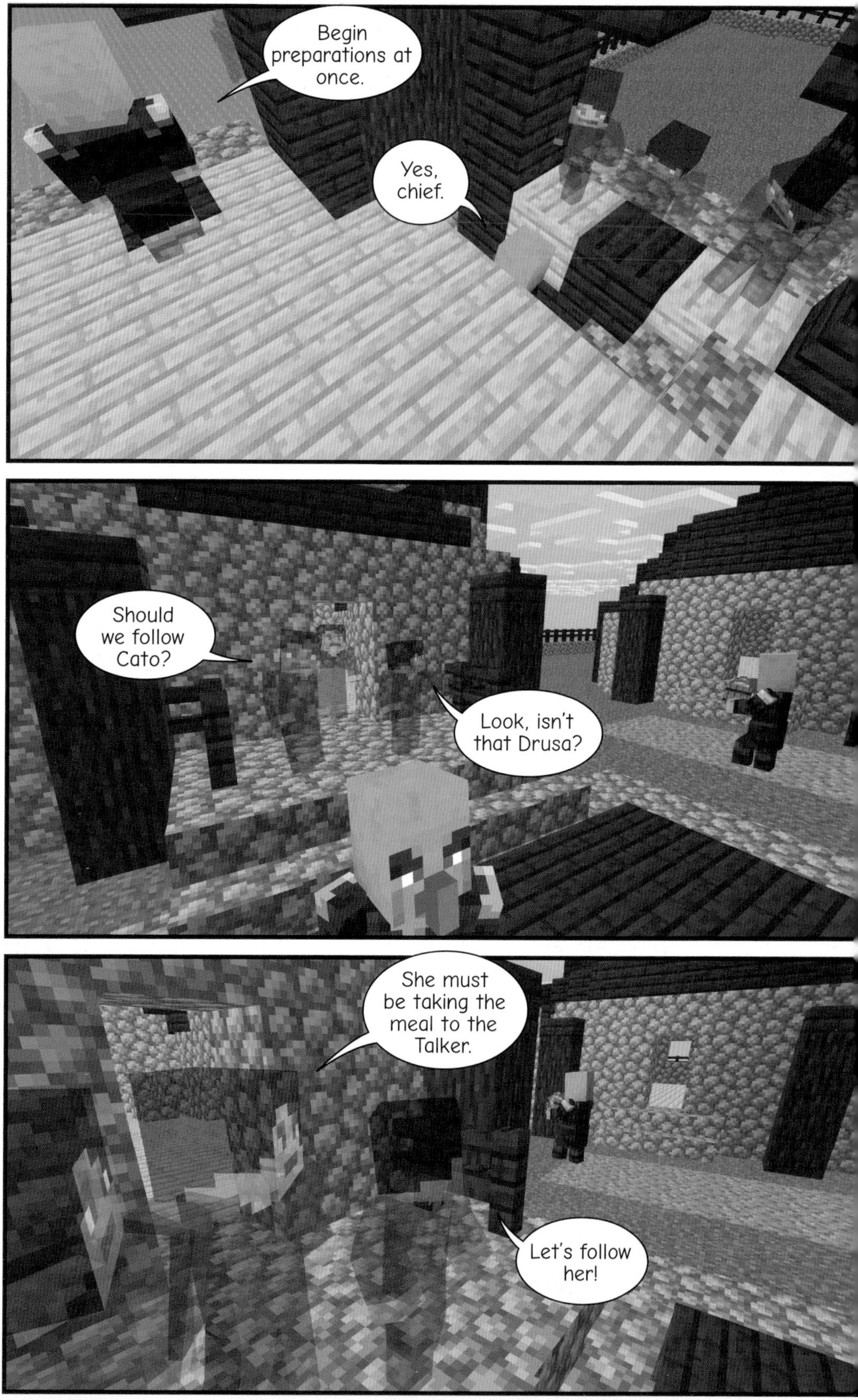
Begin preparations at once.
Yes, chief.
Should we follow Cato?
Look, isn't that Drusa?
She must be taking the meal to the Talker.
Let's follow her!

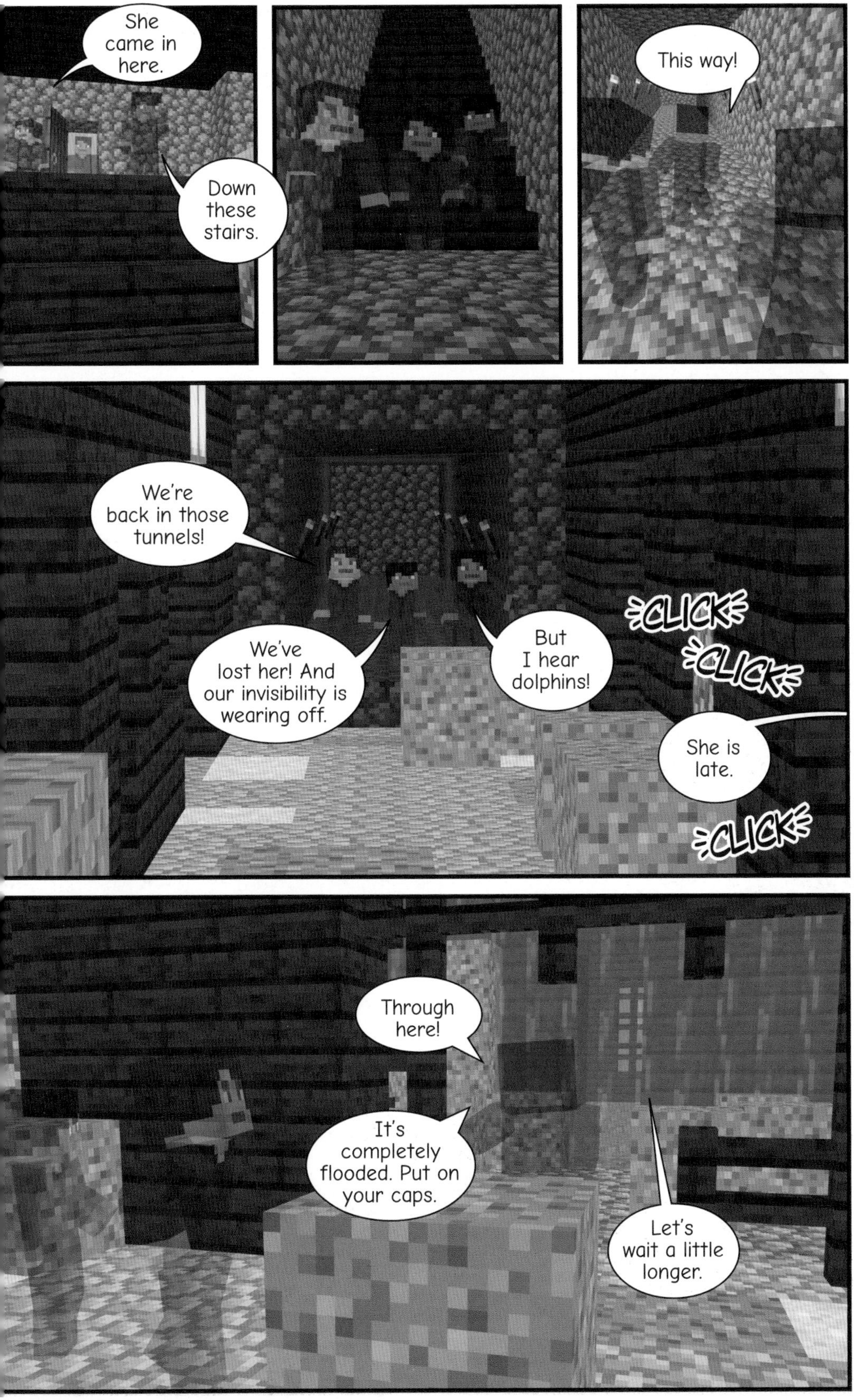
She came in here.
Down these stairs.
This way!
We're back in those tunnels!
We've lost her! And our invisibility is wearing off.
But I hear dolphins!
CLICK
CLICK
She is late.
CLICK
Through here!
It's completely flooded. Put on your caps.
Let's wait a little longer.

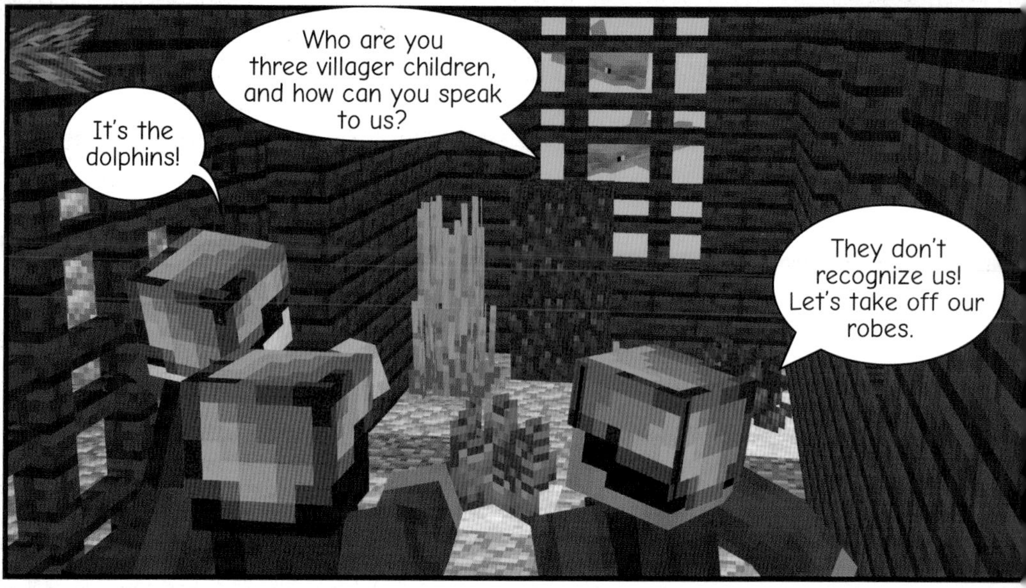
It's the dolphins!
Who are you three villager children, and how can you speak to us?
They don't recognize us! Let's take off our robes.

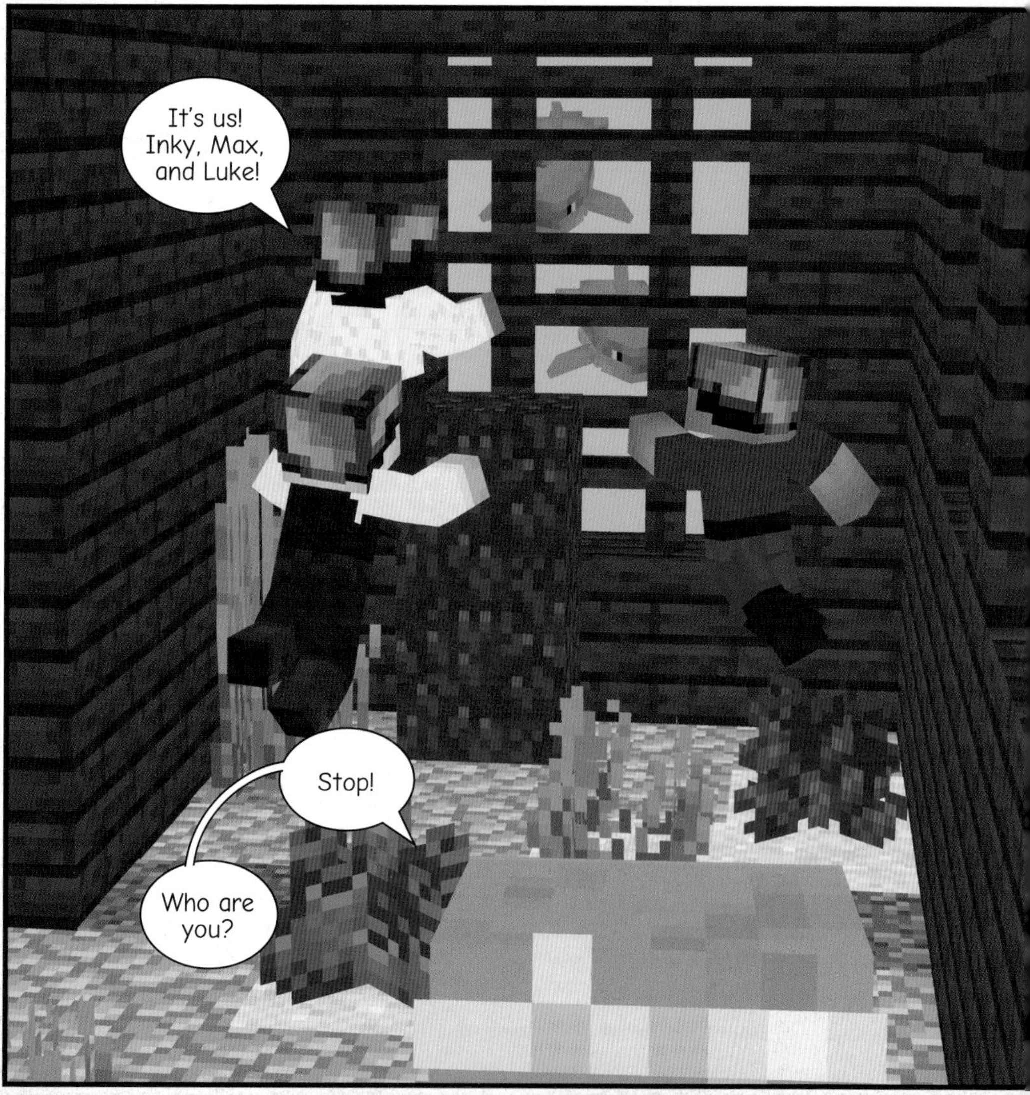
It's us! Inky, Max, and Luke!
Stop!
Who are you?

Chapter 10
Beware of
Stray Arrows

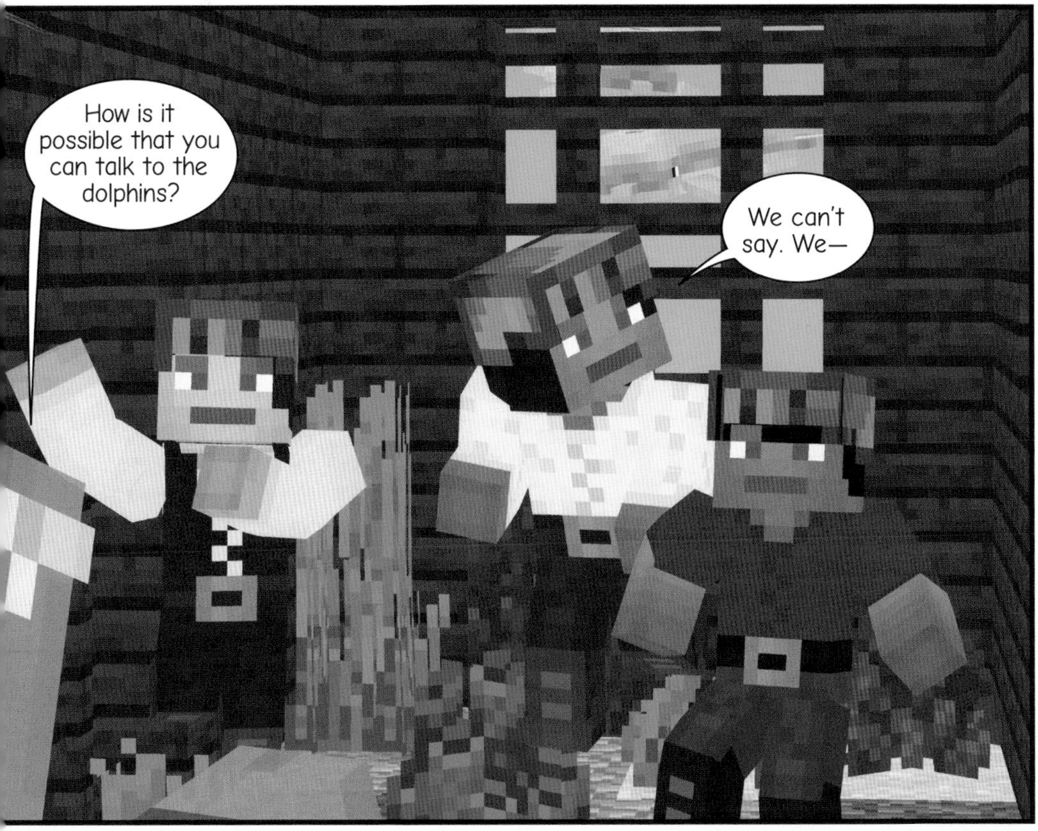
How is it possible that you can talk to the dolphins?
We can't say. We—

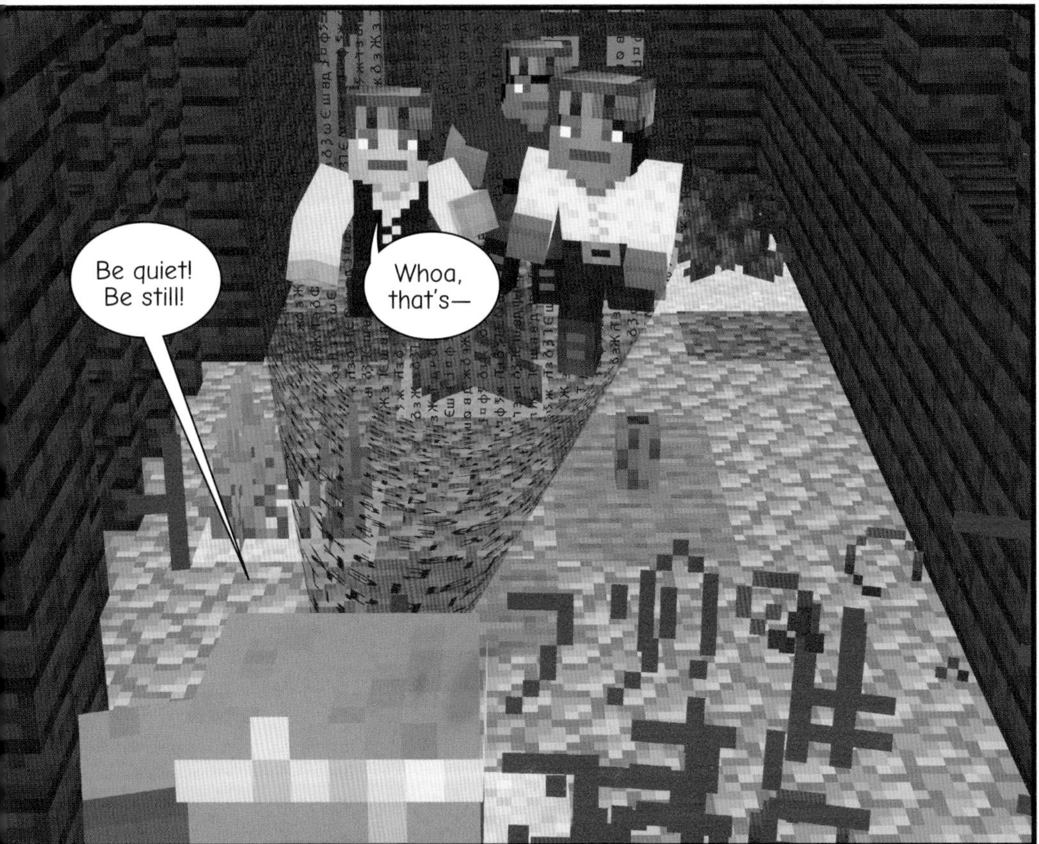
Be quiet! Be still!
Whoa, that's—

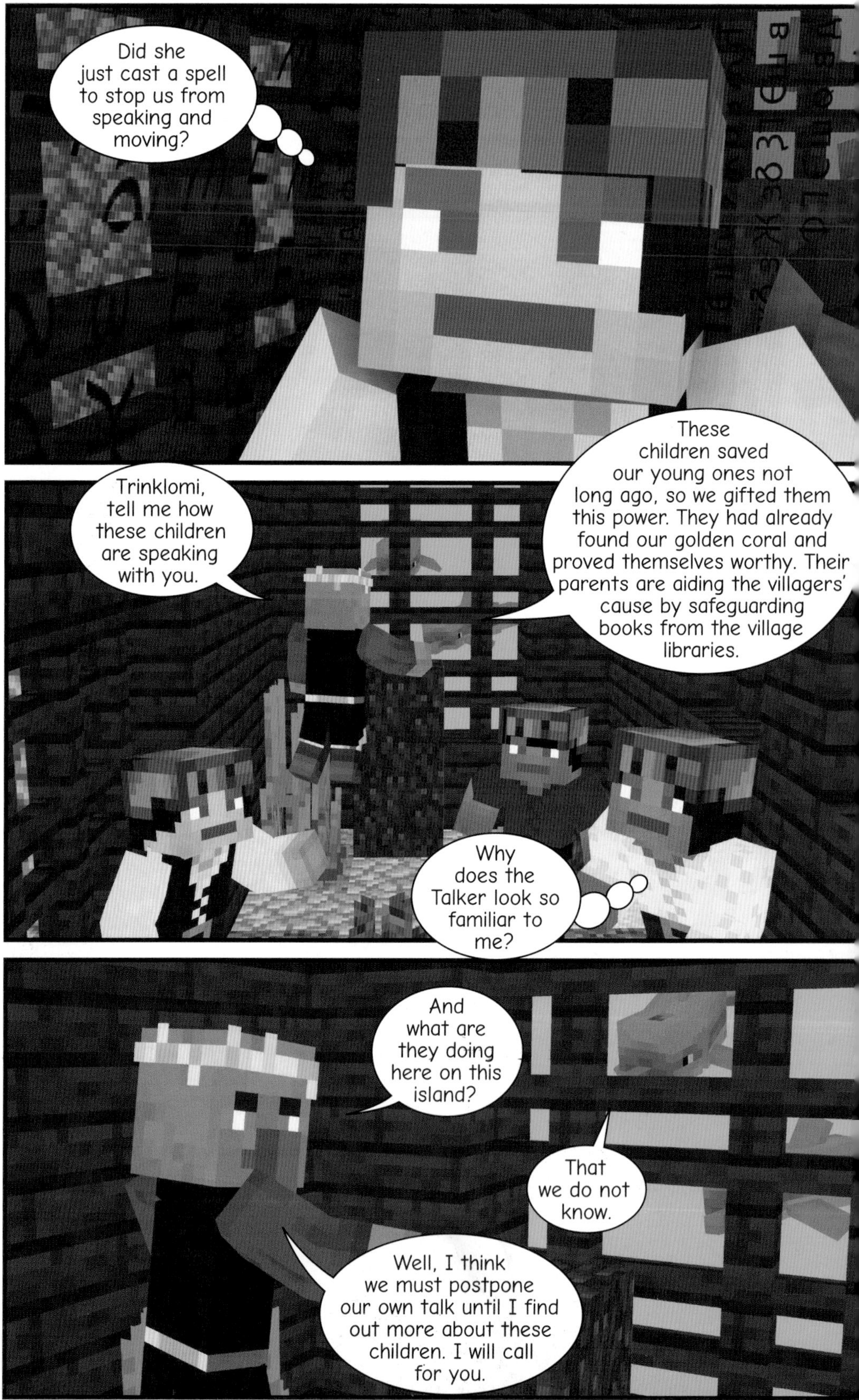
Did she just cast a spell to stop us from speaking and moving?
Trinklomi, tell me how these children are speaking with you.
These children saved our young ones not long ago, so we gifted them this power. They had already found our golden coral and proved themselves worthy. Their parents are aiding the villagers' cause by safeguarding books from the village libraries.
Why does the Talker look so familiar to me?
And what are they doing here on this island?
That we do not know.
Well, I think we must postpone our own talk until I find out more about these children. I will call for you.

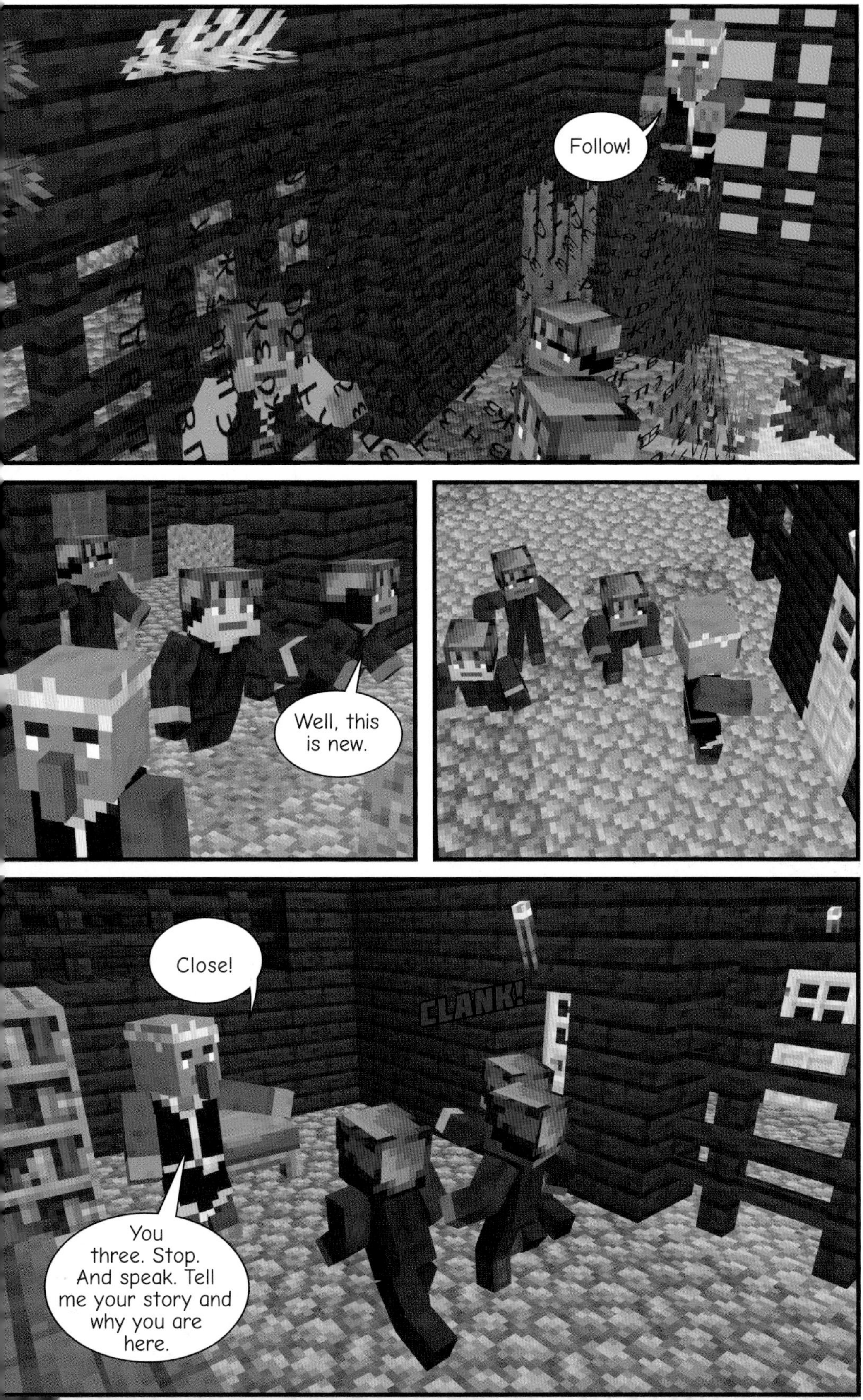
Follow!
Well, this is new.
Close!
CLANK!
You three. Stop. And speak. Tell me your story and why you are here.

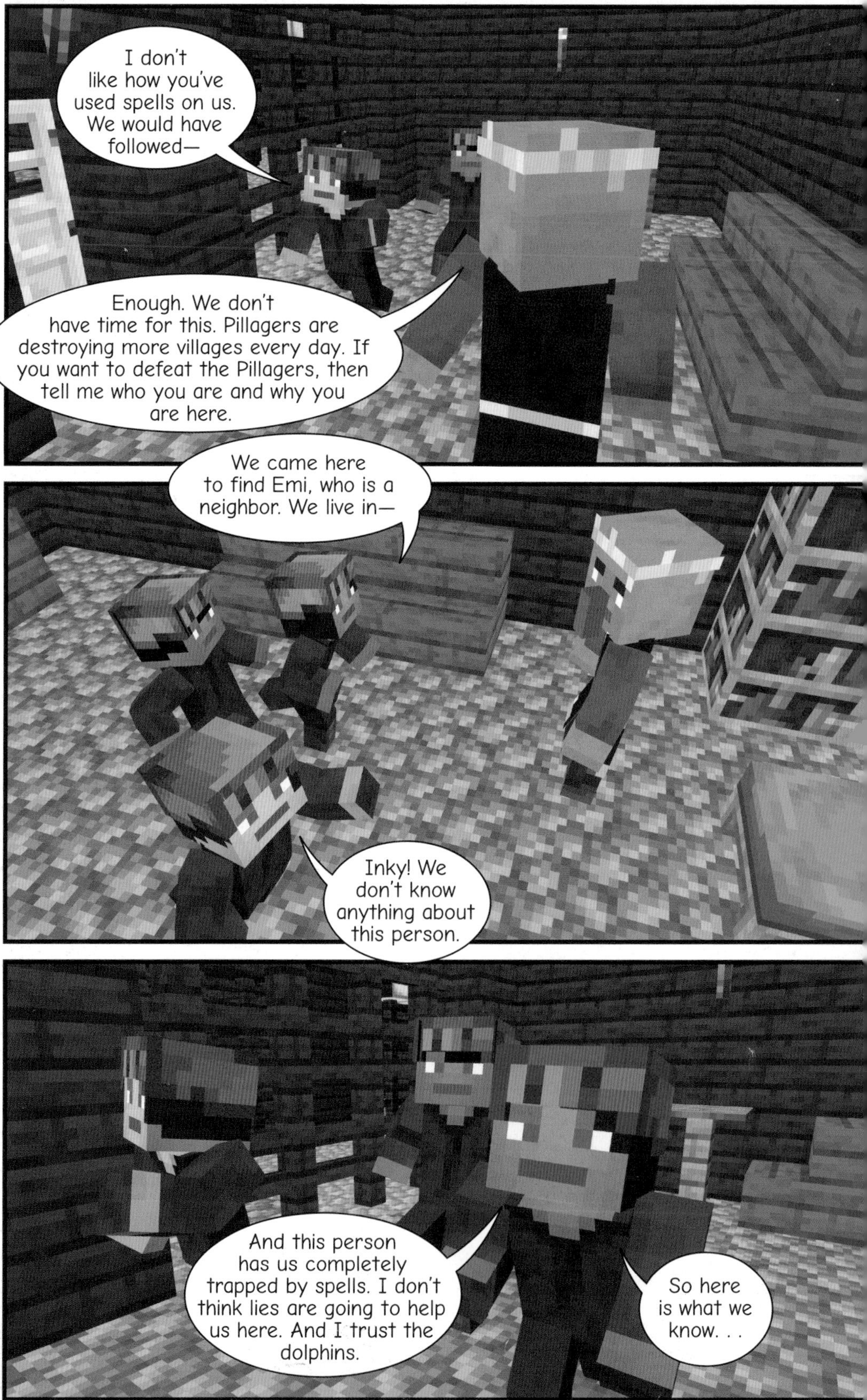
I don't like how you've used spells on us. We would have followed—
Enough. We don't have time for this. Pillagers are destroying more villages every day. If you want to defeat the Pillagers, then tell me who you are and why you are here.
We came here to find Emi, who is a neighbor. We live in—
Inky! We don't know anything about this person.
And this person has us completely trapped by spells. I don't think lies are going to help us here. And I trust the dolphins.
So here is what we know. . .

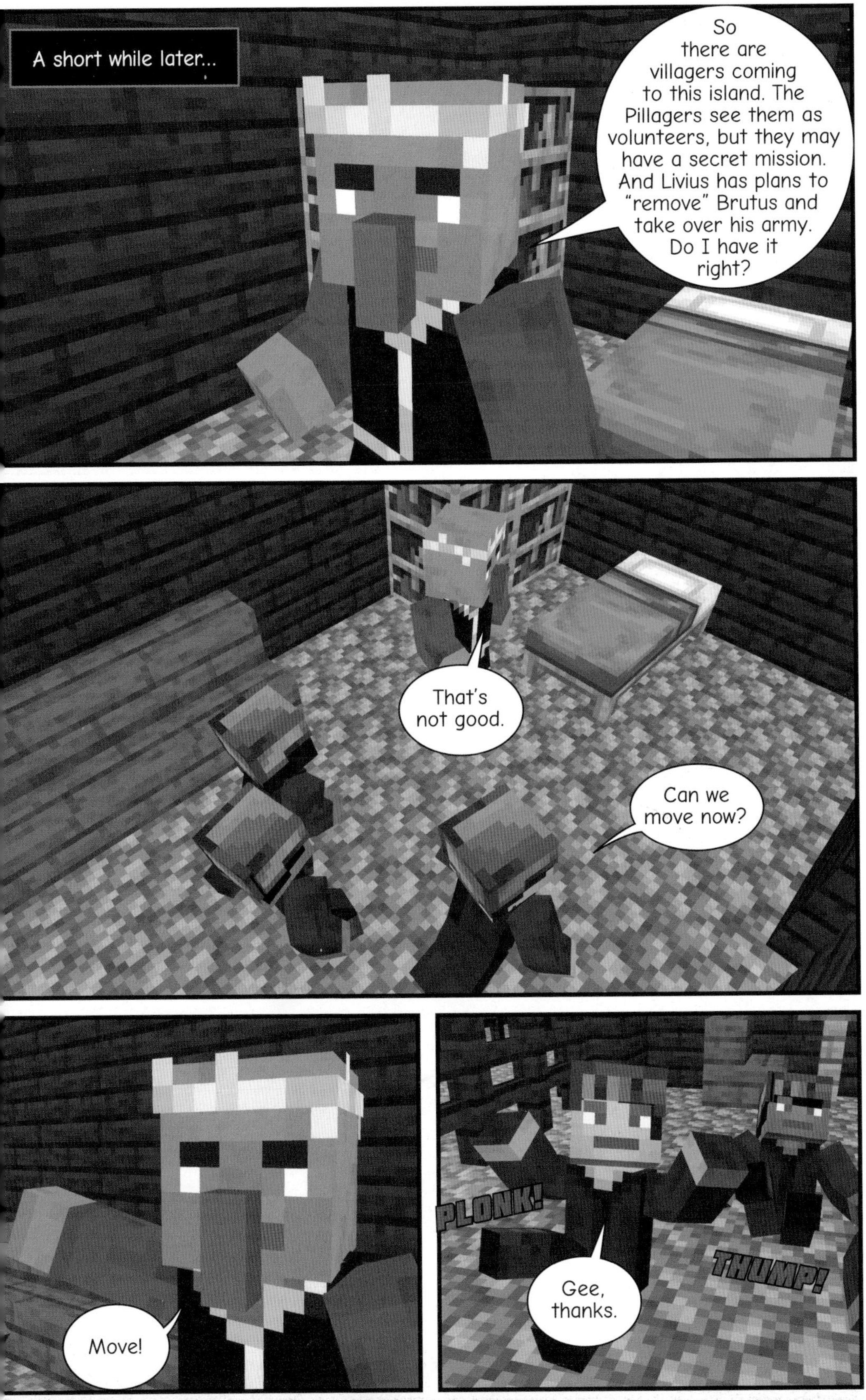
A short while later...
So there are villagers coming to this island. The Pillagers see them as volunteers, but they may have a secret mission. And Livius has plans to "remove" Brutus and take over his army. Do I have it right?
That's not good.
Can we move now?
Move!
PLONK!
THUMP!
Gee, thanks.

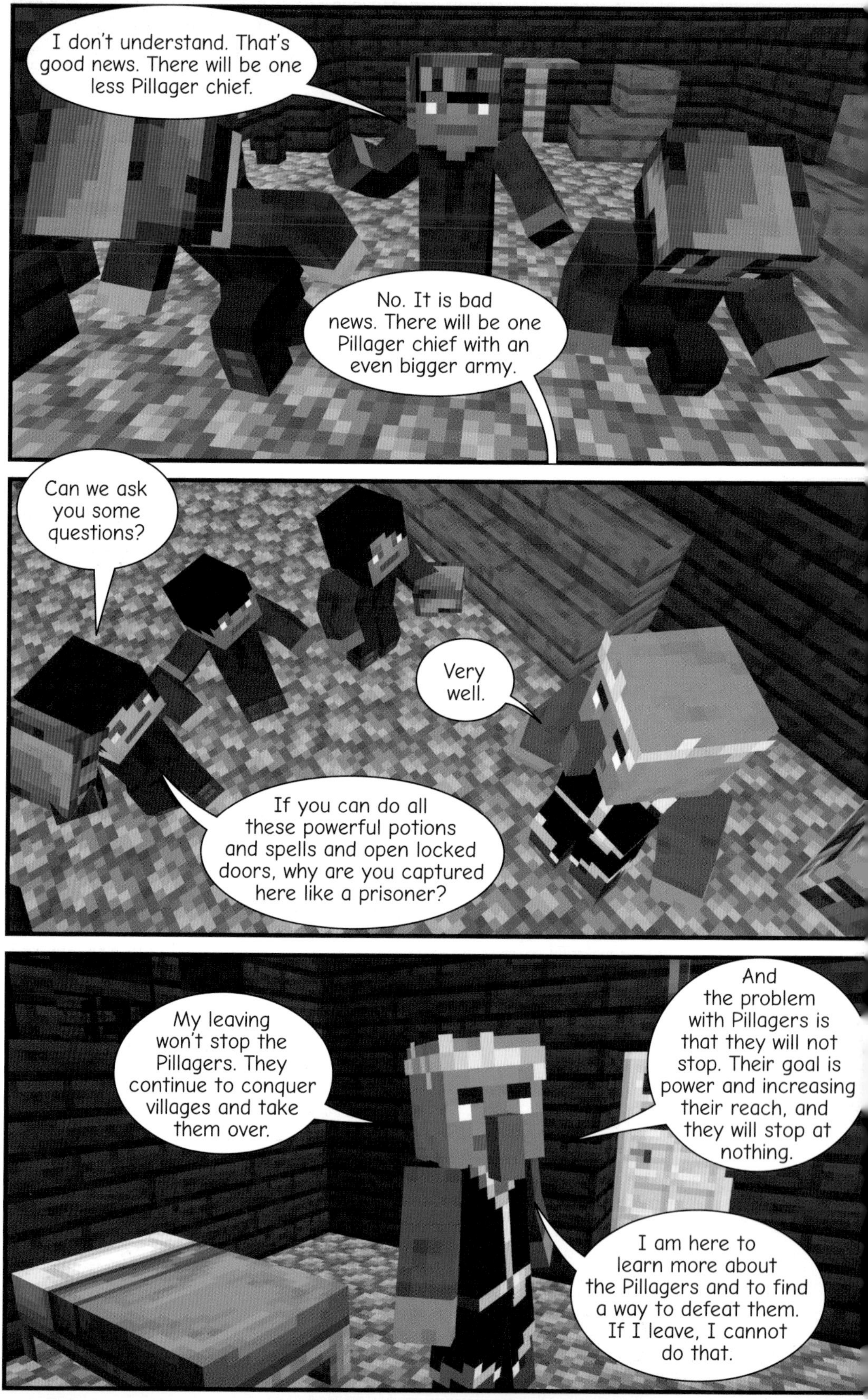

I don't understand. That's good news. There will be one less Pillager chief.
No. It is bad news. There will be one Pillager chief with an even bigger army.
Can we ask you some questions?
Very well.
If you can do all these powerful potions and spells and open locked doors, why are you captured here like a prisoner?
My leaving won't stop the Pillagers. They continue to conquer villages and take them over.
And the problem with Pillagers is that they will not stop. Their goal is power and increasing their reach, and they will stop at nothing.
I am here to learn more about the Pillagers and to find a way to defeat them. If I leave, I cannot do that.

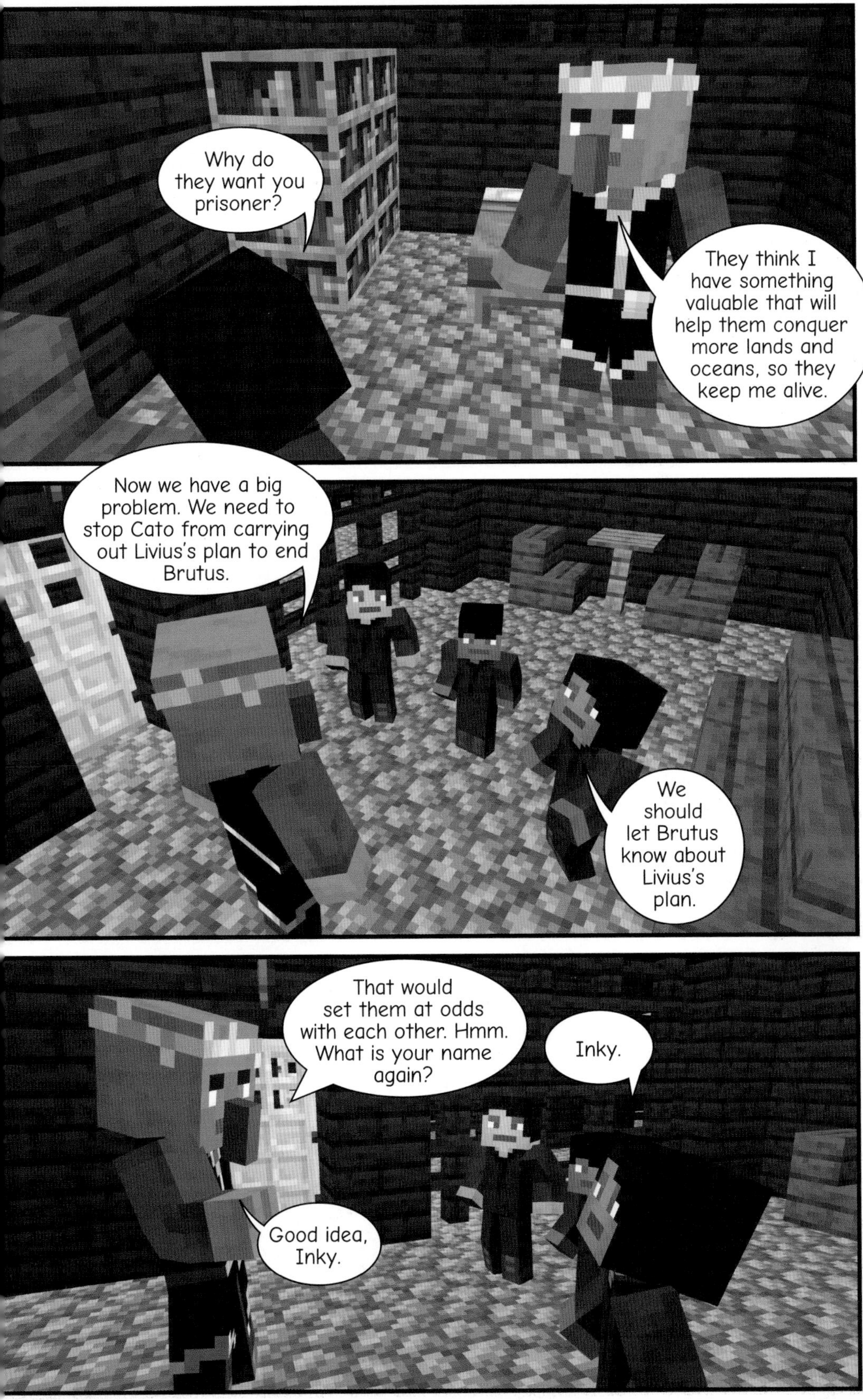
Why do they want you prisoner?
They think I have something valuable that will help them conquer more lands and oceans, so they keep me alive.
Now we have a big problem. We need to stop Cato from carrying out Livius's plan to end Brutus.
We should let Brutus know about Livius's plan.
That would set them at odds with each other. Hmm. What is your name again?
Inky.
Good idea, Inky.

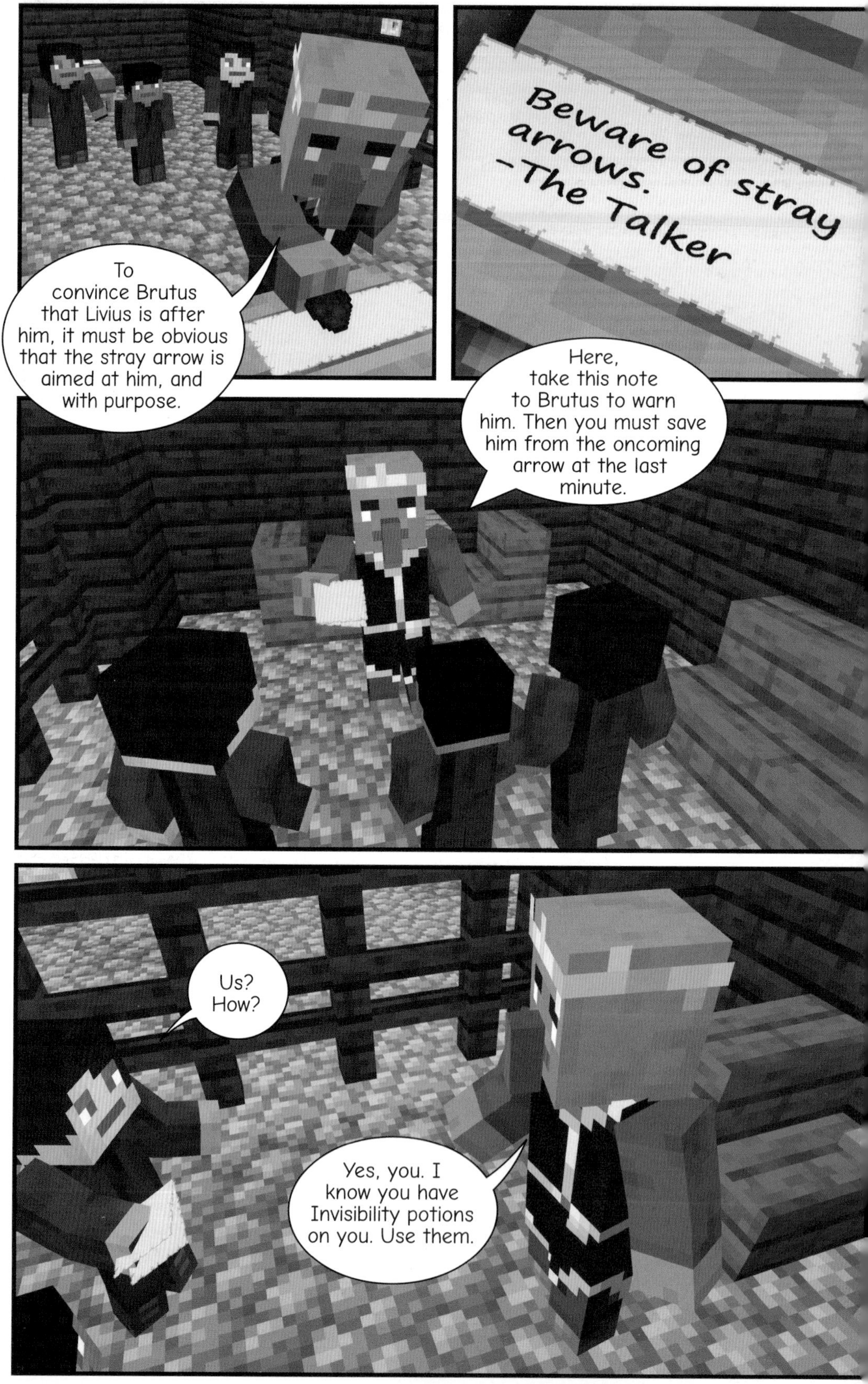
To convince Brutus that Livius is after him, it must be obvious that the stray arrow is aimed at him, and with purpose.
Beware of stray arrows. -The Talker
Here, take this note to Brutus to warn him. Then you must save him from the oncoming arrow at the last minute.
Us? How?
Yes, you. I know you have Invisibility potions on you. Use them.

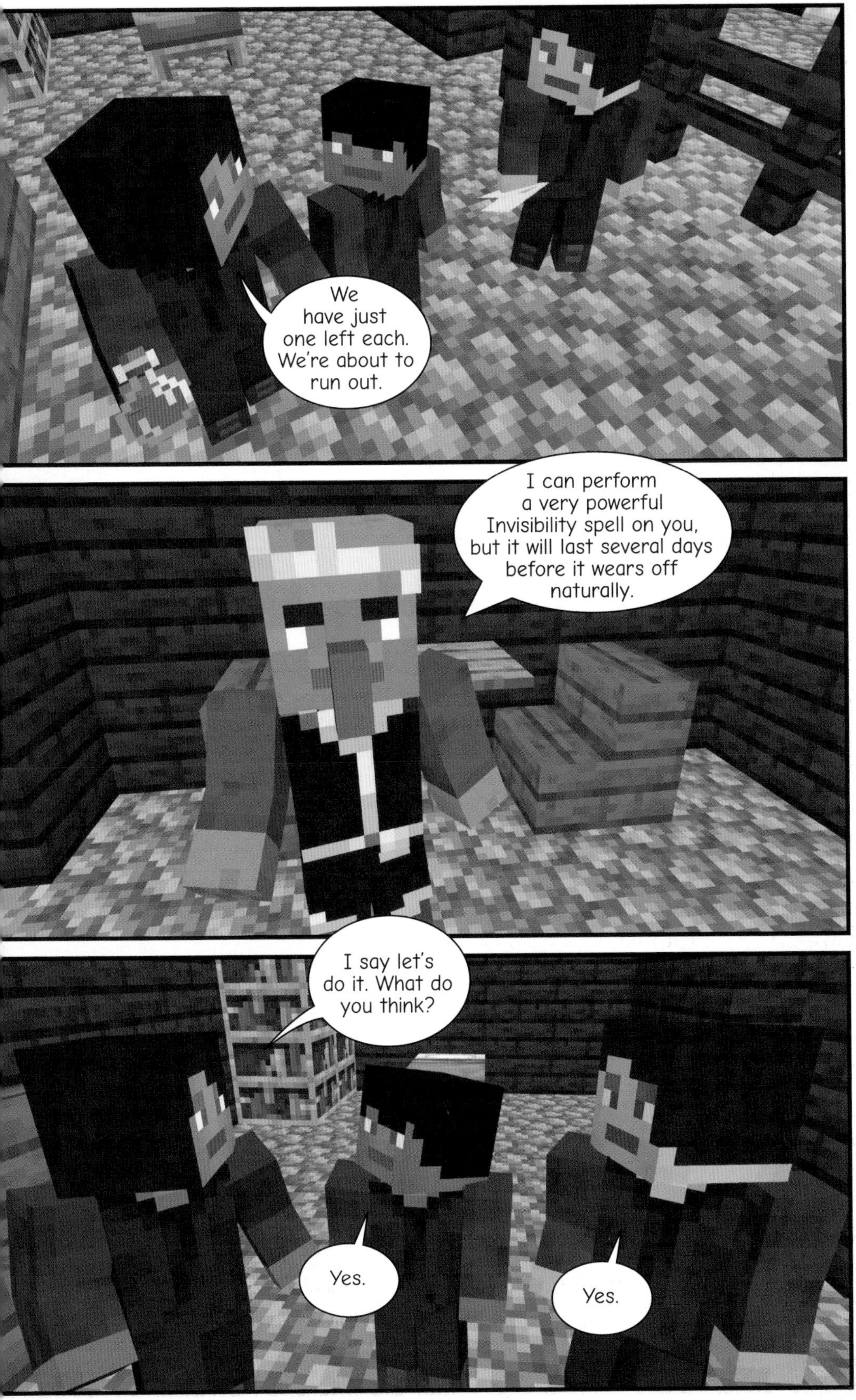

We have just one left each. We're about to run out.
I can perform a very powerful Invisibility spell on you, but it will last several days before it wears off naturally.
I say let's do it. What do you think?
Yes.
Yes.

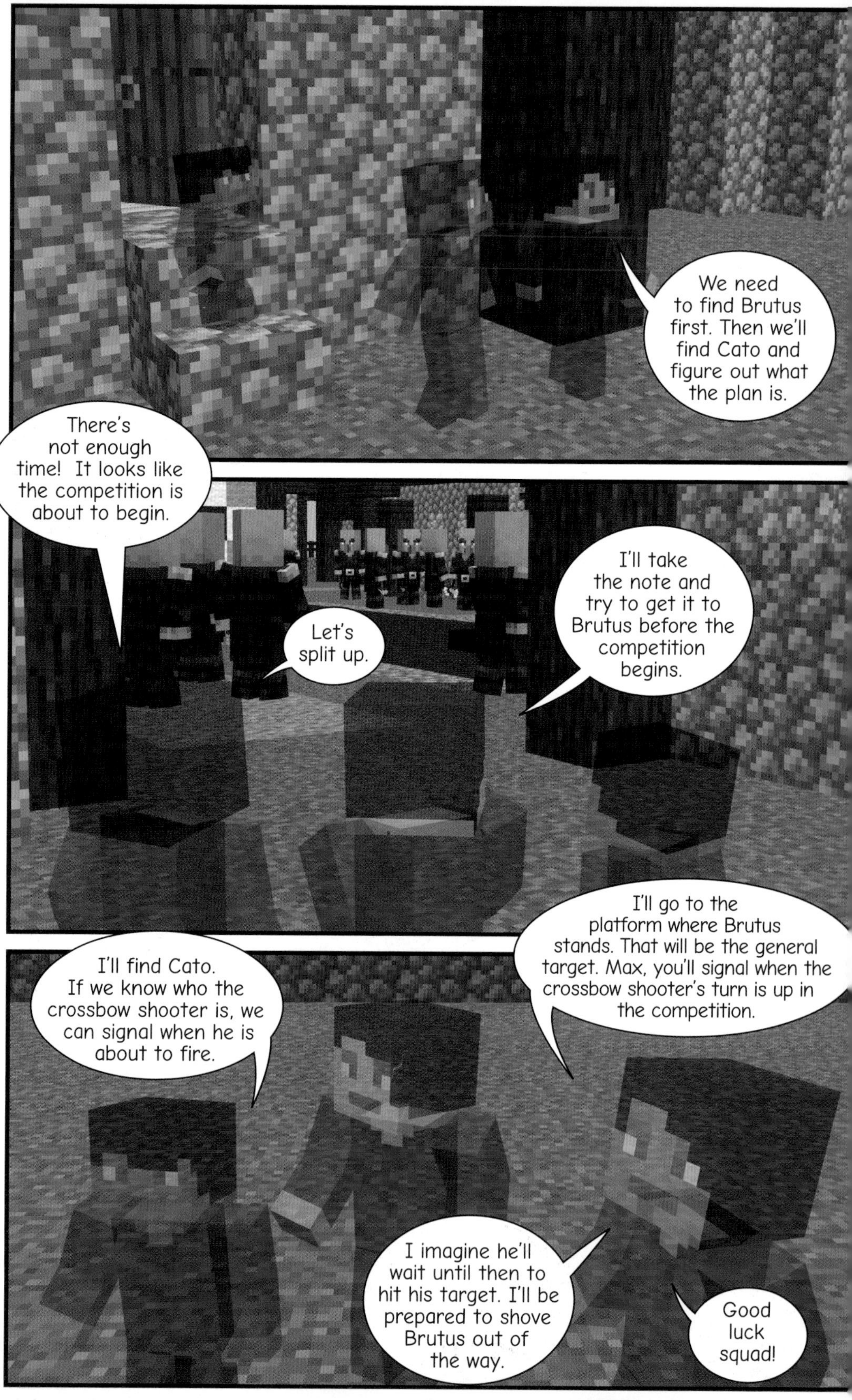
We need to find Brutus first. Then we'll find Cato and figure out what the plan is.
There's not enough time! It looks like the competition is about to begin.
Let's split up.
I'll take the note and try to get it to Brutus before the competition begins.
I'll find Cato. If we know who the crossbow shooter is, we can signal when he is about to fire.
I'll go to the platform where Brutus stands. That will be the general target. Max, you'll signal when the crossbow shooter's turn is up in the competition.
I imagine he'll wait until then to hit his target. I'll be prepared to shove Brutus out of the way.
Good luck squad!

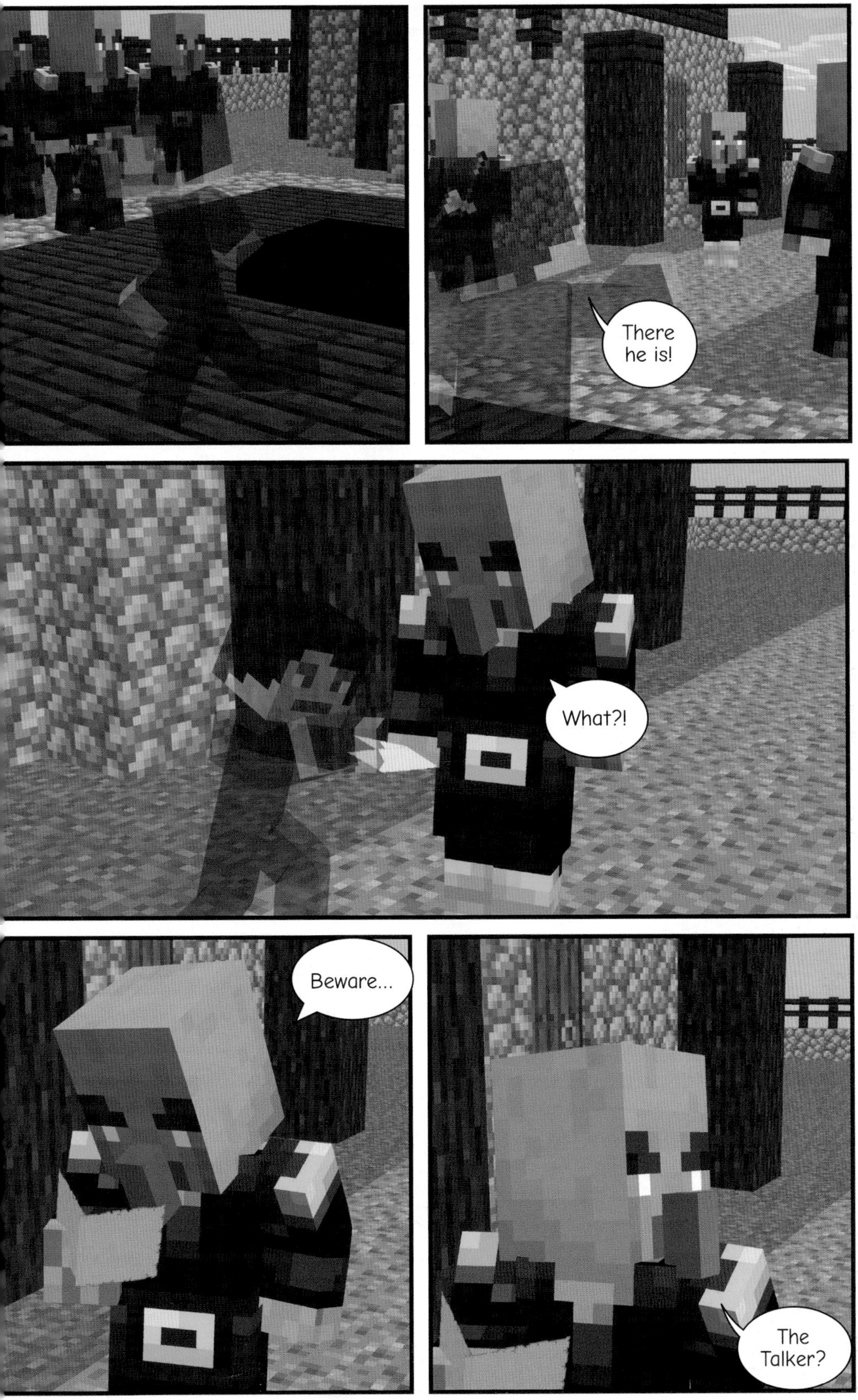
There he is!
What?!
Beware...
The Talker?

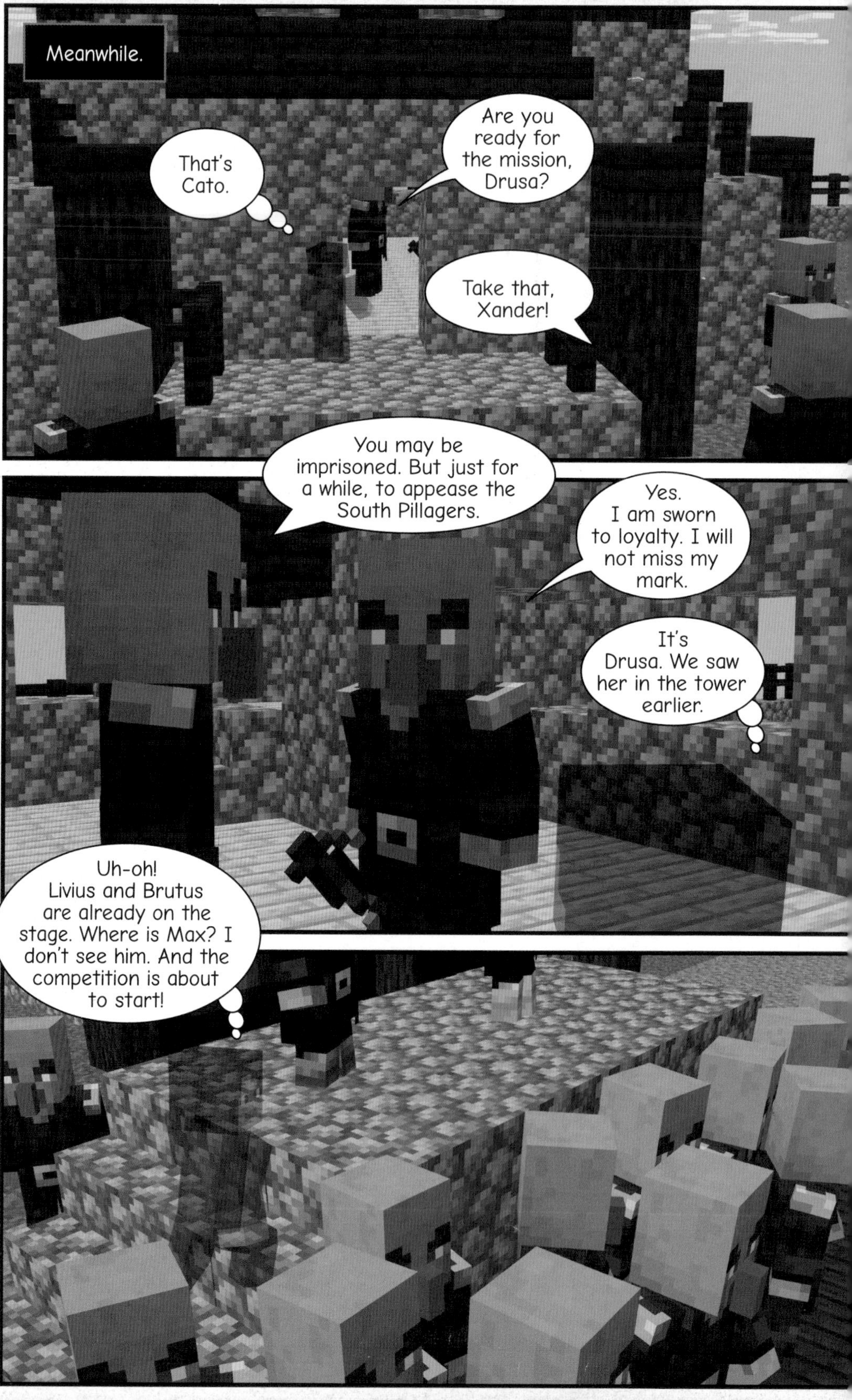

Meanwhile.
That's Cato.
Are you ready for the mission, Drusa?
Take that, Xander!
You may be imprisoned. But just for a while, to appease the South Pillagers.
Yes. I am sworn to loyalty. I will not miss my mark.
It's Drusa. We saw her in the tower earlier.
Uh-oh! Livius and Brutus are already on the stage. Where is Max? I don't see him. And the competition is about to start!

Chapter 11
Crossbows
v. Axes

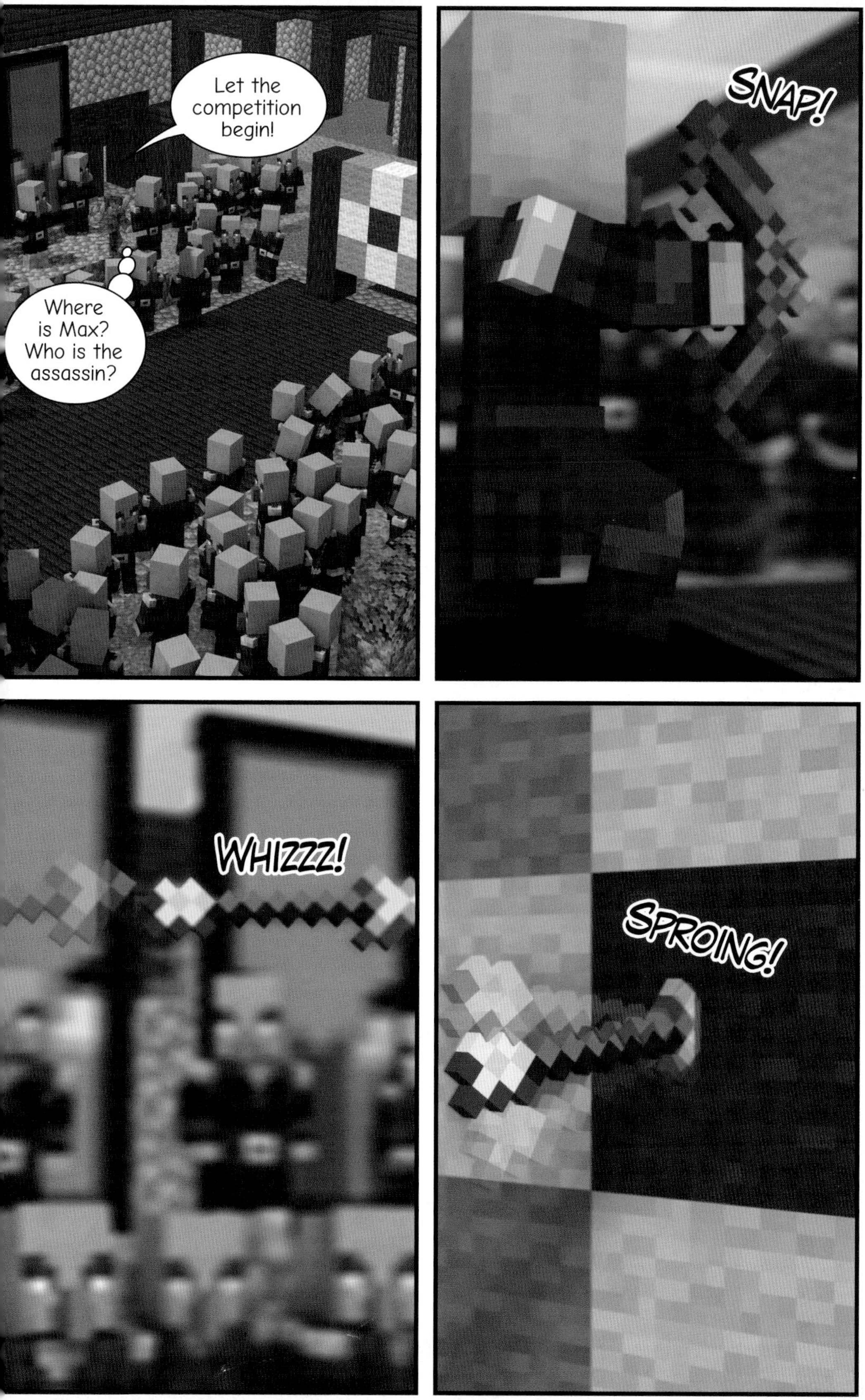
Let the competition begin!
Where is Max? Who is the assassin?
SNAP!
WHIZZZ!
SPROING!

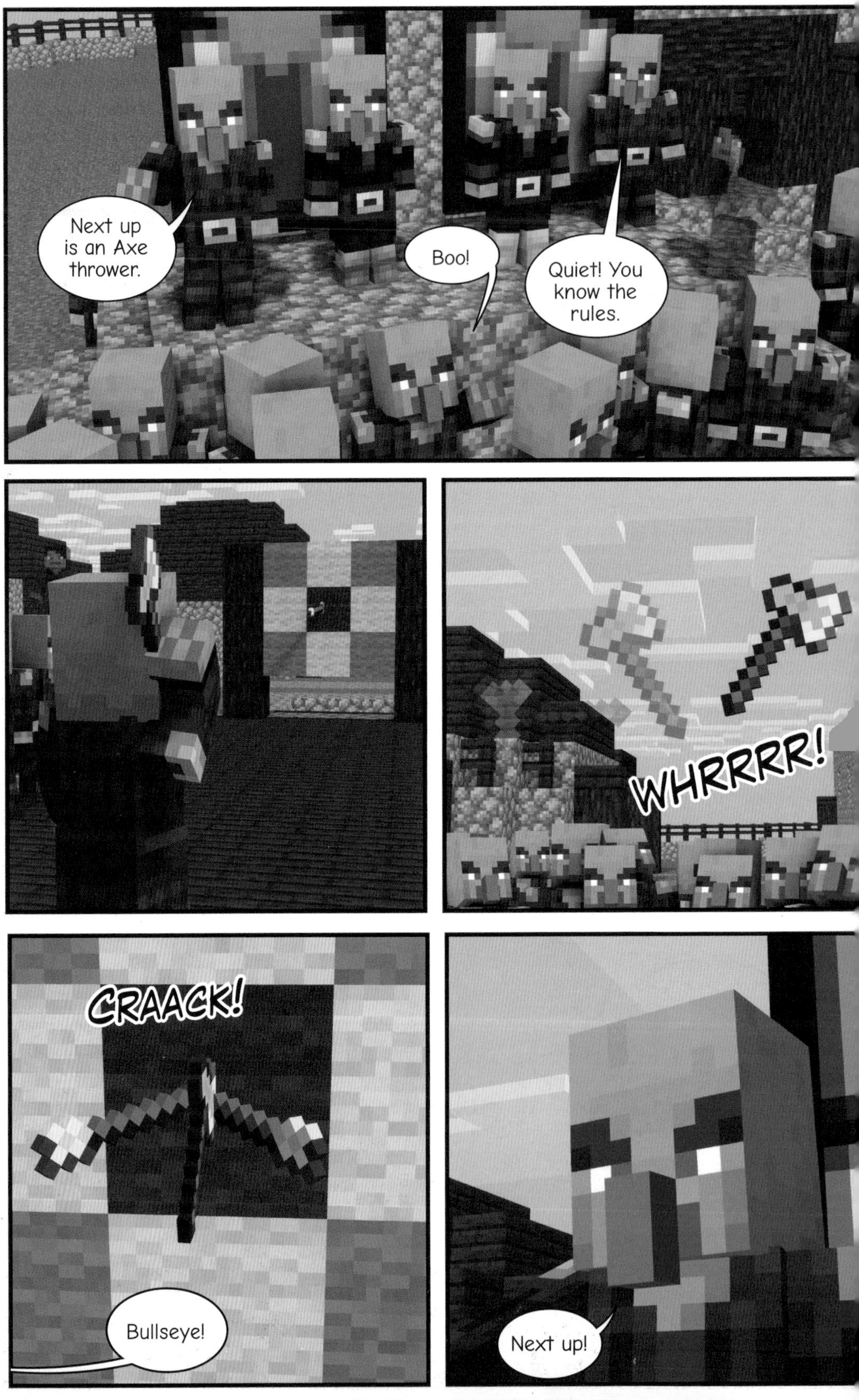
Next up is an Axe thrower.
Boo!
Quiet! You know the rules.
WHRRRR!
CRAACK!
Bullseye!
Next up!

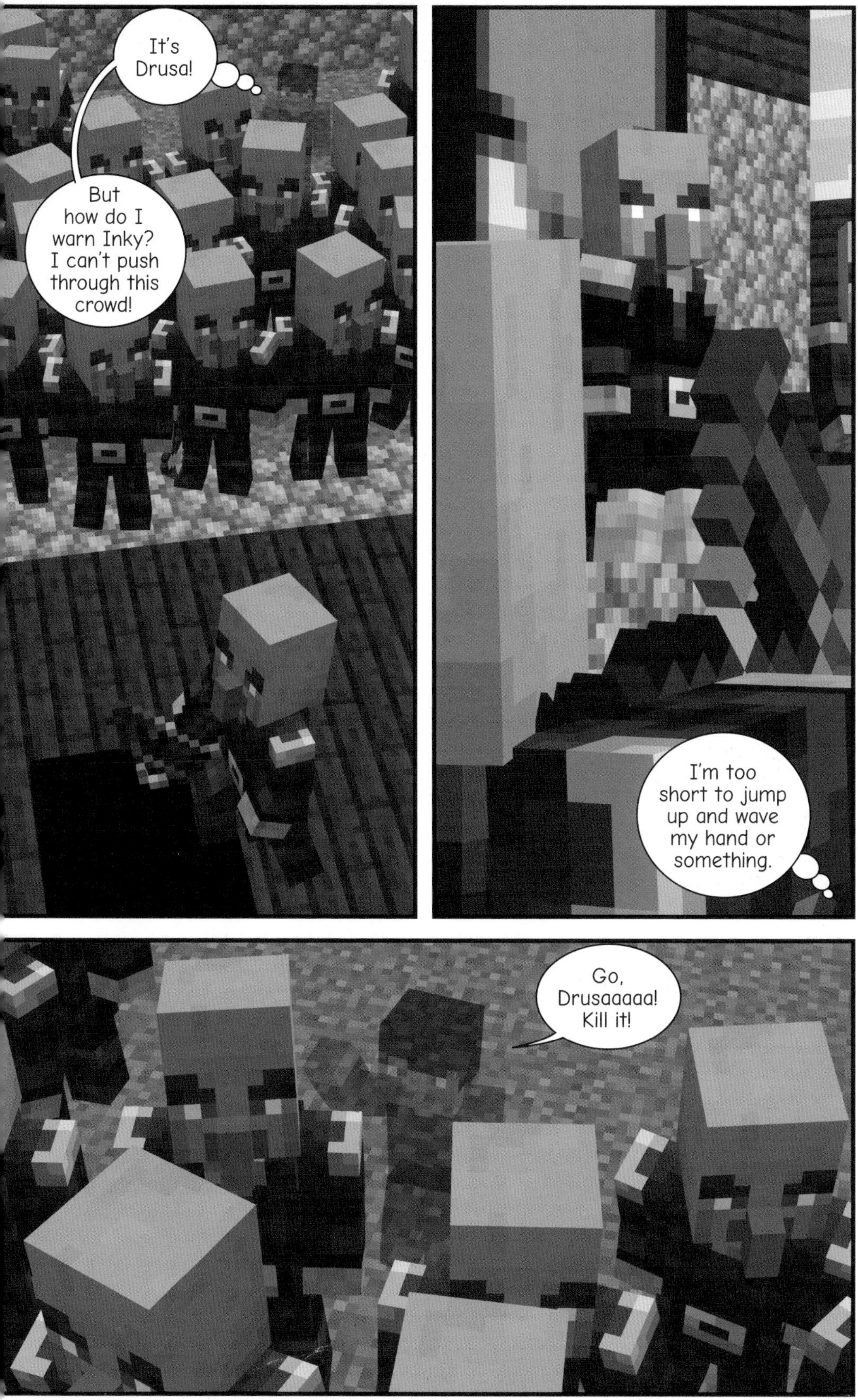
It's Drusa!
But how do I warn Inky? I can't push through this crowd!
I'm too short to jump up and wave my hand or something.
Go, Drusaaaaa! Kill it!

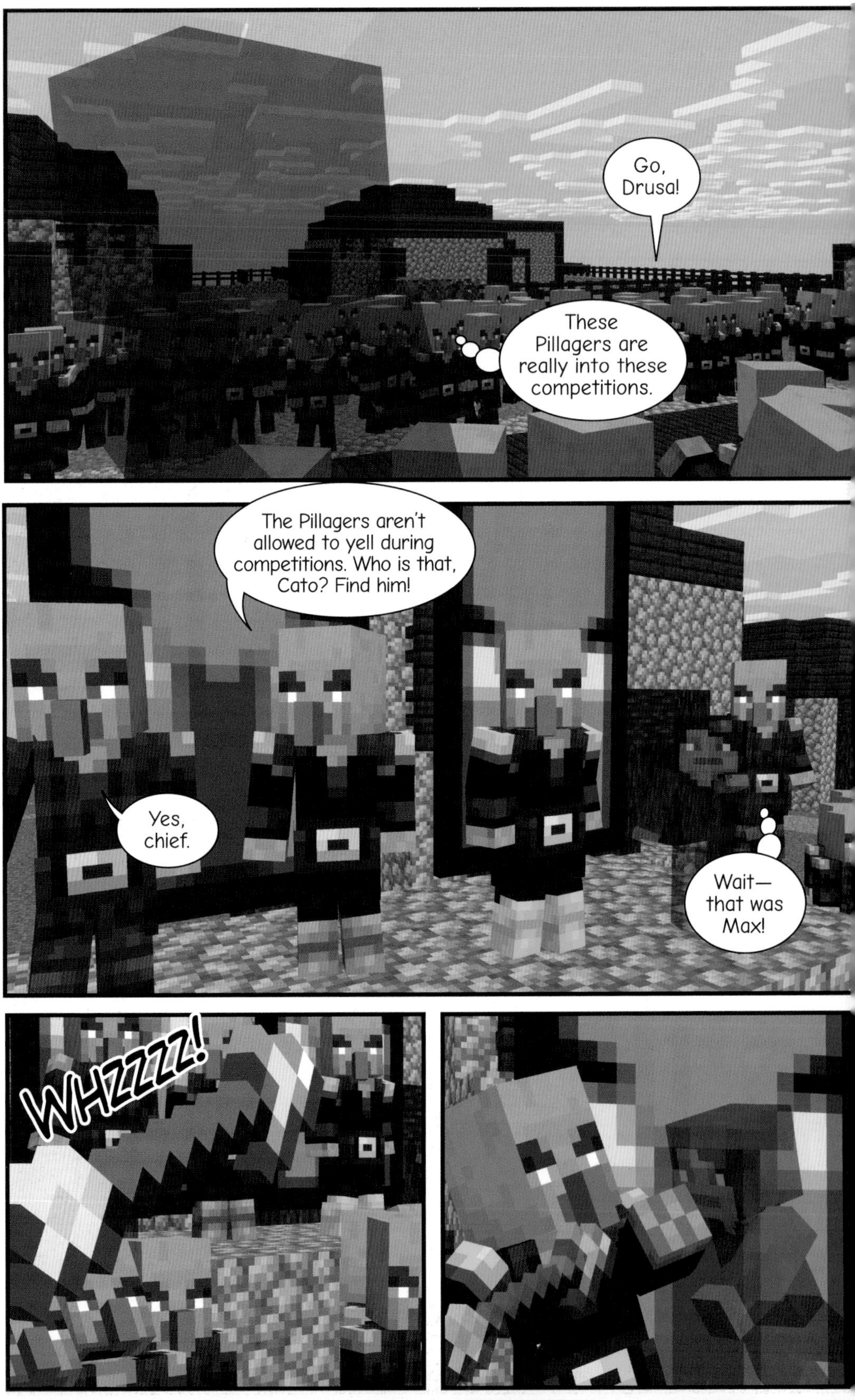
Go, Drusa!
These Pillagers are really into these competitions.
The Pillagers aren't allowed to yell during competitions. Who is that, Cato? Find him!
Yes, chief.
Wait—that was Max!
WHZZZZ!

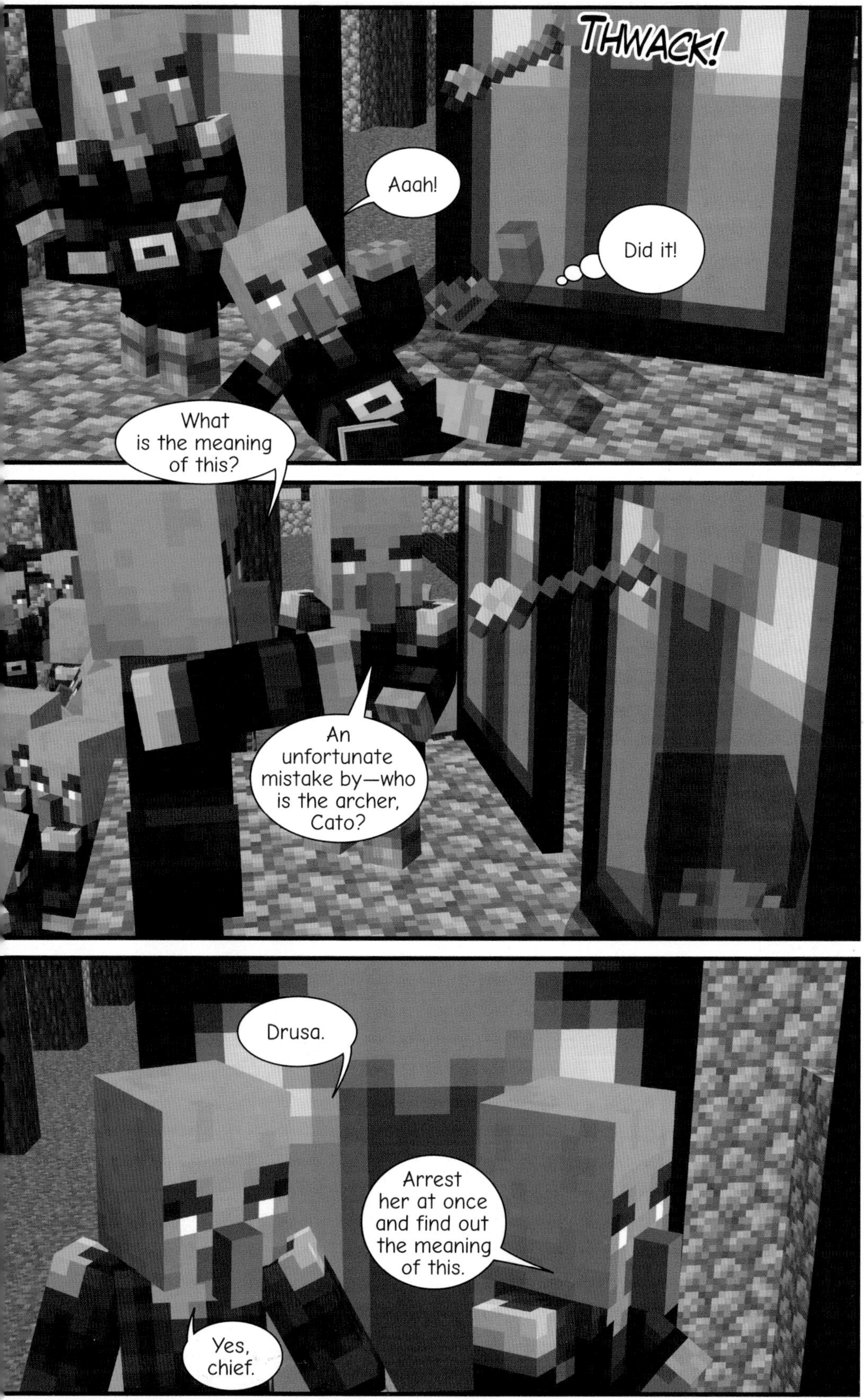
THWACK!
Aaah!
Did it!
What is the meaning of this?
An unfortunate mistake by—who is the archer, Cato?
Drusa.
Arrest her at once and find out the meaning of this.
Yes, chief.

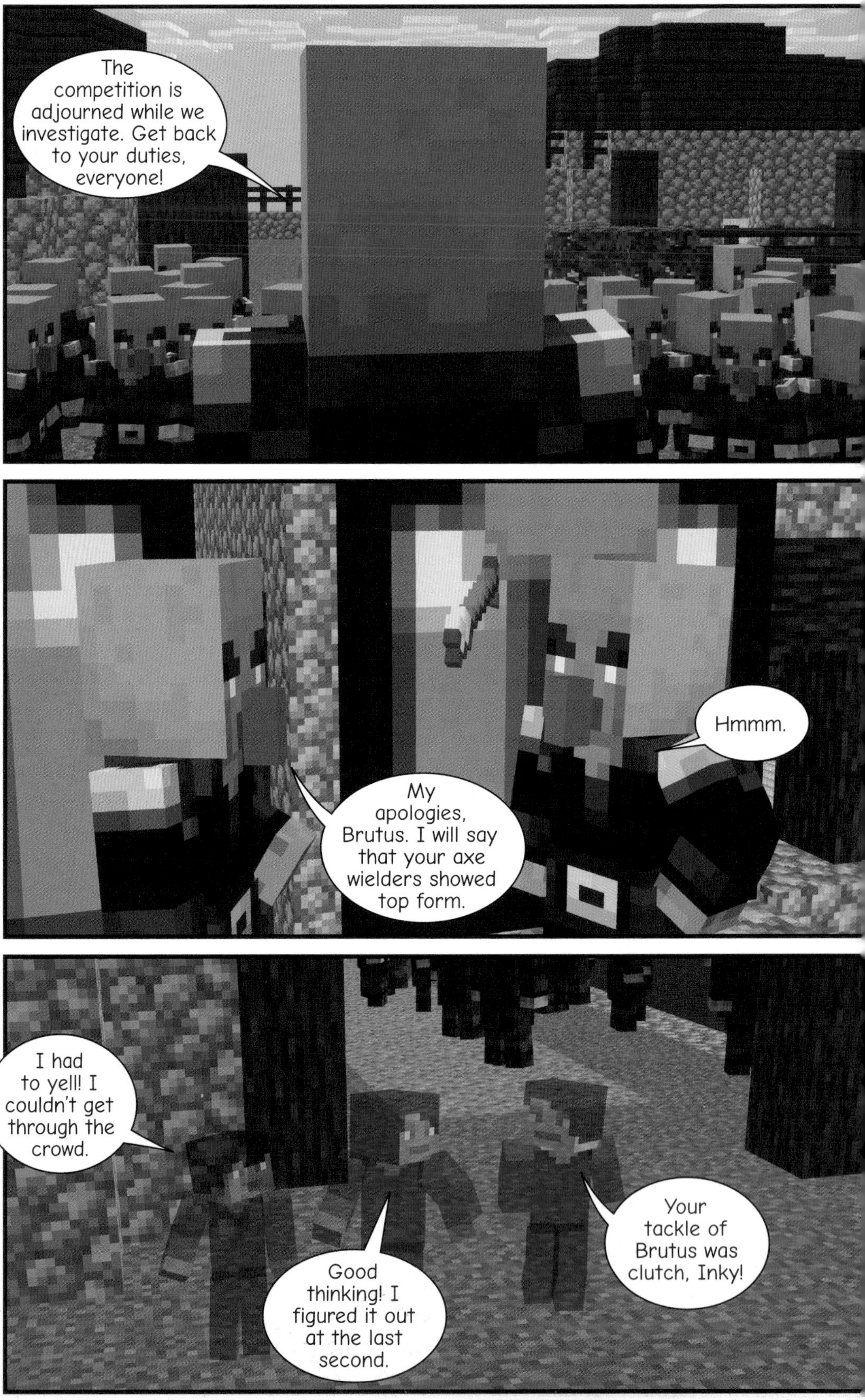
The competition is adjourned while we investigate. Get back to your duties, everyone!
My apologies, Brutus. I will say that your axe wielders showed top form.
Hmmm.
I had to yell! I couldn't get through the crowd.
Good thinking! I figured it out at the last second.
Your tackle of Brutus was clutch, Inky!

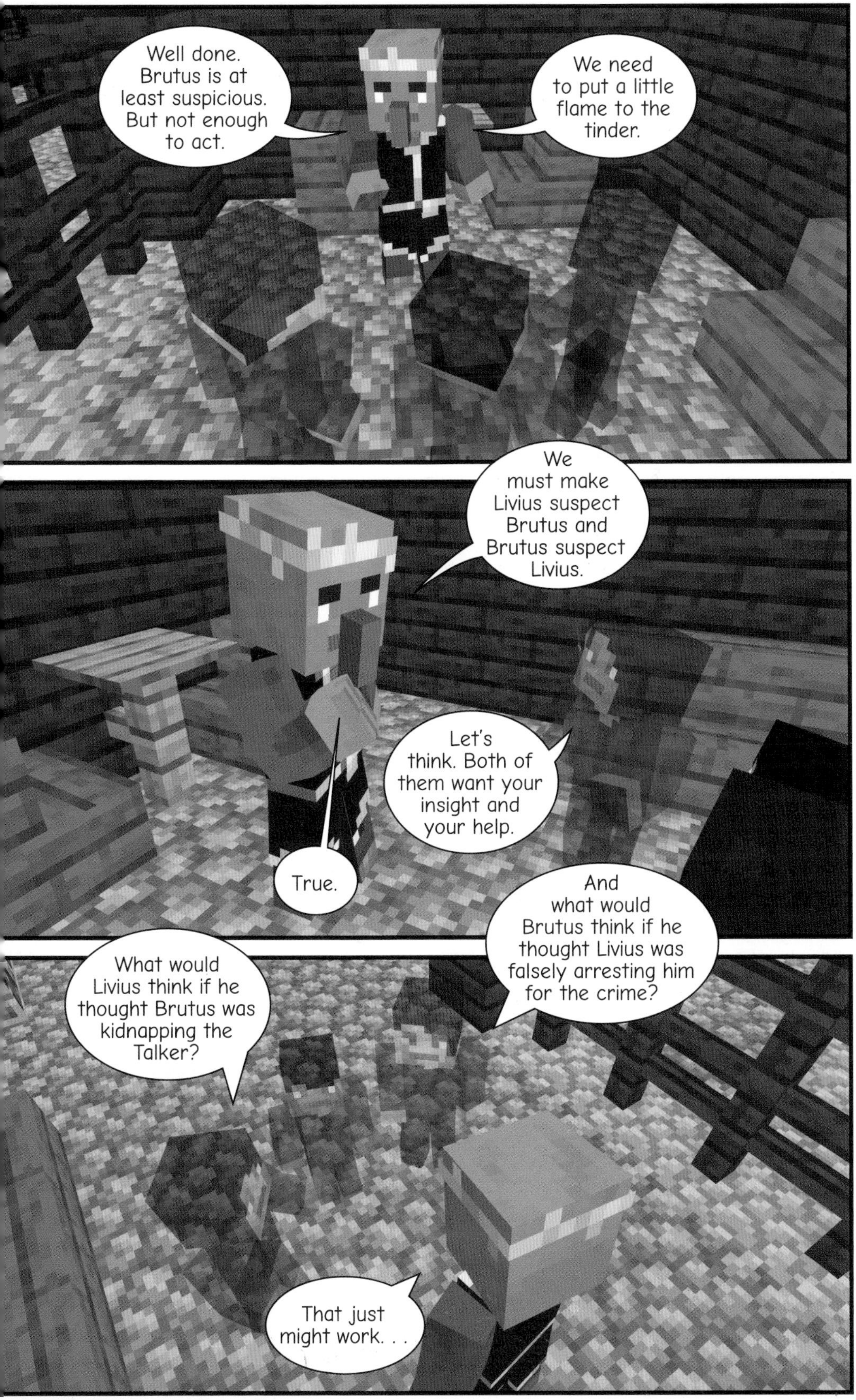
Well done. Brutus is at least suspicious. But not enough to act.
We need to put a little flame to the tinder.
We must make Livius suspect Brutus and Brutus suspect Livius.
Let's think. Both of them want your insight and your help.
True.
What would Livius think if he thought Brutus was kidnapping the Talker?
And what would Brutus think if he thought Livius was falsely arresting him for the crime?
That just might work. . .

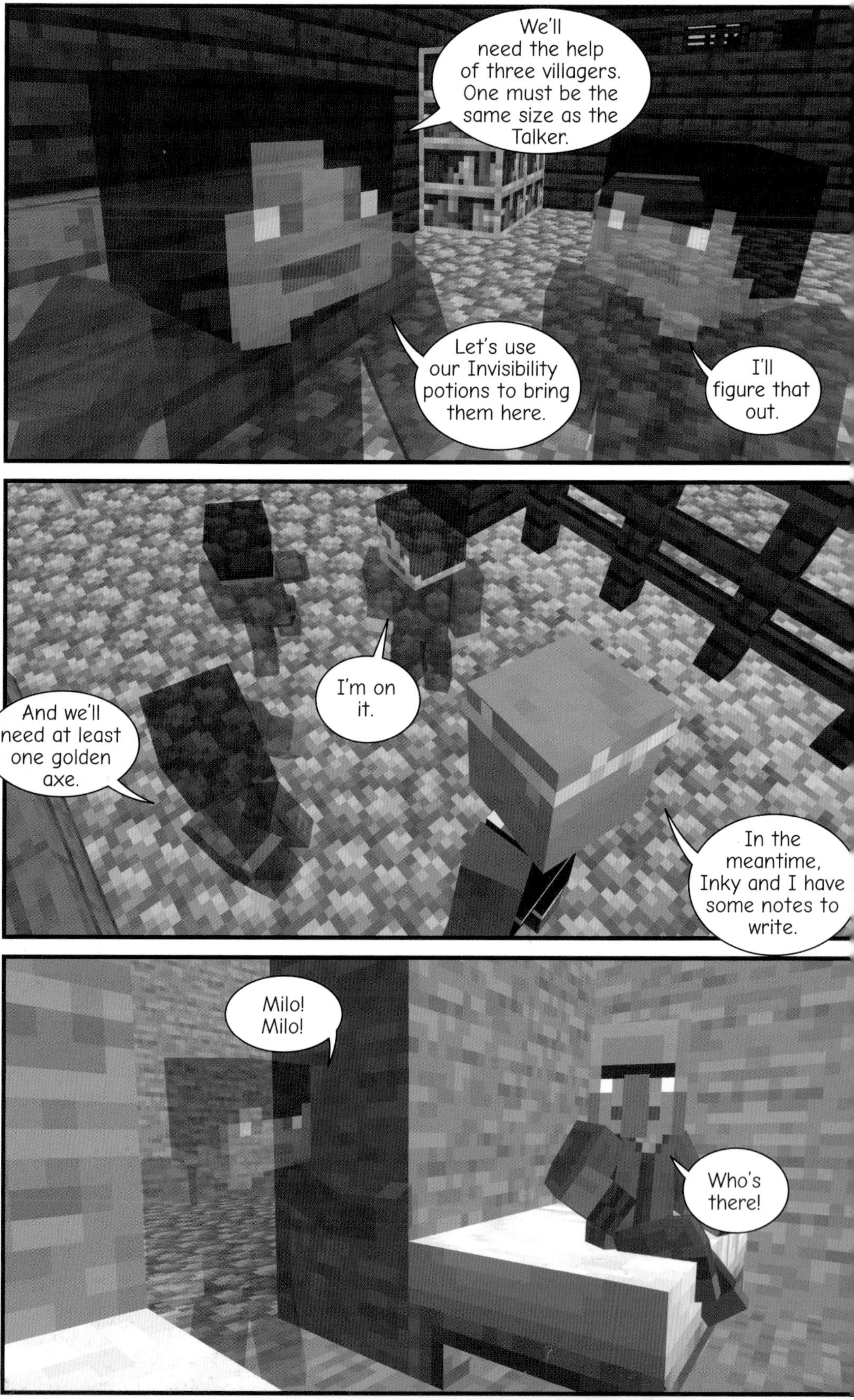
We'll need the help of three villagers. One must be the same size as the Talker.
Let's use our Invisibility potions to bring them here.
I'll figure that out.
I'm on it.
And we'll need at least one golden axe.
In the meantime, Inky and I have some notes to write.
Milo! Milo!
Who's there!

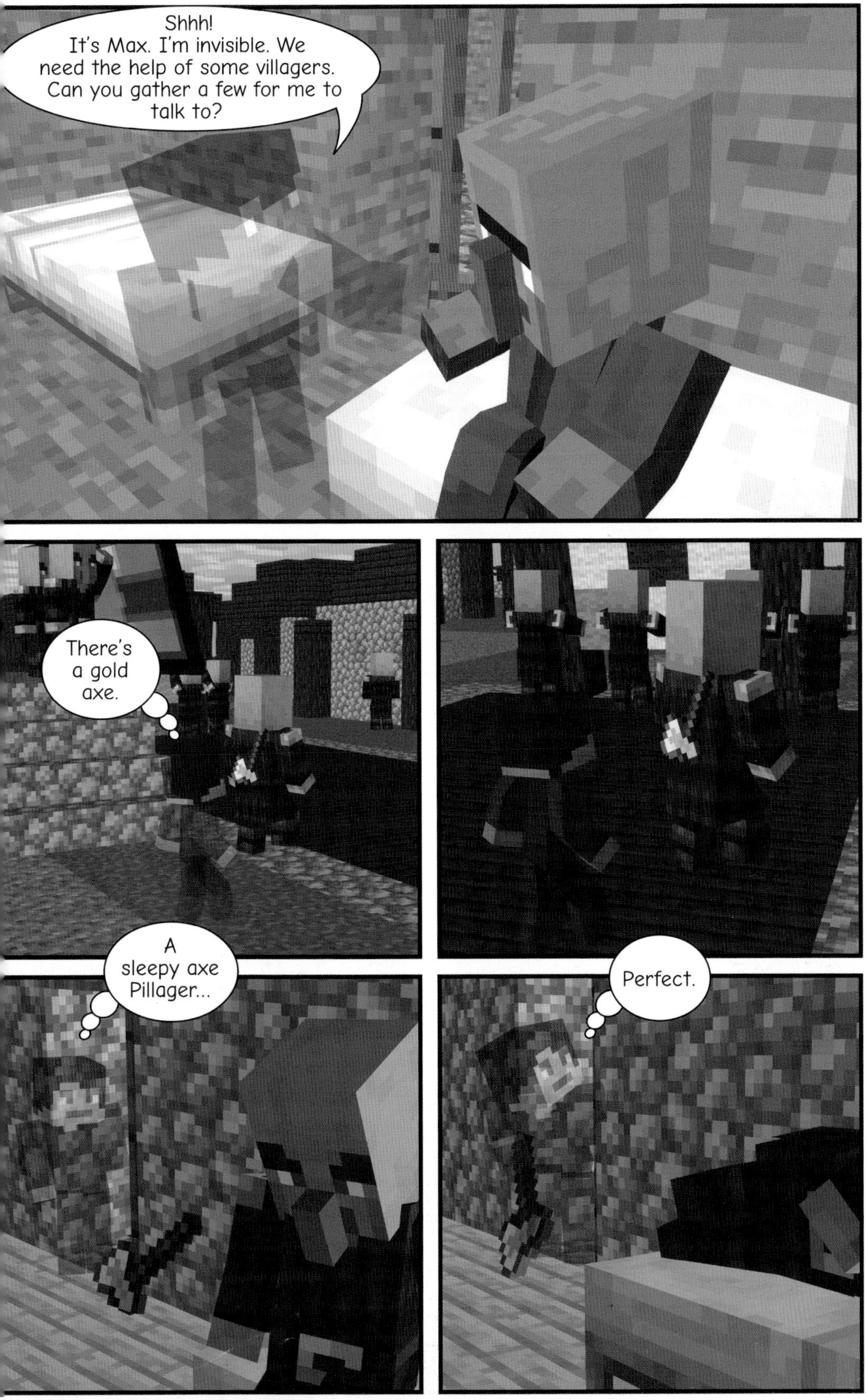
Shhh! It's Max. I'm invisible. We need the help of some villagers. Can you gather a few for me to talk to?
There's a gold axe.
A sleepy axe Pillager...
Perfect.

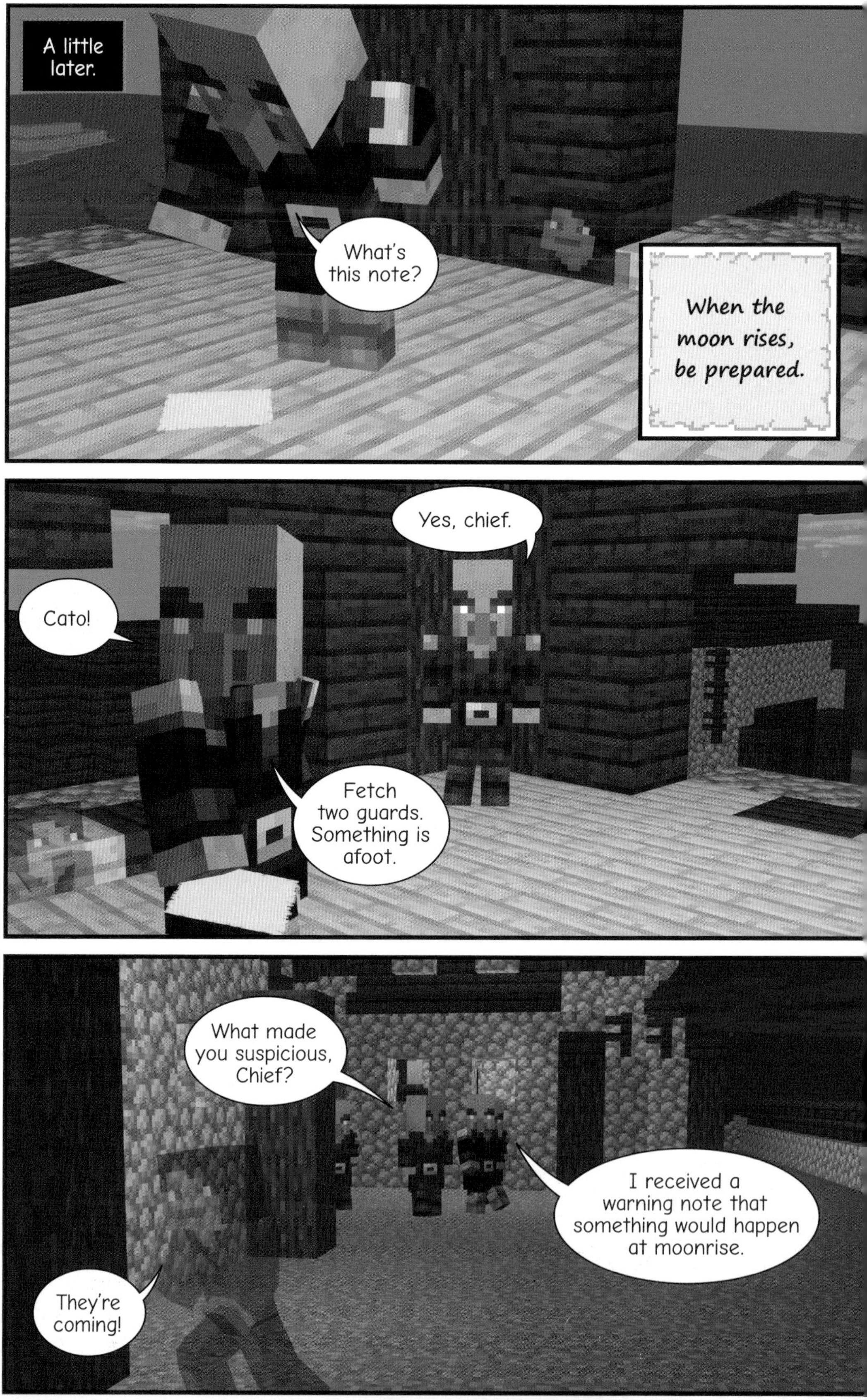
A little later.
What's this note?
When the moon rises, be prepared.
Cato!
Yes, chief.
Fetch two guards. Something is afoot.
What made you suspicious, Chief?
I received a warning note that something would happen at moonrise.
They're coming!

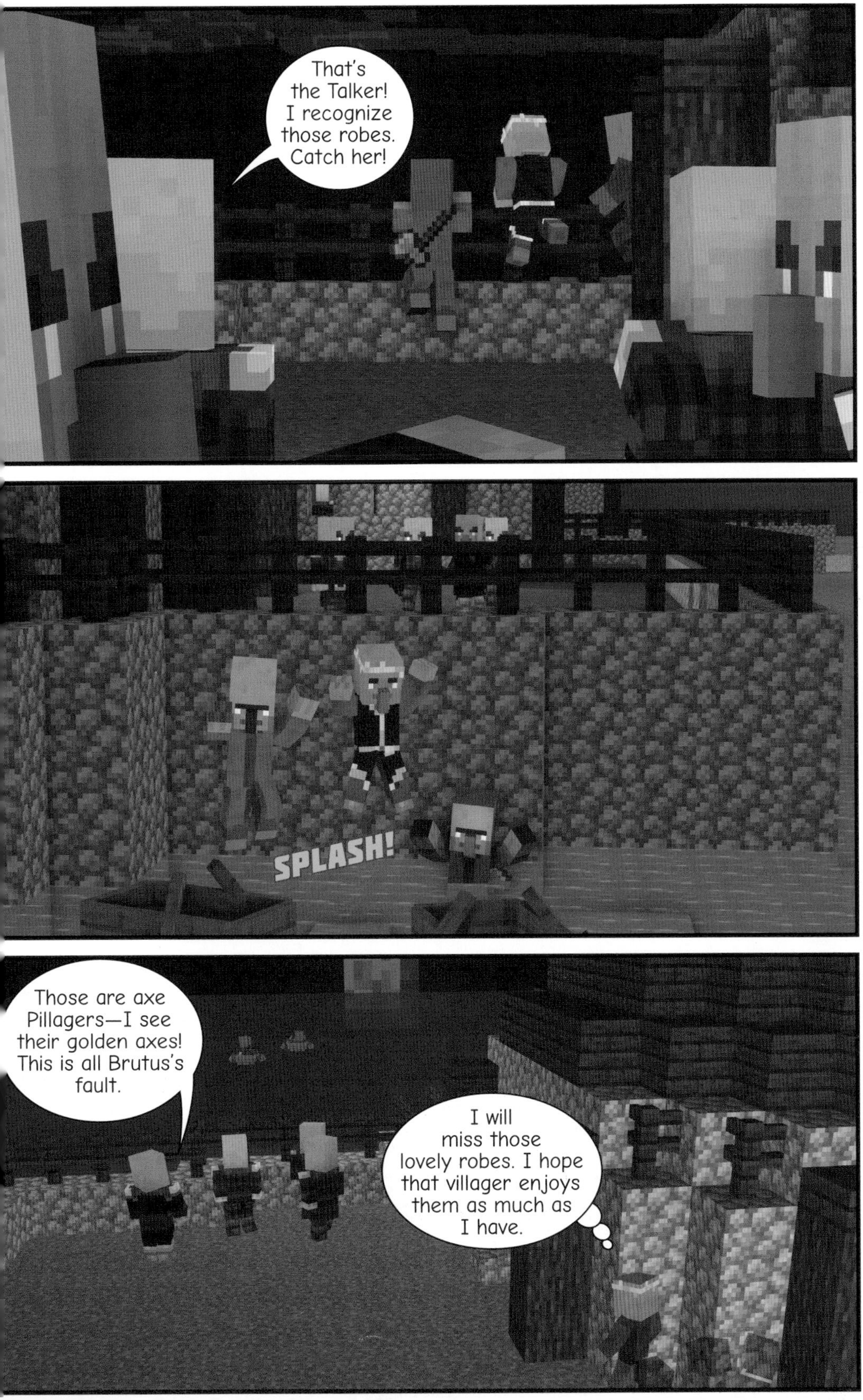
That's the Talker! I recognize those robes. Catch her!
SPLASH!
Those are axe Pillagers—I see their golden axes! This is all Brutus's fault.
I will miss those lovely robes. I hope that villager enjoys them as much as I have.

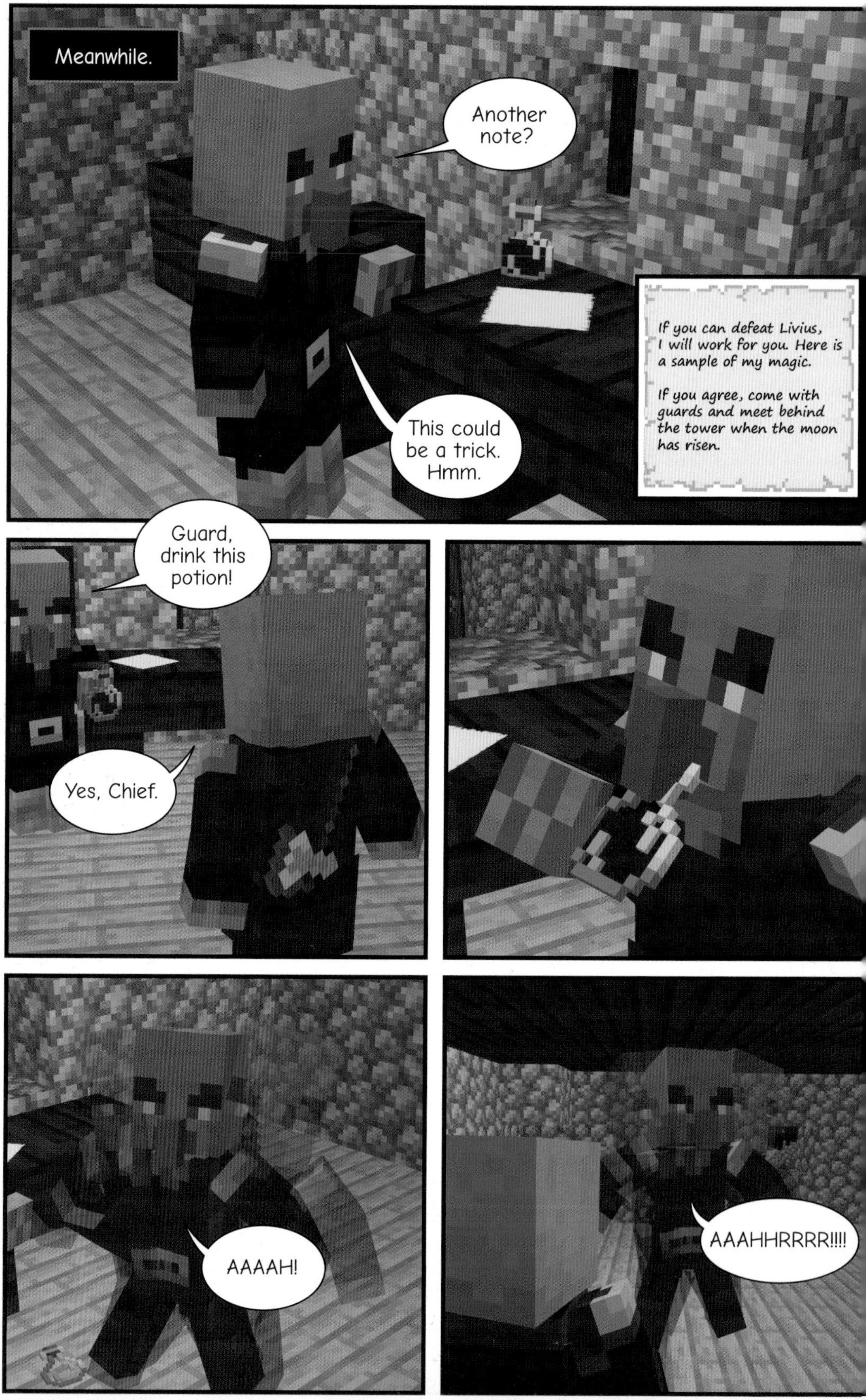
Meanwhile.
Another note?
If you can defeat Livius, I will work for you. Here is a sample of my magic.
If you agree, come with guards and meet behind the tower when the moon has risen.
This could be a trick. Hmm.
Guard, drink this potion!
Yes, Chief.
AAAAH!
AAAHHRRRR!!!!

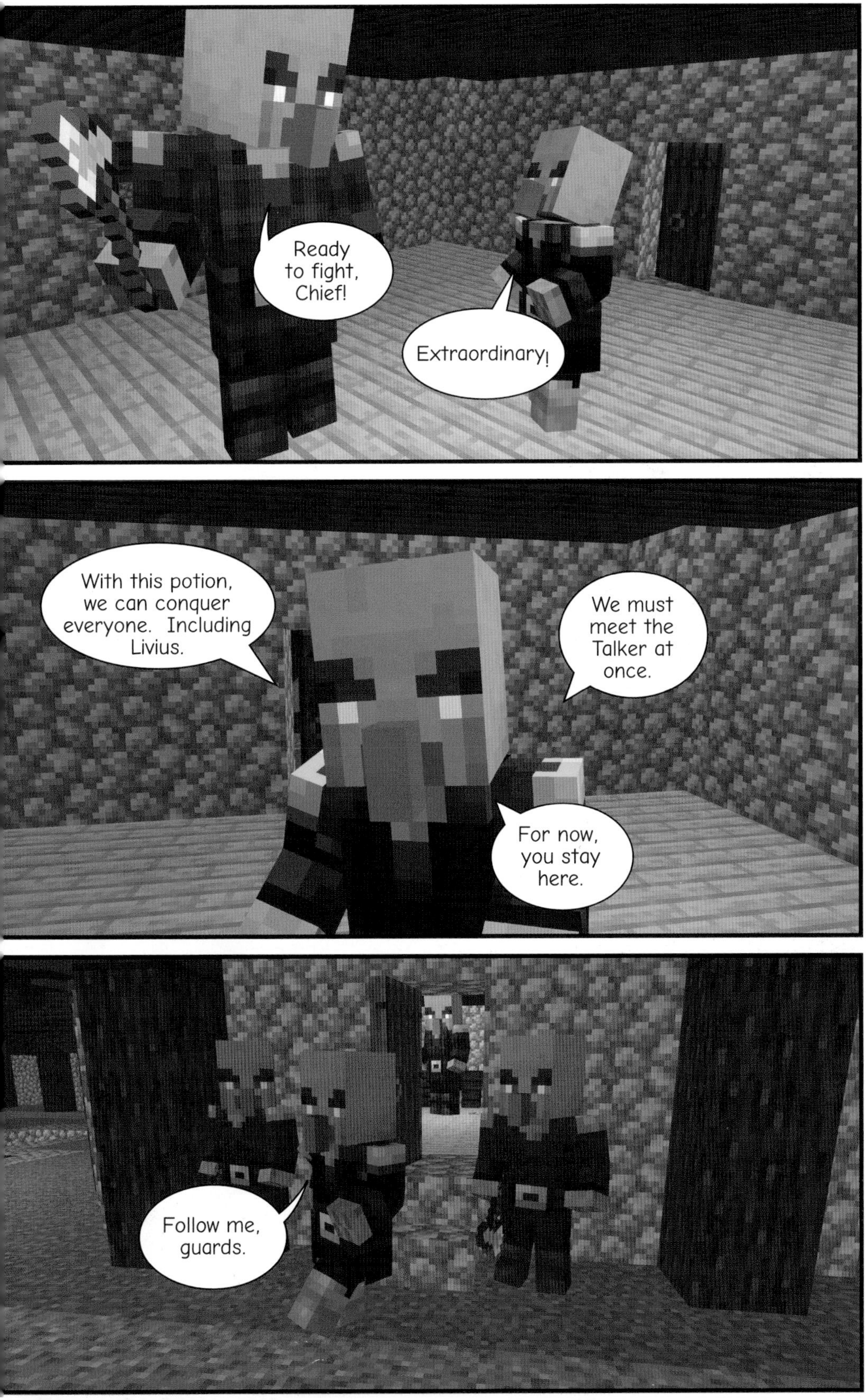
Ready to fight, Chief!
Extraordinary!
With this potion, we can conquer everyone. Including Livius.
We must meet the Talker at once.
For now, you stay here.
Follow me, guards.

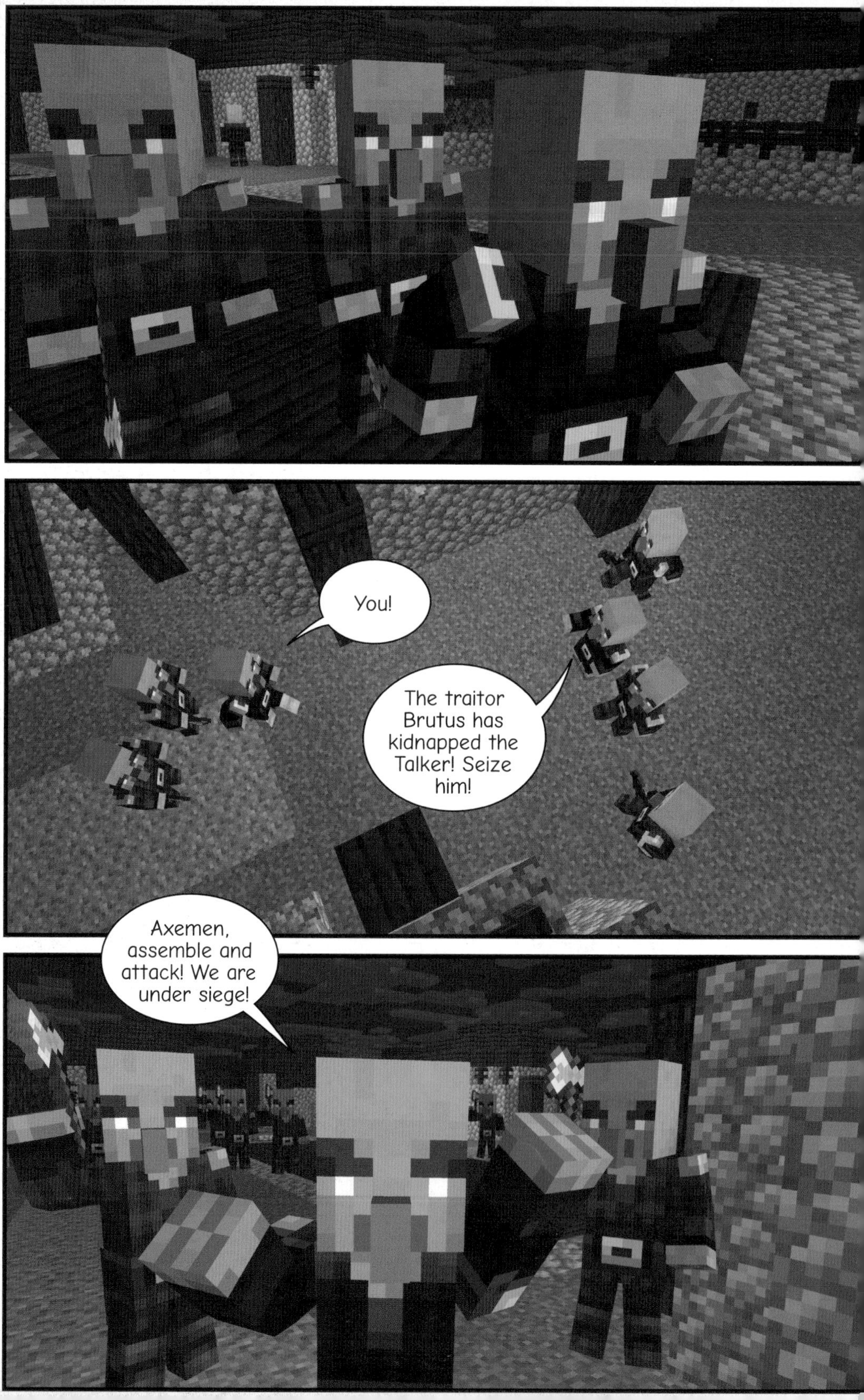
You!
The traitor Brutus has kidnapped the Talker! Seize him!
Axemen, assemble and attack! We are under siege!

Chapter 12
A Battle Begins

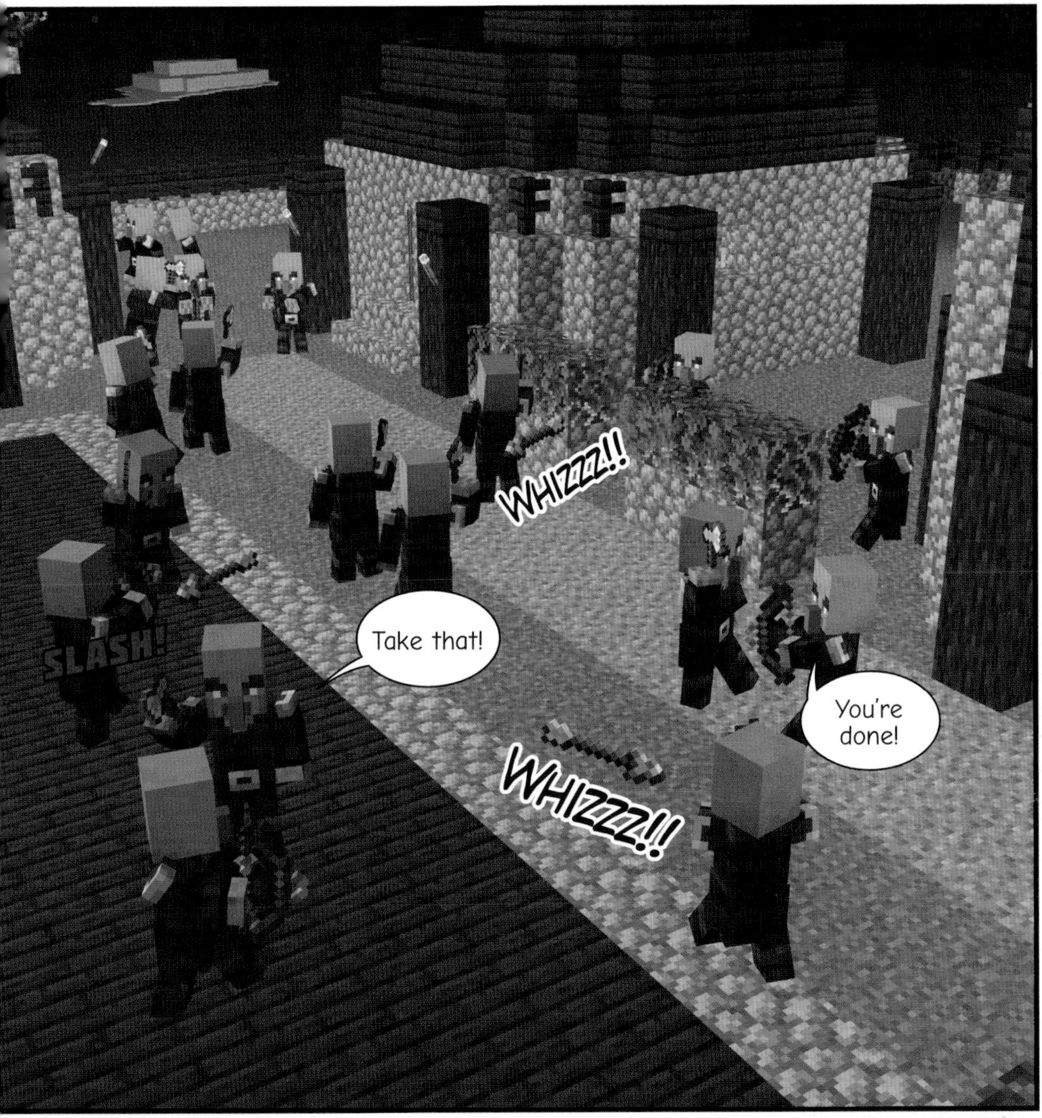
WHIZZZ!!
SLASH!
Take that!
You're done!
WHIZZZZ!!

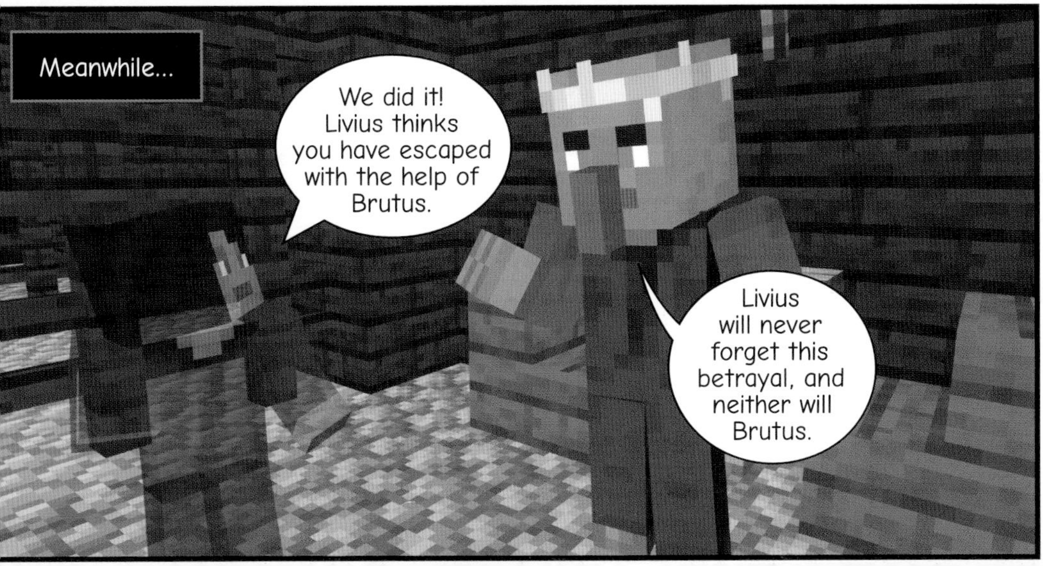
Meanwhile...
We did it! Livius thinks you have escaped with the help of Brutus.
Livius will never forget this betrayal, and neither will Brutus.

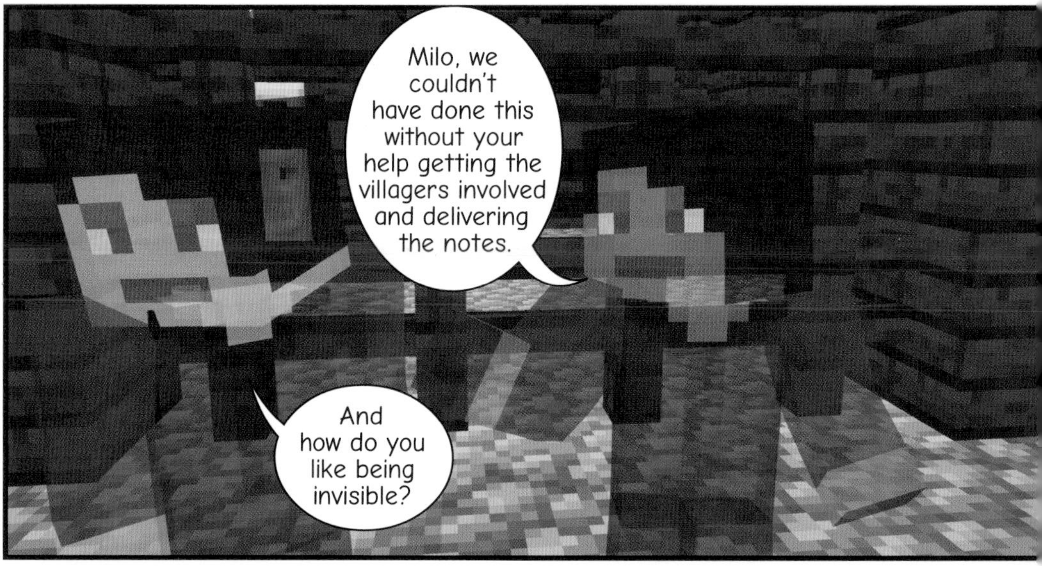
Milo, we couldn't have done this without your help getting the villagers involved and delivering the notes.
And how do you like being invisible?

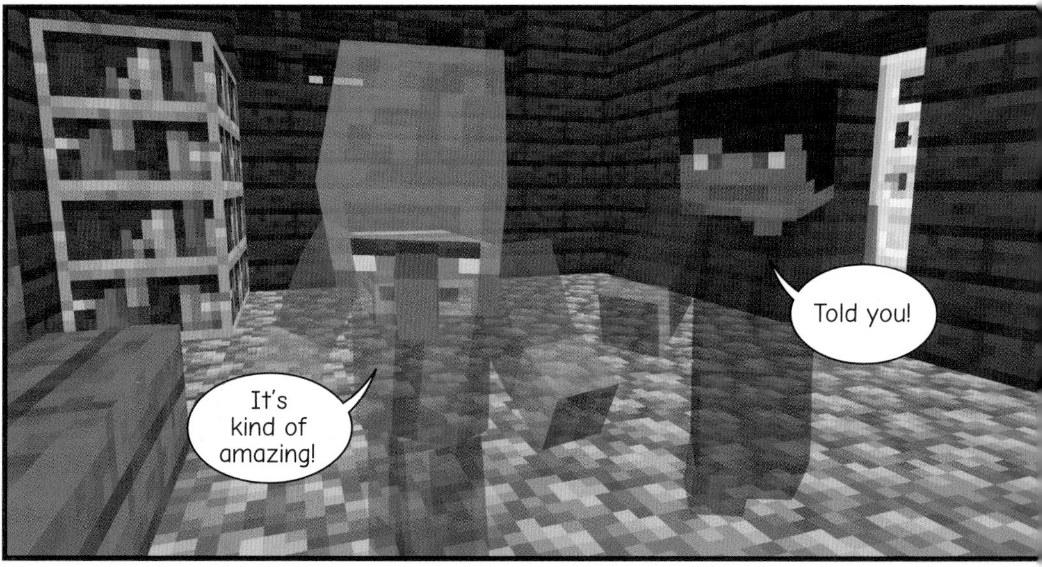
Told you!
It's kind of amazing!

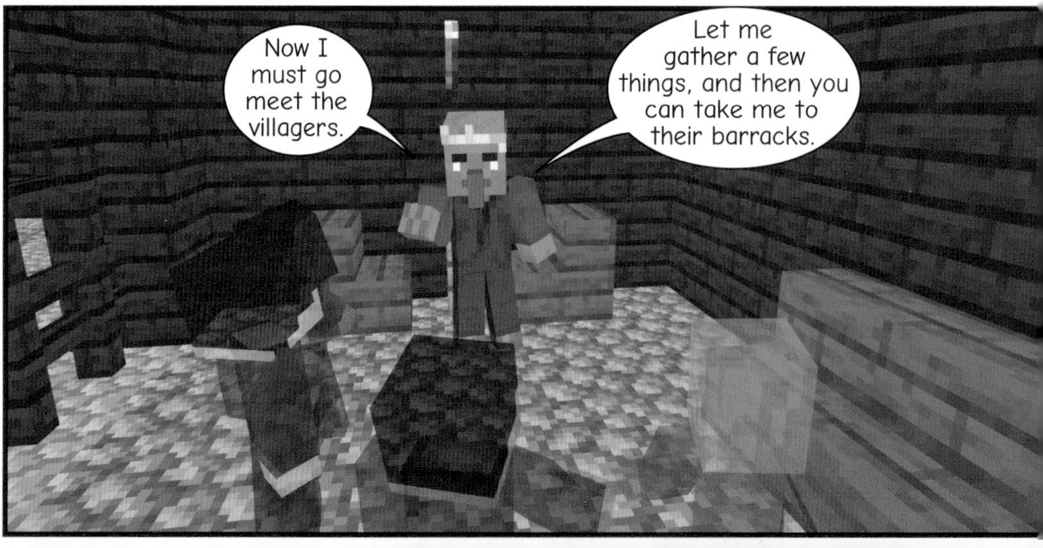
Now I must go meet the villagers.
Let me gather a few things, and then you can take me to their barracks.

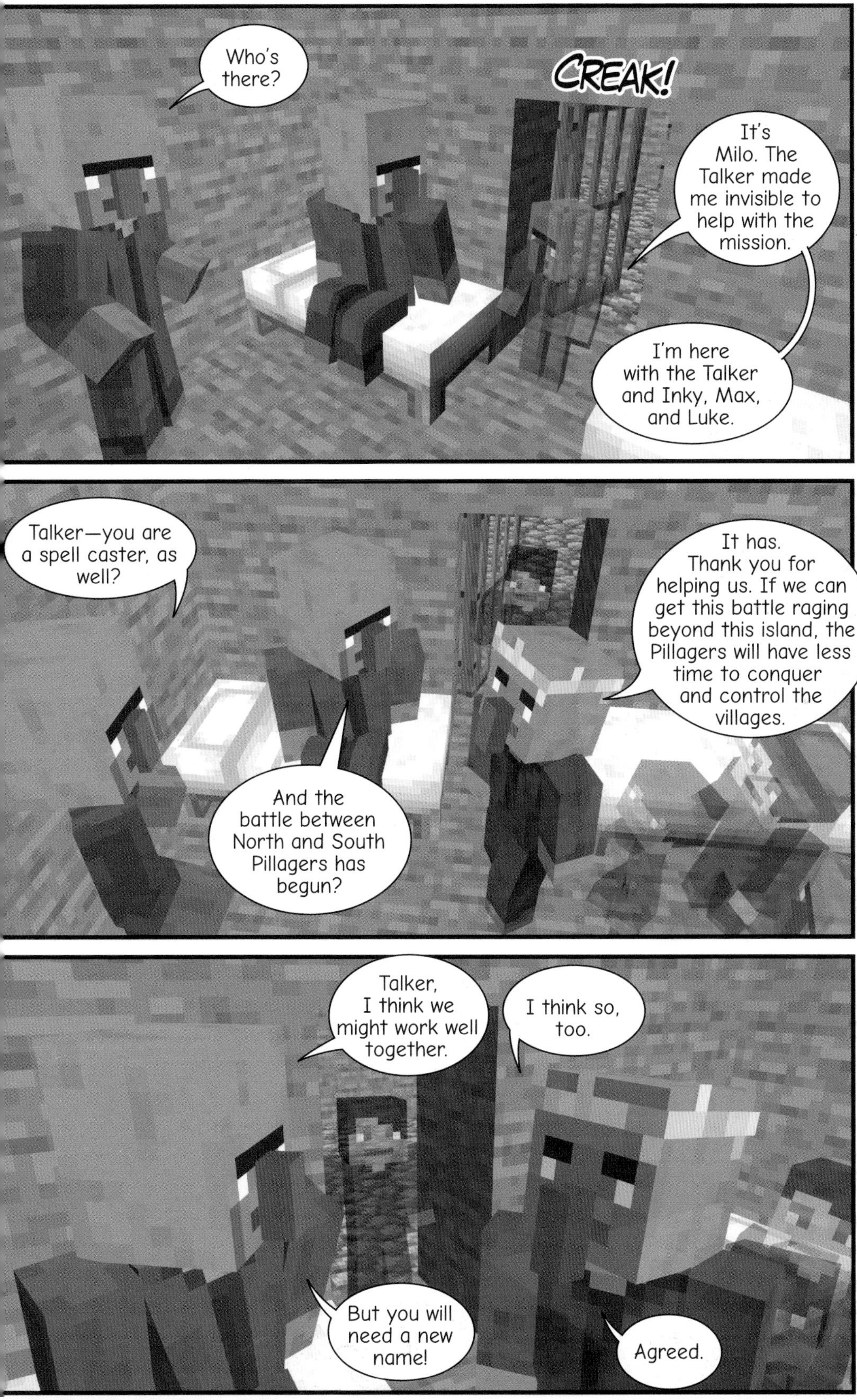
Who's there?
CREAK!
It's Milo. The Talker made me invisible to help with the mission.
I'm here with the Talker and Inky, Max, and Luke.
Talker—you are a spell caster, as well?
And the battle between North and South Pillagers has begun?
It has. Thank you for helping us. If we can get this battle raging beyond this island, the Pillagers will have less time to conquer and control the villages.
Talker, I think we might work well together.
I think so, too.
But you will need a new name!
Agreed.

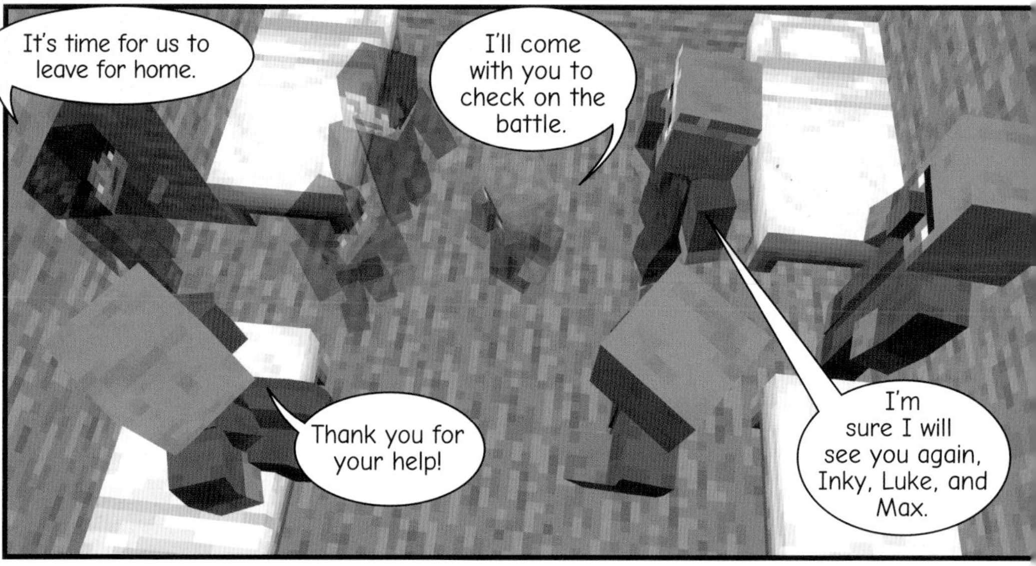
It's time for us to leave for home.
I'll come with you to check on the battle.
Thank you for your help!
I'm sure I will see you again, Inky, Luke, and Max.

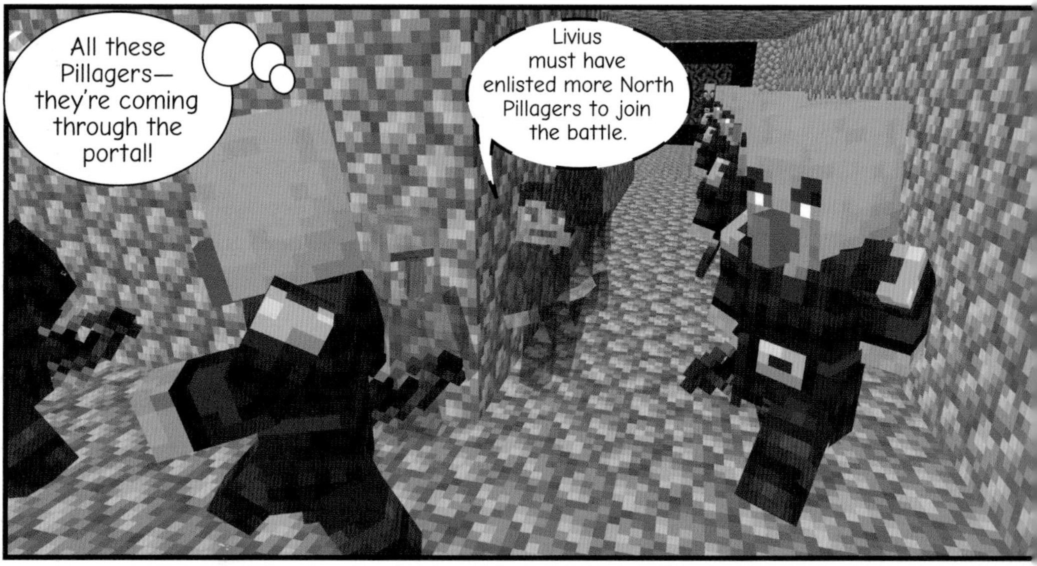
All these Pillagers— they're coming through the portal!
Livius must have enlisted more North Pillagers to join the battle.

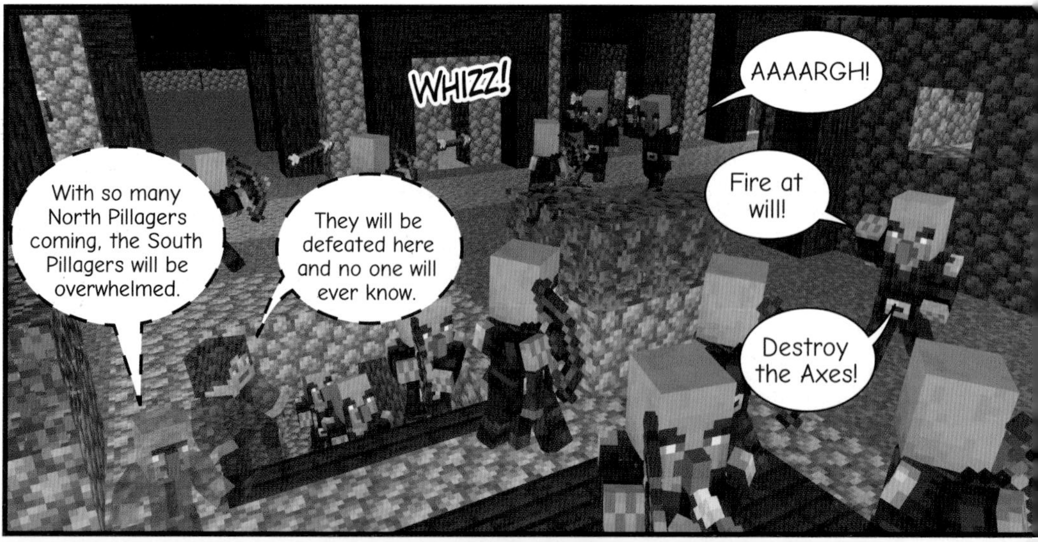
WHIZZ!
AAAARGH!
Fire at will!
With so many North Pillagers coming, the South Pillagers will be overwhelmed.
They will be defeated here and no one will ever know.
Destroy the Axes!

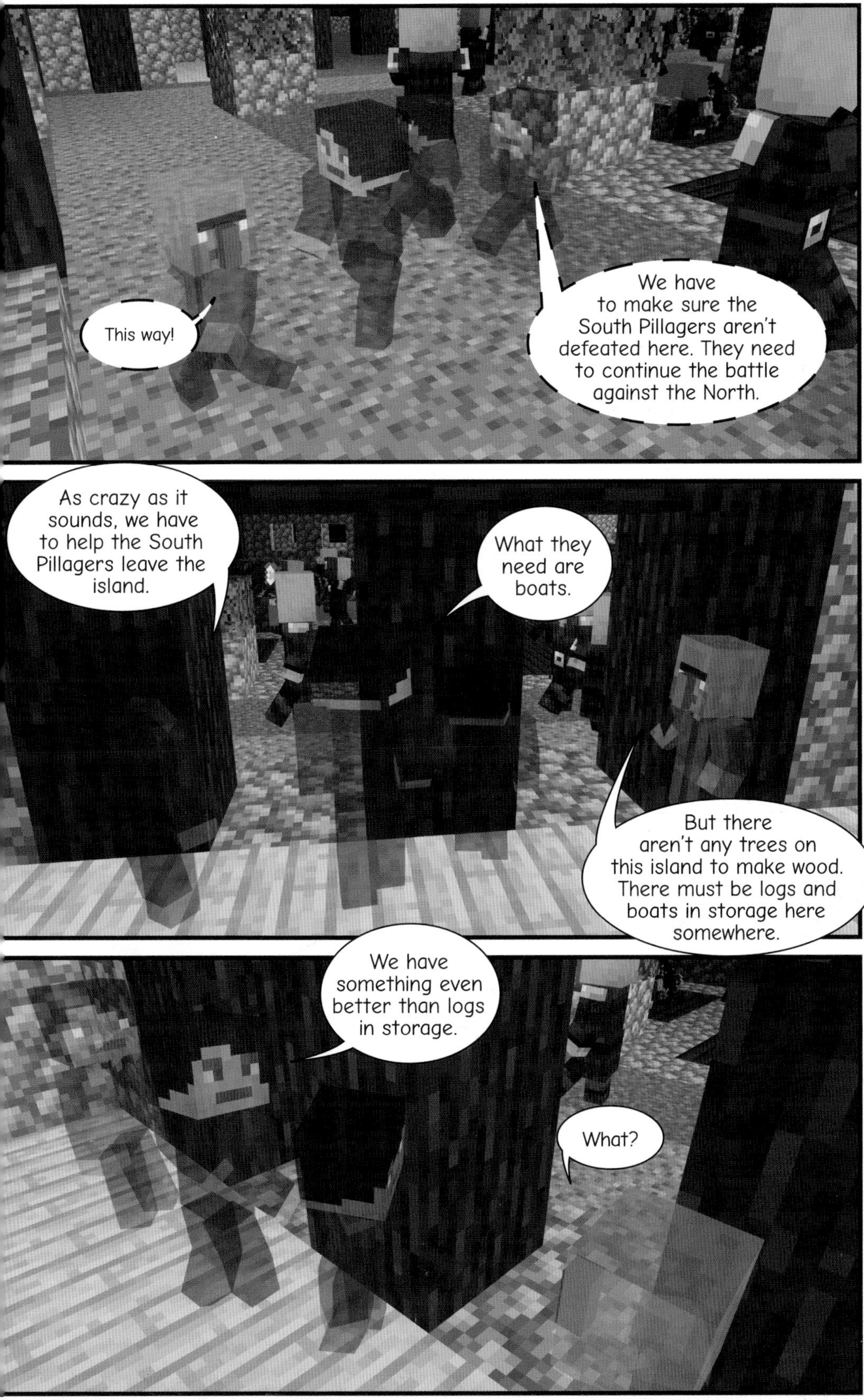
This way!
We have to make sure the South Pillagers aren't defeated here. They need to continue the battle against the North.
As crazy as it sounds, we have to help the South Pillagers leave the island.
What they need are boats.
But there aren't any trees on this island to make wood. There must be logs and boats in storage here somewhere.
We have something even better than logs in storage.
What?

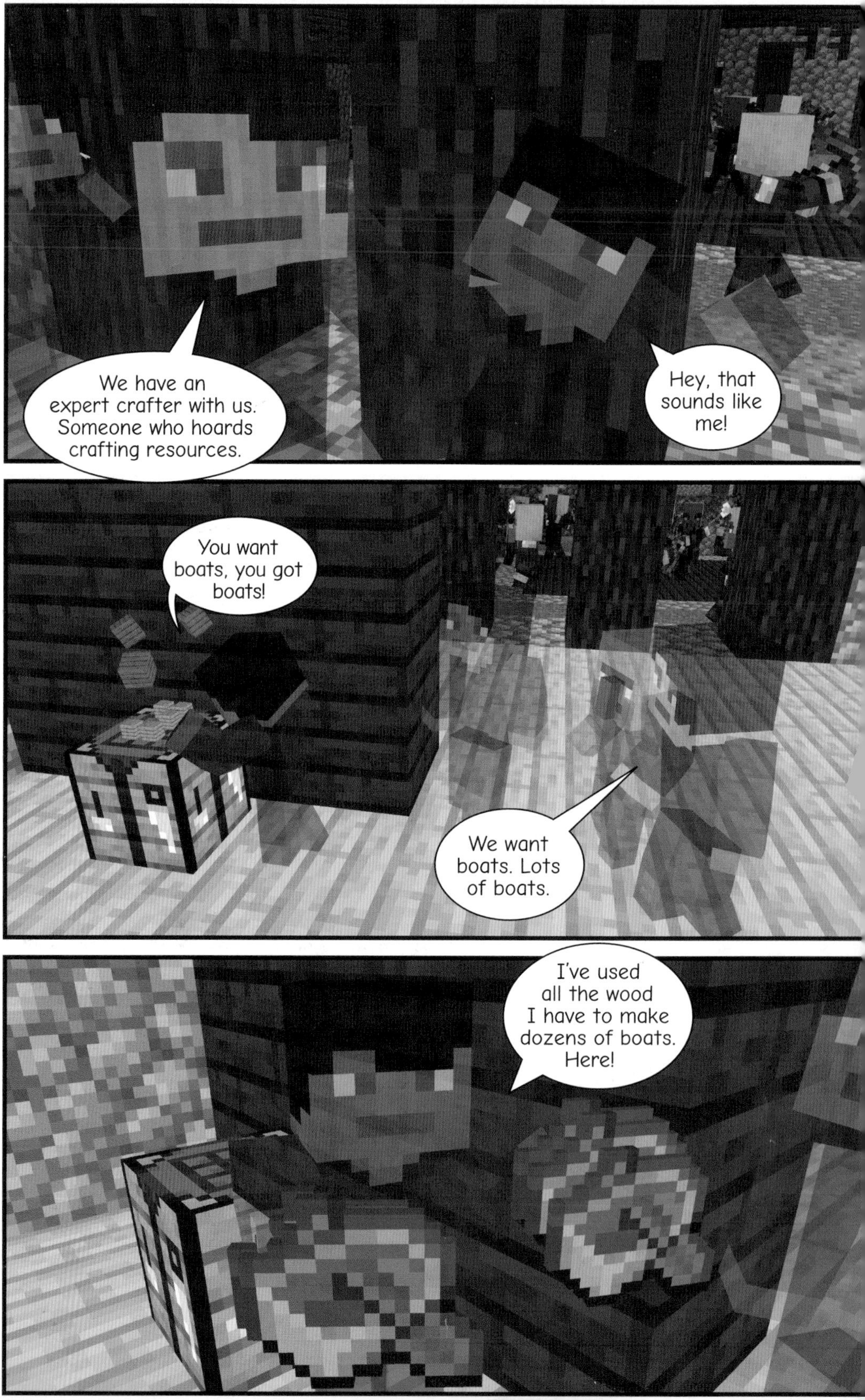
We have an expert crafter with us. Someone who hoards crafting resources.
Hey, that sounds like me!
You want boats, you got boats!
We want boats. Lots of boats.
I've used all the wood I have to make dozens of boats. Here!

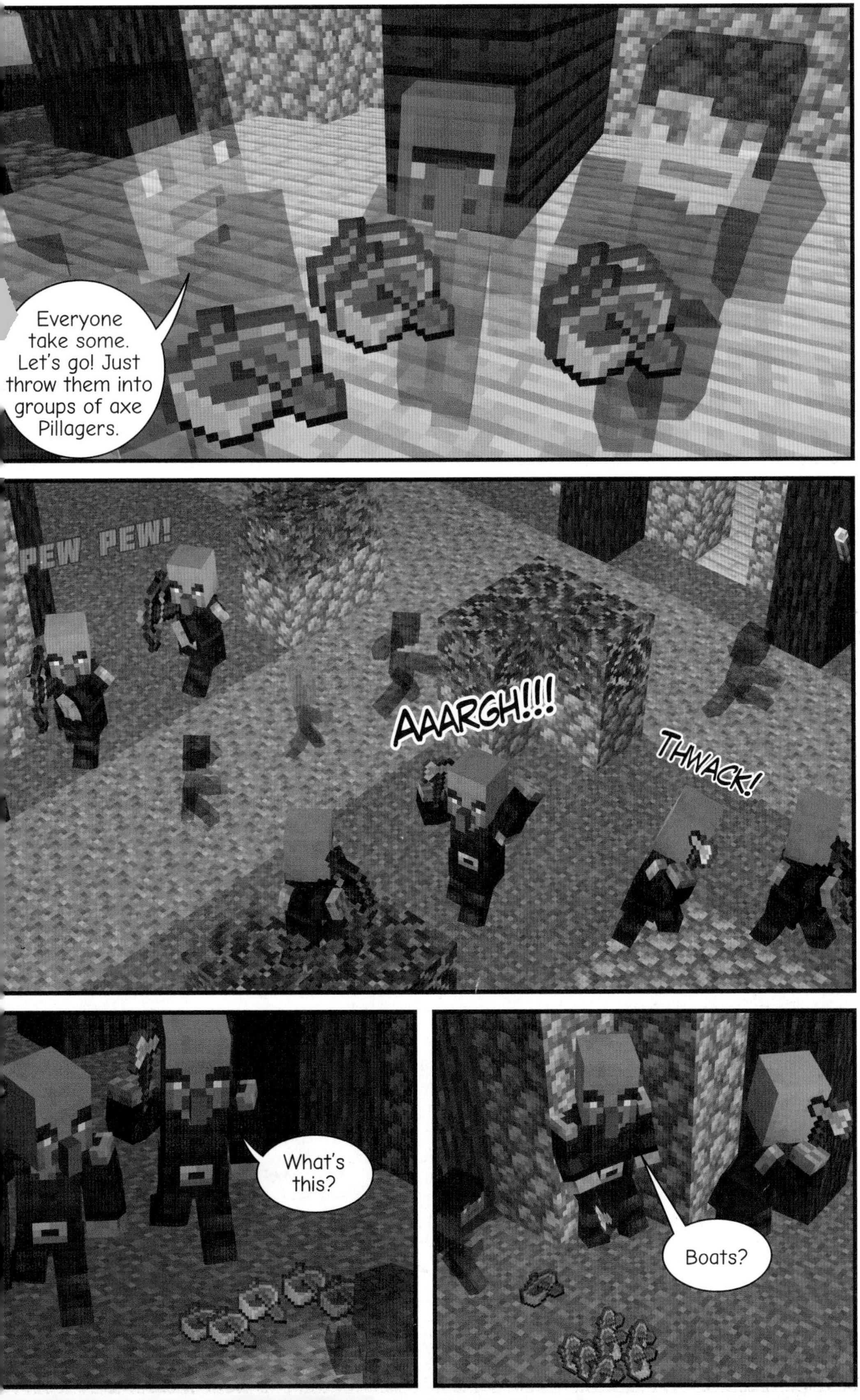
Everyone take some. Let's go! Just throw them into groups of axe Pillagers.
PEW PEW!
AAARGH!!!
THWACK!
What's this?
Boats?

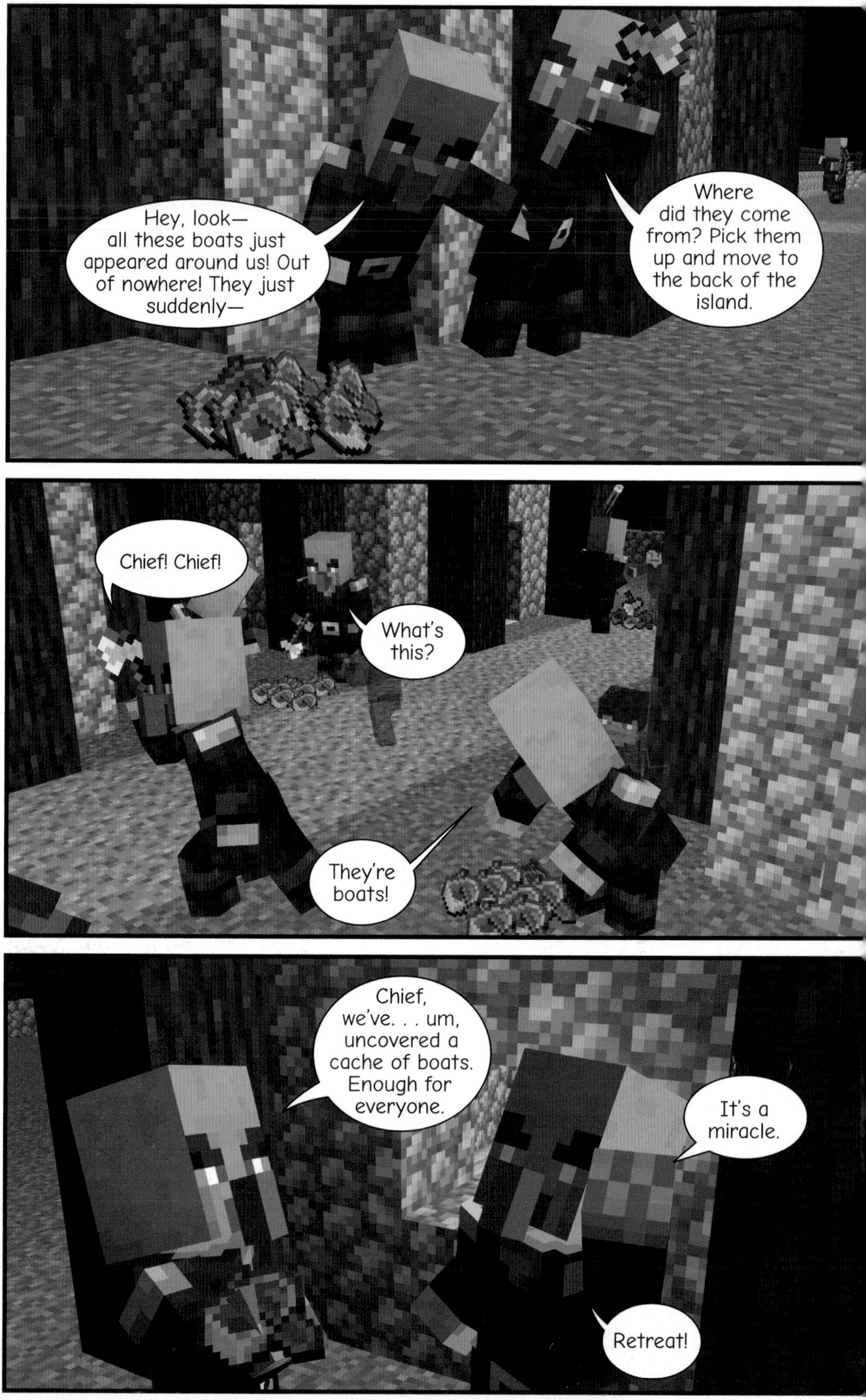
Hey, look—all these boats just appeared around us! Out of nowhere! They just suddenly—
Where did they come from? Pick them up and move to the back of the island.
Chief! Chief!
What's this?
They're boats!
Chief, we've. . . um, uncovered a cache of boats. Enough for everyone.
It's a miracle.
Retreat!

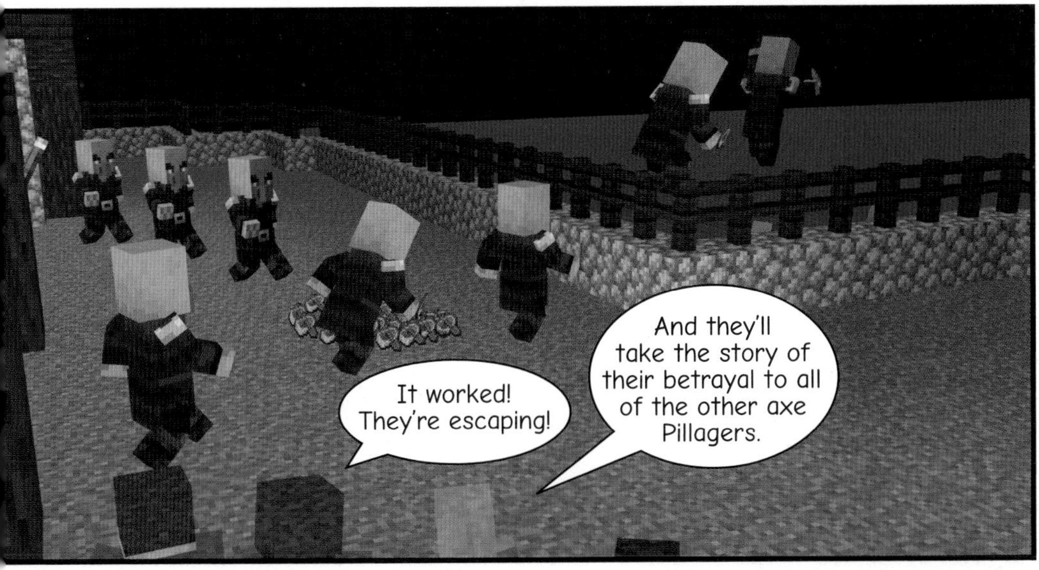
It worked! They're escaping!
And they'll take the story of their betrayal to all of the other axe Pillagers.

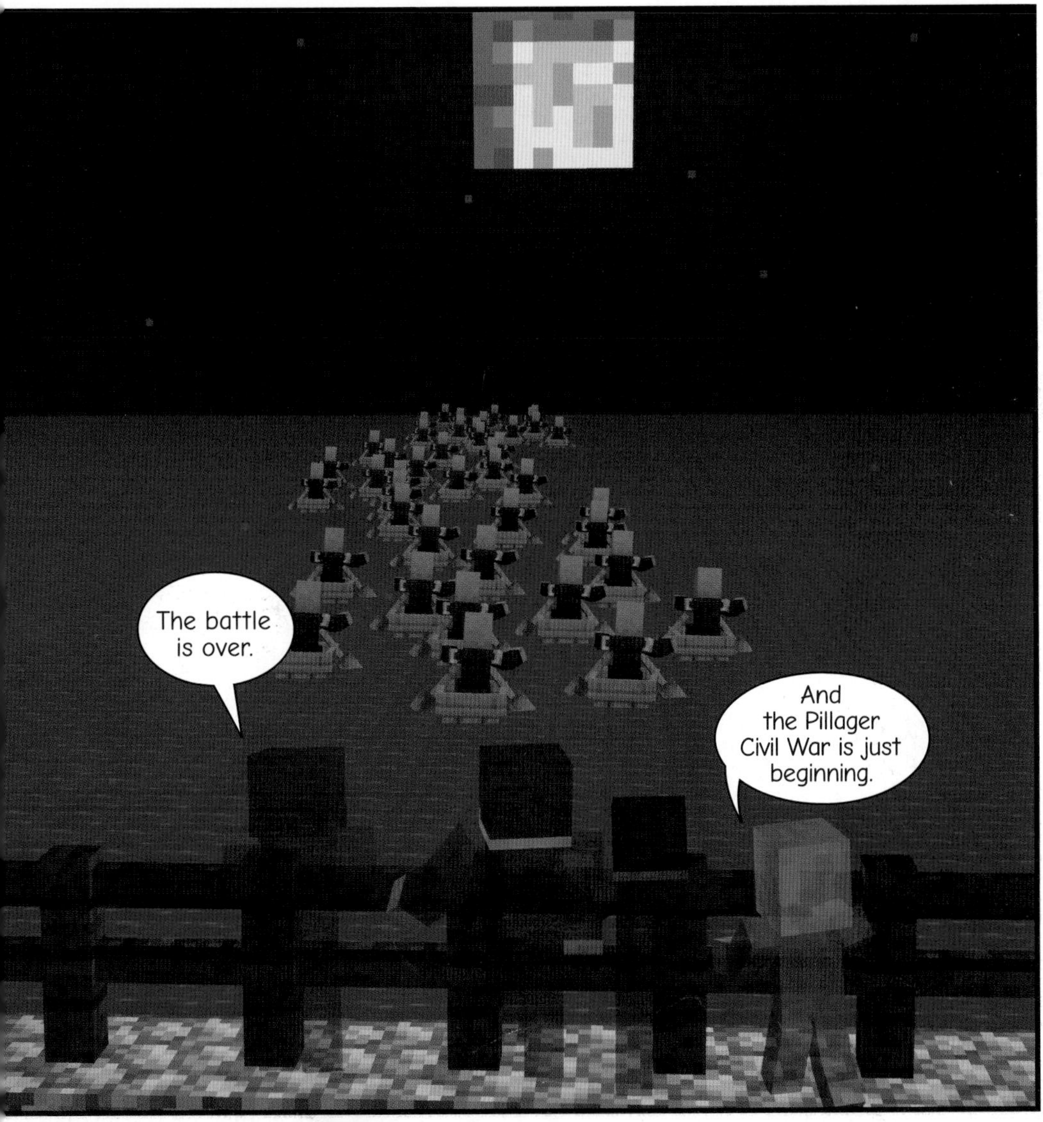
The battle is over.
And the Pillager Civil War is just beginning.

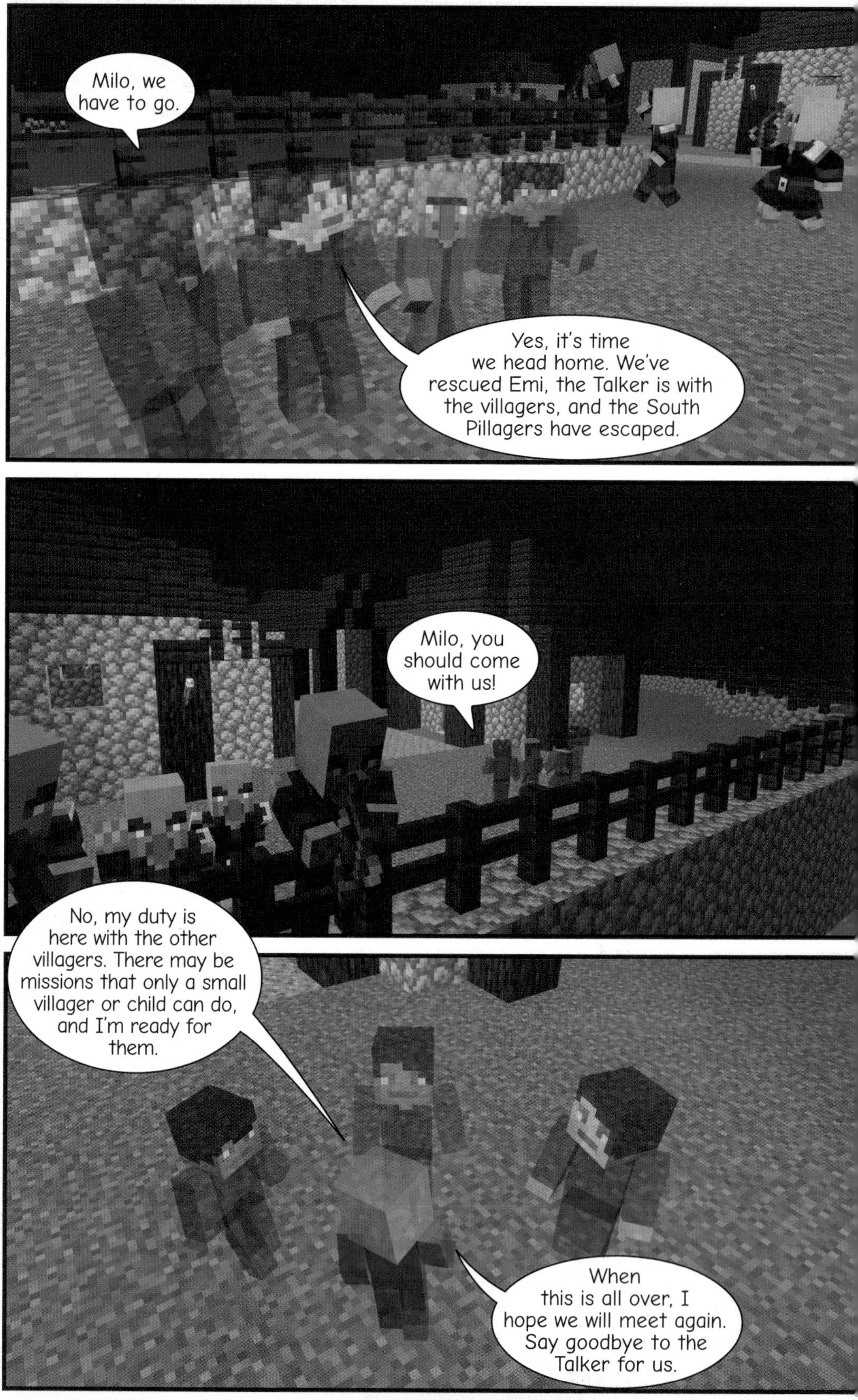
Milo, we have to go.
Yes, it's time we head home. We've rescued Emi, the Talker is with the villagers, and the South Pillagers have escaped.
Milo, you should come with us!
No, my duty is here with the other villagers. There may be missions that only a small villager or child can do, and I'm ready for them.
When this is all over, I hope we will meet again. Say goodbye to the Talker for us.

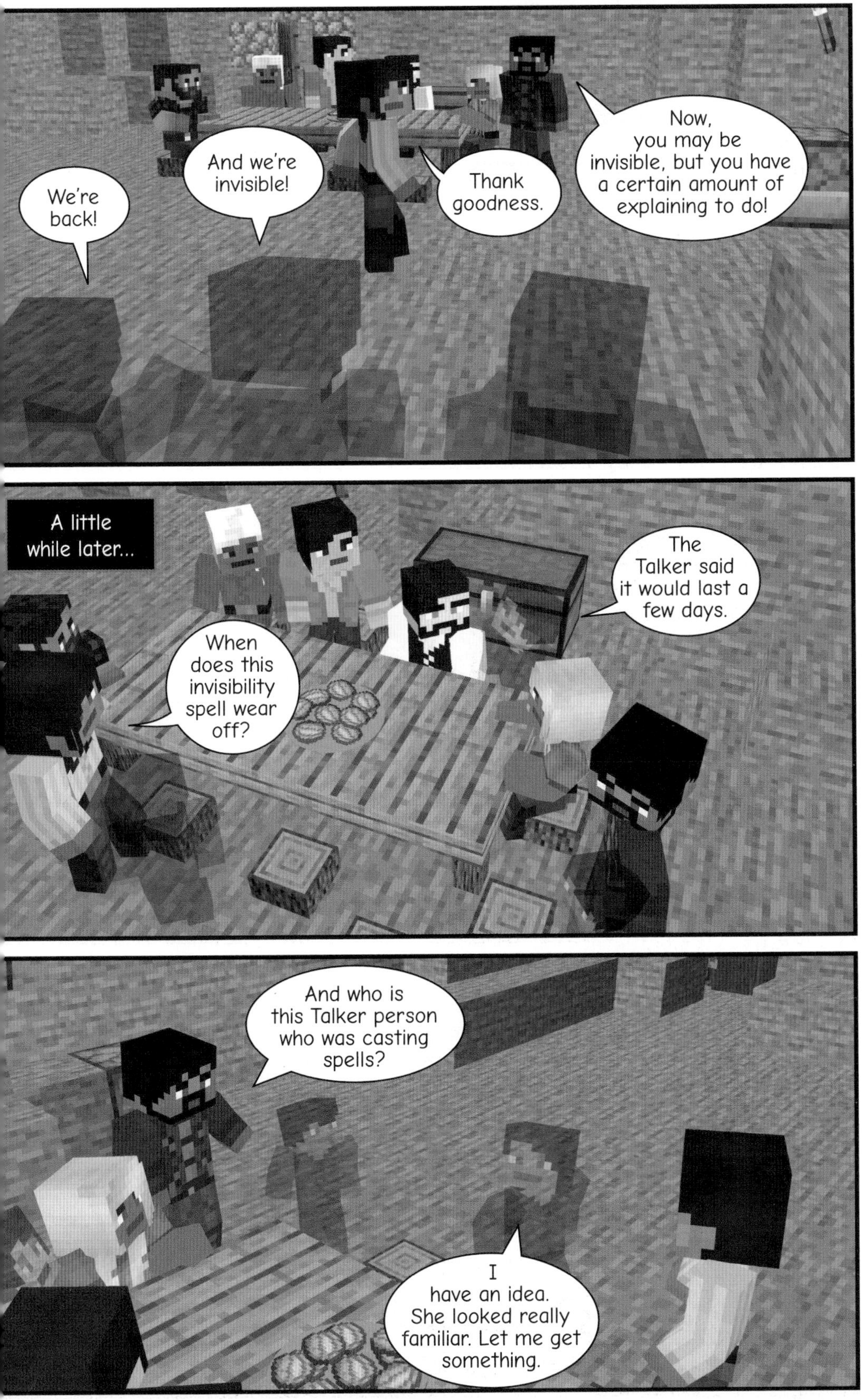
We're back!
And we're invisible!
Thank goodness.
Now, you may be invisible, but you have a certain amount of explaining to do!
A little while later...
When does this invisibility spell wear off?
The Talker said it would last a few days.
And who is this Talker person who was casting spells?
I have an idea. She looked really familiar. Let me get something.

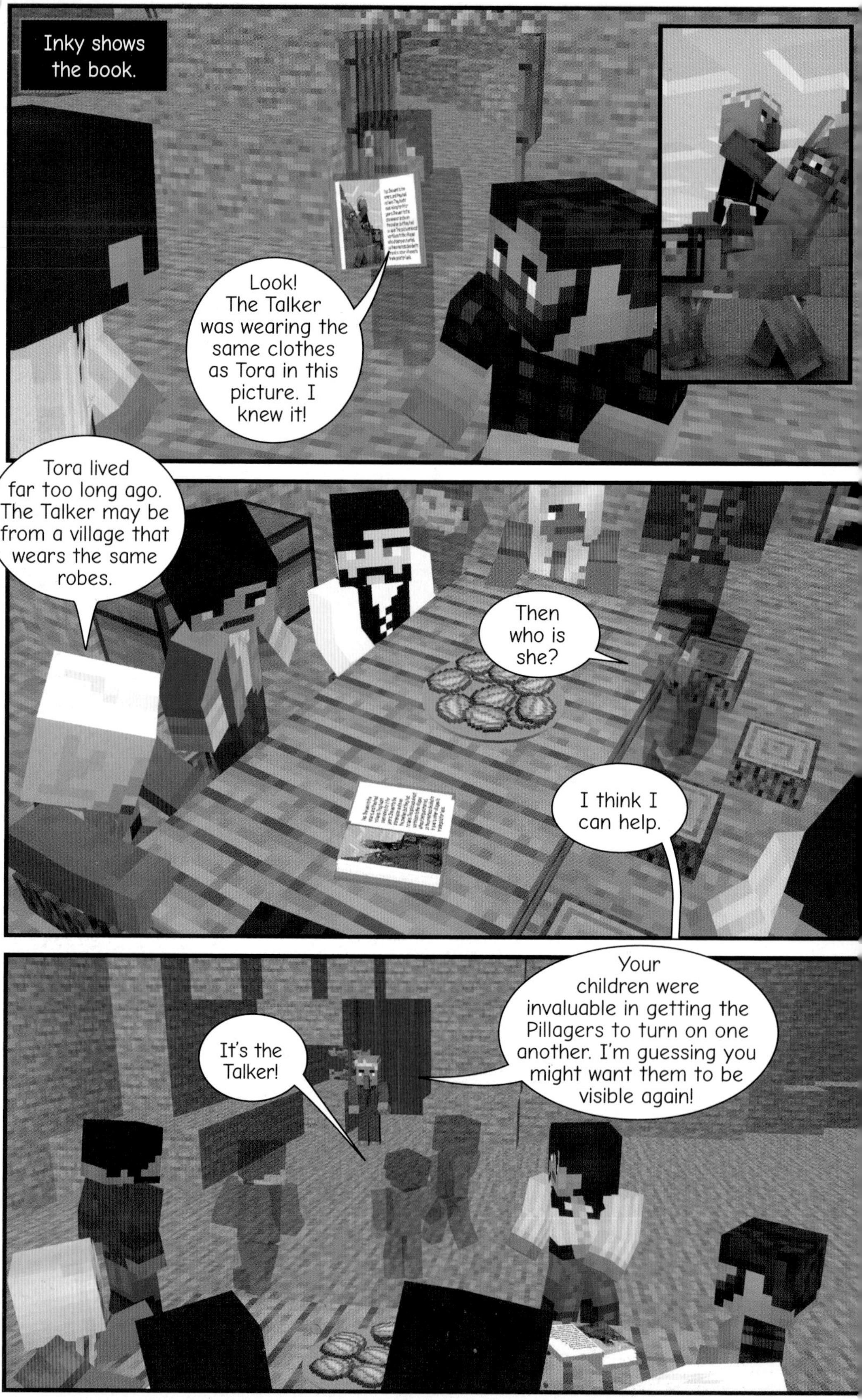
Inky shows the book.
Look! The Talker was wearing the same clothes as Tora in this picture. I knew it!
Tora lived far too long ago. The Talker may be from a village that wears the same robes.
Then who is she?
I think I can help.
Your children were invaluable in getting the Pillagers to turn on one another. I'm guessing you might want them to be visible again!
It's the Talker!

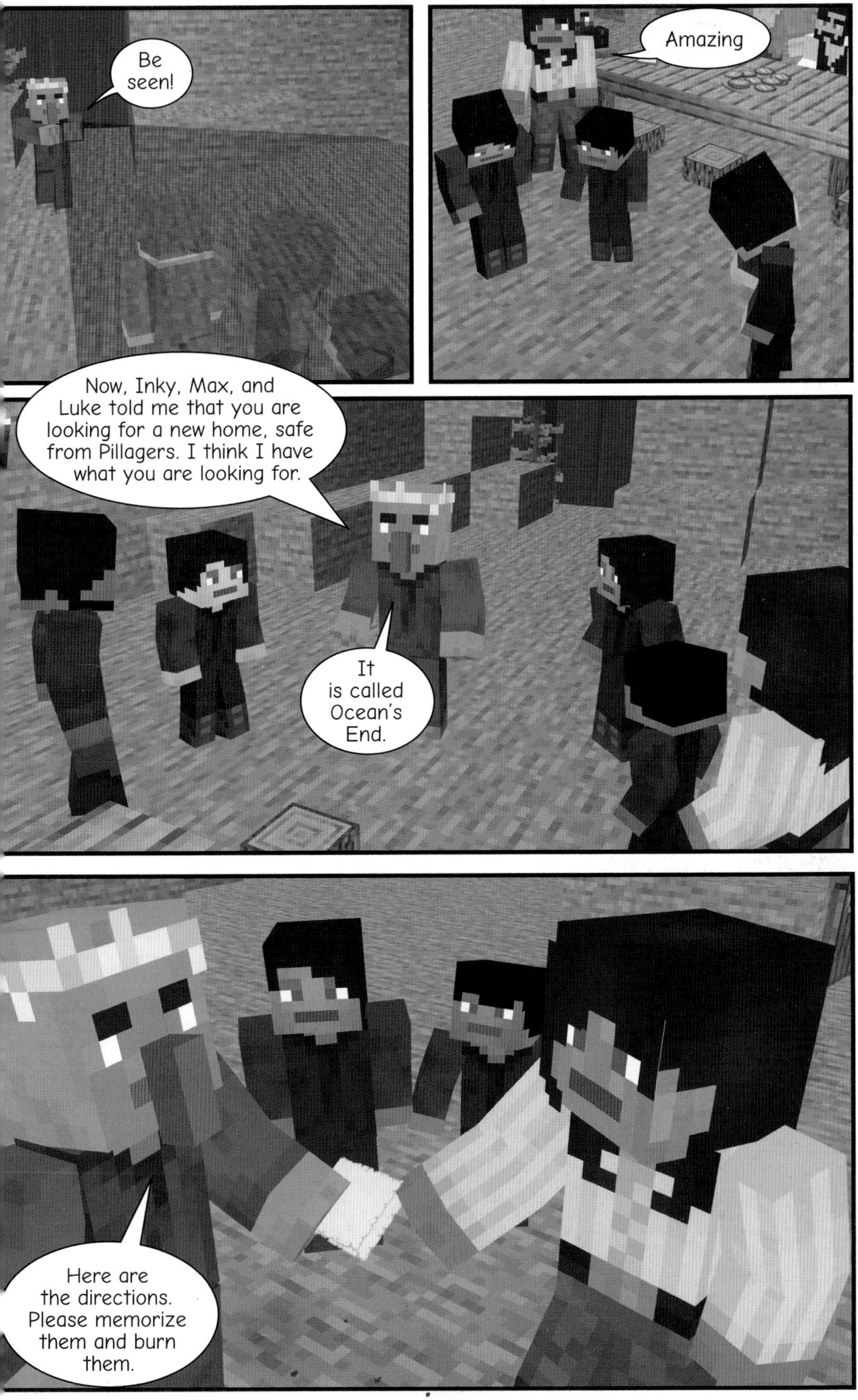
Be seen!
Amazing
Now, Inky, Max, and Luke told me that you are looking for a new home, safe from Pillagers. I think I have what you are looking for.
It is called Ocean's End.
Here are the directions. Please memorize them and burn them.

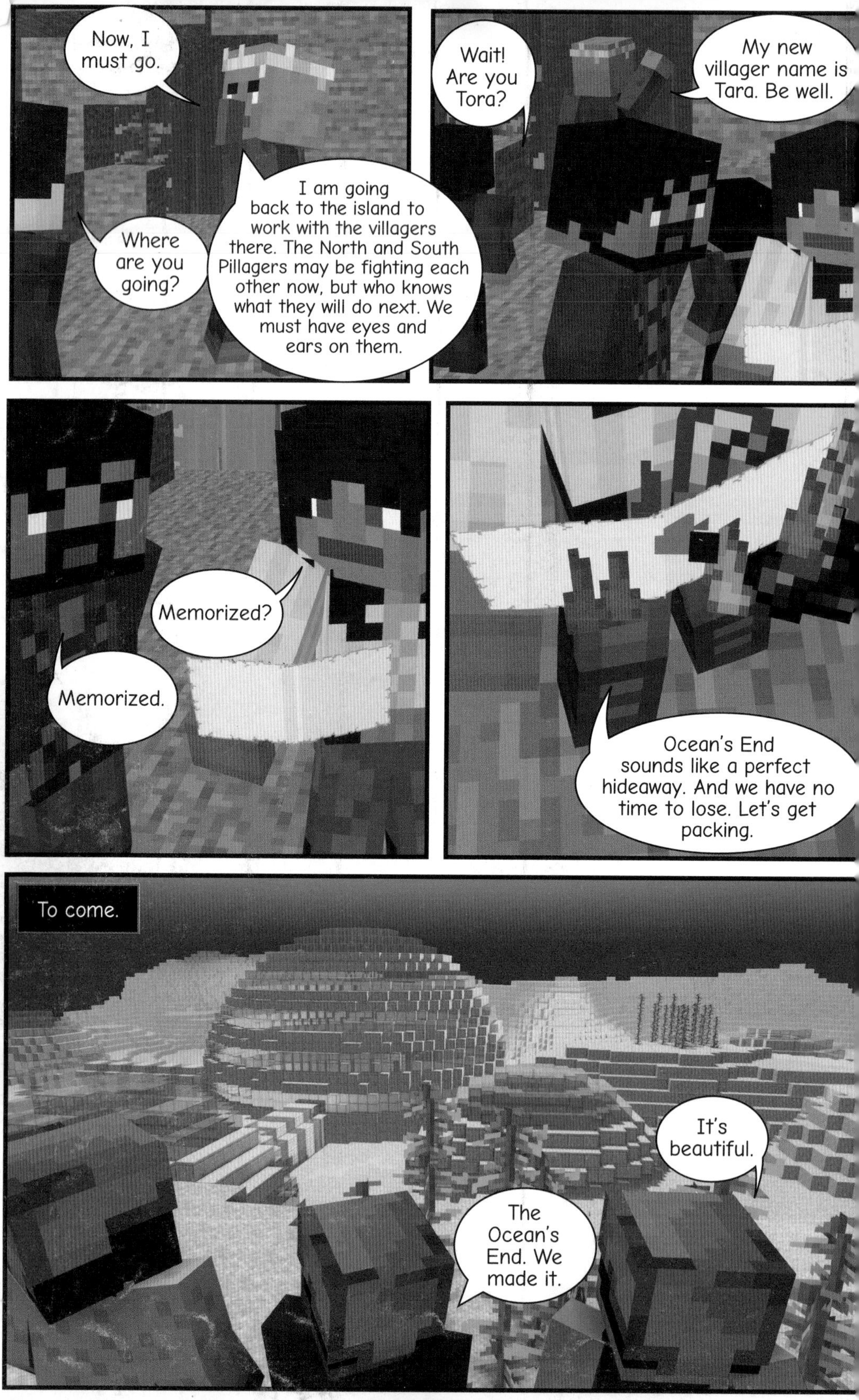
Now, I must go.
Where are you going?
I am going back to the island to work with the villagers there. The North and South Pillagers may be fighting each other now, but who knows what they will do next. We must have eyes and ears on them.
Wait! Are you Tora?
My new villager name is Tara. Be well.
Memorized?
Memorized.
Ocean's End sounds like a perfect hideaway. And we have no time to lose. Let's get packing.
To come.
It's beautiful.
The Ocean's End. We made it.